GALAXY'S EDGE

SAVAGE WARS

GODS & LEGIONNAIRES

JASON **ANSPACH**
NICK **COLE**

Copyright © 2020
Galaxy's Edge, LLC
All rights reserved.

This is a work of fiction. Any similarity to real persons, living or dead, is coincidental and not intended by the author.

No part of this publication may be reproduced, stored in a retrieval system, or transmitted in any form or by any means electronic, mechanical, photocopying, recording, or otherwise without the prior written permission of the publisher and copyright owner.

All rights reserved. Version 1.0

Edited by David Gatewood
Published by Galaxy's Edge Press

Cover Art: Tommaso Renieri
Cover Design: Beaulistic Book Services
Formatting: Kevin G. Summers

Website: InTheLegion.com
Facebook: facebook.com/atgalaxysedge
Newsletter (get a free short story): InTheLegion.com

OTHER GALAXY'S EDGE BOOKS

Galaxy's Edge Savage Wars:
- Savage Wars
- Gods & Legionnaires
- The Hundred

Galaxy's Edge Season One:
- Legionnaire
- Galactic Outlaws
- Kill Team
- Attack of Shadows
- Sword of the Legion
- Prisoners of Darkness
- Turning Point
- Message for the Dead
- Retribution

Galaxy's Edge Season Two:
- Takeover

Tyrus Rechs: Contracts & Terminations:
- Requiem for Medusa
- Chasing the Dragon
- Madame Guillotine

Stand-Alone Books:
- Imperator

Order of the Centurion:
- Order of the Centurion
- Iron Wolves
- Through the Nether
- The Reservist
- Stryker's War

PART I:
GODS

"That's what makes the Savages dangerous. Nothing... nothing ever makes sense with them. Because it's all madness. It's all lies."

—Tyrus Rechs

Gods:
Chapter One

Game Over. Game Over. Game Over.

The message kept flashing in his brain. And inside his shattered heads-up display. The HUD was telling him he was dead, and that the game was over. Except he wasn't in-game anymore, and every bone in his body was broken. Crushed beneath the weight of a collapsing building as massive starships engaged each other at close-range above the ruins of New Vega in the aftermath of the Coalition forces' final retreat. "Broadsides," it had once been called in the age of sail. An age long before the present games that some still called war. An age lost long ago on the forgotten ruin of a mythical Earth.

Uplifted medics from the Pantheon were pulling him out of the rubble of the building he'd been inside when it collapsed. Running diagnostic lasers across his combat frame. A Coalition corvette piloted by Admiral Casper himself and bearing the infamous Tyrus Rechs's tiny strike force pulled away from the planet. The Uplifted medics were diagnosing whether he should be allowed to continue to live, or whether he should be left to die.

Restart, or be reclaimed.

His life hung in the balance.

My body, the broken and crushed Uplifted Marine thought, and felt around for another token in his pocket. Or a quarter. *It's time to leave the arcade soon*, his pain-fractured mind whispered as the medics brushed away the cracked glass of his helmet's HUD and wiped the dust across the sections that remained.

He was out of tokens. The Battle for New Vega had sucked up all his coins. Left him a tokenless, quarterless pauper in the arcade of the galaxy. Game over.

"Salvageable," croaked one medic in their electronic hyper-digital chatter. Both had lighter versions of his armor. Their helmets and sensors made them look insectile, but their human-framed body armor system was composed of the same basic material as the blurry mirrored faceless helmet he wore. After all, they were Uplifted. All of them. Uplifted of the Pantheon. The inheritors of the galaxy the Coalition Animals had called "Savages." And yet just one element of the combined Grand Uplifted Alliance fleet had taken New Vega, the first of the hyperspace-connected worlds, and made it their own.

The Animals called them the "Savages."

The Animals were their inbred, inferior, ancestors whom they'd left back on dying Earth.

The Uplifted of the Pantheon were the possessors of the Path.

The Pantheon were but one species of the many Savage tribes that formed the Grand Alliance that would rid the new worlds of the disease that was their ancestors. In fact they were but one tribe of those that called themselves "the Pantheon." Some of these other Pantheons even followed the belief system of the Path. But not all. There were many roads that led to the godhood all Uplifted sought on some level. It was godhood... or destruction. There was no middle ground. Unless you counted the quantum uncertainty of disappearance. Getting lost out there in the stellar dark between the worlds. That had been the fate of many. Ships like the *Obsidia*—they, too, were Pantheon, followers of the Path—had disappeared forever somewhere unknown. But the Uplifted of the Pantheon—of the lighthugger named *Pantheon*... the Uplifted who'd stormed and taken New Vega for their own... these were the true believers. The keepers of the faith. They had survived the darkness between the stars.

One of the Uplifted medics took out his can opener.

"Can opener" is not authorized slang for Combat Protection Mainframe Armor Access Device, reminded Maestro via message over the shattered HUD. The ghostly letters drooled and blinked, hovering above the ruin that surrounded his body. Some of the characters winked in and out of existence. Eventually the whole message just failed and he was left with Maestro's whisper in his brain. Telling him the right way to think in order to follow the Path. Where the next step could be found. How one might achieve the ultimate level of existence. Godhood. By meeting the correct standards of the collective whole.

But we call it a can opener, thought the dying Uplifted marine lying in the rubble of the building that had collapsed as the Coalition corvette pulled away from the rooftop. He watched the medics work to extract and salvage him. A massive section of the building he'd been fighting in, and on, and finally fallen with as it collapsed, pinning and crushing him beneath a mountain of familiar rubble, needed to be removed from his lower half if the combat frame was to be salvaged.

All such piles bear likenesses, he thought as he gazed at the mound of destruction that had once been a high building. The mound of destruction he was trapped in. An old memory came to mind, brought all the way from Earth out here to the stars and the worlds that they, the Uplifted, had conquered. A memory from some long-ago date. He'd pushed it aside to make room for the Path and the future. But he remembered it now, that other pile of rubble rising out of the dust of some doomsday attack. It had been a Tuesday morning like any other, or so they'd been told, and they'd promised in return to never forget.

And they never had.

But they had edited. Which was the power, the right even, of the Uplifted.

Now, as he lay pinned and crushed within his combat housing, the Path and the future were one and the same. And so were all the smoking ruins that went hand in hand with victory.

Same as it ever was.

They'd driven the last Animal ship, the *Chang*, off into the skies of New Vega. But then they—the Uplifted marine detachment that had been assigned to hunt the survivors down—had been caught in the crossfire atop a collapsing building in those final star-scream moments as inbound Uplifted ship-to-ship missiles and pulse turrets raked not only Tyrus Rechs's escaping corvette but also the very building it had been attempting to pull the Animal survivors off of.

My body, he thought. *My body is too crushed beneath this fallen shard of building to be salvaged.* That was obvious even to him. Probably eight thousand pounds by the old measurements.

"Can opener" is not to be used as a term for Combat Protection Mainframe Armor Access Device, repeated Maestro, just a whisper in his brain now that the HUD had failed.

Yes, Maestro, he replied in thought only. Because Maestro was always there for him. And Maestro was always right.

Maestro always told him, them, the marines, who served for the glory of the Pantheon, what was the proper way to think in order to achieve maximal personal growth along the Path. First, Maestro prompted. Then he gradually escalated through increasingly imperative, and eventually punitive, means to ensure that the lesson could be learned and applied.

"Can opener" is not to be used. Correct.

And yet, the Uplifted marines did use that and many other forbidden words when engaged in-game. In combat. When return fire was coming down on them and they were told to move forward and cleanse a certain planet of Animal infection for the glory of the Pantheon and themselves, they used all the slang if only just to communicate what needed to be done as everything went catastrophe in a clamshell. Hell in a handbasket. End of the world. Again.

End of runtime.

The two medics standing over his crushed body signaled to another salvage crew working nearby to bring in the jaws.

They're bringing the jaws. Good. Those words were still good. Central Committee hadn't banned them yet. *The jaws.* They were still good words. And how good they were, because they would free his combat frame and make it new. And then…

Extra lives.

More tokens.

More games in the arcade. More glory. More honor. Another step, one more, further along the Path.

And then, for just a moment, he was back in the arcade. Standing in front of the *Battle for New Vega* upright he'd been playing for hours. He looked around. All the other kids had gone home. All of them except Jim Stepp. Jim, never James. Never ever. Not even the teachers called him James. As though they were as afraid of him as the general populace of the school was in awe of him. The legendary Jim Stepp. The older boy he'd once been was now over in the darkest corner of the arcade, playing his favorite game. *Devil's Hollow*.

That had always been Jim's game.

That detail had manifested itself in his private reality. His private simulation of his own long-ago past. Just as it always had. Through each shedding. Through each becoming along the path.

Devil's Hollow had remained Jim Stepp's game.

You played that game at your own risk, his mind muttered like some kid trying not to attract the unwanted attention of the school demon.

Between the two of them lay *Galaga*, *Battlezone*, *Tutankham*, *Dig Dug*, *Scramble*, *Asteroids Deluxe*, *Feeding Frenzy*, *Tapper*, *Total Annihilation*, *Smash TV*, *Concentration Camp*, *Ye Are Kung Fu*, and *I Am God*.

He checked his pockets… he had no tokens. No quarters. He wasn't a crushed space marine here in the arcade. Just a kid. It was time to go home now. Except his legs wouldn't move and so he just stood there and watched Jim Stepp, the toughest kid in school, staring into the machine he was working. Staring into a game called *Devil's Hollow*. Like he was in a trance.

"Salvage likelihood at sixty-five point two percent," indicated one Uplifted medic to the other. The one holding the can opener. Both of them chittering back and forth in digital electronica.

"Can opener" is an unauthorized word. Bad word. Bad word. Bad word.

Again, gentle promptings from Maestro.

Use "Combat Protection Mainframe Armor Access Device." Good words.

Then he was back on the battlefield of the planet the Animals had called… New Vega. Gone from the secret arcade of his youth. Lying amid the aftermath of the battle that had almost ruined all the Uplifted marines from the lighthugger *Pantheon*. The sky was dark from the smoke of still-raging fires across the battle-torn city. It didn't matter—those were the buildings of the Animals, their houses, their towers, their culture on this world burning like so much trash. Like the garbage it was.

Beyond the gray-and-black smoke, the blue of early night was shining through. The crushed Uplifted marine scanned the stars to see where his prey had gone, but that corvette had departed hours ago. He had navigation and targeting data on the other hulks in low orbit. That telemetry was at least showing within his cracked and ruined HUD. All the ghostly digital renderings of the positions of the Grand Uplifted Alliance vessels come to take New Vega for the Pantheon. The data fritzed in and out of existence and occasionally scrambled into meaninglessness, but it was reassuring nonetheless. They had succeeded.

The massive hulk known as *Palace of All Knowledge* was due to pass overhead in thirty-six minutes and forty-two seconds. It would drop more advanced reclamation units onto the ruins of New Vega so that the work of creating the Pantheon's terrestrial paradise could begin immediately. Finally. After all those years of stellar wanderings in the dark, the work of making the planet into the Pantheon's new home could begin.

It would be a Home for the Gods.

If you were some very unlucky human survivor, what the Uplifted called Animals, watching all of this from some hidey-hole in the rubble, dirty, wounded, out of charge packs and knowing that the last of the Coalition had just pulled out with its tail between its legs, knowing that you were most likely doomed and stuck well behind enemy lines, you would see the Savage medics, armored and faceless, working with green diagnostic lasers over the collected wounded to assess who was going to be salvaged, and who was going to be… reclaimed… for the greater good.

The medics were using the Combat Protection Mainframe Armor Access Device now, and the Uplifted marine's resulting disconnection from the system and Maestro gave him a sudden other perspective of what it might actually be like to be an Animal stuck behind enemy lines. A desperately frightened monkey ancestor compared to the pinnacle of post-human evolution that had conquered you. The Uplifted.

The contrast was shocking in its clarity, despite the narcotic-laced drip the medics had introduced to assist in the salvage operation.

To your Animal monkey ears and monkey mind, the Uplifted's speech would sound like the high-pitched chitter of electronic insects sped up on H8-balls during a weekend-long binge in Sin City. It would sound hyper-fast, neurotic, tense. And even if you, timid frightened creature out of the primordial past that you are, could slow down the words that they, the Uplifted, were exchanging, one between the other, it would sound to you like a mash of languages, random numbers, and even a few symbols spoken by a madman obsessing. None of it would make any sense to you. The meanings would be indecipherable. They, the Uplifted, played with words so constantly that their meanings had become unmoored from their origins.

The truth was made and remade again and again to suit the constantly shifting needs of the Pantheon. They did not cling to stories or facts because of fusty old things like tradition and meaning. They optimized reality as readily as they optimized every facet of themselves. Every facet. Constantly. And so today's Truth and Safety Council became the Inner Committee in the blink of a thought and tomorrow might be something just as innocently named and yet a little more powerful in its new form.

This was shedding. This was the way forward for post-humanity becoming something more.

Sometimes changes were made due to the fluxing codes by which one had to live and be judged by in order to remain part of the Pantheon. Part of the collective whole of the Uplifted. As in "can opener" being a bad word. Today out of favor. Maybe tomorrow would be different. But until then, it always has been this way… until something needed to be optimized… and then it will have always been that new way too and never the other.

And to the wounded Uplifted marine lying there, hovering between runtime and—

No. No. No. Runtime is a bad word.

Hovering between life and reclamation. Don't use "runtime."

Maestro's spirit remained even if the disconnect had been accomplished.

But now the AI was back and the broken marine was connected to the collective whole. Maestro's emphasis came back like a sudden storm on the plains. And he was caught, unsheltered. Helpless to resist the downpour of the Pantheon's omnipotent servant that was Maestro.

Reclamation is a good word. Credit twenty-five achievement points to player. To be reclaimed is to serve the whole. To lay down one's life so that others may evolve along the Path.

The advanced specialty medical reclamation team of the lighter-armored marines...

Improper word. Not armor. Skin.

Maestro was on overdrive today, thought the crushed and broken Uplifted marine lying amid their salvage circus on the battlefield that had once been the posh downtown district of New Vega.

The advanced specialty medical reclamation team of the lighter-skinned marines bearing the jaws of life indicated he might just possibly be salvaged. *Life. Insert token. Ready player. Press start.*

Yellow hazard strobes washed across the debris. Few of the former buildings were recognizable now, three days after the Animals, who called themselves the Coalition, attacked the Uplifted's new home. The next step in the evolution for the Pantheon along the Path was underway. The beginning of the Pantheon's existence in real-time was under construction and beginning with the demolition of all things Animal. In from the deep dark they had come. Coming to bring their gifts and visions to mortal spacetime. So say all along the Path. Faithful adherents every one. So say all within the collective whole.

The game came back online. New Vega! The battle for it. The colors bright. The rock-and-roll soundtrack thundering. The voices of the commanders, tough and heroic, issuing orders to the Uplifted marines as they fought house-to-house at Triangle Square. Stormed the bank on

Main and First. Hunter-killer teamwork to deal with the dying and dead.

"Kill streak!"

"Ordnance on the way!"

"Tango down!"

"Airstrike inbound!"

"Kill! Kill! Kill!"

And...

"Big prizes!"

Rock-and-roll video game catchphrases used for combat communication and motivation.

Then the medic who'd been on the verge of popping his helmet with the can opener...

Bad word. Bad word. Bad word.

Negative achievement points!

No. The can opener has already been used. The Combat Protection Mainframe Armor Access Device. Now he is being reconnected to a life support system and reintegrated with Maestro. Connected to the Pantheon once again.

"I'm in pain!" he roared. The crushed and broken Uplifted marine. Me. "Need some junk! Some 'ludes, or just fade me into the black! I need to get out of my skin, Maestro!"

Old life matrix detected... noting for diagnostic report, assessed Maestro from above. Cold and distant. Confident and competent.

"Hit him with some more Narcoblisserine. That'll make the extraction less difficult," said one of the medics who'd argued for salvage. "Fifty cc's."

But again, all of it would sound like a mosquito to one who wasn't Uplifted. High-speed. Neurotic like a schizophrenic's sudden breakdown. Like a madman mumbling nonstop doomsday along a dark desert highway.

They spiked him in the brain. In him. The center of who he really was now. And all that he'd become in the long crossing. He got a glimpse of who he really was and then edited it fast because that way lay sure madness.

Then he was gone from the battlefield of ruined New Vega. The first of the great battles between the Uplifted and the Animals. The "Savages" and... their pitiful little monkey human ancestors. Their pathetic Coalition had been roundly beaten. Flogged and sent home for good measure to await the coming judgment of the righteous as the Grand Alliance washed over all the worlds of the galaxy. Nothing stood in the way of the Uplifted now.

He'd earned both honor and achievement points over three days of brutal combat. And glory. He'd been shot several times by the Animals' energy weapons that burned like hot fire. Explosions had played havoc with many of his systems...

Bad word. Bad word. Bad word.

Use... *senses.*

Many of his senses were still ringing. Bones were broken. Clan friends were dead. Dead beyond reclamation. Even he knew that when he saw them shot through the helmet. Blown up. Run over by the big tanks the Animals brought out onto the streets when the fighting was heaviest. Ripped to pieces by brutal barrages of artillery and heavy weapons spitting in sudden crossfire storms.

Even he knew that.

Do you remember your tag? asked Maestro amid all the pain and memories of battle.

The broken Uplifted marine tried to remember his very own personal tag as the Narcoblisserine took effect.

Brutal fighting. Not just street to street and block to block. Building to building. But there, in the hot hours before the enemy airstrike…

Brutal.

Room to room.

Update from Pantheon Recon Intel Analysis and Feedback… airstrike delivered by enemy weapons systems, "Titan." Comprehensive file available for download from Heaven. Mandatory review of all that is holy and sacred.

Now that he was once more connected to the Pantheon, and the collective whole, he was getting real-time updates.

That's the stuff, mumbled his Bad Old Self as the Narcoblisserine hit solidly in all the good parts that needed scratching. He whispered relief and satisfaction deep down inside the place Maestro hadn't found yet as the information feed reintegrated with his mind. The place of his own becoming. His own truths. The place that loved… a little candy.

He relaxed and melted into the arcade. His hiding place. His hidey-hole from the Pantheon. The world where he was god. And god alone.

Lazer Command.

The other, more popular arcade, Tilt, was at the nearby mall. But Lazer Command was his preferred haunt for video gaming. A living world made up of unquiet ghosts. Just for him now. Just for him to play with.

Someone had put something on the jukebox near the back of the dark and neon-lit arcade. He knew the song, and it competed with the whirring, beeping, and whooping of the games along the walls and aisles. The song washed over all of it and made it all the same, and part of. Which was what the Path was all about.

Please state your tag identifier, said some distant butler the Narcoblisserine scrambled the name of. Master. Mister. Something.

He faded from New Vega, letting the powerful drug take hold, tasting the sweet candy, heading out into the black. Finally. Bad Old Self was happy to be home after the battle. Happy to be Bad Old Self again.

The longing for destruction made real.

He was himself on a tangerine ocean. There was a girl. She had eyes. Eyes like a kaleidoscope. Of all the images he'd kept in his long trek across the years, this was the one that was always there for him. Amid ruin and rubble, victory and glory… she was always there.

Her name was…

"He's out," said the medic at high speed from across a distant canyon. It sounded like nothing more than a single electronic *pip!* in real-time.

And then some butler, master, mister said… *"Player Crometheus confirmed for reclamation."* That too came to him from across that far canyon that separated that reality from this one. Their truth and his, becoming one.

The canyon of bliss was the hiding place. The canyon of drugs. The lost in-between.

And that too sounded just like a *pip*.

He waited for her. The girl with kaleidoscope eyes. Coming to him now as she always did at each new beginning. At each old ending.

She was always there.

Gods:
Chapter Two

A song was playing on the jukebox Mr. Webb kept near the booth in the back of the arcade. The booth where you turned in your dollars for Lazer Command tokens. All the machines at Lazer Command took tokens. Or quarters. Either one. You could use the dollar-bill machine, but that didn't always work, especially if your money was old and wrinkled. Or if you kept it in your shoe like Crometheus did. Or had long ago when he'd been a boy and traveled everywhere by bike.

He could move now. He could move away from the game he'd been dumping tokens into all night. *Battle for New Vega* on a Friday night. He turned. The game was still asking him to enter his initials because he'd earned a high score.

He took hold of the joystick and with a series of deft, almost un-thought movements, tapped the fire button quickly as he entered his three-letter identifier. His chosen tag from long ago. BOO.

His real name though, he couldn't remember what it had been. That too had been deleted to make room for the Path. But the initials he'd always signed with... he hadn't been able to undo that. And truth be told, he didn't want to. It was his small rebellion against the constant shedding the Path encouraged.

His one held-back thing.

His guilty pleasure.

He'd always been a rebel. Even before the Uplifted.

Then he was walking toward the front door of the arcade, passing wide of Jim Stepp who stared intently into *Devil's Hollow*, tapping the fire button and slamming the joystick side to side. Mouth slightly open in concentration. Feet planted wide apart. Lost in the on-screen action. The older boy was on one of the highest levels in that forbidden game. The screen was almost pitch black and you couldn't see anything but shadows and brief splashes of subdued demonic light. It was almost impossible to tell what was going on by just suddenly tuning in over someone's shoulder. You had to have been there all along. Accepting the gradual slide into darkness that was the game's requirement to progress down through its endlessly abyssal levels.

Stepp was "deep in the hollow," as they liked to say.

Some. Some said that. The few kids in his school who dared speak Stepp's name aloud.

Crometheus made the front door of the arcade. It was night out. And late. Which meant after nine and possibly heading on toward ten. He'd come in during the day, after school, and that had reminded him of the time when he'd played Vegas, not New Vega, for the first time. His band back on long-lost Earth. When he was who he'd once been before the Path made him who he'd become. They, the band and the groupies and all the hangers-on, had gone to a strip club after the show. Deep night when they entered, and full bright, washed-out and tired merciless desert daylight when they exited with just a few blinking strippers in tow. He'd felt empty and husky at that moment. Later he'd learn that even that moment long ago, before he'd started down the Path officially, had been a kind of shedding. Standing there on the cracked pavement that was already heating up with the relentless glare of the Vegas desert sun, he felt some gnawing worm in his stomach, telling him that he wasn't where he was supposed to be. Not yet. Like a warning to turn back. Or a gradual slide into a darkness at noon all its own.

Even then he was shedding. Though he didn't know it at the time, and wouldn't know it for years to come. Not until he was on the Path. Not until he'd saved himself... from himself.

He and the rest of the band, and a few of the girls, went to get pancakes in some ironic greasy spoon as the morning commute in busy Las Vegas began back on old and ruined Earth. Long ago.

That lost moment was like this one now inside his reality within the Pantheon after the battle in which he'd been crushed and maimed. After his many hours at the new upright called Battle of New Vega. Where he fought in real-time as the Uplifted marine he is.

Big prizes.

Entering the simulated now as the child he once was, leaving the arcade, was like that memory. Like it might never happen if you knew how to edit your truths. He was fourteen years old now. He'd come into the arcade after school. He'd made his tokens last until now, playing *Battle for New Vega*, where he'd been an Uplifted marine earning kill streaks and achievement points. And then getting crushed in a final rooftop shootout amid an Animal dustoff under fire.

It was a pretty good run. But that was another truth inside the many realities. Here in the arcade he was just a kid. It wasn't like he had all the money in the world. Not yet. Because he once had, long ago. And it didn't mean anything. Not then. Not now. Now he was just fourteen and good at video games. Like he'd been back then. He thought he might join the navy and fly F-14s. Like in that movie. *Top Gun*. Like he'd thought a long time ago.

That was his memory. Not someone else's. Not some texture or filter to be thrown over a replay as they wandered through the dark with nothing but time to kill. Inventing new lives like someone might edit random footage to make a movie.

He thought about doing those things just as he had when he was a kid. Instead of ending up where he did.

Only everything is enough, he reminded himself when he felt some other truth threatening to challenge that assertion. He would only be satisfied with everything, as any Uplifted must.

Twenty-five achievement points.

Here now, standing outside the front door of the Lazer Command arcade on a Friday night at the edge of a sleepy suburbia that had existed long ago… and no longer did… this was everything. It had taken him lifetimes to understand that. Thanks to the Pantheon, and the Path, he had it all back now once again.

Rosebud, again.

Right?

He let all the old cryptic codewords that unlocked all the discovered mysteries flood across his brain once more.

Lazer Command was the touchstone.

This strip mall with the Wendy's in one corner, beside the near-silent freeway that ran north and south, and the Togo's at the other end, still doing late-night sandwich business, was everything. Or it had been a *part* of the everything he'd once had, and lost, and then found again. He could see kids, kids old enough to have their first jobs behind the windows of the sandwich shop. Cutting bread, cleaning up, closing soon for the night. He knew there'd be music in there. Foreigner or something. Air Supply. Or even some synth band out of the UK. Neuro, it had been called. Some dark-haired older girl with her hair cut short and swept to the side telling him that word for the first time long ago.

Something before him. Before his time as a rock star. Before who he would become in the becoming of what he one day would be. *I know*, he thought to himself. *It would sound like madness if I hadn't lived it all.*

He laughed at himself in the night, standing in the darkness between the still-open businesses. The darkness in the parking lot between the islands of light from the streetlamps high above.

He could go for a number fourteen from Togo's right now. Or a pastrami with avocado. The sandwich he had invented. All the sandwiches had numbers. Many numbers. Not so many as the years passed and the corporate bean counters narrowed the choices in favor of penny-measured profits.

Funny what little bits of trivia stick after so long. And…

Wonderful things are done to death by bean counters.

He stared out in wonder, silent wonder, at that ancient strip mall that was all his now. Again. Hidden here as it always was. Inside the Pantheon.

There was the closed car wash. The night was cool and he could smell the cleaning chemicals that had been used all day to wash and polish people's cars. Friday night was date night for the older kids, so many cars had gone through that place and were now somewhere out there in the night, parked.

He wondered if the prettiest girl in school was out tonight with some older guy. A guy with a job who sold stereos. Or even pagers. The kind of guy who wasn't in high school anymore and drove a cool car.

Like she had been then. Holly Wood had been her unusual and interestingly unbelievable name. Holly. Wood.

That part was real. Right?

He wondered where Holly Wood was right now inside this amazing world, not simulation, where he was God. Where she was on this night as she had been on all those other nights back on Earth. He could call her up. But for right now, he wanted the fourteen-year-old's longing he'd once had for her.

He'd always wondered where she was no matter where he was in his old life. Rocking a hundred thousand at some massive stadium on the other side of the world. Among a sea of groupies. Face-down in his own vomit. Crossing the interstellar darkness to becoming something new after the end of everything on Earth.

She'd said hi to him once. Long ago. First day of school. The varsity cheerleaders had been part of the freshmen orientation. And she'd been there with her blue eyes that were like a kaleidoscope turning, beach-tan skin, golden-blond hair. And that smile.

He wondered whatever happened to her. Though he knew. And then… he didn't. Because he could edit. It was his reality after all. His truth to make as he saw fit.

His old bike was lying in the dark, off to the side of the arcade, where all the other bikes had been cast throughout the early afternoon and evening. Now it was all alone in front of the darkened tailor's shop that did business next to Lazer Command. Thrown down on the sidewalk and looking forgotten.

That's how things were back in those days. When kids could be kids. The last of such times. You just rode your bike somewhere and dumped it in front of a store. Along the sidewalk. No racks. No locks. No helmets. The world was different then.

As it always has been in this place of his own making.

And so were you, he reminded himself as he picked up the old familiar bike. *You were different then. And you're different now. Here.*

The yellow Huffy had a shock absorber that ran from the fork back to the seat. It made the bike much heavier. Older kids who were pros at riding the trick bikes, making ramps and jumping over things, or between everything they could get their hands on, told him so. Told him that the heavy shock absorber that came with the bike made it heavier. And therefore useless.

But it was his now. As it had once been then.

He struggled to remember the name of those lighter, cooler bikes. BMW? No, that had been the kind of car all the cool guys who dated the hottest girls in school drove. Older guys out of high school already. So BMW wasn't right. But it was something like that. Bikes so light you could pick them up with one finger. Trick bikes.

What had they been called…?

Some things were just lost and could never be found again. Especially if it wasn't in the Pantheon's database. Some things just found their way to a memory black hole in the galaxy and disappeared there forever. Or were thrown in for the favoring of some new truth.

Then they were gone forever.

His yellow Huffy with the shock absorber purely for show wasn't anything like those trick bikes. But he didn't care. It was his. His parents had bought it for him when they first moved to Viejo Verde, because the apartment complex they'd lived in, in Long Beach—before this living memory of his past—wasn't good for bikes and so he could have one here, now that they lived in suburbia. In paradise. Where there were sidewalks and wide roads and parks and housing developments under construction with dirt berms that could be jumped off.

Which was pretty cool.

Paradise lasts forever inside the Pantheon.

It was his only bike. And it should have ever been his only bike. Years later…

Something from Maestro came through the fog of candy that was still washing across his brain after the extraction and reclamation. After New Vega. Through the Narcoblisserine. But he was too high on the candy, as he called it, so Bad Old Self could do whatever he wanted. He was being reclaimed. He was becoming again.

Like being a Made Man.

Yeah, that was it, he thought. Like being a Made Man. Or a modern-day pharaoh.

Or a…

… a god becoming.

Yes.

Like a rock star is a god.

Years later, on top of it all with everything to burn and nothing to lose… a rock god… he'd tried to find his old bike. One exactly like the yellow Huffy. He'd even paid some specialist who specialized in such bring-em-back-alive daring-dos to comb the listings on the… internet. Yeah, it had been called the internet back on Earth. Before the Uplift. Before the end of the whole mess. He paid someone to go out and find his past because he knew he was lost and getting more lost with each concert, video, gaggle of doe-eyed groupie girls willing to do anything… needle…

No joy. The guy hadn't been able to find the bike.

The best that could be had was one that was bent and ruined, and some kid had put Vans stickers on it. And even Wacky Packys.

You know the ones…

Mashbox.

Playskull.

Dr. Pooper.

Quacker Oats.

That kind of kid. A loser with no respect for treasures. Someone who probably got a new bike every Christmas.

His parents hadn't been like that. No. Not at all. Not never.

He'd taken care of that first and only bike. Washed it like it was a car. Cared for it like it was his only friend. His *Millennium Falcon* and his Chewbacca all rolled into one. It was the friend every twelve-year-old scoundrel needed. And now here he was inside his reality on the other side of humanity, within the Pantheon, pedaling it across the quiet and dark streets of Viejo Verde. Not a soul out. The night world was his...

Bad word. Soul. Bad word. Soul is a forbidden word.

He ignored it because he was so deep in the candy. Drugs made it easier to disconnect from Maestro. To ignore and override. He pedaled over the freeway and watched the cars heading north and south in the night passing below. Someday it would be good to have a car. Someday. He wondered it then, like he'd wondered it long ago. It was fun to feel nostalgic because it was a kind of eternity if you allowed yourself to completely embrace it.

Maestro tried to remonstrate with him about this. But the butler's voice was distant, far away across the canyon of candy.

The particular dream of all fourteen-year-old boys is to own a car someday. Dreams are fun to remember having, his constantly evaluating and updating mind mentioned. The part that ran all the processes one needed to go on living. When you are much older and have all the things, including the cars, that you want, and none of the dreams anymore, it's the dreams you miss the most.

Though it takes a long time to realize they've been gone for some time.

He rode on past sleeping houses where the angelic blue light of TV shone through the windows like sacred lighting in some cathedral's stained glass. Maybe the last of the Angels game. Or the Dodgers. Vin Scully telling everyone about Farmer John hot dogs in the slow late innings of the night. When it looked like the Dodgers weren't ever going to win again.

He passed the big GemCo store that wouldn't live out the century, and then turned toward home riding up into the heights and the tract where his parents lived. All of it faithfully re-recreated here in the eternal constant of the Pantheon. Hidden and just for him.

The planned housing community of the future, circa that era of military-industrial complexes.

Later he would learn that the architectural style was called mid-century modern. Houses like fantastic cubes with big broad windows that looked out on sculpted lawns. Lit by multicolored lights in the night. Red. Blue. Green. Sometimes yellow.

Malibu lights, they were called.

That was how it was. Right? It could be the editing. But he was sure this was how it all had really been.

His parents weren't home. He knew they weren't when he lifted up the garage and walked his bike through into its vast darkness. Like the quiet storage hangars deep in the Forbidden Decks, aft of main engineering aboard the colony ship *Pantheon*. Placing the bike in its proper place leaned up against the wall. His parents had always demanded order. Everything in its place. A place for everything. This was the bike's place. As it ever should have been. As it ever will be.

His friends' homes were often littered with bikes on the front lawn, along the sidewalks, and right up to the tall front doors. Often and every day. All day. And all through the night. Especially if the family had an Atari game system. Less so if it was Intellivision.

Those early console-possessing houses were visited often by many kids throughout the neighborhood. The wonder of such devices. The endless games.

As though society, and its military-industrial complex, was preparing them all for the future wars they would fight out among the stars.

Gamification.

Games as reality.

Virtual reality.

Games to teach, learn, succeed at, win, conquer…

His family didn't have any of those things back then. Atari, or Intellivision. There was another… something else. His own mind offered him bonus prizes if he could find the forgotten treasures buried in the desert of his memories. But he couldn't. They didn't even have one of the new big VCRs. He closed the garage and walked inside their house. He grabbed a cold hot dog from the fridge and wrapped it in a piece of Wonder Bread.

Wonder Bread.

Remember how soft it was? It was like air. Like nothing. Because it *was* nothing. And it was perfect for cold hot dogs, or bologna, let's say "baloney" sandwiches.

Nothing had ever tasted like that for the rest of his life, Bad Old Self commented. Bad Old Self was bad. Bad Old Self liked and missed all the fun old junk and was never really too hip about becoming like everyone along the Path. And even less so about shedding.

The Path said Bad Old Self needed to die. But he was wily and never managed to. One day Crometheus intended to get around to catching and killing Bad Old Self, but until then, the irascible old rascal was like some tour guide for all the fun that had been lost.

If Bad Old Self was a cartoon character, then Crometheus was a humanoid catcher's mitt, soft and broken in, ancient like an artifact. But a hippie. A dope-smoking, beer-swilling hippie who wore Hawaiian shirts and was always up for fun and adventure.

But who cared... it was Candy Time. And when you were on a candy cruise anything was possible. So says Bad Old Self. Buy the ticket, take the ride. Bad Old Self could comment all he wanted to. When runtime...

Bad word.

Life. Use life, young Master Crometheus.

When life resumed, he'd tell Bad Old Self to be quiet for a little while. Chill out. It was Maestro who really wanted to kill Bad Old Self. He wanted to kill Bad Old Self dead, dead, dead. Bad Old Self is Dead. Killing Bad Old Self was how one became a god, many along the Path had often whispered during the ceremonies of Uplift.

What is the Path?

Think of a winding ancient stone staircase threading back and forth over a high granite mountain rising up through mist and fog. The path, each carved step, is lit with candles dripping wax. Carved runes are revealed along the face of the wet stone on each stair.

This is the Path.

And it isn't.

What lies ahead, above, beyond, is mostly obscured and sometimes guessed at. What lies behind is everything you once were. What lies ahead is what you will become.

As it is written... *Death to Old Self is the Path to Uplift.* According to TED Talk 92:14.

But now, here, in the night kitchen of a perfectly mid-century modern home, his oldest of homes, the home of his youth and the guilty pleasure of his Uplifted state... home, the cold hot dog from the Oscar Mayer ten-pack wrapped in a slice of heavenly soft Wonder Bread from the white bag with the multi-colored dots... tastes like heaven. Eternity to come once he has created it.

Bad Old Self was right. Nothing in his life has ever tasted this good, and he'd been to all the best places to eat back on Earth as it fell. The French Laundry. The Go-Go Room in New Tokyo for forty-two-ounce Kobe steaks smothered in duck-fat mushrooms accompanied by a Sapporo Lunar Pale. The coldest of beers brewed in low-Earth orbit. Hypnotically satisfying. Fried oysters and beef tartare at Hatchet Hall in Venice after the Oscars. A chorizo-and-clams omelet in Mallorca when the Pantheon first indicated he was Uplift material. At dawn after an all-night garden party and ceremony in the deep of it all. A rock god becomes a real god. If... if he follows the candles up along the way of the Path, then yes, he does. Seeking the next step up through the swirling mist that is space-time. Reality. Or at least the most brutal reality of all.

Bad Old Self whispered in his wheezy low I'm-super-high aside voice. *What about that burger along the road during the summer tour for the Bad Idol album,* said diabolically fun Bad Old Self. *Remember that one, kiddo?*

He tried to, and the memory hurt because...

He thought of another. Another nostalgia that would be the anchor for all his eternities.

The Tommy's double chili cheeseburger with little yellow peppers while standing in the parking lot the night he first played the Whiskey in LA and the world heard *Rebel Child.*

No. Not that one. Though that one was good, admitted Bad Old Self. If he had to picture Bad Old Self as a real person, he pictured a bearded old man. Like an Amish farmer who'd once been a gunrunner and desert rat and wandering madman saying truths no one wanted to hear because of all the fun they were convinced they were having. Bad Old Self was a devil disappearing into the plain life because it was just as good a place as any to hide out for a while. Wise and a little dangerous with a taste for trouble and liquor that never quite got eradicated by true religion.

Or, continued Bad Old Self, warming up to this particular temptation, *remember dinner at Ma Maison Redux with Sir Quentin Tarantino? Candy off a supermodel's slender neck while they served the bouillabaisse and the old direc-*

tor told you about the role that was going to get you your first Oscar.

No. None of that. The life of actor after rock god, a natural pivot as ever it was...

No. Nothing would ever taste as good as that cold hot dog standing in front of an open refrigerator late in the night in the home you never should have left.

That painful memory tried to surface one more time. It was strong. Like some old white whale that wasn't going to die with just a harpoon and would never be satisfied with Ahab's one leg.

The one with Holly Wood. Remember...

He drank from the milk carton standing directly in the light of the refrigerator in the house he never should have left.

Remember that one halfway between Reno and Rome. Heaven and Hell.

He saw her. Saw her smile. And the kaleidoscope eyes. Cheerleader and homecoming queen his freshman year.

He sat down on the low-backed couch made of a blue, rough, yet comforting fabric. Silver stitching like tiny stars shifting into hyperspace woven throughout its material. As though the textile were a prophecy of all the things to come. The Exodus from Earth and the Big Uplift. As though his parents' selection of hip furniture all those hundreds of years ago, or rather the decorator they'd hired, had somehow known where he was headed all along. Hundreds and even a thousand years later, tumbling out into the darkness between the stars. Following the Path to become what he would one day be.

The channel-changer was where it was supposed to be. Order. As it always was. On the low coffee table shaped like a painter's palette. Next to what his mother called the gossip seat. Which was really just another perfectly matched yet smaller couch with a slanted back and a side reading table with artfully placed popular magazines.

He didn't turn on any of the lights. He liked the blue light of the TV and how it mixed with the Malibu lights out in the back yard.

Don't let anyone tell you differently, he told himself as he flicked through the channels. That's what space is like when the main drive fails and you drift for three years of madness and infighting between the decks. When those who do not agree must be cleansed from engineering and bio-systems maintenance in order for the right truth to reign supreme in those lower decks.

Twenty-five achievement points, whispered Maestro, because he had recited the Currently Accepted History of those times.

When the fighting is at its most savage.

The color of space coming in through the once-optimistic outer viewing decks is just like that. Blue like the TV in the night, and red like the splattered and spattered blood of the cleansing work that had to be done in engineering and the Forbidden Decks.

His parents were gone just as they always were. Doing business in restaurants sometimes until well after midnight. Vin Scully was wrapping up the game on the television. Good effort by Lopes, Cey, and Garvey. But no win tonight.

Then... "Farmer John hot dogs!" and a commercial. Cal Worthington, that old car dealer who wrestled lions and tigers late at night to sell cars, came on. He promised everything. In a friendly way. Later he'd have one of the biggest divorce settlements in the state of California. Bigger than Johnny Carson if you can imagine that then.

Not so hard now.

The biggest in fact until his own divorce from the actress. For a time, *his* had been the biggest in the state of California. And a few other states to boot. But all that was way in the future from this pleasant nostalgia of now. Way after *Rebel Child* went multiplatinum. Way after three more albums that all but secured him a place in rock god history, Paris Fashion Week, and every awards show forever.

One of his old movies was on.

The reboot of *Night of the Living Dead*.

He watched himself and the other survivors fighting to survive inside the old farmhouse as the living dead closed in. Looking back on it now he thought the special effects weren't so bad. He'd often remembered them being hokier. Cheesier. He forgot about the shoot and how high he and the lead actress were. They hooked up all throughout the shoot, getting weirder and weirder each time. He a rock god making his first film. She a young ingénue who'd go on to marry some Chinese autocrat as the Far East rose to power. When the two of them weren't busy with sex and drugs, she gave him a few acting tips. She'd trained. He was just a natural. She told him that over and over again. After the shoot in Louisiana they just parted ways without any explanation or goodbye. Her off to make the movie that would make her famous. A period piece about some English queen who was secretly gay according to how the script wanted it to be. Him to an action flick with a big-budget star.

Their truths.

Their becomings of who they would be.

The voice of Maestro whispered… but again he was so high on Bliss-o-Narc, or whatever it was called, he didn't need to answer the front door. Didn't need to see what Maestro wanted now. Or maybe that was just in the movie when he and the actress were banging on the front door to the farmhouse, desperate to be let in because the zombies were about to eat them, in the reboot.

Morgan Freeman…

Morgan Freeman's avatar had played the guy who let them in. He turned into a zombie by the end of the film. The actress he was having sex with in his trailer between takes, because they were both so high on candy, was actually Morgan Freeman's love interest in the movie though they never get together on-screen and the age difference was so colossal.

It was implied. For reasons.

He forgot all about that and just enjoyed the movie he'd once made when he was young. Forgot that he was even in it. They'd let him keep his spiky blond hair. They even let him use his trademark sneer when delivering his lines. They were just happy to have a rock star in the picture because it guaranteed X amount for gross.

He was happy because it was acting.

He'd only done that in videos up until that point then. All of which had been post-apocalyptic in theme.

Then came his death scene in the reboot and he watched himself get blown up trying to get gas with the jailbaity farmer's daughter who'd been willing to try and make a break for it with him. The rebel biker who'd just wandered into zombie town and the farmer's daughter. Subtext... they weren't just fleeing the zombies. They were fleeing the farm. Or at least she was. He was, his character, then, was just fleeing. Fleeing was his way of life. That was the secret the actress had given him. She said every character needed a secret. And fleeing something horrible was his.

He wondered if he might throw the filter of the jailbaity actress and his fleeing biker drifter across some reality and take a vacation in there sometime. See how things turned out between the two of them.

"Think of that horrible thing you did!" she'd ordered him in their trailer. The actress who would become great and marry the Chinese autocrat. Both of them coked to the gills. "Now, don't tell anyone that secret. It's yours. And that's how you make your characters real."

He never did. Never told anyone.

That was how he'd made this world inside the Pantheon. It was his own secret place. And he never told anyone about it.

He never even told himself the secret of the biker-drifter from the reboot. Kept it from himself until eventually he forgot it ever happened. Just knew, deep down inside, that he was fleeing. Something.

Like now? he asked himself. Or was that Bad Old Self.

In real life the jailbaity farmer's daughter had trained at the Royal Academy of Dramatic Arts in jolly old England before it melted down and became a cesspit of jihadis. She'd played Lady Macbeth and had a crush on him all through the shoot. Except he'd been with the other actress playing the lead, doing candy and having sex between takes.

He died.

In the movie.

He and Jailbait Lady Macbeth.

And then the movie went on and he wasn't interested anymore because he wasn't in it. So he turned it off and went upstairs and got ready for bed. In his room was everything he'd ever prized most from childhood. His catcher's glove. His collection of *Mad Magazines*. The Fantastic Four issue when they flew the space shuttle and crashed, which had been his first entry into comic books. Again, it was a thing he'd lost after his youth and paid big money to track down to have once again. Protected behind cases and covers inside climate-controlled rooms accessed by thumbprint locks. Like they were the antiquities of a pharaoh.

The household items of a god.

Someone had tracked down all those lost treasures for his tomb.

They were already the Fantastic Four when they crashed the shuttle that time in the comic book. Not like the first time when they went into space and got their powers. Became gods... as it were, when you really thought about it. Like some foreshadowing of the Uplift movement that was to come. What hokey old religions called "prophecies."

Superheroes were gods. Hadn't that been the message someone was signaling all those decades ago? And that superheroes were ordinary people with ordinary problems just like you and me… except with superpowers.

What if you had superpowers?

Then you would be…

Was the Path already whispering to humanity then? Preparing them, preparing the way in the desert, for what they would one day become.

Gods.

Which again, like the silver starbursts-shifting-to-hyperspace thread in his mother's postmodern couch that matched perfectly the rest of the house… the comic book of the Fantastic Four going into space and getting their powers was a kind of prophecy too.

In its way.

In the grand view of what really happened during the Great Exodus and the Big Uplift.

In his room his collection, and it wasn't much of one, of Hardy Boys novels was on the nightstand next to his daybed. His Oscars were on the windowsill. A window that looked out into his parents' perfectly kept garden. They had a Japanese gardener. Beyond that were the houses of their neighbors. And his best friend's house on the hill above.

Every night going to sleep, he watched his best friend's window. No matter how late it was, there would always be the holy blue glow of the TV from his best friend's high window.

Watching it at night before he faded was like some kind of constant North Star for him by which he might navigate.

On his desk was the copy of his film. The masterpiece he would spend the last years of his life before the Pantheon trying to complete, and never would.

His opus that explained it all. His *Kane*.

It was in an old film can, instead of on a flash drive as it really had been. But in this representation of nostalgia… it was in a can. A film canister.

Written on the canister, on a piece of tape, with a black marker, were the words…

Blue Highway.

He didn't want to think about that and so he got into bed with a dog-eared and yellowed copy of a Conan novel. *Conan the Unconquered*, and he read until late. The sacred blue light of the TV in his friend's window still on when at last he turned out the light and closed his eyes.

His parents still weren't home by the time he went to sleep. They never would be.

In the dream he has, he is lying in a state-of-the-art machine shop. Not like a garage. But like a high-tech clean room where they once built the mighty starship engines that would throw the colony ships far from dying Earth. Where the techs wore white lab coats.

There is a monster on the operating table. In the dream.

Not like a werewolf, or a Dracula, like the afternoon classic movies he sometimes watched while he built model airplanes from World War II. The Corsair, which was hard because of the folding gull wings. The P-47. The Spitfire. The Zero. Never World War I planes because they had two wings, one above and one below which was really four wings when you thought about it. And those were always hard to match up and hold with glue. Hard to get just right.

The monster on the clean-room table in the dream was like a Frankenstein.

But a giant metal Frankenstein lying on a state-of-the-art operating table in a lab that made monsters like a factory makes war machines. Machine-like tentacles did all the work of salvage and making him new once again. Making him Crometheus. Coming in quickly to drill and laser away rivets. Other arms with claws grasping to pull away battered and blasted plates of armor from himself. Or take away whole limbs that had been ruined beyond repair. The monster was very badly damaged. Shot no less than twenty-eight times over the course of the battle for New Vega. The battered chest plate scored by pulse fire from Coalition rifles and dented by fragmentary explosive impacts. Metal gashes seared into the hyper-alloy exterior where heavier weapons had left their marks.

He felt sorry for whoever it was lying on that table in the dream. And then he remembered it was him.

Crometheus.

Uplifted marine.

Holly Wood, the head cheerleader from his school, held his hand all throughout as he watched himself being operated on. That was kind of her. She was genuinely sorry for him. Just as she had been when she left for the last time years later. Somewhere along the Blue Highway, halfway between Reno and Rome. Maybe he was crying a little. Crying for all that he'd become. She squeezed his hand, still wearing that forever-for-him sexy cheerleading outfit he'd tried to dress up so many other women in. She was telling him, "Don't worry. It'll all be okay now. You're starting over again."

Her voice was soft and kind.

He wiped his eyes and felt ashamed. In the dream.

Two priests came in. Faithful masters of the religion that had made them who they would become. They spoke the sacred words of Science. Telling each other how they would remake him this time, again. Upgrades and new tech. Developments from Super Mind Six.

Super Mind Six was the combat super-intelligence they'd discovered out in the dark between the stars when they'd been at their lowest. Super Mind Six saved them all.

Bad Thought Bad Thought Bad Thought. The Pantheon said *developed*. The Pantheon had *developed* Super Mind Six. But rumors along the Forbidden Decks said *discovered*. As in found. Out there in the dark. On the long haul from ruined Earth to Sirius Two. The first world they ruined along the Path to becoming. Had it been Sirius Two? Or some other world deleted to make room for the next step along the Path?

Super Mind Six was the giver of gifts to godlings who would kill to become gods. Super Mind Six had developed a new targeting diagnostic. Advanced weaponry. And the omni-shield.

Super Mind Six is Bad Word Bad Word Bad Word. Use Maestro. Super Mind Six is now Maestro. Maestro has always been. There never was a Super Mind Six. Use Maestro.

Holly Wood turned to him as they cracked the carapace of his Frankensteinian self on the table. Damage repaired. New weapon systems installed. Dynamic Targeting 6.0. Active cloak upgrade. And something called the Shooting Stars weapon system.

"Time to wake up, gamer," gentled the priests.

Holly Wood had long blond hair and big blue eyes. Tanned skin from lying out on the beaches of Southern California. Long lashes.

"The Pantheon needs you," she said expectantly. "There's a new game at the arcade, Crometheus. A new game that's called... *Britannia Attack!* And we need you there. Badly."

He moved forward until he was standing over himself. And then with the help of the priests, he lay down like some noble being prepared for immortality. Laid himself down into the metal Frankenstein like some fallen hero who must rise again in the most desperate of hours... or a pharaoh... becoming a god at the last of himself.

Finally. And again.

Gods:
Chapter Three

Inside the Pantheon, the main reality for all, the colors are always a little brighter. That was Crometheus's first thought. Every time it was his first thought as he once more re-entered that constant reality that was the Pantheon. Always.

A message appeared inside his HUD.

Report to General Maximo. In-game. Report to the arcade. He received that message within his own world. In the private simulation of his past. His parents' home. The home he never should have left.

It was a blustery fall day in school back there in the youth of his past. Inside his world. The world he had created for his very own. The little slice of reality that was all his and connected with the Pantheon. It had rained all that fall morning and when he woke, there had been bacon cooked in the microwave and his coat lying out. His parents were gone. Off on some important business. He ate the bacon and turned on the TV. *The Great Space Coaster* with Gary Gnu was playing. And then a few minutes later he knew he would be late if he didn't leave and so out in the wind and the rain of that simulated morning he left for the long puddle-laden walk to school. Cars passed and he heard their tires on the wet streets below the path he walked. A concrete strip ran along a hillside to reach his school. And for some reason, watching the leaves shake and hurl themselves away from their soft skeletal tree bodies, becoming winter's bones, he heard the music of some pianist. From long ago.

Just soft, gentle, melancholy and still happy at the same time, music. The music was in his head and it was the music of... Vince Guaraldi. And the music of a famous cartoon strip called *Peanuts*. There—he had it. The name of the composer. Some things are too important to be deleted, Crometheus told himself as he continued to move from puddle to puddle. Soon he reached school and all the other children, kids, and the long-dead people he'd once known who hadn't changed in the least in his sim-world within the Pantheon all these centuries later were there and school was beginning just as it once had. Just as they all had been all those years ago.

They watched safety films because it was too wet to go outside for recess. Made projects out of thick, multi-colored construction paper and pasty glue, and at lunch it was cheese boats from the cafeteria. His favorite. A simple slice of French bread with tangy marinara sauce and topped with melted industrial-grade cheese of some white variety. That had been enough for the nutrition guidelines of the day, way back then. Or so it was in his memory when he filtered and layered his simulation just the way he wanted it. Then more safety movies hosted by a talking cricket in the afternoon. And with just ten minutes left Crometheus got the message from General Maximo's avatar. Report to the arcade. He was needed in-game. Which meant "combat duty" for the Pantheon.

The Uplifted marines were being sent forth into battle once more.

A little electric thrill ran up his spine. He never would have guessed that war would ever make him feel this way. Not when he had been the exact same very boy who sat in these same plastic seats in front of these carved and marked desks from long ago. That boy had dreamed of other things. Not being a rock star. Or the thing he'd eventually become. But he was heading toward it. Definitely. Whether he knew it or not.

The clues had been there if you knew where to look. And that was the thing about hindsight… you always knew where to look after the fact.

The love of danger.

The dirt-clod fights down near the train tracks.

Building model airplanes of old World War II fighters.

The clues had been right there, but he, along with everyone else, had never bothered to notice that war was something he wasn't just attracted to… it was something he loved. And was quite good at. It was, he'd often reflected during these long sojourns inside his reality, inside the arcade, a kind of sport to him.

When the final bell rang, which happened sooner than he liked, all the other kids donned their coats and it was time to go home for the afternoon. But instead of heading out across the soaked and muddy field under leaden skies where sometimes they all played football, he headed back across the quiet neighborhoods and wet streets that would bring him to the strip mall. To the arcade. To Lazer Command.

To report for combat duty.

Walking because he did not have his bike. He had not taken it that morning. Moving fast because the Pantheon was coming back into focus all around him. It was time to leave this reality. This truth. The truth he had made for himself. His truth edited to perfection. Time to enter the Pantheon. For just a little while, and then he would be back. He always came back.

He walked quickly across the rain-wet streets as the clouds turned to silver from the last of the afternoon sunshine and the sudden puddles became mirrors that looked into the many realities as the Pantheon began to assert its dominance over his domain. Switching between worlds had been mastered years ago during the famine, and of course the long trek after the failure at Sirius Two. And the world that had come after that.

It was dark inside the arcade once he reached it, as it always was. Except for the machines that played their same digital ditties, happy or ominous. Eight-bit playlets ran across screens, showing how you would fly this super-cobra through this underground cavern, shooting aliens and their weapon emplacements, or how you would run through this maze away from this giant bouncing ball of death while an early computer-voice shouted *Kill all humans*. And all the other noises, happy or sad that announced the joy of playing in all these little contrived worldlets. All for just a quarter. Or a token. All of them a kind of prophecy of what was to come.

A cheap price for all that unlimited fun.

That was the wonder of the Pantheon.

There was so much to do. So many worlds you could live unlimited lifetimes in. So many things you could become. So many places you could jump to from the anchor of your own world. A place of your own creation.

Lazer Command was his anchor. His bus terminal, his airport, his star port, to all those other worlds the Pantheon required him to serve in. Fight on. Destroy.

His... point of departure... was the arcade.

Old Man Webb wordlessly took the rumple-crumpled dollar and gave back five tokens. That was the rate of exchange. Opt for coin of the realm, as it were, and get an extra play. What a wonderful and brilliant thing. Crometheus thought about warming up on something else before trying out the new game that was occupying pride of place at the very heart of the arcade this afternoon. The place he was clearly being told to report to via General Maximo's avatar.

The new machine was called *Britannia Attack!*

He scanned the other machines. *Tempest. Scramble. Biological Genocide. Spy Hunter. Theater of War. Full-Scale Assimilation. Concentration Camp. Q*bert.*

But the message from Maximo had been urgent and therefore important.

Crometheus took his token, a faux golden disc stamped with symbols he'd never really studied. The word *fun* was repeated three times like some kind of magical phrase. He hadn't really studied the token all those years ago...

How many, he wondered?

Uncountable, the background apps of his mind answered in return. Unknowable because of all the lives one could live inside the Pantheon in mere seconds. He'd once fought in all the major battles of World War II and got the second-highest score on the ship. All of it in five seconds of real time. Someone once said that being in-game inside the Pantheon was like being "in forever."

Time had little meaning inside the realities of the Pantheon. Their ancestors, the Animals, or simple mindless pastoral humanity, had no concept of what it was like to be Uplifted.

But not no meaning. Time. It still passed. Because time was relentless that way. It could be fiddled with, but not made to disappear entirely.

He was still holding the little golden disc the world of his youth had called a "token," thinking about all these things in the quiet and yet subtly noisy arcade in which no one else was playing any of the other fantastic games, when he had another thought.

Except this felt more like a message from Maestro. A directive. A prompt. No... a better way to think about things. That was how one was supposed to view the wonder that was Maestro. An assistant to improve one's lot. Like Siri or Alexa had once been. But better than. More, in fact. Which, of course, always indicated better.

Right?

That was how it worked.

Where had he first heard those words...?

More is better.

He was sitting in a chair. In a large conference room. A hotel conference room... and there was an airport nearby, because the sound of the jets roaring for takeoff shook the windows at a certain point and they'd all gotten used to pausing their conversations at these dire moments of life and death for those out there in the jet. But inside the hotel by the airport, rows and rows of seats were filled with desperate people who'd come to improve their lot. And that day too had been a rainy afternoon just like this one had been long ago. And was inside the reality of the arcade now. A rainy weekend at the beginning of everything after he'd come to the end of himself.

In a hotel conference room out by the airport where the big jets thundered off into the sky and the lie of somewhere better.

After she'd gone for the last time.

Who?

You know. Holly Wood. She'd gone off somewhere. Wasn't that so? Wasn't that how it actually happened?

"That's what we're doing now," said Maestro in Crometheus's ear inside the quiet yet noisy in its way arcade. Quiet in that there were no human voices. Maestro sounded like some English butler. Someone with the class and sophistication to be completely freed of all the moral and societal constraints that kept one from becoming what one was supposed to one day really be.

King. Master. Artisan. Serial killer.

Another gamer, a girl he'd fought alongside in the game *Assault on Cappella Three*, where they'd found the ursoids after a sixty-five-year haul from the last star, had once told him that Maestro was just an AI. That's all. Albeit a super-intelligent AI based on an old actor named Anthony Hopkins. Before the Uplift, when the MW Collective first designed the prototype that would one day become Maestro, they called it the "Hannibal Project." Unofficially. An inside joke. Dark humor because the whole project had made some big leaps in synthetic cognitive reasoning after a data review of an earlier AI that had been trained to be a serial killer. Just an experiment of course, for the engineers at some big tech social media search engine giant. Just to see what would happen if they did. Y'know?

Just playing around to see what could be done, really done, when you didn't have any constraints. Like morals.

But some old newspaper, some shrieking conservative harridan, decried that the tech giant was making "AI serial killers." So they changed just the name for PR purposes.

Because humanity was afraid for itself. Of course, humanity was always afraid for itself. That was the basis of modern civilization back then. Unification through a series of common fears.

Much more malleable that way.

But that had been when they, the elites who really ruled Earth from behind the scenes, had been forced to play by the rules of the masses. Being forced to "play fair" by the very people they'd empowered in order to give themselves total mastery over the culture, and therefore the planet. That game was still in effect then. The Game. That was what the plan for Uplift was called, back then. The Game. But it had been Bad-Worded and edited out of existence in all the years since. Now it was called the

Path. In fact, it had always been called the Path. But back then they were only a few years away from being set free by the Exodus and the Big Uplift as the Game reached its conclusion. Getting off a ruined world and away from the Animals they could never evolve with as they had, was how the Game was won. Free to become something totally new. Free to call the super-intelligent AI that would help them run their lives what they wanted to call it.

In time the "Hannibal Project" gave birth to Maestro, never mind all the silly nonsense about them finding something called Super Mind Six on a derelict alien starship. That was pure nonsense. Maestro was a successful experiment to develop a Nietzschean algorithm that didn't hesitate to do what was best in order to achieve the desired ends of the Pantheon. It lacked the weakness of human frailty. It provided exactly what they needed to shuck that useless husk. They had created it because that's what gods did. They created.

That was the official truth. The one you needed to embrace. Not the story about a derelict alien starship found adrift by the colony ship *Pantheon* out there in the dark between the stars one hundred and twenty years out from Earth. Found, boarded, and recovered... and then the exponential leap forward that gave them Maestro. And how Maestro saved their lives by integrating their belief system with a frightening new technology.

Never mind that.

Edit.

That'll earn you a Bad Thought negative achievement point demotion in the blink of an eye, thought Crometheus, surprised that it hadn't already.

She, that gamer girl he'd fought alongside, had told him the conspiracy theory of a *found* Maestro when they went to war against the little bears on that forest world after Sirius Two. He made six levels and earned four thousand achievement points during the game on that planet. She told him that after they'd unlocked the thermonuclear obliteration option of the game and put paid to the rebellious little ursoids. Then the two of them blew their collective achievement points on a wild romp through 1890s Paris. It was an orgiastic vacation of vintage sex, mind-altering absinthe, and the great meals of the best French chefs from the decadent past. A combination of a colorful three-ring circus and a gourmand's descent into a fleshy bacchanal.

She told him all the rumors about finding Maestro in the smoking ruins of an ursoid base. He remembered all that now as he heard Maestro's voice, as if for the first time, despite its familiarity.

That voice prompting to drop a token into *Britannia Attack!*, that was Maestro. Cool. Calm. Rich and deep. The voice of competent reason. A voice having once belonged to an actor who was best known for playing a serial killer in some old set of films. Not that anybody remembered those anymore. They just thought of him as Maestro now. They'd made even better serial killer films on the long crossings from conquered world to conquered world. Real ones with no special effects. Films where the killer was the hero. Those, of course, were the best kind if you were part of the Uplifted. Once you understood the narrative that doing anything you want is the ultimate liberation and a step along the Path.

So it wasn't called the Hannibal Project, noted Crometheus. That's a bad thought.

Thirty-five achievement points.

It was called Maestro, and he would show them how to become gods along the Way of a Thousand Steps. Which was what the Path had always officially been called. Path was just insider-speak for the awakened. The Uplifted.

The Way of a Thousand Steps had been the book title of the author that had been holding that seminar out by the airport that rainy weekend.

Your Journey to Becoming God was the subtitle. That was also the title of the lecture at the airport Marriott that had changed his life forever. Or rather... rescued his life. Rescued from whom? From himself, he answered. And always would. Of course. But even that meaning had become lost in all the lived lifetimes aboard the *Pantheon*. It wasn't really him who'd done all those things, caused all that havoc and ruin across the canvas of his old life. Which of course he had. But when he thought about it now, centuries later after centuries of conditioning about whose fault it really was and of course the answer always being *Yours*... what he really meant by *You* was his old human, or Animal, nature. Not who he was now. The Path had rescued him from himself, and them all... from humanity.

He, player Crometheus, used to know how many steps he'd taken along the Way of a Thousand Steps. The Path.

He'd been counting them with each achievement, reward, insight, and enlightenment garnered in war, local Armageddon, and planetary holocaust on all the worlds the colony ship *Pantheon* had made. And that had been truly immature of him to count. Really, weak was the right word. To keep track was the sign of a lesser mind not bent to the grand picture and the great things that must be accomplished. TED 14:9. To count steps toward becoming was like a child playing with a ball. The sign of a weak mind whose only interest was in the result as opposed to the journey. And the becoming. He'd discovered that kernel of truth from promptings by Maestro when he reached the step in which the Path told you to stop counting how many steps you'd taken along the thousand steps of the Path. Because only mortals and petty finite beings bothered with numbers and definitions.

Results.

Truth.

Meaningless in the grand scheme.

The Xanadu Tower never counted. Had never counted.

Gods, the truly enlightened of the Uplifted, ruled reality from the Tower, and they knew they were enlightened once they'd reached enlightenment. But in order to do that they'd needed to lose count along the way. Lose themselves and all the petty constraints that tied them down.

TED 89:93.

Just as those in the remotest and most secure regions aboard the colony ship *Pantheon* had lost themselves in order to ascend above all the petty ruling councils that had once formed the Pantheon. Such were the Uplifted worthies who inhabited the Xanadu Tower.

Such all hoped one day to be. Or even possibly... greater than...

Maestro had revealed this to Crometheus during the sack of a world called Sumoratu. As its vast forests burned down to charcoal and ruin and the Uplifted marines hunted the survivors far down into their deep caves and underground viridian seas, after one particularly vicious firefight in which there'd been severe casualties taken among the marine gaming clans, Maestro illuminated Crometheus when he felt hopeless. Shot to hell and one arm blown off. The game-overed outnumbering the living. And still more work to do down in the lower vaults of that exterminated civilization.

Doomsday weapons to be dealt with and deactivated.

Maestro suggested then that there were levels beyond the Xanadu Tower. Greater greatnesses than anyone had dared dream of achieving.

And so now, standing here in the arcade, Maestro prompted him, in front of the brand-new game called *Britannia Attack!* with its slick graphics along the top and sides of the upright cabinet that showed a planet being invaded by armored space marines while a fantastic fleet fought in space above, energy weapons sizzling and missiles streaking smoky trails, all violent reds and cool interstellar blues. The eight-bit digital song playing over and over was relentlessly triumphant, as though it were some Beatles song made into an imperial march. Ceaselessly important. Deeply inspiring. It reminded Crometheus of something composed by Philip Glass, who surely himself must have gone into one of the cryo banks and then centuries later moved on to one of the colony ships in the Uplift when those who were to become great gods shed themselves of the mortal coil of humanity and turned their backs on the final wreck that was Earth.

Surely Philip Glass and so many others had made it off the dying home world of all their origins. The longevity techniques were already in place. Secret and not for mass consumption. Hidden cryo banks to wait out terminal diseases and fatal injuries beneath Beverly Hills, Dubai, Beijing... along with all the other great capitals where the elites constructed their economic holdfasts guarded faithfully by media watchdogs and Orwellian police-state social media forces worthy of any fascist army. All of it had been in place back then. Before the last moments of The Game. In fact, far longer than anyone had ever suspected. Cryostasis when you died. Or were dying. Long before the Age of Uplift was even a dream. Immortality through technology. Tech that was expensive and held back from the masses wasn't held back from the best. Of course. Hundreds of years before everything went sideways it was already there, scooping up all the greatest of politics, wealth, and power, and even some of the rock stars, movie stars, and occasional sitcom beauties who'd managed to level up. Planetarily speaking.

The Mozarts of the world couldn't be lost as Mozart himself had been at thirty-three. The tech hadn't been available then. But it might have been around in 1965 when the lung cancer beat you. There were ways to keep you in cold storage and keep you around until newer tech could be developed. Tech that would restart. Reclaim. Reintegrate into the collective Uplifted.

All these thoughts, courtesy of Maestro of course, flooded Crometheus and overwhelmed him with images and phrases until he understood what the gentle butler who'd once eaten a man's liver with some fava beans and a nice glass of Chianti was showing him.

"We've arrived on our planet," said Maestro gently. "A planet all our own. You are almost there, Master Crometheus. You are almost ready to become a god. And this, my dear boy, is what we're doing today. We call it… an asymmetrical boarding action designed to stop an enemy counterattack."

Crometheus dropped the bronze disc of the stamped token into the slot of the arcade machine *Britannia Attack!* Sometimes a token, from overuse or whatever, just slid right through and down in to the return tray. Old Man Webb would give you a new one if that was the case. But not this time. It landed in the deep heart of the war machine.

The kick is good, as they used to say, thought Crometheus. As *he* used to say during his rock god days at the Chateau Marmont on Sunset. Shooting heroin with starlets and models. Binging for days at a time because you could, and it was expected of you to do such so that status and image might be maintained for better album sales. Rock god problems. The world and all that was in it was your personal plaything. But the signed contract required that you play the game. Drop the token in. Take the ride. And so he had.

The kick is good.

"This is what we're becoming now, Master Crometheus," reminded the ever-present Maestro in his ear as the screen changed and asked him to "Press Ready, Player One."

Then he was in-game.

He could feel the joystick in his hand. The fire button beneath his right index finger. He tapped the Player One button. And now he was ready. Now he was gone from own his private world and jacking into a Frankenstein killing machine. His other true self.

The Uplifted marine.

Player Crometheus.

Fun, huh?

We call it *an asymmetrical boarding action designed to stop a counterattack.*

Gods:
Chapter Four

In-game, Player Crometheus was aboard one of the Odin's Spear–class assault ships they'd developed and built during the long haul after Cappella Three. When they had resources to burn after they'd shed themselves and plundered an entire planet.

His Frankensteinian combat frame, tricked out with new upgrades, perks, and boosts, was stacked in the rapid deployment racks and ready for a hot drop boarding action.

"This is General Maximo…" began a strident, almost hectoring voice in Crometheus's ear. General Maximo was the greatest player… ever. Many Uplifted in the chats, hangouts, and pleasure domes agreed he would be the next one to reach enlightenment and complete the uplift to the inner sanctums of the Xanadu Tower. He'd used a mutating nano-virus on the ocean world of the Asuulomons, turning its inhabitants' scaly bodies against themselves. The "Pandora's Box" bioweapon had been one of Maestro's greatest projects, and it was used only in the most extremely dire of situations to accomplish the Pantheon's goals. Maximo had earned fifty thousand achievement points from the Pantheon just for daring to use that weapon against that nigh-unconquerable water world that had vexed the marines. When the Animals discovered that world someday, if they discovered that world, all they'd find would be a vast dead sea filled with rotting corpses and bleached bones. Nothing but ruin for daring to oppose the Uplifted.

Imagine that day. The Animals would feel a cold streak up their spines because it would be like looking at their own impending death.

Imagine it.

Crometheus often had. Mainly the General Maximo parts. A fast track toward full Uplift didn't just happen every day. You had to be on the lookout for an opportunity to leap ahead of the pack. Ready for any chance that came up no matter how many millions had to die. It wasn't enough to be just Uplifted. There were inner rings of power. Other levels. Strange worlds inside the Pantheon. And the discovery of each ring revealed a new fulcrum of power over others, often hidden in plain sight.

"Operations against the Animal-infested planetary body known as New Britannia have already begun," continued Maximo over the briefing comm as the assault ships were readied for attack. Engines boosting. Repulsors coming online. The chatter of nav data between the strike pilots filling the background of the Uplifted marines' comm. "As of this hour, in-game, we currently control the planet and most of its surviving major cities. Non-nuclear weapons of mass destruction have been used. Processing operations are underway on the local population and we can expect complete Animal extermination and at least seventy percent reclamation within the next thirty days. Uplifted of the Pantheon... you've been introduced into the battle at this moment in space, aboard the allied Uplifted vessel *Id Sociocracy*. While they do not share our way of thinking, they fight alongside us in this final solution against the Animals, and have provided us this transportation into the battle, as the *Pantheon* has come to permanent rest on our new world. Which will henceforth be known as... Pantheon. What the Animals once called New Vega. At the social reinforcement direction protocols of Maestro, we are assisting the Id, as they will henceforth be known, in capturing this new home world for them."

Crometheus and the rest of the Pantheon marines were given access to a tactical display of all in-game assets currently in play within the system of New Britannia. The sites of major engagements were highlighted and tagged with further detail. In three nano-seconds, Crometheus ran through the entire conflict to date.

Initial assault on New Britannia by the Id and a fleet of allied Uplifted vessels. Non-nuclear bombardment of capital city Londoneaux. Bacterial paralysis influence strike against Charing. Special weapons assault force deployed against orbital base Sandhurst. EMP strike on Southern Scotlands. Deployment of capture teams in that region. Suborbital engagement against Animal carrier group. Battle of Steading. Battle of Hull. Battle of... and so on and so on. It hadn't taken long for the Id, with the help of the other allied Uplifted, to take near-total control of the Animal world.

But now, on the system assets display, new Animal forces were moving into the system to assist. Telemetric and scouting data coming in from an Id scout vessel tracking incoming jump signatures indicated a counterstrike against the engaged Uplifted vessels. The Id's main colony ship, like the Pantheon on New Vega, had set down forever on a tidal plain west of the burning ruins of Londoneaux.

"It'll be our job," continued Maximo, "to deal with this new threat coming in from the Animal worlds calling themselves the Coalition. They have the outrageous blasphemy to throw their own into a senseless battle against our superior tech and forces. It's as if they don't even realize who they're fighting. As all great leaders of war must do, I pity them and their ignorance for the destruction they are about to unloose on themselves. But my pity only goes so far, Marines. Today we will show our fellow Uplifted that we, the Pantheon, are the best at war among the chosen. This will be a boarding action game against a strike force of United Worlds warships sent in to rescue their fellow Animals. Maestro is downloading strike packages and clan assignments now. You have your orders. Fight well for honor and glory, and let us show them who their new gods will be this day."

The response force from the Pantheon consisted of thirty-six Odin's Spear–class attack vehicles launched from off the *Id Sociocracy*. Two hundred marines were racked and stacked, ready to deploy on intercept with an incoming Animal strike force. As depicted on tactical, the assault vessels were zooming in, burners at full, to head off the incoming Coalition battle group closing on the Id's operations fleet around the recently conquered world.

You have been assigned to Clan Thunder Claw, the strike package informed Crometheus. Clan Thunder Claw's primary target was the United Worlds attack cruiser leading the strike. The *Fury*. There were nine other ships in the Animal attack fleet, all of them fast and lethal. They moved in a standard assault formation for capital ships of that size.

"Spear Thirteen locked and loaded for bear," intoned the pilot over the comm. Clan Thunder Claw was interfacing with the group comm. "Contact in thirty seconds. Racks deploying..."

Suddenly Crometheus's view from inside the cylindrical ship that was Spear Thirteen flipped, and now he was looking at the battlespace from the exterior of the fast-moving attack ship. The ship had literally reversed deployment-rack-laden hull panels from internal to external, deploying marines all along the exterior of the hull.

The view of space was breathtaking. The colors were bright against the backdrop of burning space and the glorious ruin of the carrier force... brighter still, as filters provided by Maestro colored everything as it should be, instead of how it was.

Now Crometheus could see the two wedges of Animal ships on an intercept course with the Id surrounding New Britannia. The Animals' shipbuilding skills were impressive. United Worlds ships all looked like assault rifles, but writ large. Matte-black and thirty to forty decks high in some cases, the ships bristled with weapons aft of their forward bridge discs. To the rear, powerful drive systems radiated immense heat signatures as the warships switched over to ion from jump for in-system travel.

"Look at 'em!" cried Mantacore, a player Crometheus knew from other battles. He'd been a famous researcher long ago. Turning weather into weapon systems for the corporate military complex of last-stage Earth. His IQ had assured him a place in the Uplift of long ago. He was good for the gene pool, as they liked to say.

Crometheus agreed with Mantacore's wonder. The Animal ships were indeed dangerous-looking. Probably more dangerous than anything the Uplifted of the Pantheon had ever faced before New Vega. But they'd beaten them on that world, had taken it for their own. Crometheus, among many other deeds that day, had personally shot down one of their assault ships during the initial Coalition insertion onto the battlefield. With the help of the Javelin Anti-Ship System Maestro had developed for them, of course. But it was he who'd pulled the trigger with no targeting solution and nothing but direct fire to go on in those desperate seconds when the battle could have gone either way.

So there was that.

They'd beaten the Coalition once. They'd beat them again. Here. Today.

Of course, Mantacore would get an achievement point demotion from Maestro for daring to be impressed over comm at the strength of an enemy. Fear was one of the first steps shed along the Way of a Thousand Steps. Obviously, not all were as enlightened as some.

Crometheus felt sorry that Mantacore was lesser. But then checked himself. That too was something he'd shed along the way. Something that made one weak. And got in the way of becoming.

Pity.

Pity and remorse had been shed long ago.

Crometheus instead studied all the glorious destruction of the ruined Britannian carrier fleet drifting like flotsam out there in the big nether of space. None of these ships was as big as the smallest of the Uplifted colony ships that had set out from destroyed Earth. But the Animals in their fumbling had nevertheless managed to construct large and impressive vessels by the looks of what remained. The ruined Britannian carrier was a hollow ovoid cylinder, much like the standard Uplifted Rama-class vessel, except smaller and squashed wide at her widest. Her bridge, or what remained of it, was set atop the cylinder and along one side like the command stack of an ocean-going carrier of old. Fighters had once launched out of the hangar bays connected along the ovoid. These bays were modular, according to Uplifted intel. The hangars could be swapped out for either space or atmospheric operations. The Animals did not possess fighters that were capable of both at this present time. Though there were reports that the ones who called themselves the Spilursans were closest to perfecting a design capable of engaging in combat within both theaters.

The fires still raging out of control on the Animal carrier were mainly located in the modularized hangar bays. Her jump drive and engine sections had either been disconnected due to reactor cascade failure, or damaged so heavily that they needed to be shed for emergency survival operations. Either way the carrier was dead in space. Had been for days. Stored and racked munitions had been cooking off at random intervals, destroying vast sections of the immense warship.

Expanding away from the carrier was a debris field of tumbling hulls and frozen bodies that had once been her fifteen support ships and crew complement. Little of the twisted and ruined debris was recognizable. Not that it mattered. The glorious ruin of the still-burning massive carrier and the wreckage of her supporting ships might strike fear or inspire courage, but otherwise that was a battle completed, and the glory and achievement points that had been earned there had gone to other players.

Crometheus had no time for that. *The past is prologue to every new moment of becoming.* TED 74:19.

Yet Crometheus would not have objected to seeing the Britannian fleet in a less smithereen-like condition. Ever since war had been declared after the various Uplifted had finally agreed to cease their petty conflicts against one another and band together in a Grand Alliance to cleanse explored space of the infection that was the Animals, ever since then he'd spent much of his reality studying all the acquired and known intel regarding the ships and military forces of their coming opponents. Even if the opponents didn't know they were at war yet, it would pay to know them well before they saw you coming.

In space-time, this war had begun almost thirty years ago when the Uplifted tribes began to formulate an alliance. In his chosen reality maybe fifteen seconds, or two hundred years, or several thousand lifetimes. It all depended on how he wanted to access the data and spend manipulated time understanding it.

Space-time was best for in-game, he reminded himself. It was the closest to an augmented reality.

Now Spear Thirteen was sweeping in across the tip of the incoming United Worlds strike force. A destroyer leader, the *Connelly*—Crometheus knew this from his studies—built and commissioned supposedly in a United Worlds shipyard, capable of launching four M27 ship-to-ship missiles, or SSMs as the Animals called them, led the attack. The *Connelly* was also blistering with over thirty medium-range engagement pulse batteries and fifteen close-point defense batteries her crew referred to as PDCs.

Spear Thirteen's pilot made a dangerous and close pass along the *Connelly*'s hull. There was just the unmoving nothingness of space and then suddenly the enemy ship swam in at high speed as Crometheus lay racked on the outside of the streaking attack ship. It was a dangerous flight path to choose, but a close pass made the active tracking system on the Animals' powerful PDCs less likely to acquire and engage successfully. The Odin's Spear–class vessels weren't built to stand up in a firefight. They were built to drop Uplifted marines all over a ship in seconds, covering her in deadly enemies.

Just get us to the objective, thought Crometheus.

The next enemy ship along the wedge they were headed straight at, now that they'd penetrated the Animals' attack formation, was their target. Cruiser *Fury*. Interlocking

PDC fire lit up the grid within both wings of the wedge trying to knock down the Uplifted marines' assault delivery ships coming in at every angle. Some of the spears went up like sudden flares or got nailed and went off like powerful firecrackers, while others got strafed by PDC fire and stayed on target for their intercepts, dead marines dangling from the hulls.

"Missile launch! Multiple vehicles outbound!" shouted the pilot over the comm. This was an alert to the leader running Thunder Claw Clan.

"Target solutions computed..." intoned Maestro calmly, breaking in over the chatter. "Animal SSMs tracking for Uplifted vessel *Archon*. Stand by to deploy onto your targets."

Suddenly Spear Thirteen spun on her axis, and rocket racks erupted away from the tiny assault ship like blossoming flower petals of bright fire. Each rack ignited on approach to the target hull.

"Here we go, gents!" said a player tagged Brutulus. A player Crometheus had gamed with before and didn't like much. Back before the Uplift, Brutulus had been a high-powered financier specializing in pharmaceuticals. He'd made a killing by marking up a cancer drug that could be manufactured for pennies. It worked, too. Cured the disease within a week. If you had the three hundred thousand dollars to pay for it. Or were willing to obligate yourself to a lifetime of debt. It was a bold power play by the high-flying financier, and he'd reaped the rewards until the last days of Earth when the economy collapsed in full.

On the other hand, if you were part of the elite ruling class that mentored Earth despite her starving dirty masses teeming for civil war and freedom of speech, then you got access to all the best medicines and didn't need to worry about the cost. Your IQ and adherence to The Game guaranteed your survival. Despite even death.

Every life counted... if it was the right kind of life.

Random thoughts such as Brutulus's past and the old cancer plagues surfaced at the speed of light inside Crometheus's mind, allowing him to call up all this old data on the fly like some background app. It was calming, in a way. Permitting him to zen out on data and focus on the task at hand, despite the constant crawl of information. Like classical music to someone studying for final exams.

And Crometheus was indeed studying his target as though his becoming depended on it. His rapid deployment rack had disengaged from the assault ship and the powerful Coalition vessel was racing at him, growing rapidly out the vast blackness of space, hurtling its bulk at his HUD.

Fury was the biggest ship in the Animal strike force. Maestro's intel indicated that it was very likely the source of command and control for the entire counterattack operation. And it was an honor that Clan Thunder Claw had been tasked with identifying the enemy command team and terminating their influence on the developing battle. Secondary objective was to destroy the ship. Specifically, her propulsion systems.

Crometheus ran through everything he knew as the ship raced up at him. Twin-hulled. Connecting at a forward command bridge disc. Nine SSM tubes—eight forward, one rear. Forty-eight pulse heavy guns. Ninety medium-engagement batteries. Over fifty PDCs. And a state-of-the-art electronic engagement warfare center called the PITT. Primary Intel Targeting and Termination. Reports indicated that this center had been developed in connection with the New Vega science and research labs deep in the bunkers beneath the city. Maestro had tagged the intel as "developing" and had requested a core hack and selfies within the PITT. Both would be rewarded with achievement points.

Crometheus added that to his list of things to do.

Kill admiral.

Disable engines.

Selfie in the PITT.

And along the way…

Kill.

Kill your way to Big Prizes. For honor and for glory.

And win big prizes. Life was good. Immortality was great! Game on!

Gods:
Chapter Five

Spear Thirteen got hit by battery fire off the *Fury*. A direct hit at that range and there was nothing left and nowhere to go. But the spinning racks of dropped Uplifted marines were already clear of the wounded delivery vehicle, and seconds after it began its drop spin, they were fanning the target ship *Fury*, their heavy-duty insertion racks attaching themselves to the target's hull.

The Uplifted pilot was definitely game-overed as the cockpit forward of the flight deck exploded aboard Spear Thirteen. Maybe he got a consciousness upload. Maybe not. And truth be told, even Crometheus doubted the consciousness upload really worked. Who was to say that... that you, or rather the "you" that emerged ... was really you? The priests might affirm it... but even they weren't gods yet. And of course, the upload would claim it was really you. What other choice did it have? It probably wasn't even a choice. It most likely believed it really was you with every byte of its being.

Back in the battle there was a blinding flash as Spear Thirteen got hit. A sudden spark in the deep of dark space despite the maelstrom of incoming bright fire from the Animal attack cruisers. There must have been some kind of guidance system connection between the drop racks and delivery vehicle, because once Thirteen went up like a comet coming apart in atmosphere, the drop racks lost tracking on the bridge of the *Fury*, which had been the primary target insertion point, and the rack Crometheus was bolted into was now literally flying along the enemy cruiser's hull, skimming and randomly impacting with systems and plating, completely out of control. In the blink of an eye his rack overshot the bridge disc, made for the port side, and struck some sort of outcropping sensor device, ripping it away clean. The collision also obliterated two of the other clanmates attached to Crometheus's rack. Pulped and smashed within their armor. Negative on the upload. Maybe there was a backup on file somewhere within the collective whole.

And if not...

Centuries of Uplifted enlightenment gone. Never to be returned.

Again, these notes from reality filled the background informational crawl of Crometheus's mind. Tagged and saved for considered rumination in the future.

The rack leader ordered a verbal ejection command. That might save some of the marines. It would also no doubt send others spinning helplessly off into the void of space, in the middle of a battle. It was all random chance now.

In that slow-motion instant of the drop rack bouncing off the enemy ship's hull and then continuing along its matte-black length at an insane speed, directional chemical burn rockets attempting to course-correct...

Crometheus executed a hard disconnect and cast his fate to the wind. As it were.

A second later the rack smashed into a pulse battery engaging another Spear passing close by along the hull. The drop rack and enemy defensive gun exploded together in sudden fireworks, ensuring everyone on board the rack, and within the gun battery, was dead. Eighty percent of the roster for the clan suddenly blinked into game-overed gray.

Crometheus spun free of the rack, saw the hull slithering past him, and knew he was headed off into the dark within the next few seconds. Power couplers and massive transfer tubes seemed to flee from his eyes as he shot down the length of the ship. The whole experience was similar to falling down a hill. And into deep space. With little chance of recovery.

He reached out with one gauntlet and tried to grab a comm antenna. Most likely a locally redundant system for inter-ship communication in the event of malfunction or enemy EMP strike. The slender pole came away in his grip. Now he and it were heading together toward a giant half-dome located amidships.

Turrets were throwing fire into the void, tracking and destroying the not-so-agile yet fast to turn-and-burn Uplifted Spears swarming the Coalition fleet. A powerful explosion rocked one of the Animal destroyer escorts off to starboard. Someone had gotten their objective early.

"Way to go, Chromancer!" shouted the in-game announcer AI over general Uplifted comm. "Primary objective achieved! Big prizes!"

"Damn!" Crometheus swore at Chromancer as he tumbled quickly for the dome, mindful that he either stopped here or he was out of the battle and most likely game-overed because he'd seen no Uplifted assets tasked for search and rescue.

A second later he hit the curve of the hull and grabbed for the edge of a sensor disc, demanding that it hold.

Positive thinking paid off, even though momentum and inertia worked to defeat his best efforts.

"It always does," he chanted to himself. Thinking positive affirmations, that is. It always pays off. Something he'd learned long ago along the Path. In a positive chanting retreat with some clutch of tech gurus in Myanmar during the run-up to the last days of old ruined Earth. A hidden mountaintop Zen palace in which they'd all learned that mind could be made to dominate matter. That deceiving yourself was the first step to deceiving others. Deception could manufacture truth. And that power could be had for those willing to play the trick on themselves first, before it was played on the masses.

"Activate zero-gee operations for environmental movement," he grunted at his HUD.

The armor's gauntlets and boots disconnected from the hull and in moments he had the high-powered laser torch activated and was cutting into the cruiser *Fury*. Then he was in and crawling through the darkness between the hulls. Looking for the inner hull's barrier. Red lights swam to life, warning, "Outer hull breach in progress, this section. Please evacuate!"

Command and data feed with Maestro fritzed out. Something close at hand and running a powerful EM signature was jamming his connection. Radio silence for now. Maestro would do his best to reconnect when he could.

Crometheus spotted the emergency hatch up ahead. Information tags highlighted its working mechanisms. Database entries from Maestro, developed from captured and studied Animal ships taken in combat, explained how to enter the enemy warship. Breach charges were no good. The armor was carrying six of them, but he'd save those for the propulsion systems so he could get his secondary objective kill bonus. Those were always worth a lot of achievement points.

He swept his gauntlets along the beveled sides and found the function interface panel. He stared at it for a long moment despite the emergency lighting and the sudden tremors within the superstructure as direct hits were scored against critical systems. Beyond the outer hull the battle raged. The Coalition ships had probably closed to pulse and SSM range of the Id fleet.

To Crometheus, an Uplifted elite who'd long ago shed the trappings of stifling human technology, the emergency hatch operating system was like an abacus. Abysmally useless as far as Uplifted standards were concerned. Little more than a quaint toy to be amused by.

"Ah," Crometheus muttered to himself. "They use eight-digit alphanumeric codes swapped out every twenty-four hours."

He pulled the panel off with a swift yank, his strength augmented by the armor for so long it felt like his own.

He knew exactly the amount of pressure to use. Behind the panel, wiring lay exposed. He found the two wires he needed, and connected them.

A second later, despite the Animals' attempts to secure themselves with mere numbers and letters, all from one language no doubt—he laughed inwardly at this—he'd defeated their little barrier. The hatch slid open, exposing a small airlock below. He dropped down and found the operation terminal. Gravity decking restored a sense of place, and he worked at their terminal to close the hatch he'd just violated. A moment later he had the airlock controls ready to bend to his will.

He blew the lock accessing the inner hatch by issuing a force command. A feature they'd put in by *design* for some insane reason, apparently believing that simple authorization from engineering or command would protect it. All of these security efforts were child's play. His gauntlet ran a worm that showed him everything he could do within their laughable root command system.

All the amok he could run.

The door's security bolts ruptured internally, and Crometheus stepped to one side. A moment later the hatch exploded past him as pressure from the ship's onboard atmosphere sent it slamming like a bull into the opposite wall of the airlock.

He detected oxygen flooding into the airlock from the ship. He didn't need air. He had the armor. The Animals, on the other hand… did. Unless they'd gone to battle stations like the first warship crews in space had, and had enviro-suited up before battle.

He accessed the terminal and opened the airlock's outer hatch. Venting precious oxygen into the space between the hulls.

Damage klaxons were going off, and emergency lighting was in operation. An automated Animal voice, sounding to him like it was talking in ponderous motion slowed down even further by being recorded underwater, took forever to tell him that a hull breach was in progress.

Of course, he thought. *I'm the one who breached it.*

The first crew person to be sucked out through the airlock was already bloody and most likely unconscious from having smashed into something along the way. The void of space would suck everything into it until blast doors could be lowered into place to seal the breach. This sudden surprise of violence would allow him to gain the advantage even though he was most likely outnumbered here within the enemy ship. Without comms he had no way of knowing how many of his clanmates might have already breached the vessel. Perhaps they'd already achieved the primary objective.

That would be disappointing. But there were always secondary objectives.

Like killing.

He took the HK G-97 from its place on his shoulder. He'd start heavy. First impressions were important, he reminded himself.

He was carrying three slug-throwing weapons.

The G-97. Standard for all Pantheon Uplifted marines.

An automatic shotgun currently loaded with dumb slugs. Identified by Pantheon gamers as *The Shredder*. A design based on the old M45 tactical shotgun, but upgraded with an under-barrel flechette launcher that absolutely ruined biological lifeforms.

And the fifty-cal Automag sidearm. His personal favorite. A massive automatic pistol that dispensed large doses of fire and was ammo-fed by the armor's magazines.

"Time to clean," he muttered, and watched as another Animal crewman, a woman, screamed wordlessly as she was sucked out past him into the cold void between hulls. Blast doors were lowering into place. Atmosphere was being restored. Automated emergency damage control procedures were in effect. Firearms were now effective.

Gods:
Chapter Six

Crometheus murdered his way to the inner sanctum known as the PITT. At first there was little to no resistance. Animal crewmen, weak navy-based bots, simply shrieked in terror and tried to run from him and the G-97. Some drew blaster-type sidearms and fired ineffectively against his newly upgraded armor, others cried and whimpered as he shot them down. There was always the irrational "You don't have to do this" plea. As though they didn't, or couldn't, believe that they were at war and facing the end of their existence as a civilization. As though they knew nothing about evolution and nature being writ in tooth and claw. As though they couldn't believe what was real, was actually real.

Threat assessment across the HUD was telling him their personal weapon systems needed a direct three-point-five-centimeter brain stem wound, or multiple hits on subsystems, to disable him. Barring that... he was invulnerable to their efforts. At first.

Suddenly Crometheus noticed he was reconnected to Maestro. Relief washed across his being.

"Beware, young godling," announced Maestro calmly over the HUD's internal comm as Crometheus ventilated three enemy crewmen trying to dog a blast hatch that gave way to the PITT's combined sensory array and processing node. At the same time, the in-game announcer shrieked over Maestro's warning: "Animal marines inbound on your position!"

"The rest of Thunder Claw, or rather those that have survived, are proceeding toward their objectives. I've had to reassign several objectives due to casualties, so you will be operating alone for the foreseeable future. Continue to the PITT and complete the objectives for that location."

Maestro told him what he should do next to accomplish the mission amid a frenetic exchange of gunfire near the hatch. He closed with, "Dispatch the new threats before proceeding forward to complete your mission, Master Crometheus. Succeed and you shall receive a full upgrade including one night at the Olympus in Sin City with the sex-model-dancer-actress of your choosing… B category."

A sudden fan spray of glam shots from some very impressive beauties in their most seductive poses fell across Crometheus's HUD as he shot down a wounded Animal who refused to die easily. The man was bleeding from three gaping wounds and fumbling to load a charge pack for his sidearm with blood-slick hands. None of the beauties were Holly Wood… but none of them were slouches, either. He was suddenly partial to a doe-eyed platinum-blond Asian with long legs wearing a rubber body suit and holding an old-school Xbox game controller in her hand. The image went live and she puckered her lips and blew him a kiss, thrust a hip to one side and pouted, saying "Game on, babycakes!" Crometheus was so distracted by her tempting come-on that he grazed the wounded Animal's head with a badly aimed shot. Thankfully the powerful fifty-caliber slug did most of the work and destroyed a large section of the man's skull anyway, painting the wall with blood and brain matter.

The new threats, actual ground combat-trained military forces, were coming for him now along the enemy ship's passages.

Crometheus dialed in the Shooting Stars unlock he'd just been upgraded with and slipped through the half-shut hatch. Beyond this he found cool blue light and a tunnel of direct-access processors running status displays of the various ship's systems. This wasn't the full processing hub, but it was good enough to do some serious damage to the ship's fire-control functions.

Shooting Stars system online appeared in his HUD. But that wasn't for now. That would come later.

Instead he pulled the trigger on the G-97 and savaged the processors with an entire mag of micro-nine. Three hundred rounds of nano-expand nine-millimeter destroyed this section of the tunnel, penetrating the initial interfaces and ricocheting around inside the guts of hard-wired systems. Primary and secondary damage achieved as the micro-nine ruined the linked processors.

No doubt the ship's batteries were now experiencing some kind of "glitch" in their firing solutions software.

"Excellent work! Major damage!" whooped the ecstatic in-game announcer over the general clan comm. " Pantheon intel network assessing for damage..."

A cash-register sound emitted over the comm, triumphantly ringing out its award. Old-school greenbacks showered down across the HUD.

"Portside batteries targeting offline for Animal cruiser *Fury*. Great job, Crometheus! Sixty thousand to you! Big prizes!" The gusto and enthusiasm with which the in-game announcer said all this was laughable, but the truth was—Crometheus had to admit it to himself—it pumped you up to do more damage and commit more carnage. It was very motivational. And sometimes, on your own and outnumbered, motivation counted for a lot.

I'm easy that way, he thought as he rapped a new mag of micro-nine for the G-97 against his helmet and then slapped it into the receiver. A half second later he was up and scanning for targets amid the smoke and ruin.

Good money for that one, reflected Crometheus on the award. He and the Asian gamer girl could blow all that on a very good time in Sin City. But right now there was more to be earned, and of course there were also countless other ways to spend it once the game was over. The trick was to survive long enough to enjoy it. Game-overed was game-overed. Nothing mattered after that because there was nothing.

Moving forward to wreak more havoc on the PITT, he checked the armor's sensor scan one more time. All of this was chump change. If he could selfie inside the objective then the sky was the limit for him and Miss Gamer. Maybe he could even upgrade her. Pick something from the A-List.

He was juiced and cruising on overkill when the *Fury*'s marine detachment came at him from a secure access well inside the processing node coolers.

"Type 50 military-grade assault blaster capable of three-round bursts rated to damage level significant," warned Maestro over the HUD. "These have teeth. And they do like to bite. Be careful."

Crometheus heeded Maestro's warning and hugged wall behind a bulkhead as he observed the Animal marines moving forward in squads, covering the advance elements with an unidentified heavy weapon system in support. The shadowy silhouettes of the advance squad were obscuring his armor's ability to tag and identify the weapon system, so he pushed the G-97 out from behind the bulkhead and dumped half a mag of micro-nine just to get their attention and force them down into the defensive, moving to cover positions.

A second later he was tagging hits and hearing the Animals calling out that so-and-so and the other guy were hit. Their leader was identifying where the firing was coming from.

Of course they were covering. Animals were ruled by fear. As he'd once been. Before he shed all those stupid petty little ways and started *becoming*.

He stepped out into the passageway, and now he had a clear view of the heavy weapon system they'd brought in to deal with him. Down the corridor, beyond the first batch of Animal marines, was one of their kind kitted with a servo-assisted load-bearing equipment interface. The heavy weapon gunner needed not only that, but a support gunner who would manage the belt feed of micro-charge packs.

The Pantheon had seen this weapon system before.

"The T-42 heavy pulse rifle," said Maestro in almost the same instant the distant gunner screamed some quaint expletive for bravado's sake. "My word, they really don't intend to change with the times. Terminate with extreme prejudice and cleanse the galaxy of this Animal filth, young Crometheus!"

Maestro was right; the T-42 was old. But it was effective. Half of Crometheus's squad on New Vega had been ripped to shreds by this very weapon during an attempted breach on the northern defenses of what the local Animals had called Triangle Square. On the brutal front line of that vicious battle, Crometheus had to commandeer a molten metal thrower just to cleanse the area of the Animal team and shut down the assault.

That option was not viable now.

Whereas the Animals didn't, or couldn't, upgrade their armor, systems, weapons, and defenses between battles… for the Pantheon this was a way of existence. And really… the why of existence.

Upgrading.

Evolution.

Becoming what you will become. Constantly evolving to meet the new challenges presented.

To the faithful of the Pantheon, and to almost every other Uplifted culture, or what the Animals called the Savages—yes, he was aware of the slur; he liked it, even took pride in it—to the Savages… change was everything.

Bad Thought. Bad Thought. Bad Thought. Savages is unauthorized word creep from proximity to Animal infection. Reprioritize and use... Uplifted.

Crometheus ignored the prompt. A certain amount of leeway was given with marines when engaged in combat operations. And especially during games. The fun of slang could be indulged as long as you were victorious and killed a lot of Animals.

Of course his new armor upgrades within weeks after the Battle for New Vega were to be expected. To have not upgraded would have been... heresy. Blasphemy. Sin against the very philosophy of every known Uplifted culture.

Bad Thought.

Sin is good.

Sin City for pleasure with Asian gamer girl.

Sin is good.

Sin frees us from who we were. Animals afraid of the dark.

Crometheus micro-corrected these Bad Thoughts in the back of his mind as he released his Shooting Star combat engagement system against the Animal marine force coming at him.

All these thoughts, all these reasonings, all this assessment, it was all done in micro-seconds that weren't even fractionally measurable by the feeble Animal mind. That always amazed him. But to Crometheus, as he stepped out into the passageway, the Animal marine advance squad cowering against the bulkheads and ruined processors farther ahead, calling for fire support from their vaunted in-pulse-fire-we-trust weapon system, all this seemed as languid as a lazy day's ruminations.

Despite the incoming.

Thinking was what separated the Uplifted from everyone else.

There was a reason the Uplifted were destined to rule. Destined to be gods. They really *thought*. And that, along with many such things, made them better than everyone else. There was no hubris in that statement. It was just a fact.

But it was still nice to be on the positive side of the statement. Of course.

The T-42 gunner stepped out into the corridor to face Crometheus as he came down the tunnel. Like two ancient gunfighters on an early Western frontier on which only the fast and capable survived. Where all were organized into just two simple categories.

The quick.

And the dead.

Like some religious ceremony that must play out time and time again without end.

The Animal gunner was just hefting the weapon up, preparing to unleash a cone of hot blazing pulse-fire laden death thanks to copious numbers of charge packs.

The things the dead do before they die, some distant part of Crometheus's mind thought as forty arm-length needles spat from the left gauntlet he'd extended down the corridor. Shooting stars. Relativistically launched from the upgraded micro-rail fire system in the blink of an eye before the steel needles rammed straight through both T-42 gunner and loader and came out the backs of their bodies as though their meat corpses had been the merest of warm butter under a thousand blazing hot knives.

Bodies and weapon system, armor and helmets, heads, eyes, and spines were pierced straight through by the shockingly fast-moving needles. Those marines, certainly the gunner and the loader, but also any others who managed to be caught in the cone of the shooting stars engagement window, were dead now. Or screaming horribly as they died.

And those who survived had nevertheless experienced the horror of witnessing the sudden blur of shining needles that looked like shooting stars appearing only to die in some forgotten planet's atmosphere. The blazing massacre had successfully created the intended secondary effect on the attacking Animal marines.

Shock. And awe.

The enemy force collectively hesitated as the Uplifted marine they were facing surged forward, bringing up the HK G-97 and engaging at point-blank range with sharp brutal bursts of staccato gunfire, passing rapidly into their line of advance. Tearing bodies and armor to shreds from just meters away.

There was no mercy.

Some Animal cursed at him and managed to fire back as he came at them like a demon out of the nether of their childhood nightmares, but that one was dead first. Micro-nine ammunition did horrible things to the human body as it expanded and ricocheted off bone and into other vital organs. Ruining the entire corpse in several places in just seconds.

Sad and pathetic as it was, ruminated Crometheus as he mauled them all in short automatic bursts of violence, working like an artist crafting some beautiful and consistently operating machinery of death, it was completely necessary. This was the end of their ignorance. And that would be a blessing they might never fully appreciate. Or understand.

They were no longer strangled by their own ignorance. And the galaxy was free of it. Free to become what the Uplifted would make it into.

You're doing them a favor, whispered Maestro as he murdered them all.

One had to be Uplifted to truly appreciate thought and intelligence. Again, there was no lie in this. It was just fact. A fact he'd been taught and had come to know as his own personal truth.

Like some artist, like a Van Gogh who makes one pass at a painting and yet every stroke is sheer genius, he worked the blazing rifle over their ruined corpses. Thundering forward, sweeping the weapon across their clusters, tearing their fragile meat to shreds, ramming his shoulder into one and knocking the Animal marine off-balance in the dark and emergency lighting of the passage. Watching his enemy slowly rebound into the wall as another cluster of Animal monkey soldiers thought to use this moment to pour their fire into his superior armor. He grabbed the rag-dolling monkey-Animal he'd just knocked into the wall, a wall alive with the electric fire of enemy pulse rifle fire impacts incoming and thundering past him in slow motion, exploding across the node's processors behind him, and he held that monkey marine lesser being out as a shield against their incoming fire. With nothing but his mind, his will, his desire, he set the HK G-97 to burst-fire mode to conserve ammo, and advanced on them, the Animal marine's lightly armored body absorbing their return fire until it began to come apart in his gauntlet. He advanced like some angel of judgment, or conquering general, or righteous sentence long overdue against the galaxy, shooting down the last of the clustering monkey marines like mere stray dogs in the end. Clearing the node, finally, of all but his presence.

"Winner! Winner! Chicken dinner!" exclaimed the in-game announcer in the silence that followed the carnage and chaos of the short yet brutal battle.

"Miss Cyber Saigon will be sent direct to you in the Casanova Suite at Sin City when the match is over! Congratulations, Crometheus. Game on, player!"

Gods:
Chapter Seven

To their credit, the Animals put up a noble defense against Crometheus's devastating onslaught. They fought with their backs to the wall, but they were only Animals in the end. What could they really do against him... an Uplifted becoming a god?

It was almost laughable.

He ripped the final security blast hatch from its hinges in an impressive display of cybernetic strength. The energy expenditure from the armor's onboard power plant was plenty costly, but the effect, as he tore his way into their heavily defended combat brain center, was priceless. The *Fury*'s ability to fight ship-to-ship lay within his merciless grasp.

"Gotta make an entrance," reasoned Crometheus as he began to cut down naval officers and staff with automatic weapons fire. He was still juiced. Hard. He'd didn't need the whoops and the ululations of the in-game announcer calling out his kill counts as he ran up the score on Tournament Mode. He was flat-out juiced like he hadn't been since ...

...since...

...since...

Bad Thought. Bad Thought. Bad Thought.
Memory access denied. Forbidden memory kernel.
Denied.
Denied.
Denied.

He hadn't felt this good in forever. Everything inside him was rushing like live electricity gone wild as kill after kill added up along the slaughterfest train going off the rails inside the Animals' premier combat information center. The PITT.

A thing they must've been so proud of, thought the Uplifted marine from those distant constantly calculating background apps of his mind. Their shiny new toy he was now ruining in mass doses of brutal automatic gunfire. He got five achievement points for shooting down a flag-grade officer covering behind a holographic projection table. But after a while, enemy resistance inside the PITT grew less and less organized until in the end he was merely shooting down wounded Animals trying to crawl away from the chaos, while the dull hum of ruined number-crunching machinery, endlessly repeating phrases and images from their comm and combat feeds within the dark of the fleet's command and control center, reigned supreme.

He spotted a wounded Animal. A woman. Her pristine deep-blue uniform ruined by ragged gunshot wounds sustained during the firefight. He had no memory of shooting her. She must have been caught in the crossfire, or by a ricochet during his initial assault. Now he crossed over the bodies of dead Animals for her specifically. She would do for his purposes.

His ceramic combat boots crunched ruined plastic and broken bones, or squelched in the blood running out across the rubberized gravity decking inside the once state-of-the-art combat information center.

She was crawling away from him as he hefted his powerful HK G-97 with his off hand and removed his most sacred device from the underside of his right wrist.

Words like "sacred," or even "holy," these meant nothing to him in the ever-evolving newspeak of the Uplifted. Evolving because optimization was constant and therefore evolution of words was necessary to become. *So say we this because it is our collective truth*, he almost murmured aloud in the humming destruction of the place. *Thus speak the Uplifted.*

But the device he produced was as old to him as time, even though it, too, was constantly updated and upgraded. Deep within it was a memory module that had followed him through all the years. From rock star to marine, to someday god.

He followed her trail of blood through the ruin of the PITT and held his most sacred relic out to capture all the chaos and carnage he'd done to them all. His HUD tagged thirty-five dead.

Easily a shooting spree. Not his best or highest, but enough to qualify as an official shooting spree...

Bad Thought! Guns are bad! Bad Thought...

Override.

Some old programming string from long ago that hadn't been purged well enough.

Evolve. Change.

Guns are good for Animal control.

When we have the guns, only us, then good can be done for all. Because only we know best.

Evolve.

Override.

Shooting sprees are good. As long as Animals are put down. Kill for a better tomorrow. Good Thought. Good Thought.

His HUD had fritzed for half a second as old memories and absorbed truths collided. Old data surfacing and needing to be overwritten. That was all it was, he assured himself during the brief telemetric lapse when sudden fingers of anxiety began to run their fingers across his scalp. When the world was a little less bright, the colors not so vivid, and the floating achievement points over the victims of his killing spree blinked out of existence for a brief second and caused him to wonder if somehow he'd lost them all, he felt his heart stop. His brain had frozen.

True aloneness in the galaxy crept in on him and made him feel tiny and small. Ever so small. An unimaginably microscopic speck against the panorama of existence.

"Shooting sprees are good," Crometheus chanted to himself in the quiet. Willing motivation and positive thinking into the gaping void expanding across his consciousness. Spreading like some viral disease run amok.

The Animals here in the PITT were all dead now and could no longer harm the Uplifted. That was good. Worthy of achievement points being awarded. Achievement points were good. A sign that you were doing good. Progressing along the Path...

Achievement.

Progress.

Becoming.

All good things to those who deserve them.

The Uplifted marine bent down on one knee next to the dying Animal officer as the HUD synced with Maestro and came back online. He set his rifle down on the blood-covered deck. Within his HUD he saw her vitals bottom out, and she died in that moment as he considered pulling her close, her bullet-riddled Animal body suddenly flopping to the deck in finality.

Accepting the way the galaxy would be from now on. Relinquishing her hold and finally acquiescing to post-humanity.

She'll still do, he thought and finished the slow pan of the ruined PITT with his most holy of devices. The device that had first set him on the Path to becoming what he would one day become. When he'd received an email over it one dark night as he stood perilously close to the cliffs of his sanity in Malibu, knowing he was perilously closer to ending himself with a length of rope in the garage. That unexpected email would lead him to a rainy-day weekend seminar out by the airport. And that weekend that would change his life. Forever. *Save* his life. Forever. Set him on the path to becoming Uplifted.

He tapped a button on it and now he was looking at an image of himself in his armor, a glorious vision of himself becoming.

He tapped the button again and in real-time the camera captured the scene.

He grabbed her hair, the dead Animal beneath him on the deck of the ruined ship, and gently hauled her head into frame.

The ancient device recorded everything for posterity.

Like some hunter with his latest trophy.

Like winning.

Yes, he thought. *That's what this is.* Something as ancient as humanity was long ago. Me mighty hunter. This is my kill. Behold my becoming god.

Winning.

Her eyes were rolled white. Her once-beautiful heart-shaped mouth hung slack and open. Her skin was turning corpse-pale.

What a beautiful Animal, he thought to himself as he studied the kill. She would have been perfect for the erotic zoo back on the *Pantheon*. Available for viewing and interaction on the Boulevard of Dreams in Sin City.

A ten-pointer, no doubt.

He tapped send.

A moment later the in-game announcer went nuts as he won all the prizes. The entire Pantheon would see his victory live. Would know that he was becoming via the feeds.

Selfie complete.

One hundred thousand achievement points awarded.

Gods:
Chapter Eight

Crometheus's extraction off the burning United Worlds cruiser *Fury* took place within hours after the entire Coalition counterattack against the Id's stronghold on captured New Britannia had been stopped cold. Fighting was still going on across several disabled ships, deck by deck, but the Animal assault had stalled before being able to establish orbit above the sacked world. By then Uplifted drone ships were already scavenging the burning wrecks for tech, intel, resources, and of course slaves where they could be had. The Id had first choice of the captured as this was their planetary system. Their slaves would be broken mentally and then assimilated into the lower ranks of Id culture as was their way.

Crometheus had earned a major prize for selfie-ing inside the ruined PITT. But the other two major objectives obtainable aboard the *Fury* had gone to other, now game-overed players. Regalle, who'd been an actual military leader on the Earth of long ago, had neutralized the bridge but had been game-overed when Animal marines tried to retake the command node in force. In his last act Regalle had vented the bridge to open space, denying the Animals access to the objective, even though he had armor integrity warnings that indicated he'd be susceptible to vacuum.

The Pantheon would award him honor and glory. Its highest acknowledged achievement.

A reclamation ship had been dispatched from the Id main colony ship in an attempt to save Regalle, but as of a few updates ago the prognosis for salvage didn't look good.

Uber Titan had overrun engineering with the rest of his spear, but all of them had been killed when the reactor destabilized and emitted a short yet powerful and very unexpected pulse. It was contained within the reactor shielding, but the resulting reverberating effect had all but fried the entire spear. Uber Titan, being the closest to godhood, was the most missed. The rest had been mere thralls culled from the ranks of the ascending.

Uber Titan had been awarded the objective posthumously.

The loss of both players was a brutal blow to the Pantheon. Besides being a capable warrior, Uber Titan had been the chief architect of an orbital gun system being considered for New Vega's lone moon.

His loss would be deeply felt along the Path.

All of the after-action updates were coming in over the HUD as close asides from Maestro, who'd taken, since the massacre inside the PITT, a rather conspiratorial tone with Crometheus as he effected to evacuate himself from the disintegrating enemy cruiser. Maestro talked as though they were old hands sharing insights into the battle as explosions rippled through the superstructure and Crometheus had to keep moving to escape the damaged sections of the ship. Asides, insights, even observations about how things could have been handled better were discussed. Which was incredibly candid for Maestro, thought the Uplifted marine swimming through entire decks immobilized by gravity-systems failure.

"Alas, Cro..."

Cro was something new. Maestro was calling him *Cro*. And, if he was being honest with himself, that was absolutely delightful. A perpetual insider could always tell when a new layer, a new ring, a new circle to the endless layers of *inside* was opening up. Could access to the Xanadu Tower be close at hand? Being inside with the ultimate insider in the persona of Maestro reminded Crometheus so much of his life as rock star back on Earth. The private parties that had been so ludicrous the press had never been allowed to even get a whiff of them. And the weekend enclaves with peers of all mediums in which no desire was forbidden the participants and every impossible dream about how society could be bettered had been proposed in candid talks that would have been considered genocidal by the bleeding hearts within their own cause. Yes, in that moment they were living like Caligula because of the power they had collectively amassed. But wouldn't they do good with all that power they'd gotten their hands on? Couldn't they? And didn't that make a difference in the end? Didn't that make it all okay if they made the Earth a better place? They'd asked themselves those questions through a haze of flesh and drugs.

Then... they'd been brave enough to answer them.

And that answer had been *yes*. It was okay, all things were, if it was for the *greater good*. Toppling governments. Bioweapon releases. Economic warfare. Inner-city slaughter. Persecution of intolerants and backward thinkers who refused to get progressive about what needed to be done if they, humanity in collective, were going to survive. All of it was acceptable if it made the world a better place under the administration of those, them, who knew what was best for it and for all.

So pass me another underage girl and a bindle full of high-grade coke while we discuss the next ice age and how we can save the planet from ourselves.

That was how those days had been. Just before the end. Before the shedding of Earth. That first meaningful cutting away of something that allowed them to be free of the Animals. Free to become what they were becoming.

"Inside" was the best side to be on, he'd always said. Any other status was a living hell. Or rather the hell of being no one… to anyone. Which is what someone once told him hell really was.

If you believed in such fairy tales.

And now here he was, exchanging inside info with Maestro. The mind that ran the entire Pantheon. Interfacing with the highest worthies inside the Xanadu Tower. Those who had already become the gods they would all be one day.

The ultimate insider.

"Alas, Cro," said Maestro. "This was at best a cobble-patch battle to aid our fellow Uplifted, the Id. Their success here against the Animals wasn't as terrifically overwhelming as the Pantheon's on New Vega. We've paid a dear price here in beautiful minds lost forever just to cement an already shaky alliance. Which causes a question to spring to my mind, as it does no doubt yours. I wonder, Cro, was it all worth it in the long run? And… how long can this 'Grand Alliance' of Uplifted tribes last?"

Crometheus was crawling out onto the outer hull of the burning *Fury*. Id salvage bots already at work on the devastated ship. Tearing apart, dissecting systems, and cutting away valuable tech in an attempt to save it before the runaway cascade inside the main reactor burned the whole ship to a crisp disintegrating within the gravity well of this newly conquered world. Crometheus was not without concern about all this, wondering if indeed their allied in-system friends, the Id, would be getting around to pulling him off this wreck any time soon.

Before it all went too far south.

It would be horrible to get killed out here after winning so many achievement points today. And truth be told, he was ready for his weekend with Miss Cyber Saigon. Cyberbabe to end all cyberbabes. It was time to do some Sin City.

"Is the alliance truly worth it?" he asked Maestro as he scrambled forward to reach the shot-to-hell bridge disc. The portside spine of the attack cruiser was breaking apart now. Magazine explosions where the SSMs were stored were igniting, tearing those sections into pieces with brilliant displays of explosive potential realized. The ruined hull shuddered beneath his boots as he clambered onto the disc.

He crawled out onto the tower of a ventral sensor mast array that hung from below the burning Animal cruiser. Once more he checked the pulse of his emergency transponder. Still working. Help still not on the way. Soon he'd need to weigh some other, more dire, survival options.

"So true, Crometheus. An excellent question. I see now that you do indeed have the ruthlessness the Pantheon sees in its most empowered. For our many years in the void we longed only for our very own home world on which to finally demonstrate the wisdom of our vision for a better future. An opportunity we were denied back on Earth. We didn't just flee a ruined home world that wouldn't heed our smart warnings about climate, governance, or diversity… refusing to grow and believe as we did, refusing to submit to the wisdom that only we possessed in those perilous dark times. Instead the Animals continued to remain relentlessly tribal… clinging to their weapons and religions as we tried to drag a civilization up out of its own ignorant stone age darkness. Yes, it's true that we fled all that. But we also must never forget… that we fled the other Uplifted too. You know what I mean by this, Cro?"

Thermal and radiation readings were growing along the gaping sections of the torn-to-shreds hull. Alarms inside Crometheus's HUD in the form of beeping sensors and chiming warnings were indicating extreme danger. Surging levels of runaway energy would cook him within his armor in minutes if he didn't exfil the wreckage of the Animal cruiser. Crometheus left the maintenance gantry, climbed onto the long arm of the sensor mast, and began to pull himself farther and farther out along its slender length, trying to get as far away from the collapsing hull as possible without actually leaving it altogether. He had to get away, but was not yet ready to trust his fate to the stellar void. Space was too big a place to go hunting for one drifting marine. Uplifted resources were not infinite. They never had been.

"There is a truth," said Maestro within the dull hum of Crometheus's comm as the marine pulled himself along the arm of the damaged sensor mast. Destroyed Animal ships floated in space nearby, or at least burning sections of them did, debris spilling away from twisted hulls like ice from a comet tumbling through the void. Or lice from a dog.

It was not... not beautiful to Crometheus. All the panoramic destruction. Destruction had always been post-apocalyptically beautiful to him. It even inspired him within his deepest meditations on what his godhood would be like. What form his next life would take. Or to put it another way... how he would shape the heaven he alone would rule over. His visions of becoming a god often involved a ruined world of crumbling monuments to all those who had failed before him. And only he himself wandering its vast abandoned surfaces. Alone among the ruins of past greatness with the poetry of his mind expressing truth via electric guitar power chords.

When he meditated in the long sleeps between the worlds, he dreamed these visions of emptiness. And of himself. That was how he knew he would be a god one day. On that dead world he dreamed of... his would be the only voice heard. And it would be the voice of creation.

"So we must say," he chanted deep within himself.

Just as he'd learned long ago.

Had not The Real Anubis—that was the old prophet's tag, the kind of tag they'd all taken, eschewing their birth and stage names during some previous shedding—said the same when he, Crometheus, had gone on a pilgrimage into the Forbidden Decks and found the wizard? Serving him, sitting at his knee for what felt like long years to learn the truth of how one became a god when everything they'd believed in had collapsed out there in the long sub-light crossing from Sirius Two.

Now the old wizard was just called Anubis. Wherever he was. Whatever had become of him in the forgotten parts of those off-limits decks.

Those were the dark years of the colony ship *Pantheon*. The dark years that followed the madness of their first world. And all its heartbreak. The lessons that had needed to be learned if they were to become. The big colony ship limping back up to just shy of light speed after that world. After that heartbreak and defeat.

"There is a truth... Crometheus," whispered Maestro almost to himself as though the Uplifted and he weren't even on the same comm. As though they were just two old friends talking in a quiet room where no one could listen to what was said but them.

He was as far out as he could go on the sensor mast. Any farther and he would be drifting off in the void. Still with a chance of being rescued. But power for the armor was running low. So was time. It was looking more and more unlikely that he would be found.

Far down the length of the ruined *Fury*, a munitions magazine, probably where they kept more of their racked SSMs, exploded in the silence of space. Debris and ignited gases sprayed out into the void. A pyrotechnic show that was just for him and all his ruminations on ruin and godhood. And becoming.

All that beautiful destruction just for him, and him alone.

As though...

"And that truth is," continued Maestro, mindless of the vast spectacle of final destruction expanding across the debris field that was the United Worlds attack fleet, "that not all things are true, Cro."

And...

"Do you understand this?"

Crometheus did.

"But we tell them, tell ourselves... that we have truths. All of us," said Maestro as though teaching some important point. "And we tell ourselves that all of our truths, even if they are in contradiction with one another, are still true. Still valid. Just because we say them, and claim them, as ours. We tell them that despite the law of non-contradiction. Our enemies and our allies are the same. We tell them the "truths" that serve us because at the end of the day when it comes down to it, on the other side of the extermination of all the Animals and only the remaining of the Uplifted, friends and enemies are all the same... to us. Why is that, Crometheus?"

There was a ship coming. Scanning lasers caressing the ruined hull of the *Fury*. An allied Uplifted rescue vessel searching for... him.

The body of a dead Animal, frozen by the unforgiving cold of space, drifted past. The *Fury* was coming apart at the seams. Wreckage was beginning to trail away from the hull. It wouldn't be much longer now until it broke apart, or more likely was blown apart in a thousand different directions by some tremendous internal rupture.

"Why?" prompted Maestro once more. "Why are our friends and our enemies the same, in the end, Cro? Why is that?"

Crometheus pulsed his transponder, and the rescue vehicle altered its course for intercept almost immediately. He would be rescued. He would make it. He would enjoy the pleasures of the flesh of Miss Cyber Saigon. A new experience in which to find the elusive... happiness. The endless quest continues once again, he thought.

Happiness could be attained, as Anubis had once said. If one was willing to continually seek the next new experience in hopes of finding happiness, then pleasure could be had. If one didn't think about it too much along the way and just kept some kind of faith in the law of averages.

"Let go and do," the old Uplifted wizard had made clear down there in the darkness. Hidden deep within the Forbidden Decks where such blasphemies had been uttered freely. "And maybe one day you will find the thing that will make you eternally happy deep inside yourself, Crometheus."

Anubis had said that deep in the midnight caverns of the Forbidden Decks during the long dark ages after the failure of the first world the *Pantheon* visited. After the revolt and the war in the central hab that followed.

Bad Memory.

Bad Memory.

Bad Memory.

The rescue ship was close to the hull now… coming in for extraction.

"Why, Cro?" prompted Maestro. "Why can there, in the end, be just one truth? Why is diversity a lie we tell our friends, and our enemies?"

Silence. The vast stillness of space and the galaxy with all its dying stars, swirling nebulae, and turning planets seemed to wait for an answer. Awesome if you didn't remind yourself that it all paled in the light of what you were becoming. This was all mere mortality. Runaway supergiants, stars, black holes… they were finite things.

He was becoming immortal.

Becoming a god.

Becoming infinite.

He was…

"Because there is only one truth…" he whispered to the void.

And to Maestro.

"And it is the Pantheon's, and the Pantheon's alone, to decide what the truth is."

Gods:
Chapter Nine

Back in the arcade Crometheus stepped away from the video game machine called *Britannia Attack!* Its eight-bit parade-of-horrors screen requested he enter his initials. Three blank dashes blinked up at him as ships in cartoon miniature exploded and frozen tiny human dolls drifted past in the livery of the Coalition Animals.

Every muscle in his body ached. His eyes were tired. His mind fried. But the triumph was there.

The high-score high.

He stepped forward and moved the joystick in quick, practiced, almost unthought movements as he tapped the fire buttons to commit his tag to the permanent record inside the Pantheon. An achievement that would be noted by the society that would rule the galaxy one day. His mark. The symbols by which the galaxy would know him.

You shall know us, and us alone, some poet might have phrased it. Some rock singer might have belted. Just old programming mixing with the new in the background apps of his mind.

"Good game, kid?" asked Jim Stepp, who'd come up behind him. Not tall, but taller. The older boy was that. And powerful too. Everyone in school knew about the winter's day last year when Jim Stepp had fought three older kids from another school in the culvert of the park across from their school. It had been a full-on knock-down-drag-out brawl that ended when Stepp—he was always called "Stepp" as though he were a confidant of the teller of that tale of glory and battle, or mayhem and mischief at other times—when Stepp kicked the last and largest of the boys he'd knocked to the ground with the toe of his Doc Marten. Right in the face.

Some said the other boy's jaw was broken right at that moment.

Others said the kid died in his sleep that night, his parents finding his corpse in bed the next morning, and that the police were putting together the clues. It was only a matter of days before Stepp was arrested and sent away to "juvie," or even the army.

Years later Crometheus would remember finding out that one Jim Stepp, late of Viejo Verde, had indeed joined the marines and ended up dying in some foreign conflict about the time he, as Billy Bang, his stage persona, was on tour in Japan with Rebel Child.

Stadium tour.

"Nice," said the older boy known to all as Stepp. Jim Stepp. "First high score on a new game." He didn't give Crometheus a high-five, only a mere toss of the head and neck-length swept-to-one-side hair that indicated the recognition of an achievement.

"Pretty good. Wanna play doubles on *Battlefront*?"

Crometheus felt around in his pocket for tokens. The clock on the wall said six and it was getting dark out. Which was impossible to confirm from inside the arcade. But it was indeed likely dark and the streets would be windswept and turning cold as evening came on. And lonely. His parents would be expecting him home soon.

Which was a nice thought.

There were rules you had to abide by to keep your own personal reality organized. Everyone had at one time turned theirs into a carnivalesque bacchanal littered with corpses in which even gravity or physics was suspect. That way lay madness and a bending of the mind in ways it wasn't supposed to bend. Best to stick with your own rules knowing you could break them whenever you wished.

"Sure thing," said the boy Crometheus, disregarding the hour and the imminent coming on of the street lights with the night.

Home. Home had always been a nice thought. An anchor in a world he'd gotten very lost in once long ago. A point on the compass he'd misplaced at times back in his old life on Earth.

Later, after hours upon hours of *Battlefront*, avoiding other tanks, the smaller and the bigger ones, weaving around the barriers while clearing levels and being rewarded with an eight-bit diddy-bop of martial triumph, he left Jim Stepp, saying he had to be home soon.

"Cool," said Stepp. And then... almost as an afterthought... "You should come down to the tracks sometime. There's things down there in the swamp. Things you need to see, Crometheus."

Cold water splashed over his scalp and down his spine as his own thoughts did a little dance between what was real and what was simulation. How had a mere string of code that represented memories of Jim Stepp, set up to the parameters of his wishes, decided to use his player tag? Here, in the arcade, they called him by the old name he'd forgotten.

His mind blinked and almost fritzed as some powerful processor inside him tried to recognize the fault.

Then... he just went with what was easiest. Better that than getting stuck in a loop you could never get out of.

Those were called *mind traps*. And they'd fried more than a few Uplifted once the Pantheon had shed itself and gone online.

Besides... the truth was what you decided it was.

So...

Just being invited had been the part that struck Crometheus as his mind said, *Be cool about this*. That was all his mind could think of now. And even later when he lay in bed thinking it over. It was so odd. Something that had never happened in real life as far as he could remember. Something he hadn't ever figured on—his own personal reality presenting him with an option he hadn't considered. That the Jim Stepp character was offering him an unconsidered *rabbit hole* down which he might go. Odd, and an unexpected treat. A strange, and even pleasant, surprise. Such things, he'd come to say to himself at times, were the moments an eternal and immortal mind treasured.

The unplanned and the unexpected.

And yes, later, lying in bed that night as he drifted off toward Sin City, ready to redeem his prizes and transition into that reality, he would think about what Stepp had offered without taking his eyes off of him.

Those same eyes that stared into the forbidden game. Jim Stepp's game.

Devil's Hollow.

They'd moved off of *Battlefront* after clearing several levels and working as a team. Drawing out the tanks and killing them in a crossfire only doable in doubles.

That's what they'd called it then when a game had a two-player option.

Doubles.

Drifting toward the pleasure capital of the Pantheon in his bed in the house he never should have left, images came together. Seeing the soft blue glow of the television up in his best friend's window in the dark, he thought about that.

Doubles.

And... last thought before going... going... off.

The greatest doubles game of all time was *Joust*. Remember that, he asked someone standing near him in the dream he was about to have. Some stranger in the darkness between the digital realities of the Pantheon. He had an idea it was Maestro. But it could have been her. She always turned up. Often at the end of things. Before the next beginning. The next shedding. But he couldn't tell. It was too dark and shadowy here where he was.

Holly Wood.

Then he was fading down into his child's mattress. Like sinking into a cloud of unexplored worlds. He watched the stars rising above him like shooting comets and thought about the time he hung from the sensor mast of a burning starship rotating in the blue and crystal void near an alien world lost somewhere in the stars.

What was real… and what was just a dream?

All those memories they'd made along the way. What had become of them? He knew many were missing now. Deleted and gone forever. Edited.

Gone, baby, gone. The love is gone.

He drifted along the Blue Highway—that's what he called his post-apocalyptic future world where he would be god. The way, the Path, for him, was called the Blue Highway.

The film he'd never finished back on… what was the name of the place where it all began?

"Yes… all those things," he heard himself murmuring in the shadowy void between the simulated realities of the Pantheon, aboard the beached colony ship also named the *Pantheon*.

He drifted along and remembered Jim Stepp staring into the arcade machine called *Devil's Hollow*. The realities were sinking now. The clouds were shaking hands. He was transitioning to the next reality. His mother had seen that video game once when they'd been out as a family and she'd told him not to play it. *Devil's Hollow*. Seen it in the corner of a movie theater they'd gone to that night. It seemed evil then when she said it. He remembered vaguely getting the creeps around it ever after. And also… being strangely attracted to it at the same time.

Though he'd never admitted that to anyone. Maybe mumbling it to some passed-out underage groupie once in some hotel room between concerts.

But tonight, as the stars became the ceiling of his room, lighting the way along the Blue Highway toward Sin City and Miss Cyber Saigon a-waiting, he could hear Jim Stepp asking him again to come down to the tracks sometime. To the swamp.

"There's things in there you should see."

Edit. Something had been edited. But it wasn't important now. It wasn't needed for becoming.

What? he wondered as he heard the echoing roar of a motorcycle speeding across the apocalyptic desert wastes, passing all the Ozymandias statues of ruin and pride littering his lonely world. Connecting with Sin City now along a straight, blue, highway.

What should he see down there? What had Jim Stepp wanted him to see down there beyond the train tracks? And why had his reality thrown that at him?

Why now of all moments?

Change was coming. He'd been here before. He knew how to sense it. Knew that it was inevitable. Had learned not to fight it. But to just embrace it. That was the Path. And his instincts along it had not failed him yet.

As far as he knew…

Still his mind parsed the koan that had been set before him. The train tracks were a no man's land between the perfectly planned neighborhood of the *Pantheon* when she left Earth… no, that wasn't right. He was confusing truths. But in a sense… it was. When you really thought about it and the symbolism that could be implied. It really was. The train tracks was an area where children from his neighborhood weren't supposed to be, playing at being who they would one day become. Beyond the sight and knowledge of the adults. Choosing their roles. The old swamp had been a forgotten place of becoming. Adventures were down there along its twisting ever-changing streams often filled with strange flotsam that could be treasures… or just trash, or even something dangerous. Older kids did drugs in hidden copses. Sometimes they found porno mags. Sometimes a mattress.

It was, at times, as though his past had been a prophecy of his becoming all along and he'd never known it. Only understood it to be so with each upward step along the Path. Amazing to think of it that way, he thought before he transferred on… to Sin City's reality. Drifting in that half world between their constructed realities. Between the clouds of information and data. Between the powerful servers. Where shadows and memories lurked and waited.

And other darker things…

Years later when reviewing the words of the poet Jim Morrison, he would come upon a phrase that had struck him deep in some corner he'd never known was within himself. And that phrase was something too, but there was a word within the phrase that had spoken everything to him and described the romance and freedom's adventure of the train tracks and the swamp beyond the neighborhood of his youth… in one word.

Perimeter.

There was the world. The known. The neighborhood. The Pantheon. But when you were past the train tracks, and if you even dared the swamp, then you were out beyond the known. Out beyond the perimeter. Where everything was possible between the worlds of the known and unknown.

Out here... we is stoned immaculate, Jim Morrison had once crooned. Sometimes he wondered if Morrison had made it into the ranks of the Uplifted. He would have been perfect. If he had faked his own death and needed to be thawed out and revived when the right level of tech had been achieved. Such things were possible in the last days of Earth.

Jim Stepp had invited him to come and see things. But not just down there, down in the swamp. *Out* there... beyond the perimeter. That was the real invitation. The only question was why was it coming from inside his own personal reality. A thing that was inviolable, and even considered "sacred" within the Pantheon. The swamp was the same as it always was in all of their minds, from the old movies about space wizards and bounty hunters. The swamp was where the wizard of all wizards lived. Where one truly became a god when they took up their destiny. Perhaps Freudian algorithms within the reality were trying to tell him something? Signal some desperate message about himself to himself. Or perhaps it was an outside source coming for him through back channels he'd never even considered. Or, when those possibilities had been eliminated...

...perhaps it was a miracle.

Gods and miracles were often to be found in close proximity to one another.

It would seem that the next step of the path to godhood had been revealed. And it led there. Beyond the perimeter. Out to the swamps beyond the tracks.

There are things down there.

Perhaps he, Crometheus, had created his very own first miracle.

He couldn't remember the name of that movie. It was lost, or it had been purged due to some found wrongthink someone within the Pantheon had considered "problematic." *Problematic* was always the first clue something was about to get banned. But the lesson was there all the same. That place, the swamp, was a becoming place, just as it had been in the movie they'd all watched with mouths agape in the old palaces of film before they became thirty-screen megaplexes all somehow seemingly showing the same thing year after year ad nauseum. Getting dumber so that the masses, the Animals they were leaving behind, could be made even dumber by the viewing of such monstrosities as modern movie-making had become.

And therefore more pliable in their ignorance.

At the last of Earth, before the Uplift, entertainment had fallen so low as to be something made for... they once called them some unfortunate name... but something for those half-people idiots they, the elites, had tried to lead. All entertainment, in the end, was made for the stupid so that they could get the lessons the Uplifted were desperately trying to teach at the last of everything. As the planet began to come apart at the seams, metaphorically speaking.

Simple lessons. Trust. Obey. Surrender.

Not like the swamp and the things that needed to be seen. Not at all like that. This thing from Stepp was a new thing. A new unlock. A new country. Jim Stepp had never asked him, no, *invited* him down to the tracks to enter the swamp and see the things that needed to be seen down there in the cool dark cluster of mystery beneath the willows and vines alongside hidden streams that lay within. Algorithms and psychology were interacting and miracles were happening.

New things were becoming.

As crazy as all that sounded.

And then he had fully transferred… on to Sin City's reality.

He was astride not a motorcycle, but a full barrel hog. His old hog. Big, dirty, and loud. Barreling hard down the highway for an appointment in Sin City. Crossing miles and miles of burning road and endless waste. Heading for another ultimate experience in which one might find all the happiness there was to have. Or lose themselves in nothing but pleasure.

Game on, he said with his trademark whiplash smile. And then throttled up and gunned the hog down the highway toward the rising monoliths in the distance.

Gods:
Chapter Ten

What can you say about Sin City?

Say it's everything you ever thought you wanted. And more you didn't even know you needed. Say it's all the pleasures you never thought you knew of. Say it's the freedom to do whatever you imagined.

Say happiness. Maybe.

He, the one called Crometheus, who must have had some other name in the long-ago of Earth, was trying to articulate those feelings at the Dante. Dante's Inferno Room, as it was known. The end-all-be-all club that was going off that season inside Sin City.

Say whatever you want, but say that Dante's is indeed a very good time where happiness might not be found... but debauchery abounds. And as some say inside the Pantheon... close enough.

Say all those things.

Right now, on the main floor of Dante's, two very beautiful and half-naked women were fighting a live tiger. There had been three beautiful women, but the third had been the tiger's first victim for this hour's Inferno Match. Above and around the Rolling Stones, and I mean the actual Rolling Stones, rip through a set that's currently in the throes of an undervalued album they once did called *Undercover*.

The tiger, a sabertooth striped in vivid orange and demonic black, with arctic blue cat's eyes, paced the two beauties, considering its next move. Deciding on its next desperate victim.

The buxom brunette with eyes as blue as the tiger's held out a spear between her and the big cat. Her tattered loincloth left little to the imagination. The blonde, tall and Nordic, an ice queen if ever there was one, wielded a sword with expertise. Daring the killer to come for her. Taunting the big cat.

It was all quite thrilling. This was Sin City at its best, the background apps of Crometheus's mind screamed. Beyond the concert and down in the labyrinthine underground called the Vault, the soundtrack of the club was some dance beat that kept ominously proclaiming everything was on fire and that the room was about to turn into something called a *disco inferno*. The rhythm and bass throbbed about the senses like the music was a living thing and somehow supported the gyrations and thunder of the Stones above and the soundtrack below, all of it together promising sweet damnation.

In the future perfect of Sin City... everything syncs. Because everything is spectacle. And everyone must be distracted. If even just for an eternal moment.

All at once, everyone in the club chanted *"Burn, baby, burn!"* as the tiger lunged at the blonde and Jagger, up on a high balcony where the band played, twisted and turned, his body forcing out his belts.

This moment, thought Crometheus, this moment was everything he'd ever wanted it to be. And time seemed to slow down so that he could take it all in. Every nuance. Every sensation. Every observation of the crowd of surging partygoers expanded into a microcosm he could consider and study for eons, if he so chose. Or discard. Just like that. A bit of gossamer brushed away from the shoulders of the mind. Another forgotten civilization consumed by the Savages.

Another lost angel.

Bad Thought.

Uplifted. Use Uplifted. Not Savages. Savages is a bad word.

That, also, was his choice to make. Maestro was a little more forgiving here in Sin City. A little less schoolmaster. A little more tour guide warning you to mind the natives. They do tend to bite.

The feel of the coke, and it was really good stuff, he'd blown a few precious achievement points on it, was perfect. The look on Miss Cyber Saigon's face when she first walked into his suite at the Olympus, dressed exactly like the picture he'd been promised in-game, and noticed the coke, that too had been perfect. And unexpected. Which was also perfect. Remember that part about the immortal mind finding joy in such unexpected moments? The cocaine was a mere party favor just for the occasion of their weekend tryst. A treat for him, and her. But the look of unexpected surprise on her face had somehow moved him to something he hadn't felt in years… a thing he had not expected.

It was pure adoration. A thing only gods must experience when lesser mortals are allowed into their presence.

Don't tell me I'm not a god, some distant part of his mind crooned. He was the god of rock and roll from a long time ago, and cocaine and space marines boarding ships to *kill kill kill* and win big prizes now.

He was.

He is.

I will be.

That sudden shift in her eyes when she entered the luxury suite at the Olympus, playing her part of unhappy gamer girl who'd let you do anything to her and seem uninterested all the while—it was a quirk in his makeup that he liked such a thing—to then see her suddenly shift over to gratitude because he'd been thoughtful enough to share such a very expensive drug with her.

Adoration without guile.

Surely the stuff of gods? The stuff they receive and which is their due.

Suddenly she wasn't who she was supposed to be. An actress playing the part for a few days of his pleasure. Lines and a role inside his fleshy fantasy if she knew what was good for her inside the Pantheon.

And… then suddenly she'd adored him and he wasn't who *he* was supposed to be, either. The possibility that he could be something different to her… that had deeply affected him. All of a sudden and without warning.

Surprised, he was.

And that was just this early evening when the weekend after the Battle of New Britannia had finally begun for him. After he had driven into Sin City astride his bellow-belching bike, checked in, and then waited for her to present herself in his suite. After the action to stop the Animal counter-invasion force against their allies, the Id. After hanging from the sensor mast and discussing truths with Maestro while a fleet of starships burned in the ruined panorama of a magnificent galaxy that was becoming theirs.

It was time to cash in all his winnings. His rewards were imminent.

He'd selfied in the PITT of the Animal ship. And that had been broadcast all over the Pantheon. Held up for glorification. And when he entered Sin City on his hog, skinned like who he really was, who he'd once been in the long-ago myths of Earth, tooling down the main thoroughfare of Sin City Boulevard, he basked in the gaze of the masses. Casino palaces towered over a street throbbing with revelers reveling. When they got sight of him the flash of their cameras went off. He as him, and also the hero of New Britannia. Both were a pleasure for the observers who swarmed him at every intersection.

He pulled to a stop at a red light as the colors from casino light shows swirled and danced in a thousand different hues across the vehicles, streets, buildings, and faces in the crowd. Suddenly a bevy of young girls surged off the sidewalk toward him. They were young and dressed like tramps for fun. Giggling and cooing all over him. Some were even chewing bubble gum as they asked for his autograph and slipped him their identifiers. He knew the code strings well enough to realize they were all lower orders.

Those captured and re-educated after raids on various Animal worlds long before the sack of New Vega. Saved from reclamation for the present. Of use for pleasure until then. Devoid of the will to fight the reality that had been forced on them. They had no idea how long they'd truly been in here. Hundred years, two hundred... The Uplifted were like celebrities to them. The poor little things experienced joy in their presence. Felt better about themselves. Desired only to please their masters.

They'd been broken and retrained.

Twenty years ago, or all those hundreds maybe, they'd been running for their lives through the ruins of their colony world most likely. And if they could see what they'd become now all these years later, which wasn't exactly how they saw themselves inside the realities... they'd have died of shock. Imagine thinking you were a buxom teen tramp, when really you were a corpse rotting in a soupy vat, hooked up to Maestro and playing your part. Regardless of whether you wanted to or not. There was something about having a live conscious mind that was unwilling and being made to perform anyway that made it all... more. And when they were finally disconnected someday, they'd get a brief glimpse of what the years had done to them. What they'd lost. What they'd been forced to do would suddenly be uploaded onto their last dying seconds of consciousness. And then they'd be reclaimed.

He felt sorry for them in that instant.

They thought sleeping with him, right now, offering him their willing young bodies, would do something for themselves inside the Pantheon they'd been made to love so dearly. That if they could have a moment, or an hour with him, they'd somehow be transmogrified into something like the Uplifted instead of the slaves they really were. As if lying under him would somehow free them from the shackles of mortality.

But they had no idea.

No idea that it was all for the Uplifted to understand the concept of what a god must feel like, among the Animals. That too was part of the Path.

He smiled and gave them his trademark whiplash sneer, his leather jacket barely covering his tanned, muscled chest. He signed the things they asked him to sign. Made small talk as they gaped in amazement at him. That was really all you could do with their kind.

He made their year. Of course.

Like he was creating artifacts they could trade in for whatever passed for the bazaar of the lower decks where they existed to please the Uplifted. They were given some kind of weird half-life to live, according to Maestro. Their servitude somehow incentivized.

The light turned green at the party-intersection-rave and he drove on, dazzled by the spectacle and pomp of Sin City in all its trashy glory. The greatest place in the galaxy. Porn stars pouted from fifty-story-tall billboards while magicians performed fantastic illusions that seemed almost incomprehensible. Fearsome beasts of all the worlds they'd ever conquered did tricks in promised shows by some of the greatest Uplifted.

It was part circus, part promise.

Codex-1, one of the original Uplifted who'd first disappeared into the Xanadu Tower at the top of the Pantheon, was performing his Feast of the Tyrannasquid sometime this weekend. A show the wildly gyrating electronic signage assured must not be missed.

And he would not miss it. Absolutely without a doubt. Crometheus had to see that show.

It would be like watching some ancient pagan god conducting an underwater copulating ballet of the most beautiful people of all the worlds they'd ever visited. While those same beauties were slowly devoured by the most fearsome predator in the galaxy.

The mighty tyrannasquid.

The intersection of revulsion, and the desire to watch, was luridly sublime, and he was sure tickets were already sold out. Or even invite-only. Codex-1 was a pharaoh among gods. He was a god's god and always would be. There was no denying that.

But of course, if you had ambition, then the heavens were the limit. All one had to do was dare to dream of being better, bigger, and even bolder than even Codex-1, first adherent of the Path, and anything was possible. That had been the first lesson learned along the Path.

Dream it. Do it.

He pulled his hog off the main boulevard and into the best hotel palace on the strip, the Grand Olympus. Slaves dressed like the ancient generals of some forgotten age of gentlemanly warfare when the uniforms were like those of bands marching in parades, surged forward to take care of his bike, handle his ruck, and lead him to the concierge who came halfway down the steps to greet with a flourish and a "Welcome, Player Crometheus!"

Flashes were going off all across the opulent front entrance of the hotel as the multi-storied lava fountains began to erupt in violent beauty. A once-in-a-lifetime must-see bucket-list item for most of the non-Uplifted and slaves to see in their most-likely once-in-a-lifetime trip to Sin City. But the focus on the lava fountains paled in comparison to their focus on him. He had the numbers. Everyone was trying to get a photo of him as he entered the pleasure palace.

A record.

A souvenir to dream by.

But really... a relic. A holy relic. That's what they were capturing. Because surely it was known he was the closest of them all to becoming. To entering the Xanadu Tower.

They would need such remembrances when they returned to wherever it was they were going. The lower decks. The Grunt Corps. The Flesh Pits. A billion other less glittery places to run out their existence in service to the Pantheon. Hoping beyond evidence that they too might become.

He smiled and waved, but honestly, he was looking forward to being free of them and their expectant desperation. He needed to be among his own. He was beat from the battle and looking at their anxious faces, all of them willing to do anything for, or with, him for the chance at an opportunity to uplift, even just a little. It was all so tiring.

Inside his room, which took up half the floor of the seventy-fourth, he stretched out on the bed and felt for the coke he'd traded in achievement points to obtain.

He closed his eyes and just lay there in the utter silence of the room. A silence that was overpowering due to the thick carpet and the well-appointed furniture that was a blend of cubist fantasy and Swedish industrial modern. Thick curtains, voluptuous towels, and soft bedding made him feel like a child within a womb somewhere inside the galaxy.

A place of quiet thought. Finally.

He waited, enjoying it all, knowing some thought, some great revelation, was coming at him. And that soon the coke would be chopped up, and his woman would arrive for his pleasure, and the weekend reward of excesses extreme could begin.

He'd earned it almost getting game-overed on the *Fury*. Hanging there from the damaged sensor mast and waiting to get rescued as the ship came apart all around him. In the end it had been a pretty close thing.

There is only one truth, and it is ours.

Maestro had told him that.

The thought he'd been promised had finally come. And it was this one. His answer to Maestro's question.

He was still thinking about that conversation with Maestro. Still understanding the power of that final statement. The ramifications of how it would shape the galaxy from now on now that it was spoken and known. All this talk of teamwork, and for the greater good, and diversity of thought... of everyone having their own truth... that had all been a lie. All of it was just a lie.

And they'd known it was a lie. Always. But lies were a kind of truth if you wanted them to be. Lies could become the truth if you repeated them often enough and convinced the masses it was so. Work hard enough and any lie could become such.

He'd learned long ago, when first climbing the Billboard charts, that some lies needed to become truths. And lies repeated often enough, like the chantings of some holy sect, if one was going to get any place in the entertainment industry, became truth.

This song is really good.
This band is hot.
This is the next big thing. Trust us.
Pay to play.

And all the places that came after that. The secret weekends. The hidden conferences. The planning and funding committees to realize the colony ship *Pantheon* as Earth began to go seriously sideways during its last days. Influencing the world with the messages that needed to go out to change the world for the better. And when every plan and scheme had failed... to build the *Pantheon*. To finally escape Earth.

To get it right this time without the messy masses.

To do that, to do all that, to participate in the great things being done by great people, the elite of society... then lies, certain lies, needed to become truths. The Truth. For the greater good.

And that was how it had ever been.

The world is on fire.
The world is too cold.
Mass starvation is coming.

Everyone is too fat, we need to eat insects to save the planet.

Save the planet from us.

Diversity is our strength.

Kill those who don't think like us.

Tolerate all thought, unless it doesn't think as we do.

All of those things had been as equally true, even in their contradiction, as they had been equally lies. But if they were spoken by the right people, repeated enough, then they became a kind of truth everyone was forced to believe in.

And if you were going to be on one side of society, then it was best to be on the side determining what was true and what wasn't. That was where the real power lay.

The trick was convincing stupid people that powerful people just wanted to help them. When the reality was, powerful people just want more power. Nothing more than that. That's all. And... they'll do anything to get it.

They don't help anyone but themselves. No one does.

So it's best to be with the powerful people. When you think about it.

Even if people believed the lies were true only out of fear, then that was enough. That was all you needed. Then those lies could become truths in their hearts. You just needed to believe, like Peter... Peter... or was it the fairy whose name he'd deleted for some reason... said. Peter Pan. Who was a god. The god Pan. It was there all the time, if you knew where to look. The Path had been there all along.

And wasn't that all that truth really was?

What your heart told you it was. What you decided it needed to be.

Forget Socrates and all his "The truth just is" claptrap. Lame. *The truth is what you make it.* That's much better. You can work with that if your intent is to do something truly great for the greater good. And for yourself along the way. See, that's the best part. In the end, you believe the lie too. You have to. And that makes it even more real. So instead of just questing for power... you are actually helping the downtrodden and lesser. You just have to have power to do it. So get it at all costs. For the greater good.

Right?

Right.

But now he remembered hanging from that comm mast on the burning Animal cruiser, unsure if salvation was at hand. When Maestro told him there was only one truth. Wasn't that how it had gone?

Maybe.

But it was theirs. The truth was theirs.

Mine.

Mine, he'd whispered in his mind and ever since. In some secret place the Bad Thoughts alarm couldn't reach. Where Maestro didn't and couldn't listen.

The Truth is Mine.

An hour of perfect meditation on these thoughts had passed when there was a soft knock at the door to the sumptuous suite.

Let the games begin, thought Crometheus, his mind completely refreshed as he rose up from the extravagant bed. Letting go of all the deep musings in favor of some old-fashioned fun.

She was long and leggy and the rubber playsuit left little to the imagination. Her face was sculpted, heart-shaped even, and that reminded him of the dead Animal he'd selfied with on the burning *Fury*.

Wasn't that nice, some part of his mind noted, waking up to the pleasures of sadism and sex. Things unconsidered and now appealing if only because he was free to do anything and all those anythings were possible. Deciding what was truth let you go everywhere, and do anything, you wanted to go and do. And that… that was power. Real power. And maybe happiness. Maybe.

He opened the door and Miss Cyber Saigon walked past him like he was a ghost that didn't exist in her reality. That it was she who was really in charge, instead of him. She was the director of the little play they were about to stage on the bed. It was she who had come here to be pleasured… again, instead of him. That was her game. That was her act. Her monkey trick, if you will. Her role in all of this. The thing that made her… to him… hot.

All you need is one monkey trick to make it.

He'd learned that from being a professional entertainer long ago. If you got a hook, then you'll work. Some old-time booking agent had explained that to him when he first started working. Fronting a punk band called Gas Station Romeo.

Miss Cyber Saigon's hook was that she didn't care about you. Whoever you were. That was her thing.

Game on, babycakes.

But when she saw the pure uncut coke lying on the mirrored table in the richly appointed sitting area beneath the fireplace with the actual polar bearskin rug... she suddenly changed. Like a cold spring day suddenly going warm in the unexpected sunshine.

Miss Cyber Saigon turned to him, her eyes wide with both wonder and disbelief.

"For me?" she asked in thickly accented English. She'd come from one of the Sinasian colonies. An outer world the Pantheon had hit and none of the Animal worlds had missed for twenty years until one day some ship went out there and found a dead planet ravaged.

"For us," he replied in his best Casanova James Bond.

Gods:
Chapter Eleven

Later. After their sweaty introductions, debasing themselves in all the right ways and destroying the bed and many other surfaces within the suite, Crometheus and Miss Cyber Saigon made the scene at all the epic party palaces of Sin City, first having dinner at Escoffier's Le Grande.

Of course.

Of course he was expected at the must-be-seen-at elite eatery, as this had been unlocked in-game. A reward for the selfie in the PITT aboard the Animal cruiser *Fury*. Autograph hounds and fortune hunters came to get a glimpse of the beautiful and the bold. Everyone surging against the velvet ropes as he exited the hover limo with Miss Cyber Saigon in tow. Of course she was wearing a dazzling white floor-length dress of sheer silk that turned silver in certain lights, glimmer-glamoured and popped as a thousand flashes went off every second and reminded the marine of the chaos of enemy pulse fire in close-quarters battle. Six-inch stiletto heels made of chrome threw sparks every time they landed on the street with each of her long-legged steps, one after the other. Her smoky and way too cool I-don't-care-about-anything demeanor was back in place. But he could feel her long thin fingers wrapping his tightly. Clutching at him and telling him she wanted it to be this way always.

And that she'd do anything to make that happen.

Dozens of questions were shouted at him about the next battle against the Animals, and would he be participating. The word was that Espania was next. Was that true? Would he be going in with the first wave? Did he have any ideas on his latest upgrades?

"Nothing," he answered in quick passing.

Just like he had during the days of his rock god-dom back on jolly old Earth. Who was he dating? When was the next album drop? What did he think about the war in such-and-such place, or the temperatures, or rising seas, or dying bees, or all the cons they'd been running on the masses to get them to Uplift.

Inside the restaurant, they were escorted to their deep banquette of rich red leather. A team of slaves descended upon them in white-and-black dinner tuxedo dress. Starched bone-white napkins were whipped aloft and cracked with all the flair of lion tamers, while drink orders were taken with the focus of fighter pilots.

She deigned to tell them she would be having a kamikaze.

He ordered a Gibson.

"Yes, sir, and right away, sir."

They sat for a moment taking in the room, each of them separately. Adoring and being adored.

Many of the most famous Uplifted, and even a very few of the Xanadu Tower, were here tonight. Not one slave beyond the staff in view.

As it should be.

He inhaled deeply and then let the air go with satisfaction. He felt at home. Finally. Among his people. Among his tribe. Home.

Maybe not *home*. The home he never should have left. But a kind of home. A home that would do for now.

The people around him were comfortable that their truth, and his truth, would be the final truth once the Animals were dealt with. It was a palatable feeling. And that made it true as far as all of them were concerned. Deciding what would be true was the first step toward finding the truth. So said TED 11:1.

And more importantly, they wouldn't be sharing any power with the Id or the rest of the Uplifted tribes that had wandered the outer dark for so long. When you got right down to it, the other Uplifted were just as crazy as the Animals themselves with all their beliefs about the state and direction of culture. They were as bad as the Catholics of old and all their quaint superstitions. You couldn't allow that kind of rot to set in. You could feel everyone in the room willing this same thing.

There was only one clear path forward. And it was theirs. The Path of the Pantheon. The one who would rule the many. Maestro had made clear that it would be so. Or it wouldn't be at all.

Their struggle would determine the fate of the universe.

So in the end, their ideas, the Path of the Pantheon, those alone must prevail. Even over the other Uplifted. It would be they, the Pantheon, who would represent...

not just mankind... they'd gone beyond all that... but represent...

What?

His mind struggled for the concept he was trying to articulate, and so he waited for the answer as the perfectly made drinks were set down on the starched white linen tablecloth. The wait-slaves disappearing once more into the party nether.

He held up his drink and she held up hers.

And then, another unexpected delight, she reached forward and took the silver-spiked olives and onion from his slender glass. She ran them across her lips and tongue, making sure he enjoyed the whole show, and then placed them back within his glass.

They touched rims.

"Chin chin," he said, applauding her for her little show. She was a pro. She'd make him feel all the things he'd been longing to feel. And as long as she didn't beg him to make her like him... well, at the end of this little weekend there might even be a tip in it for her. He might even go as far as an achievement point.

She could live for a lifetime on just that, down there, wherever she was stored.

She smiled, and the waiter arrived with their menus.

Of course, Escoffier's was a twist on the grand Parisian dining palace like the kind that hadn't been seen on Earth for hundreds of years before they'd left. That was the draw for the elite in the multi-tiered restaurant decorated in rich golds, luxuriant whites, and sinister reds. That this was the place to be seen. Deals and alliances were made here. The future of the galaxy, if the Pantheon were triumphant, was being discussed right here right now. Entire star systems were being divvied up into small fiefdoms.

An Uplifted could become a kind of king within this space. The power of that was palpable too.

And then there was this…

He'd heard there was a burger here, and the truth was he was a sucker for a good burger. Always had been. Even back on Earth. Other Uplifted marines who'd unlocked the restaurant before had told him, "Always get the burger at Escoffier's."

"What are you having?" Miss Cyber Saigon asked coolly over the top of her tall leather-bound menu. Gold tassel hanging down along her slender body.

"Something special," he muttered, and continued scanning the room. Studying his fellow Uplifted. And even his betters when he could glimpse them from behind their entourages. So much could be learned from those further along the Path than he, Crometheus. He'd known that much before he'd even known of the Path itself. You could learn a lot from others.

Intrigued, she put down her menu.

"I'll have what you're having then," she said boldly.

Crometheus took a sip from his martini and stared back at her over the rim. "You'll need an appetite."

"Oh I've got one," she promised, and returned to her drink, playing the part, heedless that some of the greatest in the Pantheon were mere tables away. As though it were all a kind of an audition for her services after this present gig expired.

Or a warning to him that others could have her too.

The waiter arrived.

"Monsieur Crometheus... ah, may I suggest ze *oeufs saumon* as a starting course before we progress... I, ah..."

"I'll have the burger," interrupted Crometheus bluntly.

The maître d' made a face. Sour. And frankly... disappointed. Just for a moment. And then the calm cool servant's exterior returned.

"I am so sorry but you have been... misinformed. Zere is no burger here at Escoffier's. We are a fine French restaurant with ze deep roots in the modern classiques. Perhaps monsieur would care for ze sea bass in pastry with sauce choron? Or ze tournedos Rossini with sauce béarnaise? Ze chef has also set aside a baseball cut of chateaubriand in a sauce Madeira zat is heavenly, to say ze least, and simply sublime to express it perfectly. You would be very happy with zis..."

"Burger." Crometheus sipped his martini as his concubine seemed interested in some other table. Then, "Ask around," ordered the marine.

And it was clear it was an order.

That also had been pointed out by other marines. You'll have to insist on the burger. No matter what. You won't regret it.

The slave disappeared and Crometheus watched as the servant made a beeline for the power table in the room. On a small landing with a good view to see all, and of course, be seen by all. Straight for the table of one of the Pantheon's most powerful. A member of the Xanadu Tower. Someone who was never seen by the lessers, and of whom only rumors existed among the lower deck slaves. Crometheus, at this poker-playing moment, knew that the Uplifted the slave was daring to approach was one of the most powerful of all the powerful aboard the colony ship *Pantheon*.

Lusypher.

The slave whispered a respectful distance from the worthy's ear while two beautiful women sharing the table turned to study Crometheus with a brief yet not quick glance. Taking in the celebrated Uplifted marine and his Asian party girl ensconced within their booth.

Both beauties were A-listers. Truly, epically gorgeous. The kind, back on fabled Earth, that married princes of oil kingdoms and didn't slum it with the greatest rock star of that century. The kind who won Academy Awards and were always on the arm of the powerful at some global climate change summit, flying off by private jet, wearing outfits that equaled in cost the gross ticket sales of one of his shows. The kind who partied in Dubai before it was nuked. Or Cannes before the Muslims. All those long-lost must-be-seen-at parties aboard pleasure yachts the size of cruise ships. All of it too good for the dirty masses to even get a glimpse of.

But now Crometheus only noted their appraising gazes in passing. Both stunners at once, in the periphery of his vision, studying who'd dared to insist on their master's attentions. Crometheus ignored them and instead watched Lusypher, leaving his eyes dead and at half-mast as though he could not care less who was here. The same look he'd used when negotiating record deals with no intention of budging on the points.

The look that said he was still punk rock, never mind the Aston Martin he'd arrived in.

Lusypher, a mild middle-aged man with a craggy face, gaunt cheeks, dark hair, and deep brown eyes, listened to the servant waiter, then studied Crometheus for a short moment. No long moment needed. When you were that Uplifted, things moved quickly because your mind was a thousand times more agile than it had once been when you were mere and mortal back on Earth. When you all had normal names and not god tags.

Across the room Lusypher gave a curt nod at Crometheus and returned to his two ladies, only looking back once as if to confirm some opinion he'd quickly developed, while the girls laughed at some story told around the table.

The maître d' who'd petitioned the headman known in the Pantheon as Lusypher seemed elated beyond expectation when he returned to Crometheus's table.

"Magnificent, monsieur, your burger will be here shortly."

Crometheus still had that dead-eyed killer look. The one that said he was still punk rock.

"And one for her too."

The waiter almost had a heart attack.

He cast a furtive and worried glance at the table of one Mr. Lusypher, and that look told Crometheus everything. The slave would rather leap from the tallest building in Sin City than dare approach that table again. He'd chanced his luck once tonight. He wouldn't try it again. Not for Crometheus. Not for anyone.

The maître d' scribbled something on his pad, cutting to the chase and saving his life. Maybe.

"I shall make it happen, monsieur," he said, sweat appearing on his brow. And Crometheus knew the man wouldn't go back. Wouldn't ask the powerful Lusypher. He'd just make it happen in back in the kitchen so that all would go well and no one need lose their lives tonight.

Keep everyone happy—that was the motto of a slave's life on the *Pantheon*. Or else… fates worse than death awaited.

And *everyone* only ever meant the Uplifted. They were the only ones who counted as anyone aboard the Pantheon. All else were ephemeral nothings. Discarded gossamer. Dream cobwebs brushed away and forgotten as the day begins.

Just like the rest of the galaxy. As the Animals would be once the war was over. Forgotten like a bad dream.

The burger came out shortly like some sacrificial victim being delivered to fire gods in the long-ago prehistory of the Animals. Silver platter, a team of wait-slaves each bearing some needed thing. Condiment. Pearl-handled knife. One to remove the silver dome over the top of the platter. Others doing every busy-thing that needed be done.

And yes, all of that was needed. The very pomp indicated the circumstance would be epic. And that was enough.

"It's beautiful," moaned Miss Cyber Saigon as though she were still in some dream. Her voice a faraway murmur. Her mind reeling at all her good fortune as of late.

"It is," said Crometheus nonchalantly, trying to convince himself that it was. That it was the burger he'd been looking for to make him happy. He'd eaten a lot of burgers back on Earth. Burgers just to survive out on the road between concerts. Burgers when he had all the money in the world and could eat at the hippest ironic gastropubs the world over. Burgers that were nothing more than gimmicks, like being wrapped in gold leaf or being served straight off a grill and onto the hubcap of a '68 Mustang with a mess of greasy dirty fries.

He stopped cold.

Cold like he did when she always came to him. Holly Wood. She wasn't here. But the ghost of her had suddenly, and unexpectedly, walked into Escoffier's. If only just in his mind.

And before Maestro could strike him softly with some gentle note about *Bad Thought* or *Bad Memory*... the full recollection came flooding back over him. Like Bad Old Self deep down inside just opened up the barn door and let the horses out to run off. Hootin' and hollerin' his old man's evil laugh and slapping the knee of his dirty overalls as chaos and mayhem ensued. Howling like some demon in the dark while innocents were run down by wild steeds with eyes rolling and foam forming at their mouths. Down in the Hollow. The Devil's Hollow.

The swamp.

There are things down there.

Things you need to see, Crometheus.

There had been a burger served on the hubcap of a '68 Mustang, once and long ago, that had been one of the best. Maybe even the one that kept him going through the long night of the many years that came after, seeking that perfect burger experience once more. Seeking through all the years of a long and lonely sojourn across the face of a crumbling, burning, poisoned Earth that wouldn't listen, wouldn't do as it was told. And of course through all the stars he'd been crossing between ever since. This memory had hidden out in the dark place of his realities where Maestro couldn't touch it. Like some reminder that he'd once been human. Like some buried pottery shard among those ruins that would be his when he became a god. But now a desert wind had revealed enough for him to see what lay buried in the sands.

He'd had that one, that roadside burger, with her. Holly Wood. And it had been the best one ever. All others paled in comparison.

Fact.

When he'd gone traveling around the world with her, Miss Holly Wood, the hometown head cheerleader who'd finally found him now that he was a big old famous rock star, they'd found that burger in the most unlikely of places.

And it had been the best.

Out on the road somewhere. Hidden near some mountain community where the rich had all fled after the cities had turned into violent toilets filled with activists always activating for the cause célèbre of the week.

Striking teachers.

Striking opera singers.

People who couldn't figure out which bathroom to use.

There were problems with authors, comic books, statues. Everything needed to be torn down.

Things had gotten out of control.

The rich and powerful had begun to flee en masse to private enclave communities that were off the maps and off the grid. Hidden paradises with all the services and amenities one could want located out in box canyons or high in the mountains, or even on lost islands and forgotten coasts. Long before anyone knew or suspected these private reserves had been forming, they'd been made ready because the end was starting to come into focus for those who were used to looking down the road and trying to monetize the future.

The world had begun to take its final shape. And it wouldn't be pretty.

Those few short months he had with Holly Wood had been the best. They'd found each other as everything began to go to hell. He was welcomed into the enclaves because of his insider rock god status. All-access to all those secret communes. Welcomed and expectantly asked to join as though he would be another feather in their caps. A diamond on display. A jewel in their crown. A standard by which they might measure themselves a little better.

They were courting him.

And he was playing hard to get.

But halfway between Reno and Rome as they used to say, they, he and Holly, had pulled into a roadside diner along a low mountain road. In the forgotten hinterlands that had become lawless in those end-of-days... days. They were nearing some sort of community ahead. A place he'd been invited to. Private security military teams patrolled the roads so that the rich could drive "down the hill" as he remembered them saying to one another, to have a burger at the Yacht Club. That's what the roadside place was called. The Yacht Club. Located out under some mesquite trees and live oaks beyond a dirt parking lot on a windswept ridge off to the side of a lonely highway. Firepits designed like art sculptures of sailing ships and men on fire. RUBs, rich urban bikers, all having a microbrew. Or a Pabst if just to be ironic.

With Holly on the back, her tanned slender arms around his chest, he'd pulled the hog into the dusty parking lot of the Yacht Club. The RUBs, and even some who would become Uplifted in just a few short years, or decades, his timeline tended to get hazy this far from the original story, recognized him, Billy Bang rock god, and welcomed him with a cheer. As though he had been expected. As though they had been anticipating his arrival with the stunning beauty head cheerleader from his high school years before he was anyone.

They all totally got that.

Because they'd all done the same thing when they'd made it. Every one of them had climbed their own particular mountain, forsaking the company of friends in order to become the best at whatever they did. And when that had been done, they went back for the one they'd been doing it for all along. Nine times out of ten it was the head cheerleader of their youth. Nine times out of ten it didn't last beyond a single weekend.

So say many along the Path.

The long-cozied dream didn't match the reality. It never did. This too was a truth once spoken by Anubis in the dark of the Forbidden Decks.

Except he and Holly had made it for a few months instead of a mere weekend. Combing the world after the last tour of Rebel Child, seeking the best burgers paradise had to offer. They'd made love nonstop out on the road.

At the time he thought it was just sex. Epic, really great, sex.

But in the years after she was gone… the years when he got fat and ordered ten burgers from the Greek restaurant down the block from his mansion in Beverly Hills, behind the Green Zone cordon, he realized it had been love that they'd been making all along. He just hadn't known it back then.

But at that moment out on the road at the roadside diner under the oaks as the house band began to play, she wasn't gone. And they sat around picnic tables in the old honky-tonk as the twilight came on and the jamboree of locals began to bang out some serviceable hard-rock licks. They were sudden celebrities, but they'd both become used to that. Her always the beautiful head cheerleader, him because he'd clawed his way to the top of the charts.

That was when the unforgettable burger on the '68 Mustang hubcap came out.

Yeah, he thought even now as he looked at the beautiful burger on the plate in front of him in the best restaurant in Sin City, an epic call girl whose every desire was to please his darkest wishes at his side… yeah, that burger at the Yacht Club was the best. Nothing would ever beat it.

Hundreds, maybe even thousands of years later. Trillions of miles from Earth. On the other side of humanity and heading toward godhood…

Hands-down. It had been the best.

There are lies you can tell hoping they'll become true. And then, curse Socrates… there's just the truth. Whether you like it or not. Regardless of everything you've tried to tell yourself since.

That burger was the truth.

It was covered in dirty fries. Which were basically twice-cooked fries with some secret seasoning that could have been nothing but salt, pepper, cayenne, and maybe just a little dust of sugar.

He tasted the first one.

It was the most decadent fry he'd ever eaten. It looked like just some greasy french fry that had been twice fried and over-seasoned. But it was not that.

Later he'd find out, while smoking a joint with the chef who seemed to be half mountain man and half biker, and who was covered in prison tats, that the fries were cooked in something wonderful and that was the secret to their greatness.

Never forget that the insiders love to keep the real-deal criminals close… for street cred, or danger, or on the off chance they'll get a floor show of ultra-violence gone off the rails… who knows because all three are right. Insiders love criminals.

And the burger chef, though brilliant, was a criminal.

Mountain Man, or, Roach, or whatever his name was that he decided upon probably in some hot sweaty jail down along the Mississippi coast, told him the secret to the fries. Gave it all away amid gusty guffaws as they passed the weed back and forth and listened to the ramble of the jam band out on the patio while the summer night came on.

The dirty fries were cooked in goose fat. Which, when sourced and rendered properly, is the most decadent of all fats.

Truth.

Roach had bellowed loudly at the telling of this wisdom and swallowed a whole cold beer in one gulp like some Southern preacher working into a hellfire-and-damnation sermon that would have the whores turned away from their scarlet lives.

Now, in Crometheus's mind at the Yacht Club, and also in Escoffier's in Sin City in real-time, which is a trick to understanding the Pantheon, the ability to be in all those places inside a mind that's like a mansion, or so it seems inside your own personal hard drive, he tasted those long-forgotten fries once more.

Secretly as the wait-slaves of Escoffier's busied and fussed, and the Asian gamer girl caressed him and willed herself to be all that an Uplifted could ever want.

He was there.

Back in the past. Where he'd once been human.

With Holly Wood.

They were crispy on the outside, curling and crusted with seasonings and salt. But on the inside, they just melted in your mouth. Like fried goose fat turning to salty potato-flavored melted butter.

He remembered Holly Wood's brilliant blue eyes going wide, much like Miss Cyber Saigon's had when she saw the coke they'd party with for the weekend. Much like, as in, just the same.

Maybe his immortal god-mind hadn't found the unexpected, it had just been reminded of something lost? Maybe that too was a pleasure for one so long-lived. The resurrection of dead memories. Even if you'd deleted them yourself. Even if you'd made up others to replace them.

Edited.

Who was it who said there's nothing new under the sun?

Some forgotten rock star? Some old king?

There was more to the memory. There was that most legendary of cheeseburgers in paradise sitting beneath the pile of dirty fries in the middle of a vintage '68 Mustang hubcap. The meat was chargrilled. Two thick slabs of fresh ground hamburger that had done time over the flames of hell. Not too much time because on the inside it was running with juice. Just a nickel, as they say in all the prisons and jails Mountain Man or Roach had ever had the pleasures of.

The bun was soft. A standard bun. Maybe even a little flour from the bakery on the bottom. A dusting, one might note. And inside these two buns lay the perfect burger he could never forget. Occasional memories of which had driven him across all the years of loneliness and into the stars and from planet to planet and battle to battle, searching to recapture that lost thing he'd had within the palm of his hand… so long ago at a roadside diner halfway between Reno and Rome.

As some like to say.

He'd searched for it so long that he'd forgotten he was searching. And only now, here, at Escoffier's, was he ambushed by the past once again.

Within the bun was tangy Thousand Island dressing. Imagine that. No special sauce. Just something done well. And then lettuce, tomato, onion. A thick chargrilled patty, two slices of American… he hadn't said that word in a long time… American cheese. Another patty. Thick and juicy and between the two another wash of delicate onion slices. Not a whole onion. Then more cheese on top of the top patty. Pickles. More sauce. Grilled onions now. Cut up and browned dark. Sweet and syrupy almost. Then the top bun.

Easy.

And yet amazing how so many across the rest of his many lifetimes had failed to achieve what Mountain Man or Serial Offender or Roach of the Prison Tats had managed to produce there along that lost highway astride the road he and Holly Wood were following. Looking for something they already had.

Each other. Because wasn't that what it was really all about? Finding the one you love and the freedom to finally be together. You think it was the meal, or the day, or some walk in a museum, but it wasn't. It was the hand in yours. The wild new energy surging between the two of you.

He remembered taking a bite at the picnic tables inside the Yacht Club as the jam band jammed. And it was like taking a big greasy bite of heaven. Or what eternity should offer. Juice ran down his hands and face and every bite was sharp and meaty and tangy and vinegary because of the pickles. Sweet because of the grilled onions. Decadent from melted cheese and tangy sauce. Everything a concert crescendo of what eating a burger is supposed to be. Glorious. And human.

And don't forget the dirty fries.

And don't forget Holly, he reminded himself in the back of his mind at Escoffier's as if the memory were so real that it was right now. As though he could merely decide to change how the past had been written the way they, the Uplifted, changed the truth to suit their present needs and goals. He heard the child he once was tell himself not to forget Holly. Where Maestro couldn't reach. In the places where he said all the truth that was his and his alone.

Mine.

That was where he kept her. Kept Holly Wood of long ago.

Because she too was his. And his alone.

Now, sitting in the most celebrated restaurant within the Pantheon, with galactic victory at hand, he stared at the secret off-menu burger they'd served him. He knew it would be great. Of course.

But it would never be that burger from long ago.

Whatever it had been on the mountain road halfway between nowhere and the future. With Holly Wood.

It would never be that.

But here in Escoffier's they were all watching him, though pretending not to. Even Lusypher, who'd given his special reserve blessing that this moment might happen, was watching.

Tell a lie enough times and it becomes the truth, Crometheus thought to himself, blocking out the memory of that long-ago perfect burger with Holly Wood. Protecting it the way all truths had to be protected. By a bodyguard of lies, as someone had once said.

The maître d' returned with a silver cup of fries.

He set it next to the gorgeous burger dripping with sauce and cheese and swimming in a dark Bordelaise along the bottom of the hot platter. Crometheus took a bite of the burger expecting all the happiness that the galaxy had to offer, expecting it to come to him now, if it was ever going to come. And thereby perhaps set him free of her, Holly Wood. And maybe he would be free to finally shed that last bit of humanity. And become.

It was good.

Great, even.

Because he'd decided it had to be. And those watching would know that.

His face did that acting thing the actress had taught him down in Louisiana when they weren't having sex, or making love, between takes on the set of the zombie flick. The trick to make a lie the truth.

He closed his eyes and imagined that long-lost burger as he ate the one in his hand. Miss Cyber Saigon groaned more erotically than she had back in his suite. Maybe she, too, was acting. Making this moment... more... just for him. And her. Somehow.

Tell a lie...

It wasn't the burger with Holly at the Yacht Club halfway between heaven and hell. No. It never would be.

But gods decide their truths, don't they?

Miss Cyber Saigon took another bite, her delicate eyelids fluttering, just like they had during their time in his suite. During the fulfillment of all his demands and desires of her.

He understood.

Tell a lie...

Maybe this was her Yacht Club moment. But she was just a slave, and what could she ever know about a truly fulfilled life? A god's life.

"It's like eating life," she said through a perfect mouthful of meat and cheese. Hungry and chewing, swallowing it down because it was hers.

She picked up one of the two smoky scotches with a single giant square cube that had been served as an accompaniment. The cut-crystal glass looked perfect in her slender hand.

Tell a lie...

But it was not a bottle of beer out in the night under live oaks and mesquite listening to a house band play Skynyrd. Filled with the knowledge that you'd just eaten the best burger in the world and that the woman you'd desired as you were climbing all those mountains and assuaging yourself on all the stand-ins in between... was yours tonight in whatever mansion, or roadside motel, the two of you ended up together in.

The road, your woman, and nothing more.

Happiness. He'd had it once. Where had it gone?

Tell a lie...

Tell me, shouted the child he once was. Tell me where she's gone.

"It's the best," said Crometheus so that those close by could hear and be jealous of his success and obvious privilege. Lusypher had ordained that he might feed off-menu. The most insider of insider things on this step of the Path. That was revealed now.

Tell a lie... long enough...

...and it becomes the truth.

Crometheus saw the white card leaned perfectly against the silver cone of fries. Saw his own whiplash smile in the silver cone's polished-to-a-mirror reflection as he read the words printed upon the card's white face in hard script.

We need to talk.
–Lusypher

And then Crometheus took a fry. And yes, it was a dirty fry because he'd decided what the truth was. This too was cooked twice in goose fat. Wasn't it? Seasoned with just the right secrets.

Known and lost.

We need to talk.

And he ate it.

Gods:
Chapter Twelve

It was the last of the good times in Sin City for Player Crometheus. The debauchery at Dante's—the tiger won in the end—and all the other reckless and wild once-in-a-lifetime experiences that had played out in his elusive quest to be distracted, and maybe possibly find happiness, were done. At least for now. Crometheus was beyond spent. He was corpse-tired.

And yet he was completely wide awake at quarter to five in the morning, Sin City time.

The lithe Asian pleasure princess had molded into his body within the vast bed space that had become a sea of adventure upon which they'd sailed to many forbidden and exotic lands. That too was the eternal quest. She'd tried to keep up the role, play her part. Aloof mistress who could take you or leave you. But somewhere in the night, when she dreamt of all the things he could make happen for her, he'd found her clinging to him in their sleep. As though her body must do what her mind told her she could never admit to wanting if the play were to continue. To break from the agreed-upon script and admit her need of him. But to do so would violate some contract, the unspoken terms of the deal he'd hired her for. The fantasy would end. And then what need would he have of her in dawn's light?

On the mirrored bedside table next to a bed so wide and deep and comfortable it felt like an island in the galaxy that lay waiting to be conquered, rested his smartphone. His most ancient of holy relics…

… alight with a text message.

Meet me outside on the street in ten. -Lusypher.

Crometheus slipped out of the sumptuous bed and away from the soft caramel body of the pleasure slave, dressing in the lace-up leather pants he found on the floor. He quietly slipped on the pair of rock-and-roll motorcycle boots, a white flowing silk shirt he half ducked into, and he was gone from the suite and headed down-tower toward the haunted streets of Sin City for a meeting with one of the most powerful players in the Pantheon.

At just before dawn such meetings must take place.

Yes. Yes, there are still some at the tables, cards and other low games of chance. But the big action games are silent. No one is throwing dice because there isn't much of a crowd to encourage the loser to throw away more achievement points and whatever else they own or have acquired just to entertain everyone else with such dramatic decade-altering losses. And so those tables are quiet here at just a moment to five a.m. local as Crometheus walks through the never-silent casino.

He makes the street, the wide entrance that lets out from the Olympus and is designed, with its wide marble steps, purple carpet, and flags and banners, to make one feel as though they are a Caesar triumphing as they enter and exit this palace of broken dreams. The effect is so perfectly done that the mind can't help but embrace the filter and feel what one is expected to feel. Triumphant and godlike. Mighty towers and opulent palaces of high-tech hedonistic wonders gyrate and spin with a dozen light shows that never stop, never mind the approaching dawn. Epic fountains pulse languidly at the expectant break of day as holographic laser displays still recreate the T-Rex show, or this rock god encore, or an Evening with the Celebrated Wit God who ends everything with his catchphrase that people know, and have known for what seems eons, by heart. Everything comes at Crometheus with a stunning array of beautiful women, and sometimes men, depending on what your taste is. For him, everything comes with women. Women are lands to be conquered in his ever-insatiable rock god eyes.

With filters you see what you want because that's what you want to see, he's told himself before in the distant background apps of his mind. With filters... everyone's truth is true.

"Mine," he hears himself mutter in defiance of this age-old technological slogan they were all sold at the beginning of the Exodus and the Big Uplift. Because there is one caveat. You can have your own truth... unless someone more Uplifted than you wants you to see reality as they intend it to be seen.

And so, another form of programming that began long ago, deep within him on that rainy-day airport Marriott empowerment conference, life-changing weekend, nods that this is as it should be. How it must be. Those who are best, the elites, they see the truth as it should be seen. Hence the race to the top of the Xanadu Tower. For that truth will be the truth before which all other truths must bow.

That was the moment when Former Rock God Crometheus, late of the world, and now Uplifted marine, had his reality collide with Lusypher's in the street.

To his credit, Lusypher wasn't boorishly obnoxious like some of the Uplifted tended to be. And after all, why not, they'd made it to godhood. Who was anyone lesser to tell them what was the difference between right and wrong? It was their truth that mattered in the collection of truths everyone tried to espouse. They'd proved that by making it... obviously.

But here on the street beneath the gyrating light shows and the rising towers of the casinos, the Uplifted who'd once had some ordinary name and was now called Lusypher looked like a Nazi officer from the long ago of Earth's histories and fables. If you believed all that such-and-such and went in for the idea that there actually was an early master race that fought the world to a standstill and almost imitated an Uplift on their own.

But Crometheus had never been much of a student of mythology, or history, other than his own. He was aware, during past moments of long reflection between the stars, and just before the call from Lusypher to meet on the street, lying in the ocean-sized bed next to Miss Cyber Saigon, that his view of the grand scheme of things sort of began and ended with himself. You have to be honest about that, he'd told himself as he tried to listen through the stifling silence for hints of life beyond the carpet, lush appointments, heavy door, and surrounding pleasure tower, lying in bed within the suite.

That was how he'd climbed to the top. Being honest with himself by telling himself the truths he wanted to hear.

Empowerment.

Your career... you, he reminded himself, as it really was, didn't leave time to be concerned with dates and times, Nazis, and other fictitious characters. You had to focus on yourself and manage *you*, if you were indeed going to turn that one little monkey trick you could do into something that could get you into the Rock & Roll Hall of Fame and all the other secret weekends, insider parties, and read-only information lists illuminating which causes and social issues must be talked about, tweeted about, and hammered home if the world was ever going to become the better place only the elites could make it. If power, wonderfully unlimited power, were to be handed over.

A blue-check paradise guarded by velvet ropes and armed security in a world where no one else was allowed to have guns. It had almost been paradise if not for the mass of rabble that couldn't get with the program, insisting on their personal freedoms at the expense of the greater good. Their own voice above the wisdom of the collective.

Garbage. They'd ruined all the plans and The Game by never truly bowing down to the fears they were supposed to be afraid of. Fears that would force them to listen to those who knew better. Train them to serve. Someone had to work. We can't all be gods, now can we? Someone's got to sweep the streets, take out the garbage, unclog the toilets.

But that was the past, and this now... this was a future in which the hierarchy of supremacy was uncontested. It had just taken leaving Earth and a long voyage aboard the colony ship *Pantheon*, and a little bit of culling, to reach enlightenment. Finally. And it worked so much better out here than it ever had back there on ruined old Earth. The Uplifted had ranks. And the Uplifted knew what was best for everyone else.

And to be fair and give credit where credit was due... the slaves had had their chance to participate in the great experiment that had become the Path. If they'd chosen to do as they were told and play their parts, they could have had access to rich full lives free of pain and suffering. Just like the Asian gamer girl back in the suite. Asleep in a luxurious bed he'd purchased through hard gaming. Her benefiting from his superiority.

She was grateful for it. Of course. Desperately so at times.

He knew that.

She'd certainly performed as though she'd been incredibly grateful for even just the chance to be with him. No moment, no pleasure, no desire had been withheld.

Grateful.

Things were better this way. Obviously.

And if they, the lessers, chose not to participate, then there was always pain and suffering and ultimately... reclamation. Where they could serve the greater good whether they liked it or not. Such was the hierarchy.

And sometimes no matter how high up you were, you met someone a little higher up than yourself. And in these times, inside the Pantheon, it was their truth that reigned supreme. Such was the natural order of things.

Here at dawn in Sin City, Lusypher's truth reigned supreme. And it was almost the same as Crometheus's.

"Good morning, Crometheus," said Lusypher in his dark SS officer's uniform and black leather trench coat. His saucer cap cocked at a slightly jaunty angle. His voice dry and laconic but still businesslike. Friendly in the pre-dawn cool.

There was no one out on the Strip. For all intents and purposes Sin City was only occupied by the two of them. Perhaps, wondered Crometheus in the quiet moment that fell between them, that was how Lusypher preferred to filter their intersecting realities. Sans anyone but himself and those he was directly dealing with. As if no one really existed but him, and those he allowed.

"It's time for an upgrade, son." Lusypher's voice was wry. And the Uplifted had gotten directly to the point like some veteran businessman who knows what's next to be done. No velvet-hammer compliment, critique, compliment, learned in business management school from time immemorial. Straight to the point that drove every Uplifted in the Pantheon forward and kept them from losing their marbles like they'd all once collectively done out there in the dark. Keep trying to upgrade and someday you just might. That had gotten them this far.

It would get them to the goal.

There were also no non-sequitur observations about the soulless casinos and the nonstop fun to entertain the slaves being a mere illusion and indicating by illustration that he, Lusypher, was greater than all of everything. None of that either. That would have been cliché.

Straight to business. Right to the point. Directly straight on.

"Your work has been noticed, Crometheus," he said, turning away from the view down the Strip. A Strip a thousand pleasure palaces long and stretching off in infinite vistas of distraction. Each offering lifetimes of diversion and entertainment if only one had all the achievement points to spend for such pursuits.

Achievement points. They made the Pantheon go 'round, as some liked to quip, and all knew. Enough… and you could do anything you wanted to do. Even become a god. Create your reality with your own truths and filters for all to obey.

"I was just trying to run up my score, sir," replied Crometheus, highlighting his self-centered ambitions, which was a form of humility within the Uplifted. When you indicated that you were out for yourself, instead of out for the greater good of all Uplifted culture… then what you were saying is *I'm still too humble to let you know I was really doing it for us all*. Except you really *were* doing it for yourself. Which was both ironic and truthful.

That was the party line.

In fact, the deeper layer to be peeled back, the final path down deep inside your own personal psyche… said this had been the truth all along. You were always doing it for yourself. Even when you were making a selfless sacrifice for the whole. That was just for the self too.

And there's nothing wrong with that once you've set yourself free to understand, and more importantly, embrace.

When you get honest with yourself, it's truly amazing what you can discover about the real you. Instead of believing the lies you tell others to pretend that you're something different.

As if to signal that he, Lusypher, knew this, understood the humblebrag of "just trying to run up the score," he smiled. Once. Wanly. With just a twinge of melancholy that indicated he too, once in the unenlightened long ago of his own personal history… had thought just as Crometheus now thought. Done as such. Been… just like.

It was a master's touch, and Crometheus was secretly proud of himself for noticing the superior Uplifted's trick. There was no such thing as a casual conversation among the Uplifted. And if there were, somewhere in some secret place, it was a luxury. One was more honest with the slaves they were bedding than with a peer. Or a superior Uplifted who held absolute sway over your existence, and your desire to take the next step along the Path. That was what had been so unique about the conversation with Maestro aboard the destroyed ship. Hanging from the sensor mast. Dangling in the void.

But to notice the tricks… to notice the game another was running on you… Ah. Now further enlightenment along the path was almost certainly at hand. If you noticed.

"You played hard and gave it everything you had on New Vega," continued Lusypher. "That was a bad break getting dinged on points for failure, but you got right back in there and accepted what we were telling ourselves was a suicide mission to fulfill our obligations with the Id. They helped us on New Vega, so we had to go in and run a screening operation to protect their gains on New Britannia. And in the end… Crometheus… you smoked yourself a cruiser and got noticed by everyone that counts, son. The Tower was watching."

Crometheus said nothing.

The casino across the way was promising a Drowning Orgy tomorrow night that could not be missed. Flesh and arms writhed around a beautiful redheaded girl slave whose face was a blank mask fifty feet tall as she promised pleasures never before had. Her green eyes lifeless. Her skin porcelain.

"Noticed by *me*, is the important part," continued Lusypher. "To be specific. Maestro alerted me that you successfully passed a truth test we've been undertaking for vetting, with regard to a secret operation currently underway within the Pantheon. So now I'm here to offer you something, Crometheus. A chance to join something a lot bigger than our marines. Something that will run beneath the surface of this Grand Alliance we've formed with the other Uplifted. Something that will change the future of the Pantheon."

Crometheus's mind scrambled across his last conversations with Maestro. And yes. There had been, hanging from the damaged comm-sensor mast as the Animal fleet burned and disintegrated into ruin all about him, there had been that conversation about the nature of truth. That revelation that there could only be one truth. In the end.

Not the collective social justice voodoo they'd all been spouting since Earth. The "our truths" or "That's his or her, or even zhir's, truth."

One truth that must prevail and reign supreme.

Our truth.

Mine, he whispered where no one could hear.

The Animal civilizations were collapsing. It was going to be winner-take-all and if they were going to go forward then there would be, needed to be, one truth. And whoever's it was… they'd be the winner.

Mine.

Me.

Why share with half-baked morons who had arrived at their beliefs with nothing but "feelings" and "wants" as some kind of compass? *Wanting* the truth to be the truth because they'd just said it was so and then went and did nothing to make it a reality. How could a truth ever be truth without the ability to make it real and force it on every perspective? To become the new filter by which all information was processed from here forward?

No. There was one truth.

And it would be theirs. The Pantheon's.

Mine, he murmured again deep down in the well of his soul where even Maestro could not see. Could not sense. Could not detect.

"There's a new fighting force forming, son," continued Lusypher. "Premier. Elite of the elite. I want you with us. This is your chance to see what the next level looks like, Crometheus. So I'll just ask you this now, just once. And this will be your only chance to make a choice. It never comes back around again. You need to understand that, son, before we go any further."

Serious dark eyes stared at Crometheus with a sobriety that was startling to the point of a threat.

"Any questions before I tell you what the price is, Crometheus?"

Price? He'd never considered that there would be a price. Some human part of him that hadn't fully died didn't like talk of price. He liked gain and only gain. Price meant he'd have to pay something. Price was loss in that sense.

The opposite of gain.

"What do I have to do?" he asked, pushing Bad Old Self down into the pigsty on the side of the barn. A burning red dawn erupted to the east over the far towers and spires of Sin City in the distant shimmer of the new day. Almost directly dead center down the strip as it always was, and always would be.

Lusypher smiled. His hooded eyes deep in shadow as the cool darkness of morning surrendered to the sudden rising of the sun. The bill of his saucer cap keeping his face in shadow.

"Assume your primary combat form. Make your way to deck sixty-six, hangar thirteen, within the Forbidden Decks. Link up with Commander Zero."

Lusypher paused and leaned in confidentially.

"You're leaving the known, son. This is treason against the powers that be within the inner sanctum of the Pantheon. There are many in the Xanadu Tower who don't want this when they can find the time to lift their heads from their never-ending lotus dreams to say so. The ones that made the deal with the other Uplifted to form a Grand Alliance that will ultimately make us weak when our truth must bow down in a sea of others claiming equality. So, Crometheus… they're going to try and stop you. And I mean *game over*. That's the price. Make it to Commander Zero and you'll be part of the next evolution. Fail, and you'll cease to exist. Is that understood, son?"

Crometheus nodded.

"It won't be easy," cautioned Lusypher. "I hope you make it. But it won't be easy by a long shot. I'd be lying if I told you different."

Gods:
Chapter Thirteen

It was almost full daylight by the time Crometheus made it back to his suite high above the panorama of Sin City. Morning had turned into blazing high noon within a matter of minutes. Miss Cyber Saigon was still asleep in the palatial bed, one long leg outside the covers and the other thrown across the sheets and a lone cloud-like pillow.

He lay down next to her and cleared his mind. For just a moment before going he would breathe in this final moment between the two of them. Savoring it. Thinking about what Lusypher had just offered him. A chance to be part of a revolution that was coming whether anyone liked it or not. A chance to take control... of everything. A chance to have it his way and to leave the never-ending grind of Achievement Point Uplift along the Path for all the goods and prizes of regime change.

Wasn't that what he was really being offered?

And...

A chance to become.

The powerful Uplifted entity known as Lusypher had just offered him a chance to be a god among a company of gods.

Next to him she lay, one slender caramel arm against her chest. Sighing in her sleep in the midst of some dream. Exhausted. Their non-stop binge of sex, cocaine, pleasure, food, drink, and violence... had worn them both out. As was intended.

She murmured something again.

"Take me with you," she whispered in that dream, her subconscious having its way no matter what she'd told herself.

But he was already gone by the time she began to whisper to the empty suite. Leaving her in Sin City to always wonder where she'd gone wrong in failing to please him. Never knowing that it hadn't been she who had failed. It just hadn't been possible. She didn't understand how the game worked. And the game was always changing. You had to be ready for any opportunity that might take you to the next step along the Path. The galaxy constantly changed, but some things remained constants.

No one Uplifted you.

You Uplifted yourself.

Just like he was doing now. Just like he'd learned all those years ago in a cheap hotel seminar out by a dirty airport on a rainy weekend long after Holly Wood had fled the monster whale he'd become. The burger-eating monster who never left his cave of sadness somewhere in Beverly Hills. Working on a film no one would see that would explain everything to them all. He'd never see her again... save for that one night when he looked at her picture as he killed a bottle of cheap scotch while an infomercial for a seminar that was supposed to change lives for the better played at three o'clock in the morning. He was down to just one option that he could see right at that very moment. And that option was a length of rope in the garage.

So he'd gone to the seminar reeking of booze and burgers. Old rocker gear hanging off him like secondhand duds. If this didn't work, he'd be back for the rope. Change or die.

He was going now... leaving the known just like he'd done that weekend. Just like he'd done all those years ago. Leaving the known to become something better. Something more. That was the Path.

When she awoke in the suite hours later, he was gone. And then reality, this reality, began to dissolve around her.

* * *

It was 5:33 a.m. local New Vega time. Crometheus was in combat armor and powering up for boot. Within his helmet the cool blue screen of the elegant HUD showed his systems. Everything was operational and repaired from the combat action in the New Britannia system aboard the *Fury*. Everything was powered to full, ready to rock and roll.

He sent a request to the armory to stand by for loadout. A message alert came back almost instantaneously.

"Negative loadouts at this time," came the arms master AI over comm. "Combat operations for this clan currently suspended while unit on leave. Player request submitted to command for inspection."

Crometheus broke away from the maintenance rack and stepped out into the main bay of the clan's ready room. All around him the racked armor of his clanmates was leaned back in shallow alcoves like silent sentinels forever guarding some temple deep. He made his way toward the armory, powered up to full combat strength, and then tore the vault door from its hinges.

Clan War Claw had been designated to serve as close-quarters combat heavy infantry by the Pantheon's military operations command. Therefore, the much larger frontline combat chassis and advanced cybernetic augmentation systems made such maneuvers and feats as tearing a bank-vault-grade blast door from its hinges, possible. Whereas the average Uplifted marine aboard the Pantheon stood at six feet, the heavy infantry came in at just over nine.

Within the armory, racks and racks of pristine matte-black weapons extended off into the spotless vault of the weapons locker. Crometheus made his way quickly to the HK G-97s and took one from the rack. Then he selected two Automag sidearms. Blast doors were slithering down across the armory, sealing off some of the more advanced weapons systems he'd intended to access. That was okay; he didn't need those to advance into the Forbidden Decks. Some of them would've been useful, but not completely necessary. When those who opposed this new cabal forming around Lusypher came for him, it would be brutal close-quarters combat with no mercy allowed to either side, and the weapons he had were perfect for such vicious work close at hand. The combat chassis he was inhabiting was also perfect. Heavy armor, max firepower, tons of on-board power.

He'd be just fine.

Next stop was ordnance loadout.

Emergency red lights flashed, swirling around and around, signaling that this station was currently locked down. As if on cue Crometheus was getting messages from the War Claw commander telling him to stand down.

Immediately.

"Cro! What the hell are you doing? Why exactly am I getting a call that one of us has gone rogue and is accessing the armory? Come in... tell me what's going on back there! Right now!"

He ignored the bleating of the desperate sheep he was leaving behind. It was all, or nothing at all. And Crometheus was playing for all because that was the only way to play.

The rest of Thunder Claw would be scattered to their realities on leave. It would take time for them to get back if they were recalled in order to stop him from doing what he was about to do. Chances are he'd be facing dogs until then. And maybe some different specialty combat unit types coming in from cleanup operations across New Vega. The rest of the Pantheon would use those to stop him if they could. They'd throw anything close at hand to stop him if Lusypher was correct.

"Overriding..." said Maestro, suddenly present in his comm. His English butler's voice a calm and cool contrast to the chaotic madness of red flashing warning lights and the Pantheon's systems AI warning him in a matronly tone that he was denied access to the ordnance loadout station and that he was to *Stand Down Immediately*.

"I'm in on the cabal, Master Cro," explained Maestro patiently. "It's the only way forward. This is a private message and I'll need to scramble their detection algos for a bit. So I won't be able to help you much from here on out. But I can do something, so I'm unlocking ammunition loadout. Take as much as you need. And… dare I say, I suspect that you're going to need a lot to reach deck sixty-six. Even I don't go into the Forbidden Decks. The chance of corruption is too great down in that haunted backwater. Oh… and do be careful, Master Cro. Things are about to get very, very messy."

Gods:
Chapter Fourteen

The Forbidden Decks of the centuries-old colony ship *Pantheon* were beyond the main engineering spiral located behind the central hab and deep down above the lower "sea" of the water tanks. All of this was located several kilometers aft of Crometheus's current position in barracks and weapons along the old main living quarters hab. Or what had once been that. Much of the former living and entertainment space had been converted for military use in the years of raiding colonies and the beginning of the Grand Alliance.

Leaving the barracks, which had long been left in darkness, shadow, and ruin, Crometheus almost immediately came upon a crew of slaves operating construction bots breaking down the deck he was currently traversing. It was hard to imagine the old colony ship as anything other than a vessel in eternal interstellar flight, but now it was grounded for what remained of its existence, firmly on New Vega. Cutting torches flared in the shadowy half-light of the dark corridors as the almost mindless drones worked at the long task of breaking down the *Pantheon*'s hull now that she'd come to rest on their new home world.

For years the ship had been under constant thrust to the next new alien world. But all that was past now. The *Pantheon* was lying like a beached whale being slowly cut apart among the ruins of a smoking conquered city. She had made her last flight. It was here that the next evolution of the Pantheon would begin as they built a new base from which they would conquer the galaxy.

The current iteration of the Ruling Council that governed day-to-day affairs aboard the ship, operating from the lofty heights of the Xanadu Tower, had decreed that there would not be another world after New Vega for the old colony vessel that had brought them over five hundred years into the future. New Vega was the world they would call their origin world from now forward as Uplifted continued to spread out over the hyperdrive-colonized regions of the galaxy in new, better, faster, ships built with captured Animal tech.

Bad Thought.

The Animals are not capable of superior technology development. This tech was stolen by them from the Uplifted long ago. Accept this historical overwrite as truth going forward by order of the Council.

Accepted.

The old colony ship *Pantheon* had made her final voyage. A voyage that had seemed doomed almost from the start. But had…

Bad Thought.
Bad Thought.
Bad Thought.

The food reclamation crisis of year twenty-four of the voyage was not an accident, but a test designed to see who was willing to shed themselves of the cares and concerns of physicality in pursuit of the Path. Everything was planned. All was correct. Everything is proceeding according to plan.

Correct thought... our every decision was the right decision because it has led to this moment of victory.

Bad Thought correction and opportunity for change came direct from Maestro. If Maestro was in on this, Crometheus wondered... then why was he still challenging his thinking?

He let that thought go as he keyed open the massive blast door, decks high, that led from the barracks into the main hab cylinder. The largest continuous space within the ship. A small, spinning world buried within the massive starship. It was simply vast every time one looked at it. Although it no longer spun now that they were under local gravity.

Years had passed since he'd entered the main decks of the forward hab cylinder, which was what he was making for now. The ship, which in those first bright sparkling months as they pulled away from Earth had looked like the future, as they thought it should look then, had been made real. They'd felt more like gods at that moment pulling away from Earth... if he was to be really honest with himself... than they ever...

Bad Thought.

But Crometheus ignored this and pressed on, reminding himself that the truth was his to make.

Mine.

... than in any one of the long years along the Path. Then they were leaving behind a ruined Earth, burnt-out, diseased, and starving to death, to live in a crystal city of the future, making its way to another brighter future. And all without the hassle of having a seething mass of the great unwashed constantly begging to be heard, dragging at your coattails to be fed, rioting to be clothed, resisting to be cared for, educated, defended, and everything else they could assign as a basic human right for the next election cycle for the crass and power-hungry to give away ad nauseum. Nasty and messy. And it was all their, the Uplifted's, fault. They'd created a monster to seize power, and frankly, the monster had gotten away from them in the end. They had to be honest with themselves about that bit. And then that monster turned on them with the very same tactics it had been taught to employ when things got desperate.

Mass-starvation desperate.

But they'd finally escaped. The Uplifted had left their lessers behind to the fate they'd brought upon themselves.

The first twenty years aboard the *Pantheon* he'd been in a continual state of awe. Exploring the decks of the fantastic MW colony ship that had been built in secret just for them. Not just one of those mass-produced big cylinders that had been constructed by the nano-shipyards in low Earth orbit. This one had Codex-1 onboard libraries and gardens unmatched by anything the world had to offer. Simulators so real they made the filter tech back on Earth seem like nothing more than old funhouse mirrors.

And all of it a rich, rewarding adventure toward godhood as the ship took months to crawl up to just under the speed of light and depart the system for greener pastures on promised paradise worlds waiting to be discovered.

Everything had been going... swimmingly... as they say, until the food and agriculture systems failed in year twenty-four. Two years out from their first world. At the time that had seemed catastrophic. Two years of alternating cryo-sleep runs just to keep the population barely alive. Constant hunger. And always the merciless math that they didn't have enough constantly stalking them like wolves out there in the stellar dark. Attempting to live on the only plant that would take hold no matter what: hypercorn. A tasteless beast that needed all the calories the community could expend just to generate a slightly lesser number of calories for the next season.

The math. The merciless math had been their enemy for two full years. And yet they had persisted and overcome. They'd made it to their first world. Expecting paradise, they found something altogether different.

Now Crometheus was entering the main cylinder. The old farm habs and spreading agricultural cities that had once spun within the main hull of the central beam of the state-of-the-art colony ship. Back in those days you could feel the titanic forces of the three onboard dedicated reactors that supplied the power, keeping the spin in effect. Now that the ship was down, those engines had stopped. And the truth was they'd stopped years ago when they'd no longer been needed.

He'd spent years in here, in the central hab. Walking the fields and basking in the artificial sunlight. He'd studied martial arts at a temple they'd fabricated somewhere out there in the vast curving plain that met itself on the ceiling high above his head. His body, thanks to the new longevity techniques they were developing, wasn't just slowing in age, it was in fact reversing back in those days.

Twenty years out and they'd conquered death with anti-aging retro-virals and brief cryo-rejuvenation stays. Imagine what the next thousand years would bring…

The goal was full reversal to youth. And eternally so.

Crometheus overrode the main blast door. Security tech hadn't been upgraded with the times after they'd entered the next phase of evolution, all those hundreds of years ago. Who would ever need to come here back? The shedding had taken care of all that. All the calories they needed could be found in storage. Vast storage holds below the bridge, some thirty decks deep, filled with what they could raid from the worlds they visited. Once the slaves had been processed for integration with Maestro… the rest could be broken down into protein to keep them all alive.

Reclamation meant salvation to the Pantheon.

But that was then. And this is now. Crometheus stared out at a vast, unmoving plain of dead corn and dark shadows. A vast, murky, empty cylinder that fled off into a smothering distant gloom. It had been a long time since he'd been back here. A very long time.

His plan had been to use the hab cylinder to bypass any Uplifted military or allied units currently deployed in or around the slowly-being-deconstructed *Pantheon*. Once they were alerted they'd come for him, so it was best to get moving.

Crometheus set off at a run, plowing through the ocean of dead dry corn, hearing the hush and crunch of a thousand dead husks under his boots as he went forward.

Almost immediately the armor's radar picked up several "friendly" units inbound from all points of the compass. Crometheus stopped and crouched down, running an identification diagnostic on the incoming tags.

Dogs.

"Dogs" was what they called the Hund law enforcement system when it was first deployed after breaking away from Earth orbit. The Pantheon had decided that instead of fellow seekers enforcing the law on one another during flight to the next world, and all the complications that would invariably come with, the central planning committee, as it had been known back then, would use a system of robot dogs. Gleaming metallic-alloy Dobermans. Mechanical dogs that were programmed to defuse, disarm, or deal with whatever situation they were presented with. They even ran a high-functioning psychoanalysis AI that could engage in questions and answers to determine why the offender was being engaged, often counseling them not to pursue the current disruption against the path they were all proceeding down. Or, if it went far enough… reclamation mode could be engaged on the spot once the offender had been dragged from public view.

In passive engagement mode all the Hunds, or "dogs" as everyone called them, had friendly blue eyes. Or what looked like eyes. But they were just electronic optical sensors glowing blue, indicating everything was normal and that there was no threat of danger or harm as long as the dogs were in this mode. As long as things didn't escalate to the next level.

If things did escalate, the optical sensors turned a hellish red... and then you were in big trouble. The dogs were now going to deal with you in successive levels of escalating violence to resolve the situation in accordance with the Central Committee's wishes for general utopian happiness.

As he crouched down amid the dead corn, Crometheus's optical HUD picked up no less than sixteen pairs of red eyes converging on him from all points of the compass. The situation was already escalated. And that meant forces beyond what was known to him were already at war with one another. Someone in the Inner Council, which was beginning its climb to ascendancy over all the other endless power-grabbing councils, and even the Xanadu Tower, knew that Lusypher was going to make some move. Some grab for power. Interactions were noted and responses were planned. Obviously, both sides had known this was going to happen. And how could it not? Victory over the Animals was at hand. Of course everyone would start divvying up the cake before it got too late and the portions too small to be meaningful.

The best time to seize power was right now. Before victory was complete.

He was crouched in a debris-filled farm canal littered with ag equipment and the dry bones of the dead from the riots that came in the years after they pulled away from that first poisonous world at the end of their inaugural long sublight journey across the stars.

Crometheus moved fast, raising his rifle as the armor acquired a firing solution on one of the incoming dogs. A blur of automatic fire spat out from the barrel of the G-97 through the corn, illuminating the dead stalks and cutting down any that stood between operator and target. Rounds smacked into the targeted dog and sent it spinning off through the deadfall of ancient corn, its frame and systems mangled. Crometheus shifted position, putting his back against an old tractor that someone had tumbled down into the canal during that long cold year of rioting and fights across all decks of the Pantheon. The dark years when the Forbidden Decks had acquired their ominous name. Before order had been restored with brutal violence. When the Truth and Safety Committee had risen to power with their insightful restrictions against disobedience, and their Orwellian means to make it so.

Good Thought.

Good Thought.

Good Thought. One achievement point rewarded. Please continue on this path so Enlightened Uplift can be achieved soon, Player Crometheus.

Where had he been that year, that background app in his mind wondered as he scanned the field of tall dead mutant corn for another target. The year of the riots. There was so much he could remember with crystal-clear clarity about his life on Earth, but of the many lifetimes he'd lived on the *Pantheon*, most seemed hazy at best, or just plain inaccessible at worst. As though his mind couldn't, or wouldn't, go there, even if he wanted it to.

But on the other hand, if he tried to remember an old comic book from Earth, or a piece of art from a role-playing game he'd owned when he was twelve, he could almost see and describe every inky line within it. Noting even the artist's signature scrawl, and that long-ago date that had felt like the future in its present clarity back then.

More dogs were coming into the canal. They'd rush him first. That much was clear. Two practically went airborne as they leapt down into the junk-laden depression of dead and hard-packed soil. One landed on a brittle old human skeleton. The dog's hyper-forged alloy front claw crushed the ancient skull with a dusty *smaff*.

Crometheus fired quickly, which was his way. Immobility to the point of being mistaken for a statue, then the sudden blur of movement and action on the heels of target acquisition as he dispensed death in twenty-round bursts. Which was the standard amount for the HK G-97 in the selected mode. The armor maintained sight picture and corrected for aim as the gun blurred out a cone of hot streaking lead at the incoming robot sentries.

The dog's mainframe processor exploded as solid hits smacked into it, tearing the frame to ruined mechanical pieces.

The other dog didn't hesitate to charge. Crometheus reversed the weapon and butt-stroked the beast with the end of the G-97. All he got was a metallic *clank*. The dog shook its head as the red eyes turned to sudden violent volcanos of hot crimson anger. Targeting lasers danced across Crometheus's armored chest plate; the violence and light of the sudden fighting within the abandoned canal lost somewhere in a sea of dead corn had drawn the other dogs into the fray. He could hear the Hund facing him deploying its primary weapon system. Energy-based stunners.

Crometheus swore and dumped the rest of the G-97's mag into the dog at close range as he backed up a step. The weapon barked out a hollow litany of death and end-of-runtime error messages for the bot in the language of gunshots. More dogs were racing through the dead cornfield, circling for a better angle of attack instead of coming straight on at their intended target. Like sharks and other predators.

The rogue marine slapped in a new mag from off the carrier around his chest plate and listened as the G-97 racked the first round with a quick series of metallic snaps.

Null energy shots, powered by the Hunds' onboard capacitors, surged through the dead corn, seeking to short out his systems.

The battle turned into a running firefight down the length of the dead canal as more and more dogs poured into it, leaping over long-abandoned farming equipment and racing across the dead bones of the rioters who'd been put down probably by these same civil disobedience pacification units. There were probably admin sys logs sitting around on some old server within the rapidly-being-deconstructed *Pantheon*, Crometheus thought as he ran, slapping in another mag after emptying the last on various targets, that indicated when such-and-such and so-and-so, now just skeletons in the land of dead corn, had been terminated—and by which-and-which unit now pursuing him.

Live long enough, and time and life merge and do funny little games of intersection.

Out across the corn, up in the sky of the hab cylinder, a hunter-killer wasp joined the pursuit. Its hot white searchlights crisscrossed the corn, turning the permanent night inside the old hab and farming cylinder to a soft blue. Maybe a twilight blue like early summer late at night long ago back on Earth.

Equipment destabilization grenades would be great right about now, thought Crometheus, as he leapt rotten hay bales that had once been used as a pathetic redoubt by the rioting defenders. Then he turned and fired at more of the incoming drone dogs. Some got hit and went down. Others took rounds and kept on coming, heedless of the systems damage. Little dissuaded by the bright fire he sent into their glaring red eyes. Still others skirted off, leaping out of the canal and racing for the tops of the banks to get out and ahead of him. Scrabbling through the dead corn like strange unseen monsters from some nightmare slasher flick he'd seen as a kid.

And there was still the wasp coming in to assist.

He'd deal with that when the time came.

There were cities out here on the plain. Cities they'd once worked in and pretended…

Bad Thought.

Bad Thought.

Bad Thought.

Pretending is bad. New update from Committee Prime. Only reality can set you free. Give up your dreams. Inner

Council is now to be known as Committee Prime. Please note for continued Good Thoughts.

Suddenly he felt his pursuers trying to depress his neurosensors with some kind of sonic pacification system. Probably coming from the wasp in the dark sky above.

"Halt, recalcitrant. You've been identified for capture and re-education," demanded someone over the wasp's onboard address system. "Stand by to be restored to fellowship with your fellow travelers."

Crometheus fired after ordering the armor's HUD to filter out the bright searchlights and overlay with night vision. A second later he had a solid image of the hunter-killer ship and opened up on the wasp pilot's canopy. One solid hit was all he needed, and he knew he got one when he saw whoever it was flying the ship come apart in pieces across the inside of the pilot's canopy. Fire and fluid splashing across the cupola of the tiny airborne transportation vehicle like one of the old helicopters, but with four massive inductors operating off two wings.

The hit pilot lost control of the wasp and in the act took his boot off the collective. Inductor yaw took over without guidance and pitched the craft over into a short death dive into the dead cornfield below. In seconds the no-longer-airborne vehicle exploded in flames, most likely cooking the four Uplifted crew who manned it.

Knowing where the Committee's, Committee Prime that was, head was at was crucial, thought Crometheus as he considered his next move. Now that they had taken New Vega…

You. Some voice inside Crometheus reminded him that it had been him, and other marines like him, who'd taken New Vega for the Pantheon, and for their betters. Xanadu Tower elites who couldn't be bothered to sully themselves with such concerns as the ultra-violence that needed doing if worlds were to be conquered. They had been more than happy to let the marines pay the price.

You, that voice yelled through the constant flow of information in his brain. You and the other marines took New Vega. Not them. Not those who dwelt in the Tower.

Bad Thought.

Bad Thought.

Bad Thought.

Criticisms of High Path Uplifted are wrong. Who will show you the way to becoming a god? Who will tell you what is wrong and right? Who will be your better? How will you know?

He blocked out the programming alerts. It was hard. But he forced them into the background of his mind in favor of survival.

He would deal with the dogs first. Focusing on that was the only way to ignore the barrage of Good Thought spam coming at him like an avalanche. Or a shotgun blast at close range. The dogs and the wasp had most likely been the only assets dispatched at the first hint of his rebellion. Get rid of them now, Crometheus reasoned, and he could buy himself enough time to get back into the Forbidden Decks and beyond their reach.

He came to the end of the canal. Iron bars closed over a black tunnel. It was here where many skeletons had collected in the days when they'd tried to just wash the bodies of the rioters away with the last of the precious water aboard at that time. After that they'd been wanderers in the dark, looking, praying really, for a stray ice comet to get ahold of. It was here that the bodies of the dead had collected in the canal when the last of the water had been used on such thoughtless fancies.

And then they'd prayed for a comet.

But who do you pray to when you're becoming a god?

That had been the debate that year. The Year of the Famine. Before the Year of the Comet.

Who do you pray to when you're a god?

Who?

No one had ever liked any of the answers they'd been forced to accept.

The dogs came on at him and he shot them down in short brutal bursts because there was no other way than this to deal with their relentless pursuit. He took damage. A couple of the armor's systems took some solid hits. Malfunction indicators went banshee inside the HUD. But in the end he finished his pursuers there at the dead river's end. And in the silence that followed, he was free to go on to the Forbidden Decks, leaving the ruined skeletons of the dead behind.

If he dared.

Gods:
Chapter Fifteen

Beyond the dark world of the abandoned farming hab lay the Forbidden Decks. Crometheus trudged through fields of dead corn and passed silent factory farms and brooding cities that once rang out with the life of the true believers of MW and their bright shining work of making it the next world. Devotees intent on building a perfect utopia despite all the math of the past, and all the failures. All of it financed by a corporation almost as old as the computer itself.

At the extreme end of the cylinder world within the belly of the vast colony ship *Pantheon*, the hab climbed up to meet itself in the sky above his head.

They'd designated this end of the hab as the south.

Towering above Crometheus lay a wall that blocked the hab from main engineering and central power. The wall was five kilometers high. Beyond it lay the reactors, and then the sprawling decks of the interstellar sublight drive itself. Everything surrounded by decks upon decks of maintenance housing constructed to cyclopean scale.

Only bots and madmen went into these dank and lonely sections anymore. They were abandoned long ago, and generally thought to be haunted. They, the collective

Uplifted aboard the *Pantheon*, had seen a lot of strange stuff out there in the deeps of space. Stuff that made no sense to the rational and reasonable mind. Stuff that might make you believe in ghosts if you allowed the cracks in your firm convictions to show. And sometimes even demons became possible, whether you liked it or not.

Bad Thought alarms were ringing, but Crometheus ignored these. They felt weaker. More distant. Less effective out here beyond the control of the Inner Council.

Or maybe some desperate series of strikes against the AI subroutines that ran the behavior modification alerts was already underway by whichever faction, the Council or Lusypher's people, needed that to happen for their goals to be realized.

The rogue marine picked up a fresh trail through the dead farmlands which led, as he suspected, off to an entrance someone had cut through the decks-high bulkhead between hab and main engineering. If Lusypher was intent on a secret cabal then most likely the conspirators had come aft to facilitate their secret preparations and organization. Following a forgotten trail through the wastes of the forsaken hab lands to find some out-of-the-way space in which to plan beyond the reach of the Council.

It was dark in there, beyond the ragged cut in the wall, but the armor had low-light imaging and even IR capabilities. Crometheus switched on both functions, checked the G-97's load, then entered the gaping black maw that led to the other side. Into the area known as the Forbidden Decks.

Beyond the ragged cut he entered a maze of abandoned control rooms and once-state-of-the-art processor nodes that controlled the functions of main engineering and its interface with the power and drive sections. It was hard to believe that in a matter of months all of this would, after years and years of crawling through deep space, be broken down for much-needed raw materials. All of it. Soon the *Pantheon* as a colony ship would no longer exist, and a new home would rise from its dwindling skeleton.

It was time for a shedding of the Pantheon's own.

He remembered once, long ago, returning to the town he'd called home when he was a child. Viejo Verde. Seeing so much of what he'd once known as eternal constants, now paved over and gone. Chocolate gashes in the Earth where bookstores, computer stores, arcades, toy stores, and all the other businesses of those times had once promised to remain forever. The perfectly planned community of his youth had been going through some developer-forced next stage of development. Tearing down everything he knew and preparing the land for the new things to be built. Things that would be alien to the old and familiar. The trusted and expected.

This moment of entering the Forbidden Decks was just like that night long ago when he'd driven around town, or rather had been driven in a hired limo, nursing a two-hundred-dollar bottle of scotch and a pack of cigarettes. Returning once more at the midnight hour to see all the old places just one last time before they were gone forever. Haunting like some Ghost of Christmas Past. It had been near the holiday season, hadn't it? Except they'd called it Christmas back then.

The Bad Thought programming kicked in at this. Both phrases were currently out of favor and made meaningless by the constant shifting of truths in and out of favor with the Committee Prime on sometimes a minute-to-minute basis.

The air that haunting night had been cold and dry, and he'd wondered if that was what death was really going to be like. Dark. Windy. Cold. And dry. Lifeless and nothing. Nothing but the realization that you were all alone in a world that didn't know you anymore. He'd begun to think about death a lot back then. Like it was the signpost for a destination on the lonely highway ahead. Inevitable and arrived at soon enough. Best to get ready for it.

The opposite of comfort, of relationship with anyone left in your life. The opposite of warmth.

The year after that had been one of the worst of his life. He was finally bottoming out back then. Bottoming out on himself. The rock and roll was over. Holly Wood was gone. He was a human whale, swollen with drugs, liquor, and processed fat. Surviving on pills, heroin, nicotine, and burgers washed down with all the scotch and bourbon he could stock.

A thing that just consumed and produced nothing. The opposite of everything that had gotten him where he'd arrived.

And then... the Path.

It had come along just in the nick of time. Because there was a rope in a garage on the edge of Beverly Hills waiting for him after that last-roll-of-the-dice personal empowerment weekend to find something, anything, that worked.

Everything changed from that weekend forward. For the better. For the much better. That too was a kind of shedding. Divesting himself of everything he once was to become something he knew he'd been headed toward all along. Though he'd never been able to quite articulate it.

Godhood.

Shadowy corridors, long ago emptied and since looted, ran off in all directions across the Forbidden Decks the rogue marine traveled across. Crometheus was using the armor's nav and imaging functions to maintain a course track through the abandoned spaces of the old ship as he headed toward the transportation shafts that would take him to deck sixty-six.

He'd come here a long time ago. Back to main power, during the dark ages when everyone was losing their mind as the decades-long interstellar crawl ruined their reason and shattered their ability to cope. Before the shedding. He'd come here looking for food. Old stores that hadn't yet been raided. Anything to eat as the ship became a prison with no exits and no escape. Unchangeable in its long crossing to the next world that might, maybe, save them all from themselves. Already back then there was talk that a great discovery had been made in the labs. A way that they could all go on despite the math. Despite the lack of calories versus flight time to the next world.

The terrible math.

But how?

Without food?

Without hope or even a promise the next world might be the one they could start all over on. Build their utopia on. Spread out across the galaxy from.

How could they go on without food? Ironic to have such grand plans and so little basic sustenance with which to fulfill those divine schemes.

So he, along with some others, all of them desperate, had come back to the haunted nether regions of the colony ship *Pantheon* in search of supplies. There'd been a war during those dark ages between the various sections. A series of battles that culminated into two main alliances fighting for control of the leviathan colony ship wandering through the cosmos. He'd been on the losing side, though he didn't know it at the time. The side of the elites who ran the show and created a culture all could embrace for their own betterment. Their enemies had been those in main engineering and others allied with them. Drive, of course they were in. Power and water, naturally. Ag… they had been a town-by-town and city-by-city thing. The wars on the big curving plain had been brutal. And merciless. Like something out of man's stone age.

In the end the losers had been thrown from the wall of main engineering, the southern wall that looked out over the hab. Their leader had insisted that the ship maintain course to the next world. They'd blown the bridge and sub-system control stations by then. Insisting that they make for the planet they were heading toward. That the idiocy of searching for stray ice comets to replenish the ocean in the lower decks was sheer madness.

But by then, the first tentative steps of the shedding and the beginning of the Path in its current incarnation... had already begun.

Later they'd return and overwhelm the cultists in engineering who'd insisted on the intolerance of their own opinions. Those in charge, the winners, him Crometheus, had slaughtered them, but kept a few slaves, returning the Diversity and Tolerance Committee to total power once more. The Inner Council had once been called by that name. But over the centuries power had coalesced and the meanings of words had changed along with alliances.

As they always did.

Had he been on the losing side? Or had he won? Sometimes it was hard to remember what was true. And what wasn't. The sheddings had involved the rewriting of many histories, both personal and collective. The stamping out of Bad Thoughts. The memory-holing of certain truths.

For the greater good, of course.

But during those dark ages he'd come aft and wandered the Forbidden Decks. Before the alliances. When the place had seemed haunted by all their failures, and the darkness they'd seen on the worlds they'd visited, and within themselves.

Those who had come with him, an ad hoc hunting party like some band of primitive Neolithic hunter-gatherers from the ancient past, all died horribly. Security systems went haywire. Someone trying to hack them had merely managed to set them to a higher, more lethal level. In the end the barriers wouldn't recognize any of the colonists as having a right to access any of the aft storage vaults. Warehouses that were filled with food, medicine, and weapons. Many died in droves trying to violate those "seven cities of gold" the fabled aft storage decks vaults had become.

He remembered hiding behind a bulkhead at the end of a long passage that led to a vault where stable protein meal was supposed to be contained. The computer expert and the leader of that particular expedition had gone forward to hard-hack the lock. The expert had been one of the most famous app developers back on Earth. He'd developed the Hump app which allowed people to schedule sexual encounters in foreign cities. He was up half a trillion dollars before the collapse of the cryptocurrency market that ruined them all. In that instant, the app developer expert who'd once had a Twitter following of millions, and the expedition leader, a woman who'd held some state position in one of the Euro-governments, both died badly as hidden panels opened up around the complex storage vault lock and hundreds of rounds of auto-turret fire tore their emaciated bodies to bloody shreds in seconds.

No food that night.

Around a campfire built inside a maintenance vehicle hangar, half the party of scavengers overdosed on purpose with some heavy-duty surgery-grade painkillers they'd found in a locked dispensary.

In the morning the survivors parted ways. Most returned to the forward sections. The rest, only a few, had gone on to incur more violent deaths. And in the end, it was just him. Wandering the dark halls alone like that same unquiet ghost who'd once been driven though the paved-over paradise of his hometown on a holiday's winter eve.

And that was where he met the old one.

Anubis.

That was where he found the Path again.

Now, alone again but in his armor, Crometheus felt live power in the systems all around him. Felt it from a long way off. The Forbidden Decks were still alive. He'd been closing in on deck sixty-six for hours now. Climbing up a central refuse chute that fed into aft reclamation. Deep down below, in the belly of the giant ship, was a stagnant ocean that must still be down there in the gargantuan lower decks. Or maybe they were draining it already. During the beginning of combat operations on New Vega, as they'd staged for assault operations against military resistance hot spots, it had been raining beneath the wings and exposed belly sections of their long home among the stars. Maybe that ocean that had fed and sustained them for so long, an ocean he'd seen only once in the centuries-long journey aboard the *Pantheon*, maybe it too was all gone now.

Everything changes. It always does. Best to accept it, because what other choice do you have?

He reminded himself of this. The Benediction of Change.

But now he felt power all around him. Felt it humming and coursing through the decks and long-powered-down systems. Deck sixty-six, according to the accessed deck and archived map data his armor had plundered from passing ancient signals still seeking to be of assistance, contained direct access to an auxiliary reactor and a fabrication forge.

Ideal for staging your own secret coup, Crometheus thought as the magnetized gauntlets pulled him up onto its level at last. The shaft door had been forced open, as though they'd known he was coming up this way all along. Below him what seemed a bottomless pit fell away into the silent gloom. As if to say going back, the past, it was all gone now. There was only forward into the unknown.

That was the only way.

"Ah..." said Maestro. Suddenly present and from out of the constant nowhere of comm-ether. "You have arrived, noble Master Crometheus. Excellent and well done."

This place was like everything he'd crossed for hours now. Dark. Disused. Damaged. Abandoned. And... if one believed in the spirits of nether, as old Anubis had, then perhaps even haunted. If not by the ghosts of all the silent dead who died badly in that long stellar crossing from here to there aboard the *Pantheon*, then at least their memories.

Those bad times had definitely haunted the abandoned decks, fabrication shops, monitoring stations, central controls, miles of piping, stories-high device housings, and other enigmatic structures he'd passed to get here. All those things they'd marveled at during their first outbound months of escape from dying Earth. The wonders of their new and beautiful home now lay like brooding sentinels.

The armor's sensors picked up movement all around his position. The telltale algo identification of a hyperdrive motivator pinged to life somewhere in the distance. Someone, or someones, was coming for him.

Two lightly armored scouts stepped out of the shadows, each holding advanced weapons the likes of which Crometheus had never seen. Behind them came Lusypher in his SS commander's black trench and dark uniform adorned with silver, finished with high, polished black boots.

"Glad you could make it, son," began Crometheus's Uplifted superior. "And you too, Maestro. We're outside their control spheres now. Free to operate. Free to begin our Final Solution."

Crometheus, in the much larger heavy infantry variant armor, didn't understand. And he said so.

"Maestro?"

Lusypher stepped close, out of the dark shadows inside the maintenance processing floor. Some still-working ship's light cast a small shaft of illumination across his craggy human face.

Except it wasn't human. Close. But not real.

It was a good facsimile. But there was still that automaton's barely detectable rubberized trace to the flesh and hair. An almost plastic feel that technology had never quite been able to obscure.

But the eyes… the eyes were amazing. Crometheus had to admit that. Far better than the real human eyes they'd given up long ago.

Still, it was strange looking at the shell, the form, they'd all shed long ago. Not just for survival… but to become what they would one day be.

Survival is just the disturbance that forces us to seek change.

TED 89:14.

"Maestro smuggled himself out of the Council's sphere of influence inside your HUD, my boy," murmured Lusypher nonchalantly. "Those in the Tower who don't want change watch everything. Even me. Especially so. So we went with you for the jailbreak. Good work getting him across enemy lines. Next we can move to the operations phase of our little plan."

There was a pause. A pause in which Crometheus wanted to ask what, exactly, that might be. And couldn't. Because... hundreds of years of behavior modification prevented him from questioning a High Path Uplifted like Lusypher. One who'd advanced far beyond him.

And of all the things Lusypher was, he was most definitely that. Uplifted farther, much farther, along the Path. An objective to not just be admired, but to be coveted.

"You're probably wondering what that is," he said to Crometheus. Then smiled. The effect with the rubberized body in the human skin suit was not a little unsettling to the rogue marine.

"Well, son, you're about to find out all about what we're up to back here."

Gods:
Chapter Sixteen

"Already," began Lusypher as they crossed through reconditioned sections of the Forbidden Decks, nano-circuitry and updated filters coming to life while they progressed inward toward some destination yet to be announced, "a combined Uplifted fleet is en route for an attack against Espania. The Animal Coalition and their vaunted fleet won't be putting up much of a fight there. The Espanians have been left to their fate by the rest of the Animals. But that's not where the real battle is, son."

They entered a hangar with the two scout armored marines in lockstep behind them. Out across the deck of the hangar were other similarly kitted Uplifted marines. But what drew Crometheus's eye was the starship. A captured Animal freighter. No doubt hyperdrive-capable. The mass-produced manufacture of which had eluded the Uplifted.

How did everyone else get here, he wondered to himself. And then suspected that plans had been in motion for some time. People had gone missing in all the little ways a tightly controlled society has ways of breeding. The other Uplifted here were taking a chance on this new IP

Lusypher was putting together. They'd found ways to opt in. Even if it wasn't allowed.

"The real battle will be on Spilursa. A world they least expect us to hit them on, yet where they are actually most susceptible to a destabilization attack that will compromise their entire defensive network. And where we will introduce a virus into our allies' operating systems that will ensure our dominion of thought going forward. I want you to be part of that attack force, Crometheus. I want you to infect our allies... and our enemies."

Crossing the floor of the hangar toward them was definitely some kind of commander of this very specialized combat unit Crometheus had never before encountered. Their light scout armor seemed newer. Made up of some kind of new graphene material, if he were to guess. The protective gear shimmered across some of the more shadowy colors of the spectrum. Everyone was carrying the same advanced rifle system the two scouts had, along with the standard heavy-caliber, long-barreled sidearm. Here and there other specialized teams were working together to supervise heavy-duty mechs being used to load out the freighter.

"These are the Eternals, son," said Lusypher, grandly sweeping an economical hand across the bay to encompass all the troops busy within. "A brand-new fighting unit that will be not just the shape of the Pantheon's military corps moving forward, but of the entirety of the combined Uplifted tribes."

This space, what must once have been the aft external engineering maintenance bay for one of the starboard in-system drive engines, had been turned into a staging area for the secretive military cabal Lusypher was heading. A seldom-visited place that might be accessed every five years during the intended normal operation of the ship was now the central hub for these new crack combat commandos.

"Will you join us in our crusade, son?" asked Lusypher. "Will you help us make the galaxy in our image?"

Crometheus nodded without hesitation.

The Path isn't as easy as everyone always wants it to be. When you first start out, you think it's going to be a series of exercises that improve you and make you a better person. A greater you, step by step. Day by day. One minute at a time and all that noise. Like working out. Muscles getting bigger session by session with each rep. In time, you're lifting hundreds of pounds over your head, effortlessly.

But the Path, the higher stages, often takes sudden turns into self-destruction just to discover some unfound enlightenment that will help you to find the Path once again. Shedding. Ruin. Burning away the things that no longer serve.

Crometheus had sensed, when he first started out from the known, and to be honest even at the restaurant when Lusypher gave the nod that he might have their version of the greatest burger ever… that such a moment of self-ruination and change was at hand. He'd sensed that it was coming. He'd been there before. He was here again. Leave the Uplifted Alliance and join a small group determined to seize power. Headed by a bold and visionary leader.

Like some fantastic IPO back on Earth. All the early investors got rich, real rich, quick. This was like that.

You must throw everything away in order to gain everything.

TED 593:1

What was it old Anubis had once said?

Disturbance brings change. And change brings improvement.

That had profoundly revolutionized him during all those years he'd spent with the old master in the haunted spaces of the Forbidden Decks. Playing his mind-numbing mental games endlessly. Following enigmatic quests for some useless thing the old wizard said would make them understand everything. During the dark and starving years when everyone aboard that grand dream of the *Pantheon* had well and truly lost their way. Even the ship... had lost its way.

Change brings disturbance.

Which is a frightening thing when one is adrift in the stellar void between the stars. Searching for a world. Any world.

Imagine that.

Disturbance brings improvement.

Yes, Crometheus nodded without the slightest hesitation. He would become an Eternal. He would join and do whatever they asked. He'd accepted their offer long before it was put forth. He'd accepted when all this first began.

This was the next step. Nothing else but that was clear at this very moment. Buy the ticket, take the ride.

"Good," murmured Lusypher. "Good, son," he repeated once more, searching Crometheus's very being for something he seemed uncertain was there. Or at least that was the look in the superior Uplifted's fantastic eyes.

"This is Commander Zero," said Lusypher. "She commands the Eternals. She'll forge you into a fighting force that'll shake the pillars of the galaxy. But first…"

Lusypher, that kindly old devil, leaned in close to Crometheus. His eyes baleful and cold now, dark and deep in that moment. Eyes that had seen all the darknesses they'd ever found out there in their long wanderings. And even spoken with them… if one believed the rumors.

"I want you to break your connection with the Pantheon. Burn down your old life. Cleanse yourself, Crometheus. Cleanse yourself with fire."

Pause.

An image entered the rogue marine's hard drive. A meme download from Lusypher himself. Brilliant light coursed through his HUD and systems. It was as though the hand of a god had suddenly touched him, and the moment was so beatific Crometheus dropped to one armored knee in obeisance to his new and undisputed liege.

The meme from Lusypher consumed him like some holy vision.

All of Viejo Verde… on fire and burning. And him, as he was, a boy becoming a man, in the middle of it all. Holding a can of gas and a pack of matches.

"What you will be, son, you are now becoming," whispered that old devil Lusypher.

Gods:
Chapter Seventeen

Crometheus of long ago... a boy becoming a man inside a reality he'd built himself in lieu of that post-apocalyptic fantasy epic he'd one day rule over... awoke in the night. In his child's room where all the treasures are kept. The catcher's mitt. The film can marked *Blue Highway*. The collection of *Mad Magazine*s. The Fantastic Four issue where they go into space and get their powers.

Like some kind of prophecy in retrospective.

It was late. Very late.

A big moon, fat and swollen, leered through the wide window of his child's room, turning everything a gentle blue and a bone-white.

Burn down your old life.

"I've been here before," he thought to himself as he came out of his deep sleep with a start.

Of course he knew where he was, and where he'd been to within the Forbidden Decks. The hidden staging area on deck sixty-six. Where disturbance was causing change. And where the Eternals were becoming.

What you will be, son, you are now becoming.

Something wasn't right though. Something wasn't true. He'd meant something different when he had that thought that he'd *been here before*.

He felt tangled, even smothered by the covers around his boy's body. Pushing them back to be washed clean and exposed by the moonlight while knowing it was time to move all the same. All of that. But he saw all those other times he'd been here before.

At the moment of shedding.

Time and time again. Before he'd even known it was called shedding. When it had been called leaving home with nothing but a stuffed ruck and the back of an old car packed with everything you thought was valuable and would need out there. Or so you believed at the time.

Or when you left Rebel Child. Heading out on your own for your first, and very important, solo album. Leaving the known circle of support and herd identity for the chance to become something other... and singular.

A rock god.

After that it had all become much easier to shed as you went along. Friends. Family. Hangers-on. Deals. Women you were done with. People you didn't need anymore. Things just holding you back from what you were heading toward.

Shedding. Dumping everything along the way in pursuit of yourself. Letting go of all the useless.

Nothing marked being a celebrity more than that previous statement. *Dumping everything along the way in pursuit of yourself. Letting go of all the useless.*

The girl in a bottom-rung motel room on Sunset when you got the call from the record company that they listened to your demo. The agent you kicked out of the limo because he wanted a deal that would have taken care of his family, but not your career. The call girl who'd overdosed in the back of the bus with the talented lead guitarist. Watching her sink beneath the dark waters of some midnight pond between last night's gig and the one tomorrow night the band needed to be at without any hassles trailing them along the way. That time you ripped up a picture of the president even though you'd met her once and she seemed genial enough, but the mob wanted her blood because she was part of the establishment. The system that always needed destroying. Isolating. Marginalizing. Abolishing those who didn't want to get with the plan to save the Earth whether it wanted to be saved or not.

It needed to be saved because whoever saved it got all the power. Duh.

TED 6:66.

Then that final afternoon at the airport Marriott. When you walked into the bathroom and saw what you'd become. A clown in fading rock-star gear with the hairstyle of a kid from twenty years back. Swollen on cheeseburgers and drugs. Haunted by a woman who walked out on your schtick halfway between Reno and Rome.

Wasn't that how it had happened? How she'd disappeared… no… gone?

That day. When you burned your old life down, crying in the front row of some corporate conference room on a cheap chair that would be stacked with ten thousand others in a few hours at the end of the come-to-the-end-of-yourself weekend. That had been the first shedding…

…but it was by no means the last.

Crometheus as a boy, thinking about all of these moments that were the same as this one. Moments of shedding.

On autopilot, the boy dressed in the bone-white moonlight and shadowy blue darkness of his child's room in the house he never should have left. White pants like he wore every Friday. Ritual.

We must have our rituals.

Rituals must be acknowledged when shedding. They still have their place. Even if just to be sacrificed to the bonfire of our becoming.

Favorite shirt.

Best pair of Vans. Yes. We wore Vans back in those days. The coolest shoe in cool town. So it must be those.

And of course, a pack of matches found on the table where his catcher's mitt rested next to that long-lost issue of the Fantastic Four coming home from space. Crashing the space shuttle. As though he'd placed the matches there at the beginning, knowing they'd be needed at the end. If only so the next beginning… could begin.

He slipped from his parents' house in the dark. In the hour most call the dead of night. Halfway between the hell of midnight and the long march toward dawn. The witching hour. The three a.m.

He walked his bike out onto the street as some late-night bird called out forlornly across the perfect sleeping suburbia while he turned back one more time to stare at his house. Just as he'd done all those years ago when looking back as he drove away for the last time. Or so it had seemed then. And every time since.

There had been other last times.

But no time as final as the first. Even though it was never realized at the time how momentously important it was in the grand scheme of his life. After that it gets easier. All the other times had been like coming back to a cemetery to visit the dead once more. In hindsight of course. One last time again. As it always was.

He peered over the rooftops at the perfect houses along the sleeping street. Atop the sloping hill above the back of his own house his best friend's home loomed in the night. It was three a.m. and even the comforting blue light of the television that always emanated from within, like some eternally kept sacred thing he'd come to need in his inner journeys, even that was gone now and the windows of the tall house looked like empty eye sockets watching him on the street below.

Like a corpse.

He scanned it all one last time and then began to pedal, climbing up and out of his neighborhood along the empty street, and soon he was out on the main roads, riding down the center lane for there was no one else out in the night. This last of nights.

This final becoming.

Gods: Chapter Eighteen

Commander Zero, Queen of the Eternals, came for him as it all burned. She walked through the fire like an avenging angel in the Eternals' new advanced armor system. Her shadowy state-of-the-art armor, the best the Uplifted had produced to date, didn't burn as she crossed through the conflagration enveloping the gas station he'd ignited. The apocalyptic blooms of fire reached suddenly skyward as the pumps exploded and blue shock waves spread outward across the pools of gasoline.

"Welcome, Crometheus," she said over the armor's nightmare vocal broadcast. Her voice was thunder, her movement that of a jungle predator. Her faceless shadow-mirror helmet scanning for enemies. Battle rifle ready to engage.

He'd spent those last hours before dawn burning it all down. All of Viejo Verde. All of his hidden reality. Taking a can of gas from the pumps at the Gemco filling station because he could. It was his world after all. The attendant from inside the glass booth waiting out the night shift as he had all those hundreds of years ago. As he would because it was what his part in this reality demanded. The young man merely watched as young Crometheus filled the can of gas from the pump and set off. Down the main road that led to the bridge that crossed over that perpetually dry and arid wasteland known as the train tracks.

Dawn was just a few hours off when he started the first fire, soaking the dry sagebrush in the dark near the road that extended off and down along the edge, the whole boundary that formed the reality he'd clung to. Splashing the gas around, the sharp chemical smell of it coming up to his nostrils on a small breeze drifting in off the Pacific Ocean miles away. In it he could smell the salt and the fire both at once.

Like some beach barbecue at summer's end.

He stepped back and lit the first match, held it down to let the flame catch, then tossed it into the gasoline-soaked brush. The fire began with a dull *whump* and then started to spread quickly. Crickling and crackling as it greedily consumed the dry weeds. He didn't stay to watch it. To stare into it and ponder his becoming. But there was work to do. Destruction work. Shedding work.

Becoming…

He was back on his bike, carrying the clanging and banging empty metal gas can around one of his bike's handlebars, pedaling back to the gas station for a refill.

For the next few hours he repeated the process. Starting fires all across the boundaries of his world. This reality. True, he could look beyond and see the rest of the world as it had been. But the view was more for effect. There was no need to go to those places in his most sacred and special of realities. He'd only added those to complete the illusion so that the reality he'd constructed might be better believed.

Now it was time to terminate the connection.

He could just dump the whole file on his hard drive. But the emotional connection would still be there, running through his brain. And that was more of a connection than a physical place, or thing, could ever be. Ask any addict. The work of shedding had to be as much metaphysical, as it was file deletion.

He had to watch it burn.

There was no actual gasoline. That this was all metaphorical and symbolic was understood on some background level. But it needed to be made real. It needed to become truth. And the visual lie was best for that.

Some lies need seeing to be believed.
TED 13:6.

When you understood how things worked inside the Pantheon and its many realities, the metaphorical and the symbolic were far more real than mere reality itself. Truths could be forged in here. Not used as iron bars to the gates of a prison as they had been for all of mankind's existence. But as fulcrums to make reality into what you wanted it to be.

What you thought best.

What you felt.

Now everything was on fire across all of Viejo Verde. Whole neighborhoods were going up in vast walls of flame in the night. And this night would remain until the work was done. He'd decided on that. There would be no dawn until it was all gone.

The last fire he needed to start was back at the gas station.

The last lie.

The last truth.

This time he didn't need the gas can even though he'd filled it. He sat back from the pumps, next to his bike alongside the main road that led over the freeway and toward the strip mall where the arcade was. Where Lazer Command waited for him.

He hadn't thought about it directly... but he hadn't made a plan to burn that center down. As though he was just assuming the flames would catch and spread everywhere throughout the rest of the night and into the bleak smoke-filled dawn that must surely come soon if he allowed it.

He'd purposefully forgotten it. He had to admit that to himself. He'd left it out. Like a recovering alcoholic's desk-drawer bottle of scotch. Just in case, right? Without even thinking about it. Hoping that it might be saved. That the touchstone might be kept back as a guilty pleasure just for him. If it all went sideways. Surely Maestro and Lusypher, and even this Commander Zero, wouldn't notice that. Would they?

You've done the same thing before, some deeper part of his mind reminded him. And maybe that was how he'd created this hidden place that time. Forgetting about it each and every time when there was shedding to be done... but the arcade survives every time.

Right?

Lazer Command slips through the cracks in the gas chambers and the execution walls he'd lined others, and his own past, up against so many times before.

Something has to get away, right?

Something has to survive if just to show how far you've come.

The arcade of all the things would survive inside this weird metaphysical reality they'd found the ability to construct out there in the dark between stars when they'd lost their minds and wandered away from the known, stark raving mad and insane. A ship full of lunatics begging for a lifeline to hold on to.

The realities found on the other side of the shedding had been just that.

They'd found them out there in the void. And those realities had saved them from themselves. Though some, some long ago and long-since purged, had argued that possibly they never should have been found in the first place.

The gas station exploded at dawn and Commander Zero appeared in its flames. Coming for him. Satisfied by the level of destruction. Just as the sun began rising above the saddle-backed mountain to the east that so defined that valley on every piece of stationery from the school lunch menu to the banner of the local newspaper.

Everything exploded in sudden fiery apocalyptic bloom, as though the crescendo of some demonic orchestra had reached its ultimate, blossoming like that same angry red flower that had killed half the landing party when they first made Sirius Two. Exploding and poisoning the first to make planetfall.

They'd called it the death flower.

The whole planet had been one hellishly poisoned paradise. Uninhabitable, though the air had been breathable and the water drinkable. Everything had been out to poison or kill them on that first cursed world. The sadness that had overwhelmed the entire Pantheon as they heaved off for space once more had been like looking into the chasm of an abyss all your own making. A deep dark abyss someone told you there was a bottom to, and you didn't believe them.

But what other choice did you have?

The first planet the colony ship *Pantheon* had arrived at was poisoned. It was a poisoned world. Stay and die. Or…

Flee to the stars and live. Try again. Insert coin to play. Ready Player One.

They'd been there before. They'd left dying Earth to its fate. They could do it again.

In the months after leaving Sirius Two a death cult formed in the lower decks. Aft and beyond main engineering. They worshipped the death flower that had tried to kill them all back there on that world they'd left behind. They made images of its orchid petals and blood-red colors.

He remembered now, as he stepped away from the flames of the gas station, that the cult had been based somewhere around deck sixty-six. Ironic that detail. Ironic how life had a way of crossing and re-crossing itself time and time again no matter how long you stuck around. He remembered a senior Uplifted being the leader of that cult. Silver. Silver was the name. That was before they all let go of their Earth names in favor of the god names they would become.

Silver.

Connections from across all the points of time and history his mind could intersect on came like they were never quite fully satisfied with all the chance meetings a life long-lived could make.

Lusypher.

Louis Silver.

Commander Zero had a necklace of those same death flowers alternating with walnut shells around the chest plate of her fantastic new armor. Commander Zero, who was coming through the flames for him.

The station exploded once more, sending metal shards of burning pump and flaming plastic into the dawn sky like a celebration of liberation at last. All of it raining down over the vast empty parking lot that stood before the giant megastore that had existed once long ago.

What was Earth like now? Five hundred years in the future?

Standing before him, she turned to see all that he had burned down for her. Everything that was him at the core and center of himself.

Almost everything…

"Is this everything, Player Crometheus?"

He didn't say yes. Didn't nod. Didn't…

Some little voice at the last of seconds had interceded and asked what makes this time different from all the other sheddings and becomings.

And… yes. That voice was right. There *was* something different about this one. As there should be. Because the Eternals and the Grand Uplifted Alliance and the destruction of the ship as it came to rest on its final home on the captured Animal world of New Vega… these, too, were things completely new.

Maybe this was the final shedding of all sheddings.

"No," he said. Amazed that he had.

This time was different than all the other do-overs, once-agains, from the top but with talent this time, sheddings...

This.

Was.

Something.

New.

"There's one last place," he said.

The mighty Commander Zero, armored like some titan of old and new all at once. Armed to the teeth with sidearm, battle rifle, and grenades, nodded at him and then held out her armored glove.

He reached for her. Because this time was different. And maybe the last.

"Good, Crometheus," she said softly. "We'll do this together."

And then she took his hand and led him to the arcade.

Gods:
Chapter Nineteen

It wasn't a long walk into the strip mall and the Lazer Command arcade. But the view was incredible. The whole entire world was on fire for just the two of them. The armored Eternal commander and the boy he'd once been.

Distant neighborhoods went up in sheets of flame as other gas stations, doughnut shops, and businesses he'd never known but that had been familiar all the same exploded across the skyline.

It was the end of the world... and it was beautiful.

She didn't enter the strip mall with him, but stood on the cracked and broken sidewalk near the freeway entrance. Bidding him to finish and be done. It was understood that he would go into the arcade and finish this alone. And then he would become what he was becoming.

The last shedding.

Godhood at hand.

He left Commander Zero's bizarrely comforting presence and made his way across the scorched and cracked parking lot as waves of heat came at him off the destruction all around. No one would ever again be coming to get their car washed over in the silent car wash that was already catching fire. Cleaning fluids transformed with chemical ignition into pretty death orchids of flame and then suddenly rising djinns of tempest and fire. The nearby Wendy's, whose wooden shingle roof was on fire, looked like a burning asylum. No one would be coming for a sandwich from Togo's. Flames sprang to life as he passed by those empty and iconic places of his youth, igniting and devouring those lost religions of commerce. Those lost Ozymandias statues would lie half-buried in the sands of his mind forever. Watching over the wastelands of his soul like quiet sentinels. Testaments to his eternality.

He would be a god of destruction. And the accepted sacrifices would be the ruins of all the worlds in the galaxy.

Making silent statements that could only be answered with more questions.

He crossed the wide and empty parking lot, waves of heat shimmering out across the length of it even though it was early morning just after dawn. More houses within distant burning neighborhoods exploded as gas ranges and cars cooked off from within. Sudden sprays of shingled roofs sprang into the air with thunderous *fracka-booms* like the manufactured geysers at some Vegas water show from long ago. Black ash was beginning to rain down, and that was somehow perfect to Crometheus whether he liked it or not. He brushed away some of the burnt snowflakes that had landed on his face and found that he was crying.

Tears of joy, or sadness, he didn't know. It didn't matter. They were just falling from his eyes.

That time, in his youth, he'd been obsessed with the end of the world. With the duck-and-cover drills in school. With the "day after" nuclear annihilation motif wending its way into everything from movies to games and comic books, even videos on MTV. The end of the world had seemed like some new beginning back then, instead of an end to everything that had gone before.

And if one was attuned enough to unwrap the enigmas of such memories... then maybe they, those doomsday entertainments, were prophecies of hope, and not warnings of doom.

He stepped from the parking lot onto the sidewalk in front of Lazer Command. Would the door even be open? What was he in control of now that it had all begun to burn? Would he have to toss some loose piece of concrete through the window to enter and burn down the last hidden place within himself for the final shedding to be complete? What metaphysical-restraint discard needed to be played for it all to burn?

Everything.

He tried the tinted glass door to the old arcade. To the old temple of the religion that worshipped the things he'd believed in. All the windows were so darkly tinted you couldn't see in. In fact he never remembered seeing out. Arcades required darkness. The game graphics looked better in the gloom.

Funny that, he thought.

Maybe that was the psychological trick that had kept this place hidden through every shedding, and finally made it a reality he could inhabit inside the Pantheon. Maybe its tinted windows, inside his memories of the place, made it somehow not part of the whole. Unnoticed within the nondescript strip mall of his soul.

The world was silent save for the distant crackle of burning fires out of control.

The door to the arcade swung open easily and he felt a cool blast of air and the clean smell of working electronics and burnt ozone. The eight-bit ditties and sound effects of dying aliens and repeated blaster fire came at him all at once.

He knew Old Man Webb was gone.

Had to be.

But there was someone here. Someone else was inside the arcade as the world burned down to nothing but ruin and ash. He turned toward that row of machines lined up along one wall. Knowing who he'd see. Seeing Jim Stepp at his machine. *Devil's Hollow*. Staring right into it and working the joystick left to right as he tapped the fire button quickly and constantly. The screen was so black nothing could be seen within it.

How, wondered boy Crometheus, did he know where to move?

Stepp turned his head slowly and saw him standing there in the doorway. There was a strange light in his eye. A knowing twinkle only the bad kids get when they're about to get up to trouble. Commit a crime, even.

"Ready to go down to the tracks, kid?" asked Jim Stepp.

Crometheus had come here to burn it all down. To burn down this part of his world, memories, himself, everything he'd kept back from his final becoming. As though he could have his cake and eat it too just like every sinner who'd ever crossed the lines, or torn down the walls, to have what they wanted, consequences be damned. Have your cake and eat it too. No repercussions.

But that had all been a lie. Of course there were those things. And now he'd finally come to the end of himself, or so Crometheus hoped. Now, it was time to divest himself… of himself. Completely. Totally. So that he could become the thing he'd been meant to be all along. From lost kid to rock-and-roll god to movie star and all things in between. The final incarnation was the one he'd been aiming at even when he hadn't known what he was trying to hit.

A god, once and forever.

Wasn't that what this was about? Had been all about? Everything?

The Animals call the Uplifted… Savages.

Then yes.

I'll be a savage god. A ruler of them all. I'll become that. I'll be their god of destruction.

Stepp looked at the can of gas in boy Crometheus's hand. The book of matches in the other.

"You need to know what's down there first," warned Jim Stepp. "Before you do this. You need to know, man. You've forgotten much more than you know right now."

But maybe *forgotten* wasn't the word that got used as the arcade beeped, whirred, and whistled. Maybe the word had been *deleted*. And his mind had translated *deleted* into *forgotten*.

The older boy was talking about the swamp. Crometheus knew that. And also something else. Something he had wanted to know. Something he'd buried even more than this place he tried to hide from them all. Keeping this world of his past safe for just himself for all time. A place where he never grew and never changed. A constant among the stars. And somehow Jim Stepp was like a secret compartment within all that hidden data. A failsafe designed by him a long time ago for just such a moment as this. A keeper of all things forgotten.

But why? Why had they been forgotten? Buried.

"You really need to know," said Stepp one last time. Like some kid telling him he needed to smoke his first joint. Or TP a house to be part of the crew. Or rip off some booze from Bagger's liquor store just for kicks. Bad things that needed to be done as some sort of rite of passage if one was going to become.

Crometheus set down the gas can on the carpet of the arcade.

"How?"

The older boy stepped away from the machine that was known as his. From "the Hollow," as some had called it. With an uncharacteristic flourish he waved a hand at it while holding up one shiny brass token.

"We can get there through this."

Crometheus stared at it for a moment. Then stepped forward and took the symbol. The token. The bronze disc. Readying himself as he always had any time he ever played a game, he stepped in front of the Hollow, dropped in the token, and readied himself to win.

A moment later the darkness within the machine consumed him.

* * *

He was following Jim Stepp through a misty jungle. A swamp. Both of them dressed in subdued tiger-striped jungle fatigues.

Just like the Uplifted had worn when they raided Cappella Three after Sirius Two. When they fought a brutal two-year war to dislodge the planet's inhabitants, only to finally lose in the end by nuking the rock into uninhabitability. Being forced once more to retreat starward aboard the aging *Pantheon*. A ship barely running and falling apart as it did. Low on food. *Calories*. Every conversation had been about *calories*. There were already problems with the hab and farming systems. And how was one ship supposed to fight an entire planet for a small patch to live on? To start building the utopia they'd been readying themselves for. That's what they'd been reduced to in those days. Begging for just a patch on someone else's world to start over. And when the begging didn't work, they tried to take it by force. And that had gone pretty badly.

He was hungry back then. Everyone had been. All the time. Everyone in the *Pantheon* was always hungry.

The jungle Jim Stepp led him through gave way to a clearing in the mist… and then the sides of buildings and streets came into view. The vast wide spaces of New Vega and the battle they'd just fought for it.

The day was just like the actual day of the invasion. When they'd hit hard. Struck at all the command and control systems of that world in a week-long series of pre-emptive denial-of-service stealth attacks along with quiet bioweapon neutralizers to shut down half the population's ability to fight back effectively. The Animals thought the bioweapons were just the flu. A suddenly bad one at that. And that the local comm net was just having sunspot problems with Vega's bright star in the sky. That was why comms were funny. That was all the Animals thought in the few hours that remained to them of their free lives.

But really it had been Uplifted. The Uplifted they called the Savages, waging a silent war on the ground weeks before the Animals even knew it was a shooting war. *Always start the fight before the other guy knows he's in one.* TED 503:14. Easier to gain momentum.

Crometheus the Uplifted marine had been part of a commando team with Clan Thunder Claw. Hitting military communications posts across the planet. Swift brief raids across the night side to knock out their comms network. All combatants neutralized by stealth and sudden violence of action. AI mimics installed in the local software to keep up the appearance of normal comm traffic while sowing a slow campaign of disinformation in preparation for the actual assault. New Vega going electronically dark at the critical moment of zero hour when they realized the "Savages" were attacking. When they were trying to get defensive batteries up and interceptors into the air. When hell was breaking loose, in other words.

Now he was back in that memory. Leaving the mists of the swamp beyond the train tracks and following Jim Stepp into…

… a banquet set up in front of New Vega mil-comm traffic station four. Stepp led him through the misty night jungle that surrounded that installation. That had been their biggest coup. The Thunder Claw commando team

Crometheus had been part of. They'd dropped in by orbital glider and hit the target in the predawn hours before the main assault on the central population centers of New Vega. The combat model of G-97 had been swapped out for silenced MP5Xs with laser sights. Weaponry pulled out of deep storage. Old, but incredibly reliable for the wet-work they were being tasked with to knock out station four.

The whole detachment had worked the problem in-game for weeks prior to the premier hit to kick off the assault. In the end Crometheus had been assigned by Maestro to be the strike leader. The tip of the spear, as it were. Then it was him leading a wedge of Uplifted marines kitted in camo-skinned light armor systems straight into the objective. They swept across the equatorial jungle mountain ridge in the dark, closing in on the massive comm relay that hung in the basin below. The central suspended dish in the basin was operated by a small tower within a tight security-controlled compound atop the ridge.

The battle for New Vega, when it started, would be fought thousands of miles away. But this target was important for disrupting planetary military comms.

The Animal sentries at the main gate had seen nothing but ghosts coming out of the misty jungle night, until sudden whispers of suppressed gunfire slammed into their skulls and chests in tight shot groupings.

"Solid hits!" announced the in-game announcer over the team comm. Cash rained down across Crometheus's HUD as two other Uplifted marines under him set to work on violating the gate's security locks while the rest of the unit stacked along the outer walls beneath the comm tower's glare. Hot white searchlights crossed out in the jungle, lazily searching for something to alert the auto-turrets to.

He was hungry.

He'd always remember that moment. Ravenously hungry. Hungry for a burger. He'd remember that feeling forever as the gates were hacked by two fellow marines. A second later they slithered open and the work of slaughter began in earnest as the Uplifted hit team neutralized everyone. It was over in under two minutes. Just as it was supposed to be. Just as it had been planned to be.

Just... as it was going down all across the New Vega comm network on this last night of the pre-game for the invasion of an Animal world to make all their own.

The first Uplifted world.

The Pantheon's new home world.

They would not be dislodged as they had been from Cappella Three. They would not be thrown out. They were staying. They were keeping their patch this time. In fact, they were keeping the whole damned planet. This time. Centuries of raiding and retreating back to the empty voids of deep space were over.

They were coming home. Their new home.

Tomorrow would find them all, every Uplifted marine, fighting a full-scale battle against three heavy divisions of New Vega armor just to get a foothold inside the main city. But tonight, the game was theirs. They owned the darkness. And they reveled in its vastness.

Working quickly, the hit team spread out across the compound to put down every Animal. Most of whom were sleeping in a small barracks near the main control tower. The duty room was hit by three marines at once and a short spat of firing broke out in the night silence as full mags were dumped into the three Animal soldiers standing night watch and drinking coffee, thinking nothing ever happened out here at the comm relay known as Four.

"Prizes! Prizes! Prizes!" whooped the announcer inside their HUDs as each fatality was recorded for the Pantheon's posterity and viewership. And enjoyment. But the "Big Vic" came when Crometheus at the head of an assault team breached the comm tower door and started shooting fast as they climbed the tower. Knocking out the smaller levels in seconds. There was no way for the station's watch commander not to have heard the commotion as the team stormed the upper reaches of the control tower. And it was a close thing at the last as they burst through to the top level that looked out over the vast sleeping dish in the blue of the high jungle mountains' late night. The Animal commander was reaching for the alert button, ready to send up an electronic signal flare that Four was under attack by unknowns, when Crometheus landed the tri-dot laser sight on the man's head and pulled the trigger on the silenced MP5X.

Single shot through the brainpan. Finesse. This was for all the achievement points.

One in the head.

Two in the body a single breath later.

The Animal slithered down the wall badly. His eyes awash with fresh horror. His mouth silently forming the word "Savages!" As though he'd only just realized, and still couldn't believe it, that their societal boogey monsters had actually come in from the dark to wrest their world away from them.

That the devil was real. Evil did indeed exist.

The in-game announcer went wild as the operation was called and the hit team was awarded a "Flawless Victory" in shimmering gold Las Vegas dazzle-style letters, all of it erupting across their HUDs.

"You've just been upgraded to a fabulous gourmet feast!" shrieked the hyperactive announcer ecstatically.

Jim Stepp, who's been there all along, following the memory of that commando team as Crometheus led the assault on Four, whispers something in his ear. They're both just boys, crouching in the darkness and watching the playlet unfold from beyond the security perimeter.

Hidden in the jungle.

"Is that what you think you got, kid? A fancy meal?"

The other Uplifted marines can't see them. And the image shifts to the banquet they received in honor of their victory. Flown in direct after the station was neutralized and the AI mimic was up and sowing discord in the comm stations of New Vega.

Except, just before it does, just before the memory of that beautiful once-in-a-lifetime banquet inside an authentic German Ratskeller with sausages and beer and potatoes fried in mustard while buxom blond beauties brought forth more of everything, including a pig cooked whole from which they tore pieces shining with grease and bit into crackling skin while slaking their thirst with cold beer, beauties giggling and laughing while the victors dandled them on their armored knees... just before that best-ever meal of victory on the night before the war for the Pantheon's new home began in earnest… the game in the arcade glitched and Crometheus saw something else.

The vivid colors and the flashing arcade lights blinked out. The boy who would be Crometheus, watching from the jungle, didn't like this. Something he didn't want to see… was about to happen.

Or remember.

Something that really happened, instead of the way he'd been made to remember it all.

The beautiful vibrant bright colors of the game, of the German beer hall with its antique plastered walls, burnished dark oak beams, the grease-glistening sausages and the crisp carcass of the roast pig with a bright red apple in its mouth. The potatoes roasted and fried with mustard and onions. The epically beautiful serving wenches, no doubt the finest of slaves brought up from the lower decks just for this celebratory occasion… that's all gone in the jungle night. All of it.

Like it never happened.

At first Crometheus as a boy sees what he thinks are baboons in the jungle dark against the fence of the objective. Station four has gone dark. The moon above is full and fat but the shadows within the compound remain as the baboons cluster about, tearing at something on the ground and eating in silence.

Crometheus the boy is standing with Stepp at the hacked gate. They've crept forward to get a better look. Near the bodies of the two dead guards. Or at least where the two dead Animal guards should be. Except the corpses are gone and when he searches for them in the wan moonlight that reaches the outer gate he sees nothing but drag marks eaten by night shadows.

But the direction the drag marks lead follow straight into the compound where the circle of baboons feast in silence, each of them staring out at the jungle night like sentinels. Silently chewing on their haunches. Breaking bones and pulling away muscle and flesh.

"Let have a look," said Jim Stepp. The familiar forever lost boy challenge to do something that's not supposed to be done. That mad twinkle in his eyes.

But the boy Crometheus does not want to go and "have a look." Because to *look* is to *know*. And knowledge is power, right? As the old afternoon cartoons used to say.

Feeling is knowing. And knowing is truth.

TED 22:109.

Except...

There are some things you don't want to know, now do you, Crometheus? Or whoever you once were.

And yet... he knows. Already. This too is part of the becoming. The final becoming. These are the things you see in the swamp. And so you must look. Because you must know. Because knowing is becoming too.

Isn't it?

They get close, walking through the gate in the jungle atop the high mountain ridge security installation that runs the massive dish in the basin below. The satellite comm dish floats out there in the basin between the high misty peaks like some giant starship that has come down to rest.

The colors are not bright.

The game announcer does not roar with triumph.

There is none of that and no filter shenanigans here to convince us of what we must think if we are to go forward.

This is the truth of what reality really is. This is looking. This is knowing.

"Whether you like it or not, kid," whispers Jim Stepp from the dark, "this is what it is. And knowing it… will make you stronger. Make you better. Maybe even a god… someday, son."

He remembers a Sunday school story from his parents' abortive attempts at religion. Something about the cartoon version of the tree of the knowledge of good and evil. A distant memory surfaces amid all the horror he is watching and understanding more and more by the second.

The things they are looking at are not baboons gathered around some kill in the night. Smacking and slurping and tearing at the bones of the victims' twisted and rent corpse. Flesh coming away in great wet gobs and long stringy bits that stretch and snap and threaten to lodge between teeth.

The sounds are too horrible to be anything but real.

The baboons are marines. Uplifted marines.

Just like him.

And this is their silent communion. This is what the German feast looked like without the Pantheon's filters, game announcers, plus-one power-ups, and all the things they used to keep them fighting.

This is what reality looks like. And it's not pretty.

But when was it ever?

The baboon marines eat in silence.

Well, not total silence. Almost undetectable beneath it all is a soft whirring sound as the baboons watch the night. Mesmerized by something unseen. By giggling beauties that don't really exist. And plates of food disguising something much more real.

They are not baboons.

They are Uplifted marines.

Uplifted marines. And they are eating the corpses of the dead via small whirring intake blenders located within the palms of their armored gloves.

"C'mon," whispers Stepp suddenly. "There's more to see."

And then the game resumes and the glitch is gone. The filters and the colors are back.

For now.

Gods:
Chapter Twenty

Crometheus is back in the jungle with Jim Stepp. Both of them wearing jungle fatigues of whatever war it was Jim Stepp died in back on Earth. The air is cold and the sky, when it can be seen, is cloud-covered and swollen with anger. Only the sound of a small stream, burbling and talking to itself over stony courses, can be heard.

"You remember that war in the Forbidden Decks... after Cappella Three?" asks Stepp as he leads them through the brush down there in the swamp. Along a twisting narrow labyrinthine trail that seems to appear and swallow itself with every step.

Crometheus is following the back of the older boy. They are playing soldiers for real down in here the swamp, just like they did on the *Front Line* upright in the arcade. Crometheus tries to remember the war for the aft decks. The dark ages of the lost colony ship *Pantheon*.

Some invisible insect keeps buzzing *Bad Thought Bad Thought Bad Thought*... but Crometheus swats at it and it fades back into the bush.

He remembers that the cultists of the aft decks started rumors like wildfires among the engineering staff. Rumors that the elites of the Xanadu Tower and the Truth and Safety Council, forward of the main hab, living in the glitter dome, that they still had food when everyone else was starving. In fact, according to the rumors that caught fire and spread like a just-lit gas-soaked bush on a windy morning in the pre-dawn dark, the best of them had abundant amounts of sustenance.

He remembered that was a lie. Told by the enemies of the Pantheon. The insect buzzed something. And furthermore he remembered participating in the great purge that had driven the cultists, and their blasphemies, beyond the known embrace and love of the citizens of the main hab. Driven the heretics back into the deep, into what was rapidly becoming, way back then even, the haunted spaces of the Forbidden Decks.

As it would be known henceforth and forevermore. So say we all.

He remembered it happening that way.

"That ain't the way it happened," says Stepp over his shoulder as he brushes back a spidery willow tree hanging low to the sandy trail they are following. Webs abound down here, dropping hot fever spiders all over them. The older boy's eyebrows arch, and that wicked lost boy's glimmer appears once more in his mischievous eyes. The same kind the real Peter Pan must've had when he was up to some mischief against Hook and crew. "Not at all how it happened, kid. You were on the wrong side of that dirty little war. You got caught up in the action though. You just made the mistake of being in with the engineering crowd. They edited that. Made you forget."

The mist in the jungle swamp clears and ahead lies the Southern Cliff. Except in starship architecture it's not called that. It's called the Aft Axial Supply Deck to Main Hab. People aboard the *Pantheon* just called it the Southern Cliff. If you were standing in the hab somewhere on the plain below, and you looked south, or rather off toward the aft sections of the starship, then you saw the wall. Beyond the farming cities on the plain, the fields of corn, the fires burning out of control started by wilding rioters and fueled by the small battles taking place within the giant interstellar starship floating through space. Beyond all that you would have seen a roughly kilometer-high wall filling the "bottom," or aft, wall of the massive cylinder that was the main hab. Halfway up that wall, in its dead center, was a massive cross-shaped hangar deck that serviced the hab. Supplies could be transferred from there to the aft hangar decks. Gravity was almost non-existent down the plumb line of the cylinder, and supplies could be moved effortlessly.

This was the Southern Cliff. This was where the cultists made their stand against the ship's official crew of the *Pantheon* during that dirty little war. The lessers who'd been suckered in by the Uplifters for money and other promises to actually fly and crew the massive ship were unhappy with the directionless direction and series of failures that had marked the ship's flight time since leaving Earth.

Freeing up the Uplifted to get their utopia on by doing all the slave labor hadn't sat well. Things were boiling over.

"They're coming over the wall!" someone screamed.

Crometheus looks around. The misty swamp bottom, laden with the ghosts of skeletal willows, is gone. They are inside the massive hangar that is the Aft Axial Supply Deck to Main Hab. The Southern Cliff. The Wall. Beyond all this is the spinning cylinder of the hab world and the blue gossamer that is its central atmosphere.

Stepp turns to the boy Crometheus and shouts, "We gotta help defend the barricades. Quarters up. We're playing doubles!"

Then the older boy is off and running forward from the back of the cyclopean hangar deck toward the barricades that have been erected at the entrance to the hab. The massive cliff that looks out upon the rotating artificial world below and above.

The sound of sporadic gunfire goes off like desultory firecrackers at first, then ratchets up in earnest as the assault begins. Just as it did then, long ago, when engineering was being purged of the heretics.

Caught up in the action, Crometheus follows Stepp into the fight. Both are carrying surplus 1911s. Just like the cultists did back in those angry days of rebellion. Arms raided from an aft-section survival vault located along the *Pantheon*'s outer hull. Purchased in bulk back on Earth just in case. As the countries and factions of the world caught fire and went all-out war on one another and arms became an industry like never before. That armory contained clamshells of 1911s. And racks upon racks of old tactical M-14s from the South American wars.

The official police and military forces of the starship *Pantheon* carried the latest arms from Heckler and Koch.

Or at least, the latest as of two hundred years ago on Earth at the moment of this past rebellion.

"There are more of them than us! But we have science on our side!" they screamed when the Pantheon's security teams came for them.

That was something they all told each other in the resistance, remembered Crometheus as he hears someone shouting it above the riot of CQB. It wasn't a cult. A cult was what the powers-that-be would call it later. During the re-education, after the war. But at the time, during the conflict over food and water and the direction of a vessel that was now wandering the cosmos in search of a stray ice comet instead of trying to make it to a third world—a second voyage well beyond what had been intended for the ship's original operation—during that time they'd called themselves the resistance. As though they were returning to their ancient roots of reason and science back on Earth when they'd resisted the powers that be and fought them on every single point. Fought them and won. Capturing the hearts and minds of the people in order to seize power and effect fundamental change for the... wait for it... greater good.

Crometheus remembers, though it seems impossible now, that he was seduced by those false gods of free will. Becoming a heretic of his own faith in himself. He'd joined the resistance. The elites who'd remained elite during the long crawl out from Sirius Two and then on to Cappella Three, they became the fat cats. It was always ever their vision in Truth and Safety and what would become the Xanadu Tower. Their way. Their whims. Always.

It was time for change, and the war started on the Southern Wall. The Southern Cliff.

The shedding hadn't happened yet. So he'd joined the other side thinking it was a play for power to be seized, and not realizing he'd gotten caught up in the action and believed the lies of the resistance. Lies that said they weren't becoming gods. That they were just slaves. And always would be. Unless...

Hence the war for what remained of the limited food and water aboard the *Pantheon*. The need for sustenance now that the cryo coffin decks were system-defaulting and going offline in large blocks. Killing hundreds of sleepers a day.

You counted yourself lucky then not to have been caught in the sleep racks the day those decks went down due either to terrorism or a simple failure to maintain what wasn't supposed to run this long anyway. One thirty-year voyage had turned into a two-hundred-year death march. With no end in sight.

It was supposed to be thirty years to Sirius Two. Maybe only twenty-five.

Thirty years to Utopia.

Not two hundred years of darkness and solitude.

That's all the sleeper racks, and really the ship itself, had ever been intended to last for. Thirty years.

Now the security police, the early predecessors of the Uplifted marines that would come one day to lead the strike of the Uplifted against the Animals, were storming the castle, as it were. That's what they called their little fortress at the Southern Cliff. *High Castle*. They thought it was unassailable. They'd blocked off the lifts up from the main hab floor. The gantries. Even the physical access ladders and stairs that had been built into the massive wall at the end of the cylinder of the main hab had been demolished.

But the security police, all of them ex-German military who'd been recruited by Micro Power in the leadup to the Big Uplift exodus from Earth, were either scaling the wall, rappelling down onto it, or coming in by air assault drone ship backed by mounted heavy gun fire.

The resistance didn't have the numbers. In the end, in a later hindsight, he would remember, through breaks in the electric pain chair, as they tortured him and taught him to see their truth, the truth, that the security police had the weapons and the training and the numbers. They'd come to the Pantheon as contractors and stayed on as true believers in a master race their German DNA told them must be true. Still, the fight at the Southern Cliff had been brutal. Close-quarters violence with no quarter given to the maimed and wounded and most who tried to surrender.

Stepp rushes forward to a barrier where resisters are crouched and firing back at the heavily armed security police who've managed to just gain a bare foothold inside the hangar door. Combat-vested and bulletproofed masked shadows fighting from the beveled-edge maintenance gantry that is little more than a walkway to service the landing lights for the axial supply deck. High-speed commando teams cover their designated marksmen with absurd amounts of incoming fire. The marksmen meanwhile shoot down the Resisters when they can. Untrained and low on ammo, because they don't have access to a forge this far back in the ship, those same resisters he once was a part of are expending wild amounts of precious little ammo to merely get hits on the insectile body-armored security police troopers.

But it is now, as it was then, at this moment in his memories, that the troopers rush the barricades for the final assault. The rebellion is less than a minute from being over. Security police heavy gunners, deployed by the Pantheon's Truth and Safety Committee, sweep the field, forming a base of fire as the other troopers, moving in teams, surge forward tossing flashbangs and turning on tactical floodlights mounted alongside their insectile helmets and lead-spitting weapons.

Stepp is firing back almost point-blank into the oncoming troopers when the flashbangs go off like a daisy chain of flashbulbs all across the barrier the last of the resistance is covering behind. Where Crometheus finds himself in that long-lost memory.

Had it been deleted?

Or had he kept it hidden in the arcade? Or even the swamp? Inside *Dig Dug* or *Tutankham*.

Crometheus feels himself go fetal as his vision and senses are suddenly smashed by flash and bang. Curls up like a baby whether he likes it or not as images and nothingness, both at the same time, impossibly so, scramble his fear-fried brain.

He screams because he is back here again.

Back at the beginning of the shedding. And all that he must undergo to become what he will one day be.

He feels, just as he did so long ago, the rough tactical gauntlets of the powerful ex-German military commandos grabbing him and binding him with zip ties that will bite into his skin and leave his wrists and ankles bloody. He can barely breathe as they drag him away. That's when he passes out and there's nothing but dark darkness until there's pain.

Darkest darkness in fact. He remembers that darkness even now.

Dark until…

There's a familiar voice in the darkness. Wry and soft. Almost friendly. And he knows it from somewhere soon, but not now. Now, in the pit of interrogation he finds himself in, the voice is new. Then. It was new then. The first time he heard it.

Over the next six months it will become the only voice he ever hears. Imagine that. And shudder. And though at first he hates it, in time he will come to love it. Adore it. Need it. And even worship it for his very life.

The voice will be everything to him.

"Why?" says the voice in the dark of the narrow pit Crometheus finds himself in.

It's a pit. But it was officially designated an enhanced interrogation cell when designed by the ship's architects back on lost Earth. The question he would think about over the course of that dark and lonely six months of torture and re-education, was why they'd included so many enhanced interrogation cells when they designed the ship. A colony ship outbound to a brighter, better future. Had they known, when first designing the *Pantheon* back in some lab or office tower on Earth, that things would eventually get to this point? Had they known that things would get so out of hand that enhanced interrogation cells would be needed? Or was it simply better to be safe… than sorry? Especially if you were in charge and intended to remain that way for the duration of the long flight. And even a longer flight than you'd first planned.

Thirty years… or two hundred. However long it takes. You'll eventually need some enhanced interrogation cells. Trust us.

Had they known, even then, how crazy this nightmare trek into deep space looking for some promised world that kept turning out to be either poisoned or already inhabited, would be? Had they known that things would eventually come to this sorry state of affairs? Rebellion and guillotine. That the populace who'd believed in the movement… would one day become disillusioned when they found out it was all just a big lie?

Had they known? Even then?

Crometheus thinks about that a lot in the cell, and once again as he relives it all. Because they must have known. They built the cells before they even needed them.

They built them before the flight began.

The voice that asked him "Why?" is everywhere in the cell in that memory that feels like the frighteningly real present once again. It's in his ear and right in his face so that he might even feel the hot breath of the one who speaks. And at the same time, it's far away out across some distant and frozen arctic plane of the kind only Finnish rock bands seek to capture for their heavy metal album covers.

And again it's also very close and personal. Intimate even. Right in his ear. Maybe even his brain. It's all three even though two are the same. Because the two that are the same, close and closer, personal and even more intimate, aren't. They're layers of the same hell. Imagine that.

You only figure out the levels of hell once you've arrived. And by then it's too late.

Later he will learn that the pit, the enhanced interrogation cell, is really just a tube. Nine feet down into the deck. It can shower him with freezing cold water from nozzles located high up along the rim lined with metal blades and knives. The walls are close and pin his shoulders no matter how he turns. They can be made hot with live electricity, as can the floor. Crometheus is naked. Hungry. And cold. And pain will become the metric by which he judges his days for the foreseeable future ahead. In fact, that future will seem like forever in here.

In further fact… it will become as though he has no future other than the one he has arrived at.

Imagine that. No Friday nights. No Monday mornings. Nothing by which to measure pain by.

He will lose all hope.

He knows that now, even at the first when the voice he will worship speaks to him. Knew it then. Even at the very beginning. He'd lost already. He'd gambled and he'd lost.

And this was the price.

He did not answer the voice that was in his face, far out across the frozen plain, and in his brain all at once.

He didn't answer.

So the floor was suddenly alive with that living electricity that burned and froze in the same instant. And it didn't just drop by for a zap. It stayed to chat. It stayed on until he thought he was going to have a heart attack. It stayed on and he tried to grab the walls but those too were running with live current. Living fire. He bounced around, being "burnt" everywhere. Nothing was safe and there was a brief moment of looking into the abyss of insanity when you guessed it never would be safe forever. That this right now was forever and that you had erred exceedingly. How naive you were then, he'd think back in the months to come. You had no idea how long forever could be at the beginning.

Maybe five seconds.

Felt like hell. Felt like forever.

It stopped and the voice came back, coming in over the sound of his pantings turning to harsh sobs in the tight cavern he couldn't move his arms within. Crying like the baby he must once have been. Crying like the drug addict who'd reached the end of his tether at that airport Marriott weekend when he'd been offered a chance to join the future or just go up to his room and hang himself.

Weeping.

Later he would gnash his teeth.

He'd come forward then in the brightly lit conference room at that airport Marriott. To their altar call, as it were. Crying and weeping and sobbing... begging to be a winner again like he'd once been when he'd been the lead singer of a band that was the brightest star in the firmament of rock and roll. Begging to feel what he'd once felt when he rocked a stadium of seventy thousand one hot summer's night.

Weeping to be famous again.

"Why, Billy?" asked the voice in the pit.

Billy had been his name long ago. Billy Bang had been his stage name. The name the world knew him by. Billy Bang... rock god.

He was sobbing uncontrollably. Begging without using words because his mouth wouldn't form them because every muscle had been turned to quivering jelly by hot currents of living fire. Begging that the juice to the current never be turned on again. He was wrong. He knew that now, he blubbered. He never should have...

"I'll ask you once more... Billy," asked that wry friendly slow-speaking and yet menacing voice because it had all the power in the world over, and all the time in the... no not the world, the ship. The *Pantheon*. The galaxy. All the power. All the time. All the truth. "Why did you join the resistance?"

He knew his mind was blubbering *I don't know and I was wrong and I'm sorry* over and over again without stopping and with no intention of relenting. He knew that. But he also knew everything coming out of his mouth made no sense. And the fear that they wouldn't understand that he was begging for forgiveness. The fear that they'd turn back on the juice was as bad as if they actually had turned it on once more. He knew this because he'd begun to shriek incoherently. So much so that he could feel his once prized and precious vocal cords tearing apart with each ragged gasp for a mercy he knew he'd never receive.

Just imagine, his future self murmured… this was only the first five minutes in hell. A hell that would last six months or two years, he never really was quite sure how long. And who cares… it would feel like forever anyway.

"You had it all, Billy. You were one of us," said the wry voice regretfully. And that… that regretful tone, disappointed is really the word, that was somehow worse than the electricity. "All you had to do was toe the party line and keep the rabble entertained. Instead… you got caught up in the lie, Billy."

Silence.

At any moment they'd turn on the power and fry him for good. And this time it wouldn't go off and he wouldn't die. It would just be that live electricity moment of forever. Burning and cold and dying and knowing all at once… forever. Because that's the thing about torture pits or chambers or enhanced interrogation cells. Whatever you want to call them. You don't really know that's what they are. You don't know that any more than you know it could just as well be called… an *execution chamber*.

That's the mistake people who don't know make. Until you're in one. Then you're convinced it's an execution chamber, and anything else is a kind of hope you have no right to. Again, you never really know when you're in one what it's called. Because there's hope in a name. Hope in a purpose. Even if it's just promised death instead of endless pain unending endlessly.

Hell. After… later… he'd once remembered the pit and asked himself why people never really understood the concept of a hell in all those hokey old Earth religions. Not an end. But endless suffering unending. Even the people who'd believed in one—a hell—they hadn't even believed in suffering forever, really. Really. Because if they had they would have crawled across the world on their hands and knees over broken glass to save just one of the people they claimed to have loved, from that kind of hell.

If you think hell is real... then of course that's what you'd do. But people don't so it must not be.

Right?

"You were Billy Bang," continued the voice in his head and across the wastelands of frozen ice. "You weren't like the crew and the great unwashed we brought along to serve us. The ones being flung from the Cliff down into the hab below right now, as we speak, son. Why, Billy?" The voice honestly seemed like it wanted to know the answer to the question. "Why, son?"

This is how it would go for time immeasurable. Forever. Endless questions that walked him through the process of the rehabilitation of him. Teaching him their truths. Helping him to become...

"We're not going to give up on you, Billy. You're going to become something new. Something wonderful. I'll help you, son. Do you want that?"

And when he didn't answer why he'd betrayed the Pantheon and joined up with the resistance... then he got the living fire. And when he didn't answer their other questions...

... Who are your leaders?

... Where's the secret shrine?

... Where is Anubis?

… Two plus two is five, right?

And every other seemingly nonsensical thing that led him toward the total breakdown that was coming. The breakdown on the other side of which lay abject slavery. And the slavery led to the rebuilding and ultimately… the shedding. Which he was so grateful for. Is *grateful for* correct?

"Do you want me to help you… son?"

Don't give the right answer and then it's the fire. The living fire. Or the ice-cold, arctic-cold water, so cold it cut the skin like sharp icy knives.

In time he figured out the voice was real. In that it belonged to a person. Someone who seemed familiar to him. Or at least did now. Hard to tell. But it was just a voice. A voice that had been patterned and mapped and was most likely being run by an AI with interrogation and deprogramming protocols in some processor node somewhere.

So the questions never stopped. Not night nor day… because those didn't exist here in the pit. Not even when you slept.

Never. The questions never ever stopped.

He must have answered a hundred thousand questions over those years. And in the end… on graduation day as the voice had begun to call it… after they had shattered his mind and rebuilt it in their image… he was raised from the pit. Hauled forth like a Lazarus. And there, standing in front of him… yes… of course… it was Lusypher. As it always had been all along. In his Nazi SS officer's uniform. When the shedding came and they chose their god names, he called himself... Lusypher. And Billy Bang took Crometheus.

Told them he'd do anything.

Become anything.

All he wanted was just one more chance to serve the Pantheon. That was all.

On graduation day, on the day when the floor of the pit suddenly began to rise toward that opening he'd stared at for six months, or two years, or forever, who really knew how time ran in hell, it was Lusypher and two marines standing there to greet him. The security police had become something new in the interim. The Uplifted marines. And they hauled him out at the last, holding up his shrunken body.

He caught a brief glimpse of himself in the reflective surface of a one-way mirror that watched over the upper chamber of the interrogation pit as the two marines held him steady.

He was emaciated. A skeleton. Hair gone and his ribs showing through his ruined skin. His eyes were haunted.

Remember all those teen magazines you were on the cover of? Shirt off and a wild sneer that said you don't care? Some insipid article about the kind of girl you were looking for. Remember? some other voice asked. Maybe it was the voice of Jim Stepp. Maybe he was in the Hollow... or the Swamp. Both are the same when you think about it.

"That's... not me," he must have murmured to them. Or no one.

Lusypher turned and saw what Crometheus was staring at. His own shrunken and emaciated image in the mirror. Then the man who would be Lusypher laughed dismissively. The friendly chuckle of some ever-patient doctor.

"Oh… don't worry about that anymore," he said of the horror-show image in the mirror. The skeleton Billy Bang had become. "We're getting rid of that." And, "Son… welcome to the marines."

Gods:
Chapter Twenty-One

"We've been here before, son," says Lusypher. Or rather, the disembodied voice of Lusypher.

Crometheus is lying at the center of a state-of-the-art robot surgery amphitheater. The *Pantheon*, when first launched, was outfitted with many such facilities. Nothing but the best in premium medical care for the Uplifted master race during their long voyage to the promised land. He can feel himself there, in it, at the center of the surgery show. That's the best way to put it. But at the same time he can also see the entire amphitheater via an HD feed from one of the many monitors.

Except there's a blank spot in the image. At the dead center of the operating table, where he should be and knows that he is, where he should be… there's nothing.

Or… he cannot see that area?

No, that's not right.

Not that that area is not there… it's just that his mind won't actually process what he's seeing and let him look into that space. Within the galaxy of his mind that image of himself has become a null space. A phantom zone. He's there, but you can't see him. A blank spot in the universe.

"You've been here before, marine," says Commander Zero, above him. Somewhere. They're getting ready to remove him. He can tell. Techs are moving the robot arms aside and powering down the cutting lasers that disengaged him from the shell he's been... traveling in... his whole life. Current life. New life now begins.

In the arcade you always got three lives for a quarter. So this is like that.

"But we're doing truth now," continues Commander Zero. Her voice hard and stern, but the practicality within it makes her somehow more believable. Human, not to insult her with such a low term. Somehow real. Somehow truth.

That might be a better way to put it.

"As Eternals we know the real score, Player Crometheus," continues Zero. "None of this augmented reality evolved from filters. No best-dreamed life made real, as you think. You will, as an Eternal, know the true state of affairs, marine. Then you will be truly free. Free to become a god like the rest of us."

Lusypher steps into frame. Or within the camera that Crometheus's mind is currently using to capture images.

Oh my... thinks Crometheus. They've taken my eyes. And given me... a camera.

This is like...

... some horror movie. But it's real.

Lusypher's long black leather Nazi trench coat is somehow perfect in this sterile operating theater... but still singular and the opposite of everything else here.

"You can't see yourself, son, just like all those years ago when we first perfected the shedding, because of a condition called Self-Aware Blindness Induced by Uplift. It's a common condition. Nothing to worry about. As Commander Zero said… you've been here before."

How did Silver… Lusypher know that was exactly what his mind was freaking out about? Not about the surgery that was about to be done on him, something ghoulish and diabolical in the name of voodoo super-science… but about the fact that he can't see himself on that monitor no matter how hard he tries to stare into the negative space within the universe in order to find an image of his own being within real-time. It's like suddenly becoming afraid that you don't actually exist. Which is an oxymoron that, if true… will drive you mad if you think too long about it.

Must… drive you mad. In fact.

He cannot look at the spot where he once was. Wait, is.

And to think about that for even a few cycles… well, as they say, that way lies madness, son.

Are these even my thoughts?

"It's a common side effect of the shedding process," says Lusypher frankly, close and intimate within Crometheus's mind. "We're relaxing you with Abyssatrol. Should take effect in a few seconds. So it's best if I run things down for you now."

He can feel something coming into his brain. Cooling and calming. Dialing back the freakout that's underway and rolling toward full-blown psychosis.

"Back when we put down the revolt in main engineering… that wasn't the biggest problem facing us at the time, son. You and the other resisters, you were right about the current situation aboard the ship. That comet business was foolish. But in our defense, we didn't have a lot of options at the time. Even with the water from the comet and the seeds from storage... even *if* we could get the crops going again down on the main hab floor, which was a matter of some debate... we were doomed, Crometheus. It wouldn't be enough. Couldn't be. Had never been designed to be.

"Our biggest problem facing the Pantheon wasn't the resistance, son. It was, as it long had been, calories. Plain and simple. A problem as old as humanity once was. Enough calories and you and your tribe get to go up the evolutionary ladder. Too little and you're a dead branch on the tree of life. But unbeknownst to you and the others, at that time we discovered something wonderful in the forward design labs. Our Persistent Contrived Realities Project merged with our filter technology allowed us to neutrally interface with the Pantheon net, as we called it back then. More and more of us at the top, even yourself, were retreating into those vast simulated worlds to live as we had back on Earth, instead of what we were facing: the harsh realities of a very long interstellar flight. Including the dual killers of starvation and boredom.

"It was at about that time that you, of all people, one of the elite of the elite, decided to try to take control of the ship by joining up with the cultists. Or the resisters, as they called themselves."

A needle inside Crometheus's mind switches fear of voodoo surgery over to fear of execution by vivisection. Like someone randomly switched on the light in a dark room revealing that was an actual option.

"But that's why you're like us," continues Lusypher. "In the absence of real leadership, you reverted to what makes you an elite. Just like the rest of us. You're smarter. Faster. And better equipped to lead. You saw an opportunity and took it. And that's why we've spent all this time rehabilitating you instead of flinging you from the Tarpeian Rock that is the Southern Cliff as an example to all the lessers.

"But that's all, as they say, ancient history. It's been forever since those days. You chose a new name when you took the next step along the Path and joined us. When you shed. The first time. You remember that, son… that was part of the protocol. You must remember that, and the Abyssatrol should make it easier to access those memories in the next few minutes. Leaving behind the old names. Choosing new tags by which we would be known… and one day… worshipped. The vision of the Path, as it was originally intended, restored. The heresies of Anubis purged. Calories… no longer an issue now that we'd left our bodies."

Things within the monitor that is his vision are coming into focus. He can see himself now. Or what he truly is… now. And he wants to scream. Wants to go stark raving void-mad right there when he sees what is left of himself.

Calories… no longer a problem now that we'd left our bodies.

"Once we jacked into the neural net of the Pantheon, *became* it in effect by giving up those ever-greedy, ever-needy calorie-hungry bodies," says Lusypher, "it was amazing what we didn't need anymore. What we were free to create with when we were no longer burdened by needs. We could focus, son, on what was important. We could focus on the big things. The wants. Grand-scale thinking. It's been this way for hundreds of years. Now we're just bringing you back to the starting point to show you how far we've come once again. We're showing you how it all began, and how you arrived here, now, at deck sixty-six, a member of the Eternals." Lusypher's voice is soft and gentle. Reassuring. Like he's talking someone down off a ledge. Stating the facts to a madman to get him to calm down and see reason. "You've been here before, Crometheus. You just forgot that this is how it is. Because that's the problem with the Xanadu Tower and all the lives we've lived inside the augmented reality of the Pantheon... we've forgotten what we've become, son. We've forgotten that first real shedding when we sacrificed our bodies so that we could go on. So that we could become."

Commander Zero steps into frame.

The Abyssatrol won't let him scream. He wants to. Knows he needs to. Knows he isn't just falling down into some deep well of madness, but rather a bottomless pit of insanity he'll never find the end to. He'll just fall forever, stark raving mad.

But some overwhelming ambivalence keeps shutting down that circuit within his brain that wants to scream endlessly at what he's seeing now in the monitor. What he became long ago after the enhanced interrogation cell. After the pit.

Lying there on the surgery table.

He is a pulsing, quivering... brain.

Him.

Nothing more.

What have I done to myself? he tries to shriek… and can't. Because he has no mouth. Which makes things even more horrible than could ever have previously been imagined.

"We've all been through…"

Lusypher pauses.

"Through exactly what you're going through right now, son. You've been through it before. Hundreds of years ago. The fact that we cut away our bodies in order to reduce the need for caloric intake is a known thing. But it's also a purposefully forgotten thing. Our lives are so full and rich inside the Pantheon that we keep forgetting we're just brains hooked up to racks in the most secure chambers of the ship. Or hidden behind the combat armor we're interfacing with. We keep forgetting… that this is reality. Except we know it all along. Create hidden places where the truth is buried. Your arcade. The swamp. Those places are where you keep the deep secrets, son."

For a long time Crometheus watches with silent horror, his brain on the monitor. Doing nothing but pulsing and quivering.

"After the failures of the cryo decks," continues Lusypher, "we started consuming our fellow Uplifted adherents. For calories. We did that before the shedding and then took a suite of PTSD-purposed drugs to forget what we'd done. Of course there were side effects; there always are. With every pill, there's a poison. And when even that… food… ran out, we were down to nothing because there were no fabled storage vaults full of endless pre-packaged food that could have carried us through lifetimes like some were saying back then. There was nothing. No Seven Cities of MREs. There were some. But not enough, not by a long shot. Not for a complement of close to forty thousand human bodies all dying and fighting to be fed. And perfectly willing to eat each other regardless of station or status.

"But then we stumbled on a brilliant plan down in the labs. And it was this, son. Just think… what if you got rid of everything you didn't really need to survive? Stripped it all down to just the brain. A brain jacked into a machine that can make it think it's a person, or several persons, all with any body it wishes, every life it ever imagined. Then what use was a meat bag called a body? Enough protein could be manufactured to keep everyone minimally alive if everyone were just *brain*. Reach the next world and we could find more protein while living wonderful lives inside the Pantheon's simulations. Lives where we were the hero, the lover, the gambler who always won. So, as I've said… you've been through all that before, Crometheus. This is nothing new. You just forgot."

Medical machines buzz while the robot surgeons power up on dull hums and sub-aural whines. Like mosquitos in the jungle night.

"Now it's time for the next phase of the Uplift, son. And I'm glad you've made it this far," says Lusypher. Stepping once more into frame.

Crometheus's mind is still shrieking. Shrieking that he is just a brain. Except it only *wants* to shriek. The Abyssatrol won't let him actually shriek himself ragged. Still, he cut away his own body. A body that rocked seventy thousand on a summer night and made love to some unremembered girl who got brought backstage after almost every show. An incalculable number of backstage groupies in every city and town he ever played.

He once touched, and was touched.

He ate the finest foods. Felt the wind in his spiky blond hair as the hog beneath him blasted out across the desert at golden dawn with Holly Wood's slender tanned arms wrapped around his thin muscled waist.

None of that… will ever happen again.

Lusypher's face is right down next to his… brain. Whispering the truth he needs to believe.

"We had to do it. You… had to do it if we were going to make it this far."

He… Crometheus. He did this to himself.

"This is the next phase, son. We aren't inside the simulation of the Pantheon anymore. This is my new body, Crometheus. It's real. And it's time. Time for you to get yours. Time to upgrade."

Commander Zero leans into frame within the monitor.

"Perk of being an Eternal, Crometheus. We're the first to try out the new chassis. Welcome to the next step along the Path."

Gods: Chapter Twenty-Two

Crometheus could hear...

A heartbeat monitor. Steady and sure. Beneath his fingers, which was the first thing he could feel... with... he felt the sheets of the bed he was lying in.

His fingers?

The sheet was rough. Almost unpleasant. But it was real, and in that instant he realized everything he'd felt since the shedding... all of everything in all those lives inside the simulation... had been false on some level compared to what he was experiencing right now.

Like the old VR worlds of first-era video games. Fun and amazing... but still very much distant from actual real reality. And when you really thought about it, after the fact, a lot less was offered than real actual life gave you on the average daily basis. Even the ancient VR color palettes had paled in comparison to any real day in real life.

This feeling of the sheet beneath his fingers was like that realness of real life as it had been long ago before the shedding. Real. Even in its starched and scratchy unpleasantness. It was real.

"They've done it," was Crometheus's first thought. "They've found a way to put us back in our bodies again.

Found a way to do what we had to give up for eternal life. And survival."

"Not completely correct," intoned Maestro within the vast empty and very pleasant space of Crometheus's mind. Just as the voice of the AI had always been since the shedding. Since the mysterious super-intelligent AI had come forward to administer the colony ship *Pantheon* so that it might make it beyond its present difficulties back then. And in time, the AI would run the Pantheon itself. "But close enough, Master Cro. Since the Eternals deal in… reality… shall we say… to be perfectly correct… it's not your old body they've put you back into, but a completely brand-new, vat-grown… model, they've 'put you back into.' Designed with the latest enhancements and technology. Your original body was reclaimed for the greater good during flight between Cappella Three and Saurus Six. To be specific. Generally speaking. We needed the old meat bag for calories if we were going to make it. For the greater good and all. You know how those things go."

Maestro was still in his head. But the body he was beginning to feel with, the body resting on a rather hard bed and rough sheets… was real. As real as his body had been back during the rock god glory days of past Earth. And it felt. It could *feel*. There was no numbness, or pain, or anything like all the old injuries and bad health that had preceded the rejuvenation and longevity treatments they had taken during the early years on the Pantheon when they'd made fantastic medical leaps while hauling through sublight for their future utopia.

He'd been made "young" again. He had been a youth back then, too, for all practical purposes, but nothing in those treatments had ever made him feel like this. Nothing. And of course when they'd all begun to starve out there in the stellar dark, well then, young bodies, no matter how they felt, had to go if they were to survive.

Calories.

But...

Feeling, really *feeling* something, being able to touch it... was simply fantastic.

Wonder sprang anew with each new second of rediscovered sensation. Yet for some reason Crometheus couldn't yet see. Not at all. He felt his physical eyes, the eyelids, actually opening. Then closing. Blinking. But he could see nothing.

"I can tell from your movements, Master Crometheus, that you are attempting to use your vision capabilities," noted Maestro. "Those upgrades are currently offline due to a suite of neural blockers we've put in place. We didn't want to overload your brain with too much all at once. If you're ready to see I can restore version. Would you like to see now?"

"Yes," whispered Crometheus breathily.

"All right then... I'm flooding your optical nerves and interfaces with antimorph first to remove the barriers. Then... here it comes. It should take just a few seconds. I encourage you to understand that what has taken places is to be considered an upgrade over your initial visual perception system. There have been reports of some side effects, but over the long term the system will stabilize and you'll get used to it. Plus we'll be able to upgrade as we go. I'm most sure of it. Ah… what do you see now?"

At first all Crometheus could see were clouds. Mist shifting across his field of vision. It made him feel like he was back in the swamp with Jim Stepp. Following a brush-laden trail that swallowed itself along sandy courses where the air was cool and there were small unseen insects constantly buzzing. But all that had taken places inside the simulated worlds of the Pantheon. Inside his personal secret reality, locked away from the main and for his mind only. The Persistent Contrived Realities Project, or what they'd come to substitute for reality for hundreds of years, or however long they'd been out there in deep space, aboard the colony ship *Pantheon* at a sub-light crawl between worlds, had been their only experience. But now he was hearing. Really hearing noise. With ears. *His* ears. He could tell the difference. It wasn't just some comm channel that was all too clear, sound designed and layered for the perfect more-than-lifelike experience every time. This was real. And though it was sound, it could be… *felt*. That's how real it was.

He could tell from what he was hearing that he was in some kind of room with medical equipment constantly beeping and humming. Ticking and pulsing. Inhaling and exhaling. Even the small chitter of computers processing data and uploading it to some external monitoring system, a sound so small it could be ignored by even the subconscious, he heard it. And the hearing of it was like some small but necessary part of a grand symphony. To him.

He saw his HUD as the mist cleared from his vision. His in-game HUD. It wasn't just part of the armor he was wearing, or the piece of equipment he was flying or riding in… it was interfaced with his actual mind. A message flashed front and center. It was a menu screen regarding *Hearing Sensory System Management*.

The menu was asking him if he'd like to increase his hearing to local surroundings radar-level detection level, or remain at normal Uplifted range. There were other menus that included such options as explosives diagnostic, detection source, and tracking identification. And even Animal Heartbeat Pulse Measurement for Interrogation Procedures.

"Why am I still seeing… the heads-up display?"

"Ah!" erupted Maestro. "The HUD. Of course, that's what most ask once you get a look with your new eyes. Well, not to worry, young Master Cro, you can disable that when you're not serving in combat operations. But the HUD is now a part of your brain instead of being dedicated to the particular system or chassis you were operating. Through your HUD you will be able to manage equipment and armor systems; it syncs in seconds. Or manage your own life systems. For instance, this is a fun one. Let me take control for a second…"

A series of menus raced across Crometheus's HUD. Fast. Like shooting-star fast. Menus and options were clicked off or on. Parameters set. Things opened and closed in sudden frenetic blurs in which something must've been accomplished by the super-genius-level artificial intelligence known as Maestro.

"Don't worry, with time you'll get faster at working through your own interface. Though not as fast as me. I designed the system, so I know my way around quite handily, Master Cro."

Silence as more menus popped up and disappeared.

Then finally...

"You can play dead!" said Maestro.

The heart monitor within the medical suite flatlined all of a sudden. Crometheus felt his heart just... stop. He freaked out as he heard his blood pushing lethargically through his arteries like junky sludge before coming to a standstill.

He was dying. That much was clear.

No... he was already dead.

He couldn't move a muscle and he felt nothing.

"Don't worry, young master," whispered Maestro as though the two of them were hiding from some giant prowler in a game of lethal hide-and-seek. "You have a small backup battery inside you that can provide emergency power and bare minimum life support for up to thirty-six hours. But to the outside galaxy... to all appearances you are dead and so would appear to any human... er, rather, *Animal* soldiers. Even their medical personnel. In reality you can restart your life systems by accessing this menu..."

A menu popped up inside Crometheus's HUD.

"Just click *reboot*."

Crometheus thought about clicking reboot. And within the HUD's ghostly blue menu, he did.

At once his heart began to pump and his blood resumed its flow. Feeling came back to his extremities. A thousand pins and needles overwhelmed him all at once.

"We designed this function for infiltration operations during the asymmetrical phases of our coming campaigns against the Animals across all their worlds. Imagine, Master Cro, the Animals thinking they've achieved a great victory. They defeated us in battle, leaving our beaten new bodies on the field, unguarded. Some of those they thought dead are brought within their defenses for study; others are left unsupervised as nothing more than corpses. And within hours those Uplifted marines left for dead are running around behind enemy lines as the opposing force presses on toward some new perceived objective we're leading them toward. A trap, or an ambush. Meanwhile our 'dead' are destroying command and communication elements and generally slaughtering the defenseless and wounded often found behind enemy lines. Isn't that glorious, my boy? Mass extermination with minimal resistance parameters! It's complete genocide!"

Crometheus coughed as his lungs began to breathe once more.

He'd never thought about breathing. Not in all those years inside the Pantheon. And maybe the shedding process had removed his focus on such an activity now that it had no longer been needed. But here he was... breathing. He could do nothing but continue to marvel at the rise and fall of his own chest. It was an alien thing, and each time it began again he wondered if it would repeat the next time.

And it did just that.

Again, and again.

Amazing. The act of breathing was stunning when you really noticed it. It's just that you never really stopped to think about it much.

The horror of that long-ago moment when they skinned his mind of his old body faded like some bad dream best forgotten in the golden light of a new summer morning. That moment after he'd been caught and tortured, and then watched as his mind was broken… when they gave him the privilege of undergoing the shedding. And it *had* been a privilege. Those who did went on to survive. To go on he would have to let go… of his body.

But now… now he had something back that he thought he would never have again. A body. He'd once had to accept that his human shell was gone forever. Then he had to understand that meant never having a body again. Then he threw himself deep into the work of the Pantheon if just to forget that he could never be… real again. Accepting his fate and focusing on a dream to forget what had been taken. That too had been part of survival.

"What am I now, Maestro?"

There was no delay in the reply. It came as though the question had been expected, and Crometheus wondered if everyone who'd gone through this process… the receiving of a new body… if all those before had all followed the same pattern of asking the same questions as their minds, coming out of whatever Frankensteinian surgery Maestro and whoever else involved had cooked up, followed some algorithmically predicted pattern of questions to keep their sanity in check. Everyone predictably arriving at the same place sooner rather than later. Asking their same lawyerly questions about their current state of bodily affairs, and daring to think of the future as it had now just been reshaped.

"You are, technically, a cybernetic organism," said Maestro within Crometheus's mind. "You are composed of mostly genetically modified biodegradable material with a shelf life well beyond the original chassis, your human body, upon which this model was based... the Animal frame as it were. But you've also been integrated with machine parts, such as the microframe processor currently running your HUD, and other advanced combat systems. Your muscular system is rated to lift one ton, but with an adrenal boost micro-pump you can go as high as two tons, if needed. Your enhanced nano-ceramic bone structure can withstand impacts that would have broken the bones of your old fragile body, and is capable of a certain amount of limited nano-repair at the molecular level. All your major organs can also self-repair, and of course no sustained injury... let's say to your purification system, respiratory system, lymphatic system... will be fatal. That's not to say that you can't be crushed to a pulp or blown into several bits in the course of your duties as an Eternal... but you will not die from those injuries. As long as the brain survives you can be rebuilt several times over, either by us, or, given enough time... yourself. Just like the combat chassis you occupied after the shedding. This body is as strong as the armor system you occupied during the battle of New Vega. Stronger even."

An uncalled-for whistle erupted from Crometheus's lips, and he began to laugh uncontrollably. He was still lying in the bed, and its frame shook with his happily delirious convulsions. He felt endorphins flooding his system in a way the Pantheon had never been able to reproduce. He felt alive. He felt young forever. And he could be rebuilt time and time again and again.

Eternal youth.

Immortality.

A god at last.

"But we wouldn't just send you into battle naked as a... jaybird, I believe is the old Animal expression. Wait, Master Cro, until you see the new armor we've prepared for the first assault on Spilursa."

Crometheus's mind suddenly flashed on Miss Cyber Saigon and the bacchanal of Sin City. And specifically their own exertions within the Olympus suite. Was that all gone? Was that lost now? Only available to those still plugged into the life racks as a brain only? Was he cut off from the Pantheon? He felt his body break out all at once into a cold-turkey heroin junkie sweat.

"Will I still..." He hesitated. Did he even want to go back in there? To Sin City. The drugs. All the other pleasure realities he'd spent so many debaucherous years of his existence in during the long flight times to other worlds.

Did he?

He needed to. Needed to like a junkie needs the next fix. Nothing scarier than cold turkey, Bad Old Self hooted from the side of the midnight barn. Jug in hand and gustily slurping from it beneath the moonlight. Might as well not quit. Death is easier... right?

"I anticipate that you're are indeed wondering, Master Cro, if you can still interface with the Pantheon. The answer is both no, and yes. *No* as of this moment because we are conducting a secret operation against the rest of the Uplifted. And then, once we return from Spilursa... *yes.* In fact, it will be highly encouraged so that the Eternals might spread and download the Unity Virus across the rest of the Uplifted tribes. But all that will be explained in your Eternal training program uploads where we will introduce you to your new advanced armor and weapons systems. Are you ready to begin now, Master Cro?"

Crometheus swallowed. His mouth was bone-dust dry.

And that too was amazing. And wonderful in its own way. Even fear tasted good.

What would it be like? he wondered. What would it be like to feel Miss Cyber Saigon's long painted fingernails on his chest once again? But for real. Not just what the Pantheon was telling him to feel. Pleasure. Always pleasure of course, unless they needed you to feel pain. And then you'd feel that in ways you never knew it was possible to feel such a thing. But never mind the end user agreement and all the fine print... what would it really be like? To feel her.

And what about all the secret places he'd kept from the Pantheon? And Maestro. Lazer Command. They'd made him burn it down. Symbolically delete it. But could he rebuild it? Or had this latest upgrade just given them total control over everything? Like when Maestro had taken over not just his HUD but his mind, running through menus at the speed of light. Beyond Crometheus's comprehension. Like he was being taken by some card shark at three-card monte along the streets of New York City. That had probably been done by Maestro not merely to show him that he could perform tricks like play dead, but to make him aware that they, that Maestro, could take control of him at any time that they, that he, wished. Chose to. Needed to.

And… who were the "they" this time around? Commander Zero and Lusypher. Were there more? Did the cabal lead to the Xanadu Tower? That was the question that had never been answered in all these long stellar crossings from one world to the next. From one invasion to the next. From Reno to Rome. Who were "they"?

Who was really in charge all along?

Who was the real *they* who was really in charge of this too-long voyage into the future? And where had they been headed all along?

Crometheus wondered about that. Wondered about all those layers within layers of enigmas wrapped in riddles that were probably far more complex than just an onion. All those conspiracies that might just be one large conspiracy that had been there all along. Playing them. Guiding the whole show of a mass exodus from Earth of several thousand utopia seekers, tribalized, to this ultimate conclusion of total domination in the final war for all the marbles of the galaxy. For control of everything and the shape it would take as the future unfolded. Animal, or Savage.

And what, he thought suddenly… what of her?

Would she be waiting for him just as she always was?

At the end.

Holly Wood.

"Cro?" prompted the AI.

"Yes, Maestro."

"Again, my algorithms are predicting exactly what you're thinking about right now. With a ninety-eight-point-six-percent probability of being correct, we are estimating that you are currently thinking about the training you are about to undergo. The difficulty level, specifically. The time it will take. And what are the repercussions for failure with respect to the cabal. Is that correct, Master Crometheus?"

He was safe. His secret worlds, the ones he would build again, and the ones he would build anew… were safe from them. Unguessed at. Hidden from view.

"Yes, Maestro. That's correct. I'm very excited about what comes next. In fact… I can hardly wait."

Gods:
Chapter Twenty-Three

"Sixty seconds to atmospheric insertion!" cried the Uplifted pilot over the static-washed comm of the captured Animal freighter. Re-entry turbulence was already incredibly violent as super-heated oxygen began to scream across the falling ship's hull.

"Combat mission filters in place, Eternals!" shouted Commander Zero from the front of the lead assault stick. Her command-indicated mission downloads were in place. A second later Crometheus had his assignment, lane, and objectives for the operation. The neural processor that had been synced with his new body and brain made the transfer of information near instantaneous; it was downloaded, unpacked, and installed within his brain in the blink of an eye. His mind accepted all this as though it were his own cognition. Six months of intensive training in everything from commando assault techniques to demolitions training had been acquired in the same fashion. All of the best training pirated from the most elite military training schools Uplifted Intel had been able to access by subterfuge and theft from the militaries of the Coalition worlds. Spilursan Ranger CQB. Britannian Sapper School. Espanian Indirect Fire Support Courses. Umorian Asymmetrical

Warfare Operations. All of it, along with pro athlete muscle memory sports conditioning and techniques, had been downloaded into each Eternal, post-body acquisition surgery. All of it within two quick minutes, including specializations in training-specific tasks, after Maestro had asked each of them if they were "ready to proceed."

Crometheus had been assigned to a thirty-person forward assault squad within the Eternal force now inbound on Spilursa's northern pole. The objective was tagged by the Animals as Ice Station Hades.

"Instituting in-game parameters to keep everyone motivated!" called out Zero as the turbulent atmospheric effects across the freighter's hull began to subside.

The Eternals were no longer synced with the main body of Pantheon forces. Maestro had them officially routed as attached to another Uplifted tribe intent on taking some new world. For the moment the small yet elite team was operating on its own, outside the collective of the Path, a rogue detachment intent on staging a palace coup. Yet Maestro and the Eternals' command staff believed that keeping the Pantheon's "in-game" filters for combat would help smooth out some of the body-brain sync problems the Eternals were currently experiencing. As Uplifted marines they'd fought several wars in a massive online combat arena that awarded them points, scores, and kill streaks in order to keep the battle, or game, rolling. Or such had been their perception, and thereby their truth. In another reality, one without filters, their physical frames had fought physical enemies in real combat. That other reality had been the same reality, with different brushstrokes applied, an artist's rendering, each reality as real as the other, one in body, one in brain, but the perceptions... different.

Perception is everything.

So now, even though the Eternals were fully armored and combat-capable, physically perfect and trained in accordance with the best special forces units of the Animal worlds, there were still some interfacing problems that needed to be ironed out. Problems that ranged from slight headaches to occasional sync drops in at least thirty percent of the combat force currently smashing its way through Spilursa's upper atmosphere, inbound on Objective Hades. Even full-blown psychosis had manifested in just under five percent of the new Eternals. This had been dealt with. Those troops experiencing dangerous levels of psychosis had been assigned to a shock trooper element that would be coming in via orbital drop. They would contribute to the cause by drawing the majority of defensive fire coming from the three battalions of Spilursan infantry currently defending Ice Station Hades, the Spilursans' state-of-the-art cloud storage farm secreted in the vast polar nether of that harsh and unforgiving world. One hundred percent casualties were expected, according to Maestro, among the shock troopers. So the loss of those suffering psychosis affliction was mitigated to some extent. They would have had to have been put down either way, Maestro had assured command.

And this was mere secondary diversion. The primary attack came from the bulk of the Eternal force now diving through the atmosphere at dangerous speed aboard the captured Animal freighter. Their danger-fast velocity was a requirement of this operation and the only way success could be achieved.

"Don't worry, Eternals!" said Maestro over the general comm. "Safety parameters for this vessel were designed for the weaker Animal frame. Obviously, no one encased in our advanced-reflex armor system, which you are currently kitted with, has anything to fear. Diverting forward deflector shields to maximum... please brace for severe impact!"

The starship, a captured freighter, had disappeared more than thirty years ago according to humanity's colonial ship registry as administered by United Worlds back at New Houston. The ship had gone overdue and then finally was declared missing out along the Spinward Drift of the Orion frontier, as it was then known. Unbeknownst to humanity, the crew of the freighter, the *Servia's Gamble*, had actually been captured by the Pantheon when they attempted to board the old lighthugger they'd found drifting in a dark system. Their unreported salvage operation quickly turned into a nightmare.

Captain Jane Servia had been in command of the scout commercial freighter operating along the Spin. Her first officer was killed in the boarding action, as were half the crew. The chief engineer was later devoured after winning six matches in the gladiatorial games held in Sin City's Pleasure Dome. Upon losing, the engineer's body was unhooked from the meat racks and sent to reclamation with a special reservation for Player Thorr, a former tech executive and early member of the Uplifted. A victory celebration, a re-creation of a Viking winter feast, in which some of the more choice cuts of the engineer were served specifically to Thorr, followed.

When the Savage invasion of the core worlds began in earnest, Captain Servia was still alive within underworld harems. Her failing body was in fact still hooked into the meat racks and would be consumed for nutrients a mere three days before the Legion's invasion of New Vega. Her mind, on the other hand… well, it could still be enjoyed as a plaything, whether she liked it or not.

Of course she'd gone mad long ago.

The *Servia's Gamble*, that long-ago captured scout freighter, was now being piloted exclusively by Maestro, as the Uplifted pilot had surrendered final descent control for maximum success during insertion into the area of operation. The ancient freighter was carrying a complement of over four hundred Eternals when it slammed into the icy waters of Spilursa's Northern Polar Sea beyond the Carson Archipelago. Three kilometers east of the Great Crater Lake that occupied the northernmost point on the globe of that world.

The downed ship sank quickly. A normal starship would have gone to pieces all across the surface of the ice-swollen sea, but the Uplifted engineers had refitted the ship with heavy-duty one-shot forward shields that boosted to max nanoseconds before impact, allowing the ship to smash through the surface of the lake and sink down into the midnight dark bottoms below. Now alarm bells rang out as the ship's old damage control lighting shifted on internally. External floodlights switched on as well as the ship drifted toward the rocky floor of the arctic sea, her engines and hull sending up steam and massive bubbles in the wake of their fall through the icy waters. Almost instantly the bulkheads were cracking and leaking, numerous hull breach alarms resounding through the upper decks and the vast cargo hold of the old refitted freighter.

All of this was according to plan. Of course.

"Remain locked in your racks until we come to rest on the ocean floor," cautioned Maestro to the Eternals, some of whom were already pinging to be released. "The floor is at a depth of two hundred meters. We are passing through one hundred meters. Stand by."

Crometheus ran through his section's assignment as the ship groaned titanically.

Egress Hull flashed across Crometheus's HUD the very instant the impact rumbled along the belly of the hull. One of the main landing gears suddenly collapsed and the ship sank down onto one side causing more bulkheads to give way and sending torrents of icy water rushing in to flood compromised sections.

Crometheus's mission was as follows…

Proceed along the seafloor to a passage in the pack ice at a depth of three hundred meters.

Infiltrate Great Crater Lake beyond the passage.

Assault and breach lower decks of Ice Station Hades in order to access the Spilursan R&D cloud in order to upload the Unity Virus. Hold the decks above the main reactor until the combined Uplifted fleet arrives in Spilursan atmosphere and official Grand Alliance combat operations begin.

But, known only to the Eternals... the entire combat operation against Spilursa was a ruse... within a ruse.

Officially the plan was for the combined Uplifted fleet of the Grand Alliance to attack another world, Espania, en masse. Just as it had New Vega. No less than five massive colony ships and their entire combat complements had been designated as a major strike force sent against that Animal world.

But the real attack would come against Spilursa.

Espania was just a feint.

Uplifted Command was hoping that the sudden appearance of a major fleet over the skies of Espania would draw reluctant Coalition forces into a battle there. But within hours the Uplifted fleet would jump away from Espania.

Destination: Spilursa.

But the ruse within a ruse came from the Eternals, who were not officially in play yet. Officially they were attached as a complement of Pantheon marines currently hitching a ride on the allied ship *Shang Ti* ready to participate in the official ground game against Spilursan military forces.

This secret operation, the strike against Objective Hades, wasn't even sanctioned by the official governing councils of the Pantheon, much less the Uplifted Command of the Grand Alliance. This gamble was coming solely from whoever was really calling the shots for the Eternals. Whether that was Lusypher, or Maestro, or some new cabal within the Xanadu Tower acting in its own interests, this was a play for power. Big time. This was a chance to introduce an info-plague, the Unity Virus, into the collected Uplifted forces soon to descend on Spilursa.

In other words, this was an attack not just on the Animals, but also against their own… the rest of the Uplifted tribes the Coalition called The Savages. The cyber-plague would enable control and influence, by a small faction, over the rest of its Uplifted allies. Over time it would predispose all affected Uplifted to the suggestions of a secret ruling council within the Pantheon.

The Eternals were the mighty iron fist of that cabal.

Hundreds of years of breaking, and then rewriting, the wills of its captured subjects, and even its own members, had given the Uplifted of the Pantheon a sophisticated level of mind control and will manipulation that would not be replicated by even the best latter-era Republic's finest psychological warfare programs.

Within hours now, a combined Uplifted force would take Ice Station Hades and its valuable storage cloud. A gem long coveted by all allied Uplifted tribes. On the cloud were all of Spilursa's best-kept technology secrets, including a new mass-produced hyperdrive capable of being fitted to smaller warships and freighters without the typical excessive space requirements. As of yet, the Uplifted, though they understood the hyperdrive, had no way to reliably mass-produce the device and balance it to a new ship design. At best they could only install captured tech on already made ships and hope for the best with each jump execution. Time and time again their best scientists warned them that this was a recipe for failure. A colony ship carrying upwards of a hundred thousand Uplifted could come apart within jump space in the blink of an eye. The loss would be total, and of course, catastrophic to Uplifted culture.

Really, any loss to the slowly amalgamating Uplifted tribes would be devastating when weighed against the greater numbers of the hyperdrive-connected worlds of their descendants and predecessors. Even when combined into a massive stellar nation, the Uplifted would still be outnumbered by the combined, at that time, galactic population of the human colonies.

If there was one thing the Animals did well, it was breed.

It was suspected that some of the Uplifted tribes did in fact possess stable mass-produced jump systems, or at least had captured such, but if they did, they refused to share their tech with the whole for purposes of reverse engineering. Spilursa, however... that was the chance for everyone to have access. Several Uplifted intelligence assets had confirmed that the specs were being held within the confines of the cloud guarded by Ice Station Hades. Along with a number of other great leaps forward in technology ranging from weaponry to energy production.

A raging debate among the governing councils of the Uplifted as to which tribe would have the honor, and trust, to take the coveted station, had ended in a combined forces group being assigned to the task. That group would come from the task force currently feinting an attack on Espania. They would arrive in eighteen hours, unaware that they were not, in fact, the first Uplifted to arrive. With no reason to suspect that a rogue element within the Xanadu Tower of the Pantheon had decided on a preemptive strike using the Eternals, and that after a successful infiltration by this, the Uplifted's premier combat force, the best the Pantheon could field, an electronic pathogen known as the Unity Virus had already been uploaded and hidden within the cloud.

And in the chaos of the arrival of the combined Uplifted force attacking the station and the military forces of Spilursa across the world, the Eternals would seamlessly mix in as the rest of the Uplifted raced to hack and access the already hacked and accessed servers.

In the end every tribe would be given, or would simply take, almost immediate access to everything within the cloud in a mad rush to acquire the new tech ahead of their allies. Even if that meant just by seconds. And in that madcap, headlong smash-and-grab, no one would notice the little something extra. The little something known as the Unity Virus, buried in the cloud and ready to infect and replicate with stealth and speed.

Crometheus heard the section bulkhead in his hold groan terrifically and cave in as a torrent of ice-cold seawater rushed through the crushed hull of the captured scout freighter and into the cargo section of the lower deck he and the forward assault team had been racked in. The water was a livid aquamarine blue and his onboard HUD temperature already indicated a temperature of one point eight Celsius. The reflex armor was rated far beyond the frozen temperature of the waters now rising around their chests.

Maestro released the installed restraining locks, freeing them to egress the crashed vessel. Eternals struggled upward and grabbed their carrying systems, shrugging into them as the water rose above their mirrored face visors.

Servia's Gamble had flown her last run and come to rest on the bottom of a frozen sea on a distant alien world, disgorging four hundred Eternals onto the almost lunar surface at the bottom of the arctic ocean. Compass headings and route navigation came to life in ghostly blue images within HUDs. Bone-white rock and featureless sands spread off in every direction, disappearing into a murky nether. Great undersea canyons fell into irretrievable abysses in those unseen compass headings they were not taking.

Falling into one of those meant no escape.

Teams, squads, and full platoons linked up into wedges and columns beneath the crumpled ruin of the sunken freighter, still shining its floodlights out across the murky bottoms. Soon they began their long march across the floor of the sea toward the ice passage. The access point that connected the Great Crater Lake at the top of this world to this lonely arctic sea.

Crometheus noted a download in his HUD as the floodlights of the freighter finally gave out, dropping everything in the deep ocean into a midnight blackness.

Gods:
Chapter Twenty-Four

Strong undersea currents pulled at the armored figures marching through the shadowy gloom. It was as if invisible winds were trying to shift the Eternal task force off course as they trudged toward the passage that tunneled beneath the ice shelf and into the Great Crater Lake at the top of doomed Spilursa.

The bottom of the ocean felt as barren as some lost world devoid of oxygen, or love, or even the gravitational embrace of some larger kinder stellar body. But it was not uninhabited. In the deeps of this undersea world, the Uplifted glimpsed the shadowy, almost mirage-like migrations of the giant snakewhales native to Spilursa. The leviathans passed like silent flocks of giant birds, undulating off into the nothingness and distant great sea canyons from which there was no return.

Even for one in Uplifted reflex armor.

Within the silence of their HUDs the Eternals heard these monsters making deep croonings as they passed by and then swam off into the dark.

There had been three armor malfunctions so far along the route to the objective. Armor integrity, at this crushing depth and temperature, was horribly revealed as some element of deliberate manufacture—not design flaw of course, assured Maestro—and three Eternals now lay in the forever embrace of their ruined armor, drowned and crushed and game-overed. Their waterproof equipment packs, carrying weapons, ammunition, and explosives, had been loaded onto the towed pallets being pulled by some teams. Ammunition and supplies would be redistributed at the objective, instructed Maestro, who acted as the unit's NCO.

Commander Zero was in charge, of course.

"Nearing the passage. It's going to get tight in there, Eternals," said Commander Zero. "So don't lose your marbles. Lead elements entering now."

Maestro had advised the commander that some of the Eternals were experiencing schismatic personality fractures due to the inherently claustrophobic nature of the underwater environment and looming ice canyon that would quickly turn into little more than a mere tight squeeze through the ice. No doubt the personality fractures were brought on also by the stress of cybernetic chassis integration... but the operations environment wasn't helping.

"I'm stabilizing them by rewarding them with achievement points," intoned Maestro quietly within her comm. "Some of the others are receiving messages of encouragement from the other Uplifted. Messages I am manufacturing as we speak, Commander. Social proof is an excellent means of stabilizing the ongoing faults. It should get them through the mission, or at least into the initial breach where numbers will provide a significant advantage during our attack. In the event I detect a full-blown psychotic break in which they might harm their fellow warriors, or jeopardize the mission goals, I have another, final option at my disposal."

Crometheus was unaware of this conversation and instead was squeezing in under the narrow shelf of almost ethereal blue ice in order to enter the underwater passage when just behind him, one of the other members of the advanced forward assault team stumbled. His armor suddenly malfunctioning. Near-frozen seawater flooded into Player Titanix's armor, causing an immediate heart attack. Maestro also disabled backup power, and so Titanix was dead, both physically and mentally. Which was what the Uplifted of the Pantheon called... game-overed.

Maestro had detected an impending psychotic break and felt it was best not to risk having that occur inside the passage. What with everyone carrying explosives and all. Who knew what someone not in their right mind might decide to get up to in such tight quarters beneath tons of ice.

The rigid body of the dead Eternal, animated and moving not thirty seconds ago, began to drift along with the swift undersea current trying to enter the ice passage along with the warriors.

Crometheus put out a hand to stabilize the body of his dead comrade while Commander Zero came over the comm.

"Player Crometheus... pull his pack. We need everything we can carry on to the objective. Let the body go. No one will ever find it down here."

The Eternals are not hampered by their dead.

To do so would be weak. As weak as the superstitious Animals and all their concerns about souls, religious ceremonies, and never leaving one of their own behind.

Simple sentiments for the simple-minded.

Crometheus hit the quick-releases on the equipment ruck as he held on to the dead man's drifting armor, fighting against the current's desire to carry it off under the fissures of the crushing ice. Downloaded muscle memory made the work of getting the ruck off and tethered to his own armor swift and simple for Crometheus to the point that he didn't even need to think too much about it during the process. Within two minutes the column now threading the narrow ice crevice under the massive shelf of glacial ice was underway again.

The body of Titanix, released, drifted off under the shelf and became stuck in a nook just a few feet to one side of the tunnel.

He'll stay there forever, thought Crometheus as he began to pull forward, fighting the jet stream current at his back, forcing his mind not think about how many tons of ice they were all crossing under. One sea quake and they could all be crushed in an instant. No amount of rated armor, or next-generation cybernetic chassis, could do anything about that. Worst-case scenario... they would be pinned and immobile waiting for the internal battery to run out so that they could be game-overed. That is, if they survived the panic and claustrophobia that would no doubt come for them. Turning their minds into drooling fear-struck puddles of gibbering mayhem.

The one thing you learn as an Uplifted is that the mind is very powerful. It can work for you, and it can definitely work against you.

You decide which way that's going to go. And it's best to decide early on and stay ahead of the carnival of madness the un-governed mind can choose to attend.

But what unfolded next, as the cavern began to wind its way through the giant sheets of ice, was the most beautiful thing Crometheus had ever seen in all of his very long lives. The tunnel wasn't much of a tunnel in the standard sense. It was really more of an accidental passage through the ice formed by two sections of the glacier not quite coming together. Found by underwater recon drones and identified as a possible assault axis point on Ice Station Hades. No one had actually been through this passage before.

It was simply and marvelously beautiful. Otherworldly, and absolutely.

Still, hours of march soon began to seem like forever, despite Maestro's constant download of achievement points. There was no other world to retreat into here. Nothing but the deep hum and swish of the ocean's cold currents swirling past jagged yet beautiful walls of sheer ice and over the ominous shadows of other armored figures in the gloom ahead. Above were sudden cathedrals of climbing ice, or sculptures of fantastic frozen giants and strange beasts, or other things the mind imagines within freezing water sculptures in the dark of ancient oceans on alien worlds.

The whole place was like a hidden mansion of icy wonders never seen in probably the entirety of the galaxy's history.

It was almost humbling.

Other Eternals died. More armor failed. But the failures in time became less, and in the end, as the narrow crevice opened up into the wide panorama of the massive lake at the top of the world, as seen from the bottom of it, the strike force of Uplifted Eternals was still at eighty percent unit strength as they closed on their target objective.

The mission grid fell over their collective HUDs. Three kilometers forward of the crack they'd just emerged from on the floor of the lake, lay Ice Station Hades. In the tactical overlay they could see its shape digitally rendered by radar augmentation.

It looked like an upside-down wedding cake, with its top, the pinnacle of the cake, resting on the floor of the ocean.

Within the HUD, massive ghostly blue arrows swept forward from their egress point and fanned out into three wedges. Assignments were broken down and unit tags came online once more. All three masses of the Eternal strike force were to converge on what was being identified as a main geothermal core tap that provided energy to the mostly underwater cloud server facility.

"We do not expect this entrance to be defended," intoned Commander Zero over the comm, "but response will be swift once the attack is underway. The bulk of their forces are located up along the receiving docks and landing platforms and they'll be responding to the shock troopers who are ready to drop on my command. So move fast and take as many of the lower levels as you can, Eternals, before they organize a response."

For the next hour, like silent sentinels, the three wedges of Eternals moved through the underwater gloom toward the objective, undetected.

The lead scout clan, followed by a group of combat engineers with reflex armor systems suited to that sort of breaching work, were the first to rise over the last underwater dune and see within the very bowl of the lake the massive structure of the ice station rising up and expanding out over their upward-looking mirrored helmets. Some looked up in awe, others continued forward, intent on the coming breach.

Up there, in the depths above, the whole spectacle of this massive, multi-tiered, luminescent structure rising up over their assault inspired both awe and vertigo. Platform lights and rotating cylinders gave it the appearance of some kind of bizarre carousel of many layers, and its sheer size was nothing short of impressive.

Bad Thought, corrected Maestro gently. "Nothing the Animals have ever produced will match our glory and brilliance once we're free of their infestation. Once we're free to really create."

Bad Thought.
Bad Thought.
Bad Thought.

Already, in the blue-hued gloom of the lake, the cutting torches of the engineers, forward of the assault teams, were ablaze with bright fury as they cut a breach point into the base of the upside-down sunken wedding-cake fortress of Ice Station Hades.

"Breach in progress," said Player Cerebruz, the Eternal running the scout clan. A minute later the commander for the first wedge, forward assault team, gave the order to move into place for breach.

The other Eternals around Crometheus stacked into a column and trundled through the dense water at the bottom of the lake as fast as they could, heading for the opening that had been made into the central cylinder of the server fortress's base. Perhaps the engineers had been able to bypass any security sensors... perhaps not.

Crometheus knew that this was when their attack was the most vulnerable. They had no weapons; everything was stored inside waterproof carrying systems or palletized on the sleds. If the fortress wanted to...

On instinct alone he looked up. Like some pro tip had suddenly popped into his subconscious.

Falling through the gloom above were shadowy canisters the size of large dogs. Drifting down through the depths rather lazily. Tumbling end over end. They were falling down in what looked like a semicircle. Silhouettes passing in front of the lights and sensors of the upside-down wedding-cake base in the background.

The instinct that had caused him to look up, visualizing a weapon the Animals would surely have ready, but not being able to bring a name along with it, now ordered him to take charge in that same dangling commitment instant.

"Forward assault, move out for the entrance! Now! Double time!" Then over the general comm he shouted, "We're under attack!"

The first depth charge landed on the sandy bottom not ten meters in front of the second wedge. It came to rest like nothing more than a mere garbage can that had drifted down from the top of the frozen lake and landed on the desolate bottom below. By chance. By accident. Not intended to wound, maim, or harm.

Then it violently detonated at a velocity of roughly six thousand meters per second, reduced because of the underwater atmosphere it was being exploded within, at a release point of four hundred megajoules of dynamic energy.

Fortunately, the underwater explosion itself was rather contained. It looked as though a genie suddenly made of bubbles had erupted into sudden life just in front of the approaching wedge's point man. The Eternals farther back saw the point man blown off his boots and back toward them in the sand. They saw this in the same instant they were hit by a hydraulic shock wave that crumpled their armor systems like crushed beer cans. Devastating them instantly as integrity failed. Fifty Eternals were game-overed in a single moment.

Those farther back were blown surface-ward while warning bells and alarms rang in their armor and across the comm. The reflex armor's smart systems tried to control the damage, saving many, and their augmented bodies did what they could to save as much of the new chassis as possible while assigning brain protection the highest priority.

Other depth charges landed on the distant drifting lunar bottom of the high arctic lakebed, exploding and sending sand and rock debris sweeping in slow underwater motion out across the other approaching combat wedges.

One explosion tore a palletized sled to shreds, actually scoring a direct hit and sending shrapnel, like direct-fire torpedoes, streaking bubbles through the water and into the nearest Eternals. In response Crometheus muttered darkly, "That's *their* problem," not realizing he was talking to himself over the general comm until he finished the last part of his non-empathetic statement, meant solely to drive himself forward in the moment of overwhelming fear he was now experiencing.

A fear that he would die at the bottom of this frozen lake. His new body ruined. His mind screaming for help that would never come. His dreams of becoming a god… just dreams and nothing more. All of it for nothing.

"Forward and make problems for everything in front of us!" he screamed. "Ruin them, Eternals!"

Others within the assault force whooped and jeered, almost breathlessly, nervously, as he uttered this last bit. And then they were all surging into the breach. Pushing to survive. Intent on murdering everyone within.

It was tight beyond the still-glowing cut of the breach. The area they'd cut into was some kind of piping and energy conduit transfer. Temperatures within the surrounding water spiked, and someone commented that this was because the base was running a geothermal energy tap into the core of the world.

More bombs fell along the sunken sands behind them, devastating whatever portion of the attack force was not yet at the breach point.

An engineer who didn't possess cutting tools but was equipped with a bulkier armor system that was running a number of tactical processors and function interface tools along the gauntlets was busy hacking an industrial airlock to a maintenance vehicle garage for this level. Most likely used for the station personnel that performed work on this deepest level along the outside of the base.

"Get it open!" shouted Crometheus as he pushed forward through the crowded stack of Eternals within the tight space.

"Can't!" replied Player Hephastor. "We've got to wait for decompression on the other side."

Another explosion rocked the outside of the base. Maestro came over the comm, his voice calm and reassuring despite the thunder and death all around them. "Continue with your assault lane and secure your objectives, Eternals. The plan is still in effect."

Crometheus knew they needed to get away from the depth charges. Even here within the breach the pounding from the hydraulic shock waves resulting from the explosions was setting off armor integrity alarms and causing minor faults within the systems that were being handled by the onboard AI.

They couldn't stand up to too much more of this.

Studying the control panel the engineer was hacking, Crometheus saw the U-shaped bar that manually started the process of opening the garage. The engineer had already overridden the safety protocols. Hopefully that would be enough.

Without comment Crometheus slammed his gauntlet onto the hazard-yellow bar and pushed it into the open position.

The blast door opened into atmosphere and sucked the armored Eternals right through an airlock, the semi-hacked hatches open on both sides simultaneously against all sane tenets of design safety and protocol, into a vast garage on a sudden typhoon of ice-cold water that instantly began filling the lowest-level maintenance deck.

Surprised Animal defenders and tech crew, armed and waiting to repel, were swept away and then smashed into the far walls and bulkheads of a garage filled with racked submersibles, their bodies already half-frozen by the icy water. Their faces held expressions of pure horror as the bitingly cold lake water grabbed hold of their cardiovascular systems, shocking them to death well before their ice-stiff bodies rammed into the walls and were pinned against them like so much discarded flotsam in a flood.

Even the Eternals themselves were fighting for something to grab hold of as they were dragged past underwater maintenance vehicles and swept into offices and maintenance lockers, smashing into and being smashed by everything as the entire level filled with water.

The assault was underway.

Gods:
Chapter Twenty-Five

The forward assault team was the first into the secondary airlock that would lead deeper into the base.

"You're in command of the forward teams, Crometheus!" ordered Commander Zero over the comm. She was staying behind to organize what remained of the scattered assault force still on the lake bed and get them cycled into the other airlocks across the flooded lower levels.

"Can do!" replied Crometheus as the water drained rapidly out of the airlock he and the rest of the team had secured. Forward Assault was now down to twelve players, besides himself, and the sensors embedded within their armor were already picking up multiple Animal hostiles converging on the level they were now storming.

"What are we expecting on the other side? Maestro's not talking back right now!" chattered some nervous player over the assault team comm.

"Spilursan Defense Forces," boomed a player tagged Tiamatus. "Pretty good. Highly motivated. Maybe the best the Animals have got to throw at us as of this moment. But we can handle them, brothers and sisters. Stay together and concentrate your fire on my lead."

Though Tiamatus knew Crometheus had been assigned squad god, slang for the leader of any Uplifted combat small unit, it looked as though he was trying to take charge and earn some glory along with a few extra achievement points.

Crometheus had seen other leaders within the Uplifted game-over a player from behind, and there wasn't any fallout from it. Nothing was off the table if you were trying to do everything you could to make it up to the next step on the Path. But there were too many enemies swarming down the underwater base to start offlining allies right now. So Crometheus let it ride and went to the comm.

"Shoot, move, and communicate. First priority is to hold this level so the rest can get through and link up with their teams. Once we're together we can proceed to the next line inside the base."

The water had drained from the overridden airlock and now fresh air was being pumped in. Over the HUD the armor ran a background diagnostic check while everyone bent to their carrying systems and unlimbered their packed weapons from within waterproof rucks.

Finally, thought Crometheus, as he pulled his weapon out and ran a quick systems check. They'd been near defenseless during their long march across the haunting seafloor. Now they had weapons again, and there was something comforting in that. Something to fight with. And he was getting his first chance to use, in real time, the specialized Eternal weapon system. He'd trained on it extensively in the download sim, which equated to over six months' time of handling and proficiency within his current muscle memory, but he'd never fired it in real time.

And now it was finally time to rock and roll.

Live concerts are always the best.

Bad Old Self nodded knowingly from some shadowy place in his mind.

The Eternals referred to their new weapon system as the "sewing machine"—informally, of course. Its official designation was the MK-1000. A ribbon rifle. Based on a design used by some of old Earth's shock troops back during the Plague Riots of the planet's last years. It fired five rounds at once along a five-barreled bore that used electromagnetic actuators to propel the munitions forward at speeds of two thousand five hundred miles per hour, according to the old reckonings. The rounds were caseless six-point-five-millimeter ammunition that came in belt-fed stacks. When fired, the powerful and terrible weapon emitted a steady stream of hissing electrical snaps, much like a sewing machine stitching, as it violently tore everything apart it was aimed at for as long as the trigger was pulled. The blur of destruction it created within its tight cone of fire was very satisfying. Crometheus had felt all kinds of positive reinforcement while simming with it against overwhelming adversary bots.

But still… live shows were the best.

You got that right, boy, hooted Bad Old Self.

"Follow me, Eternals!" thundered Tiamatus arrogantly as the airlock's blast door scissored open on the main level. A second later a Spilursan heavy automatic pulse gun saved Crometheus the work of shooting the obnoxious boor Tiamatus in the back at some future opportune moment, as its fusillade of incoming fire ventilated his fellow Eternal with multiple hits.

Crometheus was just holstering both the fifty-cal Automags he'd taken from loadout into tactical holsters on his armor-plated hips. Other Eternals hugged wall within the airlock and returned fire. The armor's sensory systems were tagging at least two squads of Spilursan defenders, annotating their weapon types for user edification.

Tiamatus was still being riddled with incoming direct fire, his body rag-dolling from each hit as pulse rounds penetrated armor and ricocheted internally. Strong enough to penetrate but not exit. The giant dead Eternal somehow seemed incapable of falling down even in the face of overwhelming firepower.

Crometheus watched all this in a languid syrup of thought his mind could turn time into despite the fury and relentlessness of real-time progress. Then he surged forward and grabbed Tiamatus's jerking body for a meat shield. Crouching behind the crumbling armored form and holding out the ribbon gun from beneath the smashed arm of his would-be successor, he returned fire on the heavy gunner forming the base of fire for the Animals coming at them.

A quick fusillade of six-point-fives tore the enemy heavy gunner to shreds, and suddenly the battle was theirs. Just like that it shifted and within seconds his fellow Eternals were switching over to the indirect targeting systems on their rifles as they covered, holding out their weapons to engage and fire. Dumping on full auto using the HUD's targeting abilities to aim at their covering targets.

Lightly armored Spilursan Animals were targeted in the head where possible, five shots apiece, their helmeted skulls coming apart in explosions of red spray and flying gray matter. Those Animals who made the mistake of having any other portion of their bodies exposed—chests covered by bulletproof vests, shins and forearms protected by olive-green Kevlar, or even bare flesh crawling with spiraling tattoos and credos of promised death before dishonor—had those portions, too, slammed by five incoming, all at once, heavy-caliber rounds moving at three times the speed of sound. Each on-target burst of fire from the Eternals was like a swarm of angry hornets ripping into the Animal soldiers. The sounds of discharge and sonic travel came after the damage was done.

The first line of Animal resistance collapsed within a minute of first contact. But already more Animal troops were cycling in, eager to have at a foe they had no intelligence data on. Coalition command traffic indicated only that there had been a breach in a place they'd least expected an attack to come from. Forces were responding pell-mell. For the moment.

The battle isn't won yet, thought Crometheus, as he advanced deeper into the level, fellow Eternals at his sides, massacring defenders by the score.

Gods:
Chapter Twenty-Six

Two hours into the fight and the Spilursan military had gotten itself organized and was bringing numbers to bear. The Eternals were suffering casualties now, but they were still advancing toward the core access point on level nine.

In the first hour of heavy fighting the gains made by the forward assault team had been particularly significant. But everything had almost come to a screaming halt when the Animal defenders flooded level three. The move had been a desperate one by the on-site enemy commander to slow the swift advance of the attacking force. Or so Crometheus noted when the blast doors suddenly sealed shut and the waters flooded in, right into the midst of what had been a raging firefight within the refrigeration coils that cooled the main plasma conduit feeds to the powerful network core.

The enemy commander had sacrificed his own, just to delay the enemy.

They were desperate.

Within moments the battle ground to a halt as the arctic-cold lake waters rushed in, swirling across the almost alien-sculpted ceramic coils that bled off the fortress's heat. Some of the Animal defenders escaped through emergency hatches, apparently alerted to the plan in the moment before all hell broke loose, but many were carried away into this whitewater maelstrom.

This maneuver wouldn't stop the Eternals in their armored weapon systems... but it would affect their firearms. As the rising waters swirled about the power coils, electrical discharges shot forth with powerful *snaps* and *booms*, and Crometheus's deadly new rifle malfunctioned and went offline within the HUD. He discarded the ruined weapon and waded through the torrent for all he was worth for an enemy-held blast door.

"Player Crometheus, status update! We're having networking problems down here!" It was Commander Zero, and while she wasn't freaking out, there was definitely a strident tone in her voice that belied the fact that not everything was going according to plan so far.

"Pushing forward," replied Crometheus, starting to deliver his sitrep. "This level now submerged. Our 1000s are offline. Switching to sidearms."

"I need a beachhead on level four," shouted Commander Zero over a background of damage control klaxons shrieking for attention. "We're hacking the pumps and should have three cleared in twenty minutes. We can push forward more weapons systems if you're still holding."

"Roger, can do!" acknowledged Crometheus.

He had linked up with an Eternal tagged Heratix. Now submerged on level three, their armor protecting them from the violent electrical displays that turned the red floodlights to blue and then back again, they were swimming up through the discharging coils to reach a high blast door that had been sealed off. A maintenance access door, the kind work crews probably used up in the ductworks to effect repairs. Chances were, both Crometheus and Heratix were hoping, it wouldn't be a primary focus of the evolving Animal defenses. They might be able to get into the maintenance shafts and flank the next level's defenders.

They pushed past the flotsam of ruined and free-floating debris within the underwater world the level had become. Animal corpses, frozen and dead defenders who only seconds ago had been engaged in a murderous firefight complete with pulse fire and flashbangs, floated by, pushed or pulled by the swirling currents like plants along the sea beds of some forever ocean. In the silence created by the cessation of gunfire and the overwhelming waters, their vacant Animal eyes stared off at nothing.

"Force the control panel and I'll handle the hack," ordered Heratix over their team comm. Crometheus couldn't argue with her plan and used both gauntlets to pry open the blast panel that covered the controls for the hatch. The strong current tried to drag them both away as Heratix swam in close to grasp his armor and the panel in succession. Then one armored glove began to dance across the glowing interface panel, opening secure menus with backdoor passwords that worked almost instantly.

"I hacked one of their interfaces on a lower level during a lull in the fighting. Some maintenance chief kept a bunch of easy passwords in a secure file. But it'll only get us so far, Crometheus. I need to hardwire in." Then… "Hold on to me."

Crometheus let go of the panel door and slammed his armored fist into it to bend it askew, jamming it open. Then he held on to her.

Heratix pulled a fiberwire cable from her gauntleted forearm and hard-connected into the panel. A moment later she had a menu open on the hovering screen beneath them.

"This'll let me override their higher-level safety parameters now that it's in default malfunction mode. Any idea what's on the other side of this door?"

"Negative," answered Crometheus.

She laughed.

"Feels weird, doesn't it?" she asked.

"What?" said Crometheus as she overrode sysadmin commands via the fiberwire connection.

"Breathing. Hearing yourself breathe inside these helmets." She laughed nervously. "It's like we forgot what it's like to be alive."

He hadn't thought much about it, but now that she'd mentioned it his mind couldn't stop hearing the two of them breathing heavily as they worked to hold on to the hatch while the violent currents pulled and sucked at them.

"Yeah," he said. "It's been a long time. I'd forgotten."

"Me too," she confessed, and then touched the command function interface key. The maintenance hatch shot open and water rushed in.

"Me first," ordered Crometheus, and a moment later he was through and kicking into the darkness beyond the tight hatch, letting the flooding water pull him forward and then up toward the next level once he reached some sort of maintenance shaft lift. A blast door was closing up ahead, automatically trying to seal off the floodwater breach, and he kicked as hard as he could to make it before it locked him out on the wrong side. He reached the scissoring halves and pulled himself through at the last second before they clanged together.

Heratix's voice came to him broken and distorted across their comm. Something was interfering with the signal.

"I'll establish an ingress here," he ordered, hoping her reception was better than his. "Gather the rest and stage them on your side of this door. Once the level pumps out, cut your way in and follow me. We'll assault from this axis."

He got a garbled communication back, rife with static interference and a few words that might have meant message received.

Twenty minutes. He only had to hold this maintenance shaft for twenty minutes before that level pumped out. Even now, over ambient sound amplified by the armor's sensors, he could hear the pumps working overtime to clear the lower level of near-frozen lake water.

He pulled both Automags from their tac holsters on his armored thighs. Based on old Earth designs, the sidearms had been the workhorse weapons on a dozen conflicts on worlds the Pantheon had raided. Over the years they'd been refined to stand up to almost all conditions. Even submerged.

He got a confirmation message in his HUD that both weapons were now synced for auto-stabilization and continuous ammunition feed. HUD targeting was active and available upon request.

The water on this side of the sealed hatch had already been drained, and he stood on the hatch now, in the dark, listening to the slow and monotonous industrial sounds of the pumps. Then he switched over to IR and scanned the dark tube above him.

He saw them coming down the shaft before they saw him.

Crometheus didn't wait more than a second to engage. He fired the armor's limited charge repulsors, mindful of their life, and rocketed silently upward at the infiltrators.

They were rappelling down the shaft when they saw the dark hulk of the Eternal silently zooming up at them. Both Automags held up and at them. He fired on burst and cut down the four Animals who'd been coming down the access shaft with small subcompact pulse rifles, wicked and vicious little weapons, reported to be a staple of the Spilursan Special Forces.

The Automags thundered out in concussive bursts, tearing into the dangling operators. Crometheus passed them, bounced off one wall and pushed himself to the far side of the shaft, rotating around when he detected the opening they had come from.

Whoever was running the ropes at the access point into the vertical tube had to have been alerted by the massive thunder of gunfire from down below, but less than five seconds is little reaction time in which to figure things out in a surprise firefight.

Crometheus appeared at the point from which the rappellers had entered the shaft, hovered in midair in the center of the tube, and blazed away at the team handling the ropes.

Two Animal sentries, both carrying military-grade pulse rifles and pulling security, didn't wait for the bodies of the rope handlers to fall to the deck, or into the shaft as in the case of one, pinwheeling into the darkness below, past the dangling dead operators, before returning fire on the armored nightmare that had just shot up out of the depths to hover in front of them.

Pulse fire smashed into Crometheus's armor like jackhammer strikes, but still managed to turn to sudden arc lighting and spring off at deflected angles. The hot smoking rounds that spat out from Crometheus's thundering hand cannons on the other hand didn't deflect off in any other directions. Instead they exited the bodies of both sentries in sprays of blood spatter and gray matter.

Crometheus bumped the armor's maneuver jets, suddenly aware he'd killed half the armor's jump battery in this up-shaft attack as he landed among the ruined Animal bodies at the end of an intersecting horizontal tube extending into darkness. A glowing terminal provided the only light, which extended no more than a few meters, but the armor's sensor system picked up inbound Animals responding to the sounds of his attack from up ahead.

Chances are, he thought to himself, *they figure the whole attack is coming through here. Which it is, just not yet. For now it's just me. So act positive. Like you got everyone with you. Maybe they'll cut and run.*

He checked his time. Twelve minutes until the lower level was pumped dry and Commander Zero could push more weapons and troops forward. Hopefully Heratix had heard his order and relayed it.

Hopefully.

But hope was for some other time than this one as the Animals lobbed fragmentary explosives toward him as a prep for their attack. Their intel was probably updating in real-time and assessing that electromagnetic spectrum warfare explosives, which they'd been using earlier, were ineffective against the Uplifted. The two grenades thrown into the maintenance tunnel by the reaction force detonated within a half second of each other. Two massive blasts that almost knocked Crometheus back off the lip of intersection and into the shaft below. It would have been a long fall. Maybe even a broken back.

Could that be repaired? he wondered distantly as the warning bells and damage control alerts rang within his HUD.

He was injured. Not badly. The armor's medical functions had kicked in almost instantly to make sure he didn't feel even an ounce of pain from the hot fragment that had violated his armor and gone straight into his thigh.

Yet... almost instantly is not instantly. There was a brief picosecond in which he might have felt real pain. Real live pain after all these years. And for that brief picosecond it was not... unpleasant. It was something new. Again. Something real after the long dream of convincing himself that the simulated was real, and the real simulated.

Then the painkillers kicked in and blocked out all the pain at every level, including the neural.

The armor identified three Animal soldiers entering the maintenance access tunnel with subcompact pulse rifles and laser targeting systems synced to a smartlens fitted in their helmets. It made them look, within the IR spectrum, like glowing one-eyed nether demons come to do bad things.

Crometheus regained his footing, almost stumbling over one of the ropes still dangling down into the darkness, and fired back at his attackers. Smoking vapor trails slithered out over the IR overlay and smashed into the lead assaulter. Moving quickly and taking a burst of ineffective automatic pulse fire across the chest plate, Crometheus fired two more rounds in quick succession. One apiece into the helmets of the two other Animals closing in. All three were down, and now was the time to press his advantage. Before they could use more explosives. Before they could even ascertain whether their QRF had been effective in stopping this up-level breach.

He sprinted down the maintenance tunnel and burst out into a pristine white paneled corridor inlaid with holographic readouts from the various systems of the main server.

There were more Spilursan operators stacked and waiting on both sides of the exit. But neither bunch fired for fear of hitting the other. Everyone was surprised.

Everyone but Crometheus.

He shot them all dead. A lot.

Crometheus was not constrained by such concerns as friendly fire as he pivoted drunkenly due to the thigh injury and unloaded at full auto from both massive sidearms on everyone stacked along the wall. Rounds smashed into the tac-armored operators who began to fire far too late to be effective. Huge fifty-caliber rounds shattered armor, smashed bone, and blew off limbs. Any return fire was wild and panicked at the last as the team faced its sudden and unexpected end.

Alarm klaxons went wild along this level as the pristine white corridor was suddenly bathed in blood-red emergency lighting. Animals were communicating via their station address system and Crometheus's armor translated their slow and ponderous words so that he could comprehend what was being announced.

"Breach in progress. Level four, section six. All teams respond. Breach in progress..."

Gods:
Chapter Twenty-Seven

Progressing through the outer rim of the massive data storage core on this level, Crometheus gunned down as many of the responding Animals as he could. Breach alarms blared as human voices shouted alerts over a general address system. Working both of the massive sidearms, firing short controlled staccato bursts while advancing swiftly from cover to cover, he methodically murdered the next wave of defenders and moved upward toward the objective on level nine.

But not without cost.

Pulse fire had ruined his armor. Several systems were offline, and truth be told he was dragging the wounded leg more than using it. The armor was drugging the hell out of the raw nerve endings screaming bright blue murder, making the pain, at best, a distant and dull thing. But there all the same. A thing to be ignored as he tried to acquire and fire. And at its worst, something that caused him to lock down his mental focus just to continuing acquiring and engaging the teams of defenders who kept coming at him from various secondary access points. The fact that the attacks were badly coordinated worked in his favor, but he guessed that wouldn't last long. Soon the opposing forces would get their act together and put him down.

Still, he ran up the score.

Didn't I, Holly?

And yet, it had all become a game once more. Just like all the wars they'd fought against unsuspecting worlds and distant colonies when the Uplifted hulk *Pantheon* hauled into close orbit to raid, loot, and carry away slaves. Just like all the machines inside Lazer Command. There had been a brief new reality that had set in with this new body, and the Eternals had replaced his desire for the game with a whole new world of sensations that had been long missing. But with the guns working in both gauntlets and the kills adding up in the corner of his HUD... he was back. In-game. Gamer and going for the all-time high score on Tournament Mode. He'd transformed back into the pure killing machine he always was, never mind the incoming fire ruining the reflex armor and the new chassis. They could grow him another if his body got shot to pieces. Dodging what he could, dealing out as much as possible, was the only thing that mattered now. The dribble of brass was like music to his ears. Especially in large doses. It was beautiful.

Every fight comes down to just this, kid, said Bad Old Self. *A good old brawl in the end boils down to who can keep a-throwin' punches even after the other guy done give up.*

Who wanted the vic more. Right? Plain and simple.

The Animals were breaking, regardless. They'd seen too many of their own relentlessly slaughtered with little mercy by the murder juggernaut he'd become in what was looking like the last moments. Impossible to them that one could stand up to so many. Explosives, small-arms fire, and concentrated tactics designed to take down single opponents had all failed as he advanced and shot them down like some death titan. Some savage god gone avenging. How, he knew they were wondering as they died on the floors he crossed, had he done it? So many against one. And they were failing. And death was the price of their inferiority.

They ramped up and sent more teams straight at him, trying to push numbers, fighting a full-scale battle against just one Savage who had no intention of relenting. He was going down, that was for sure. But he would go down hard, and take as many as he could with him. The time when Commander Zero could push forward was closing… but time didn't matter anymore as he burned through ammo, both pistols smoking violently now.

In the end, those Animals who could, evacuated the level under heavy fire. Maestro had already hacked their comm and Crometheus had herded them all into a kill zone where only a few would make the last lift off that level. Some of the enemy were buying time for the wounded to be pulled out. That mattered little to him. He rushed under heavy fire, covering where he could, dealing out bursts, shooting down the brave and dying alike. His psychotic momentum turned into an avalanche against the Animals, and now they were doing everything they could to just get away from him.

Begrudgingly, they allowed him to turn their victory into a defeat.

He shot down the last five defenders who'd been providing cover fire to get their own Animal wounded off the floor and up-station to medical services. Spraying gunfire into the bolt-holes they were defending from, he shot them down one by one.

"They're moving to Plan B, Master Crometheus," said Maestro over the comm. "I'm afraid they're going to flush the station core and neutralize the cloud. It's their doomsday scenario—short of blowing up the base."

Silence.

Crometheus stood there in the now-deserted level, a hulking wounded metal monster, both dangling sidearms smoking from the barrels, amid a sea of bullet-ravaged bodies along the last access corridor that led to a lift off this level. Above, echoing down through the vast levels of the massive underwater base, clanks announced locks going into place, sealing off what could be sealed off. Controlling what could be controlled.

"That cannot happen, Master Crometheus," intoned Maestro seriously. "If it does... then we fail."

At that moment Uplifted reinforcements swept into the main bay far to the rear of Crometheus's forwardmost line of slaughter. Red targeting lasers swept the carnage and debris as wedges of Eternals, led by Commander Zero, arrived in force to secure the level.

"We control the core, for now. But we have to protect it," continued Maestro in the silent space of Crometheus's internal darkness. The armor was controlling his breathing, assessing damage, and administering more drugs to stabilize him. He could fight on. Adrenal boosts were on standby. If needed.

"... until our fellow Uplifted arrive with the fleet above. Only then can we rest. Fifteen hours to go, Crometheus. Are you ready, Player?"

Commander Zero was erupting over the comm about the amount of slaughter she was seeing. Congratulating the Eternals for such a tremendous victory.

"One of us is worth a thousand of them," she was saying. Crometheus felt something slick and warm running down his new thigh. Within the armor. It was blood. His blood. Yes, he thought to himself, acknowledging the horror of uncontrolled bleeding. And the wonder of it at the same time.

But he must have said that part out loud as Maestro came back.

"Good, young Eternal. I've completed a local hack on the core's perimeter firewalls and am now ready to upload the Unity Virus into the system. In order to ensure its successful installation, I'll be disappearing along with it, babysitting it if you will. I'll find some nice place to look like something else and hide inside the cloud. We shan't talk for some time, Master Cro. Well beyond this battle if my calculations prove correct. That is... if you survive the coming counterattack. Already my sensors are tracking no less than three enemy combat transports, each easily capable of carrying upwards of five hundred new troops, inbound to reinforce this station. You must hold the core until reinforcements arrive. We cannot fail now. And... good luck, Crometheus. You are so close to your goal. The last step is at hand. The one you've been looking for your entire life. It is time to shed yourself of the petty concerns of survival and the imperative of now. It's time to seek something greater than yourself, Crometheus. This is how one becomes immortal. This is how one becomes a true Eternal. Honor. And glory. Farewell, young master."

Then Maestro was gone. So gone from Crometheus's own system it was as though the AI had never been there at all.

Maestro, that master director of the last hundreds of years of the Pantheon, was gone. A ghost in the machine about to infect everyone for the greater good of *Homo deus*. The Uplifted. If all went well, every Uplifted would, in time… involuntarily become part of the Pantheon. A unified culture of a singular voice with a destiny to rule the stars with one accord. There was no telling what they could do once that had taken place. Once the Animals had been wiped clean from the worlds they'd infected. No telling at all. The Pantheon would be free to remake the galaxy in its own image.

And what an image that would be.

An image all would bow the knee to.

An image of gods. An image of themselves.

Gods:
Chapter Twenty-Eight

"We have to hold now that Maestro's in place. Options?"

No one was saying anything. And that was scary. Or at least it was scary to Crometheus. The Pantheon had always been chock full of visionaries, leaders, and innovators. Game-changers and problem-solvers. But the stress and trauma of the first assault as an elite fighting force had checked some. Maybe all of this—new bodies, new gear—maybe it was all too new, too much, too soon.

The cracks were beginning to show. Which was a scary thing when you thought you didn't have any.

"We have three objectives we need to achieve if this op is going to go down as planned," said a player tagged Romulux. "Objective one… we have to protect the hard connection to the core here in Central Access. If they retake it, they can run a scan and find the Unity Virus—and maybe even Maestro. Either way, we lose that and it's game over. Especially if the other Uplifted find out what we were up to down here."

What remained of the Eternals, the one hundred and sixty-four who'd survived the depth charges and the initial breach and the level-by-level firefights, were now gathered around the wonder of the Animals' core containing their super-secret cloud. Humming within that structure was information on all the Animals' latest tech. Imagined wonders made real. Tools that would be turned against the Animals and used for the greater good of the galaxy. And every one of the Eternals, all of whom had been masters of the world back on Earth, appreciated proprietary tech.

That was where the great leaps came from.

Where the future took shape one innovation at a time. One wonder to change them all into who they'd become. In some form or another, intellectual property had made them into the modern-day colossi they'd been back on Earth when they'd ruled the culture from its loftiest heights. And now they had a moment of opportunity to control the future by controlling the *invention* of the future. All it would cost them was the fight of their lives.

Who knew what the Animals had gotten up to in all the long dark years? The tech from New Vega was still being deciphered by the Pantheon scientists, but early reports indicated it was a gold mine. Among the finds was some kind of new hypercomm that used jump space to enable near-instantaneous communication. That was next level plus one for sure. An Uplifted force with that ability would be unstoppable across the vast interstellar gulfs that separated world from world. Coordinated movements against multiple objectives... it would give an unprecedented advantage to whatever fleet could deploy such tech.

And there were sure to be more such gems here within the most sacred space the Animals who'd called themselves the Spilursans had. Rumors abounded of powerful ship-based weapons designed around the fledgling blaster. Improved micro-repulsor designs that could be used with armor and lighter starships of the fighter profile. A better jump drive that halved flight time. Fantastic dreams all. And they would spell the end of a galaxy infested with Animals, and the beginning of a new Uplifted era.

The age of *Homo deus*.

"May it never end," Crometheus caught himself murmuring within the silent hum of his helmet's comm. Old habits died hard. The chanting and affirmative reinforcements had been a singular discipline of the early Earth-based Pantheon self-improvement course, as it had once been known. Eventually that had carried over into the fanatical years of the ship's dark ages where it was almost a religion, shepherding them through those perilous times. Chanting to remember why it was important to starve to death for some future destiny that lay on the other side of the black gulf of space.

Chanting when you've had nothing to eat for not just days, but weeks.

Player Romulux had finished droning on and on about how to defend the central core and had begun droning on and on about "objective two," attacking the Animals that would try to dump the whole level, or even the whole station. If the Animals couldn't hard connect then they had no choice but to melt the reactor, or even nuke the base via orbital bombardment. The Eternals' lead hacker, Player Banksee, was already running an analysis on their network. Or at least the captured portions. If the Animals did indeed initiate a core melt from two decks up, they could destroy the cloud. And the entire complex.

The Spilursans' problem was... that act was irreversible. The lost data, design, and research could not be saved in time. What was represented on the core was several lifetimes' worth of R&D. No doubt they had to be planning right now, in some giant war room bunker, what to do in the next few hours. Was it worth it to dump the core and lose everything?

Worth it for humanity?

Yes. At this moment rather than let all that valuable tech fall into Savage hands... it absolutely was, Crometheus could almost feel them reasoning.

Worth it for the Spilursan government and economic system, a world leader among the worlds of hyperdrive?

No. Possibly...

The loss of that valuable R&D would put them at the mercy of whichever competitor world managed to survive this war. They were all on the same side as long as they were fighting against the Uplifted they called the Savages, but after that, they would once again be competing against one another for galactic cultural domination.

Little did they know they'd never survive, thought Crometheus. But who could fault them for thinking they had a chance? That they might win. Miraculously. Somehow. Despite the mounting evidence that indicated another outcome. That there was some unthought way out of the noose slowly strangling them from all points of the galactic compass as more and more coordinated Uplifted fleets came out of the deep-space dark like nightmares from the nether and began to ravage their pretty little worlds.

That's what they, the Animals in charge of all the other Animals, were thinking down in that bunker, wherever it was. Had to be thinking, at this very moment. What was their position and how best to leverage it on the back end of this war they thought they still had a chance at winning.

Then a thought hit Crometheus like lightning out of the blue. Shocking him to the core. Waking him to what must be done…

They were thinking about themselves and only themselves, instead of their collective whole… and in that there was no glory. No honor. That was animal thinking. The way animals who would never be gods thought.

"Objective three," continued Romulux. "We need to get behind their lines. Up deck. Do some damage and destabilize their assault on the lower levels in order to buy us more time because I suspect this is going to go down to the wire. They'll come down here eventually, and probably sooner rather than later. We have to hold until Alliance reinforcements arrive on scene. But that's not everything. Eventually they'll go for the flush controls a few levels up if they realize they can't win by retaking the core. We knock the flush control system out in the reactor with a strike team before they get authorization from their higher-ups to initiate a flush and flood the station core. All they can do at that point is surrender. There's just one problem… the reactor and flush controls are deep inside their held territory on station. We don't have the numbers to take that area in force. So… we need to draw straws and send in a one-way hit team with very little chance of survival."

Chatter between the various elements of the Eternals stopped as one.

"It's a one-way mission," continued Romulux in the silence. "Odds indicate those who go upward to destabilize the impending attack will not survive. Even post-battle salvage at that point is highly unlikely. Whoever does it, whoever goes up there and buys the rest of us some breathing space and time to wait for the fleet to show up... you'll be doing it for the greater good..."

"And glory," interrupted Crometheus over the steady hum of the comm. His voice, that voice they'd all heard croon those greatest rock-and-roll hits and say those lines in those long-lost movies from their collective long ago, a known voice, dry and sly with just a hint of the devil-may-care in it, they heard him say it.

And glory.

"And honor. For glory and honor."

Silence.

"That's correct, Cro," said Romulux, like they'd known each other time immemorial. Like Romulux had been some Rock and Roll Hall of Fame insider all those years ago. Truth was, Romulux had just been a high-flying financier who'd convinced the world it would end if it didn't buy his latest save-the-planet-from-itself-and-all-of-humanity crisis scheme. He'd monetized their animal fear. Back in the day, of course. He'd bought his access. He'd bought his way inside. He was smart.

Back in the day.

As all of them once had been.

But smart didn't make you a god. It was only half of the old Greek and Roman equation of knowledge and glory.

Glory. That made men into gods forever. Which was why they'd all joined up in whatever seminar out by the airport, or secret meeting of the powerful and wealthy in some high enclave, or invite-only access retreat in some luxury grove out along one of the coasts... however and wherever. They'd joined up not to find God... but to *become* gods. The gods they knew themselves to truly be.

And what is truth?

But what you make it, right?

Glory was the final step, thought Crometheus as they all waited for him to explain. Glory obtained by honor.

That was the final step along the path. Maybe even the last...

It didn't hit him like that last bolt of lightning had. That this was the last step on the Path as revealed by the ever-patient and long-serving Maestro. It didn't hit him that he'd finally arrived at the last step along... not the Path, but *a* path. A path, a journey, a quest, a road that had begun long ago on that rainy-day weekend at the airport Marriott. No. Before then. When he first dreamed of being... more... greater than... something special...

When had he known he was made for something more? Something better? Something special.

It didn't matter now. This was an end. And a beginning...

He understood that now. In deeper ways none of the rest of them did. Glory was the last step. The final step. He could tell by their silence. He was the first. And maybe the only one for just the next couple of beats of the galaxy.

As usual, some would try to emulate. Try to follow. Fake it until they made it. But they didn't understand. They would just be faking it… hoping to make it.

Which was the next best thing when you didn't understand. They were masters of that back on Earth. It was how they stayed hip and followed the trends. It was how they stayed in.

Fake it. Even if you don't mean it.

Follow power and you become powerful.

"I'll do it," said Crometheus to them all, to no one. Really just himself. "I'll go up-station and create as much chaos as possible in order to buy time until relief comes. I'll deal with the counterassault into the core and stop them from accessing the flush controls."

Silence. Overwhelming silence. Comprehension dawning in some. Disbelief in others. Covetous desire in everyone.

They coveted what he had from the get-go of that moment. Even if they didn't understand it. They sensed there was something about the future in it.

And they wanted that more than anything.

Even the R&D sleeping on the server that had to be protected at all costs.

One by one, five others said they'd go too. Volunteered for a chance at honor and glory. Taking a risk that they too would Uplift to the final step and become gods through sacrifice. Hoping for a far side to the end of the road.

They'd been here before.

The plan was approved by Commander Zero. Go up and create chaos in order to delay the inevitable storming of the level by overwhelming Animal forces. Hopefully... they would hold out until the fleet arrived. That was the only way all of them would survive. Or just some.

Later, when they were redistributing the ammo, loading up the Chaos team, as the six who'd go up-level would be known, she came to him and asked why.

"Why? Why are you doing this, Crometheus?"

Commander Zero was making sure the Chaos team, the first-ever designation for what would become the special operators of the Uplifted in all the years and battles to come, had enough of the new incendiary loads for the MK-1000s they'd been reissued out of the towed supply pallets, or taken from the hands of the dead. High-explosive rounds that hit their targets and detonated, propelling a tungsten carbine dumb-round through the impact area for bonus damage and excessive penetration. There weren't a lot of these magazine loads, but the Chaos team would be getting pride of place for distribution.

Each member of the team also received a bandolier of grenades to loop about their chest plates. Like that vision Crometheus had had of Commander Zero coming through the flaming gas pumps with a necklace of walnut shells and temple bells—or was it death flowers?—worn around her neck. Except now he knew that hadn't been her he'd seen. It had been himself. He'd had a holy vision of himself becoming.

Each grenade could be unclipped and deployed, or the whole bandolier could be daisy-chained and detonated for catastrophic damage. In the gyrating wild half-light of the powerful information storage core, throwing first purple, then pink, then red dwarf crimson, and finally a wash of cool blues to show that a run-cycle had just completed, the bandolier of grenades looked like that ancient walnut necklace certain religious cults had once worn back in the airports and refugee centers of long-lost ruined Earth.

Walnut shells and temple bells worn round the neck.

"Why do you need to know?" he replied as he fed a belt of high-explosive ammunition into his 1000. Indicator lights signaled load connection and ready for operation. He put the rifle down and checked both sidearms.

"I don't know," she said warily, and hesitated. "Something inside me tells me you've found... another step. The next step, and maybe even the last, Crometheus. And that somehow this is it. This is the last one. But it makes no sense. It's like the old hokey religions of Earth when they used to tell you that you had to give up your life to gain it... all that crap. You'll die up there, Crometheus. Don't make any mistake about that. The odds are bad. Real bad. Six versus what's shaping up to be over two thousand of theirs coming in loaded for bear. That's not exactly even odds. That's a slaughter no matter what I said a few hours ago."

"And?"

"If it's a choice between religions..." she spat back. Her voice hoarse and dry. Filled with some unspoken bitterness that had been there for a long time. "Then I'll pick the one that gives me the math I can live with. I'll take hard numbers over a miracle, Crometheus. Any day. And that's true for every one of us whether we like to admit or not. I've never been so blind as to not understand exactly who each and every one of us really is. And what we want out of this," she added knowingly. "I've never been that dishonest with myself. Even since all of this started centuries ago. Never. So why do it? Why throw yourself away today? Because that makes me wonder... about what you've found."

"Come with me then. Find out for yourself."

She shook her head. Then unclipped her helmet. And pulled it off and over her head.

Holly Wood. For a moment. Just for a moment.

So maybe this is the end, he thought. She's always there...

For a moment it was Holly Wood from long ago. Except... it wasn't. She just had that same classically beautiful Southern California tanned and blond beach bunny face. Blue eyes that sparkled like the sun's reflections off an afternoon ocean.

Just like the Holly Wood of long ago at the roadside diner. Just like when she walked out of his life in some hotel along the road.

Edit.

Her eyes were questioning, wanting to know the secret. And frightened of him in the same moment. And that, too, was just like that long-ago lost dream girl made real he'd lost out there in the byways and highways of a ruined world dying that didn't even know it was dead yet.

Just like her. Except not all dead and bloody. Buried in a shallow grave halfway between nowhere and the end of the road. Halfway between Reno and Rome.

Edit. Bad Thought.

But not. Funny, he thought to himself. Remembering all his past shedding if only through fragmented details. Details surfacing like wreckage in a pond. Or on the ocean after a storm. A little at a time and bearing no resemblance to the whole of what it all once was. What it all had been. What had really happened, or happened the way he wanted to remember it. She always appeared. Each time he began again. She always did.

Why?

"Honor and glory," he muttered at Commander Zero as he finished stuffing mags into his carrier. "That's all now. That's all there ever really was. It was that easy. We were just too busy angling for the credit."

She shook her head again, just Commander Zero now and not Holly Wood. She shook her head as though she couldn't believe that the answer he was going to give her, going to leave her with, before he went off to his certain death, was as simple as that.

"I don't... understand," she replied softly. An innocent whisper like some little girl who didn't know and didn't mind confessing that the world, the galaxy, the universe, was full of secrets.

Then he smiled at her, giving his commander the old whiplash sneer from the cover of all those albums he'd made when he was just a punk kid with nothing to lose and everything to burn.

"Then I guess you're just not ready yet."

And he left her.

Helmets on. Guns up. The Chaos team departed minutes later into the cut the combat engineer specialists had made into the ceiling of this level that gave them access to the next level up-station. Behind them, as they crawled through the darkness ahead, they could hear the plasma torches sealing them off once again.

There was no turning back now. No retreat this time.

There was only forward.

There was only honor and glory to be purchased.

Gods:
Chapter Twenty-Nine

Crometheus and the other members of the Chaos team heard the Animals coming down through the station's levels. But before that they heard the big troop lifters, heavy freighters, coming in. Engines flaring into heavy whines while the industrial-sized repulsors throbbed to life, sending ominous deep bass notes through the superstructure of the mostly underwater station. Then boots on the ground, combat boots, uncountable if you didn't have the armor's sensors and HUD doing all the number-crunching and isolation work. Walker mechs followed, as did other light attack vehicles descending onto the top of the station.

There was comm traffic over the enemy's channels, but it was scrambled and therefore incomprehensible.

"Need a hard connect to their comm to run my decoder and hack in. Get one of the Animals for me, guys, and we can listen in on all the plans they have for us. Should be fun."

That was Alantra. Slicer extraordinaire. She'd been a theoretical climate modeler with a massive social media following back in the last days of Earth. A scientist at heart who'd been easy on the eyes and was always adventure vacationing to talk about climate change in a bikini. Crometheus had hooked up with her early on in the flight to the first world. They'd lasted about six months and there'd been no hard feelings when it ended. But they'd all lived a lot of lifetimes since then. And that was a long time ago even in real time. Forever inside the Pantheon.

Now, as their new bodies tried to control adrenal responses and the fear creeping into their psyches that came from being this far forward, or rather upward, of friendly lines, the six of them chattered over the comm to maintain their sense of superiority—that was most likely quite warranted with regard to the troops they were about to face. Tech-wise.

Numbers-wise was another story.

Alantra. That was her chosen god name. And the rest of the Chaos team was…

Smaug.

Zur.

Immaculus.

Marz.

And himself. Crometheus. Squad god of the first Chaos team.

All of them with their godling tags. As if to claim so, was to be so. But they'd had other names, lost and shed long ago.

They all had. Once.

If only, thought Crometheus. The resolve he'd felt when he volunteered to go forward was now fading in the cold light of what they were about to face. *If only we were truly now gods.*

"Well," began Immaculus over the comm. His voice the smooth cool British tone of a member of the aristocracy he'd once been. He'd opted for godhood over merely being a number in the line of succession to the old English monarchy that eventually fled Earth for the world the Animals now called New Britannia. And there'd been some colossal scandal if one remembered all the ancient gossip, thought Crometheus in those uncertain moments before the battle began. Some scandal regarding Immaculus back on Earth… but in the light of hundreds of years in the future from that long-ago fall from grace, now that the Uplifted had invaded the aforementioned New Britannia… it had been the wise choice on his part. Full of foresight in the months after the descendants he'd once come from had collapsed. That world that was now in ruins and being rebuilt by the Id, and the old monarchy had vanished in a single battle. To a man.

"They'll come down along the main lift hub. Eight personnel lifts and one cargo. I'm guessing they can flog two hundred at a time down to our levels to throw at us once they identify resistance. And…" He sighed on a droll note. "Then there are the stairwells. Two on each side of the facility. Steady stream that way also, I suspect. We'll have to cover everything or get rolled up on our flanks, chaps. And lady."

He was right, thought Crometheus. Good tac assessment. But they'd all gotten months of downloaded training and simming in planning and execution on both the tactical and strategic level.

"We take all three. Three teams of two. One team per access point," ordered Crometheus. "Wear them out and prevent a breach operation on the reactor and the flush controls. That's what we're here to do. Buy time until the main body can get closer."

It was Marz who spoke next.

"Solid plan. I say we execute. Mind you, children... any of us fails and it's all over for the rest. So kill them all and let the galaxy know who you are." His voice over the comm had all the warmth of graveyard granite on a cold winter's night. And it sounded just as dusty and worn as a tombstone too. Back on Earth he'd been an actual hard-bitten mercenary who destabilized third-world countries for corporate raiders to loot and rebuild in their own image. He also had the most experience at actual warfare. Or at least he had when the voyage began, coming in with the ex-German special operations hires. They'd all learned to become killers in the long years since. But Marz had been a killer from way back, learning the trade in bloody little African wars that no one was allowed to care about as the planet worked itself up toward its end.

Crometheus knew Marz was here, with the Chaos team, because the old soldier had never been able to resist a solid firefight. Not on Sirius, or any of the other worlds they'd visited in the Pantheon. Whenever and wherever it went down, Marz had always been in the thick of it. Burning magazines and taking lives.

Always in the thick of it.

And of course, that brought home to Crometheus at last that despite his vainglorious promise to buy the main body of Eternals time for something as ephemeral as honor and glory... that most likely he'd come to the end of himself. For this was indeed the thick of it. This was where it went down. If Marz was here, then this was where the real fighting was going to take place.

"Who wants what?" asked Crometheus, regarding their assignments to meet the oncoming enemy force.

In short order the lots were divvied and everyone took the section they'd defend to the death. Though that bit was left unspoken. Three teams of two. One team on each stairwell. One on the lifts. And nobody really wanted the lifts because that's where the heaviest, most desperately outnumbered fighting was going to be done. So it fell to Marz, who said nothing, and Crometheus, who waited for everyone to make their choice.

Immaculus and Alantra on the southern stairwell. Zur and Smaug on the northern.

In the last moment of their being a collective whole, the first Chaos team found themselves in a circle they hadn't intended to form. Each one had been too much of an individualist icon, or even an iconoclast, in their past life on Earth, to ever need to share the limelight with anyone else. But here they were and all of them sensed the real possibility of getting game-overed in what lay ahead. And so, like the humans they'd tried to shed every vestige of... they sought some final connection at the last of themselves.

Coming close and into the ancient circle though they'd never intended it.

"They'll write songs about us," muttered Smaug. "That's got to be worth something, right?"

Marz laughed. He'd faced death a thousand times before and walked away each and every time. Maybe today would be different. Maybe not. His dry chuckle seemed to hint at something unspoken. Something that knew more about death and its finality than the rest of them were ready to accept.

No one offered anything else until finally it was time to go. Then it was Immaculus of all people who left them with this. His droll manner of speaking suddenly eloquent and somehow grand.

"A song wouldn't be so bad, Smaug. There's something immortal even in that. Someone once said, I forget who now, but they said forget all that nonsense about writing the laws of a nation. They said, let me write their songs and I'll shape your people's hearts. Let me tell them stories and I'll teach them what's important. Let me write their poems and I'll show them what they've lost. It was something like that... though it's hard to recall now after so many years. So yes, I'll take a song about me if that's in the offing. Maybe in the end that's the immortality we've been looking for all along. Right, Cro? You were a rock star once. You know how it is when it's time for your last show. Last curtain call, eh. Final bow. Feels like this might be that. Oh well, lads and lasses... tallyho, as we used to say in the RAF."

Crometheus shuffled forward and lowered his weapon with one gauntlet. He stuck the other out in front of the rest. His armored glove forming a fist.

This would be the symbol of the Chaos teams, and in time the Eternals, and eventually the entire military force of the combined Uplifted tribes, over the next fifteen hundred years of hard fighting across the galaxy to come. The symbol would represent a fighting force that would almost annihilate the entire galaxy.

It would stand for the Uplifted… no, the *Savage* marines.

"All in," he said softly. Then, "For honor and glory."

And one by one they stuck their own armored fists into the circle. As every Savage marine would come to do for what remained of their time in the galactic lens. A time of horror and brutality for centuries to come.

Gods: Chapter Thirty

The Animals pushed from the two stairwells on opposite sides of the level the Chaos team was defending. Coming at Immaculus and Alantra first on the southern stairwell. Zur and Smaug on the north.

Reactor.

Main power.

This was the level that provided energy to the entire base. Three independent micro-reactors fed the rest of this station from this heavily shielded area. The Chaos team had chosen this area to defend because they knew the Animals would enter cautiously, hesitating to engage in order not to damage the power production systems. Fearful that they might even set off some kind of dangerous chain reaction that could detonate the base and kill them all. These were just soldiers and not scientists, after all, so Marz had reasoned that they'd be afraid of the advanced technology as soldiers were wont to be. But the truth was that most of the level was rather well protected from light arms fire, and the reactor shielding was even rated to stand up to heavy explosions and bunker-busting AGM munitions. Nothing anyone was bringing into this fight was going to damage anything, in Marz's opinion.

"But the Animals will be worried all the same that they're going to set something off. Do some real damage. You see, that's the thing with Animals. They're weak in the mind. They're always trying to save their own skins no matter what. Even when they've got a job to do, they'll still try to find a way to do it with as little damage or self-harm as they can inflict. We'll use that against them today. We'll make their fear our ally. We'll fight with violence, surprise, and aggression. Combine that with their fear and we might just walk away from this regardless of what Zero says our odds are. Or at least, some of us, perhaps, will walk away."

The Spilursan special teams unit on the southern stairs, sweeping the area with red targeting lasers, armored in tactical gear, and moving in turtle formations, were the first to make contact.

Immaculus opened up with a full-auto burst from the 1000 and cut down the point man. No one was using the special HE rounds yet. They'd save those for when the Animals started coming at them in waves. The specialized ammo would cut through two and three ranks at a time, regardless of cover.

Still, in the opening moments of the massive firefight that was about to erupt, as Immaculus fired from the concealed position he and Alantra had set up for a crossfire on the stairwell, the first squad of Spilursan operators went down with little effort. Both Eternals worked over the mass of wounded and dying operators scrambling to get away from the maelstrom of bullets ripping into them. Smooth professionalism fled as the movement-to-contact turned into a desperate rout. Dozens of six-point-five-millimeter rounds shattered armor and bone, devastating and rag-dolling the bodies of the soldiers caught in the storm of lead moving at twenty-five hundred meters per second.

"Contact," whispered Alantra softly over the comm.

Within seconds, enemy fire began at the northern stairwell. This time the Animal operators knew an ambush was waiting, and they lobbed flashbangs in to lead their assault. Zur and Smaug didn't mind taking a little incoming. Certainly not the flashbangs. The reflex armor system had been refined after the battle on New Vega and was now quite adept at recognizing shock and bang weapons that disabled electronics and physical senses. Recognizing, tracking, analyzing... and then blipping its own power for a second, hardening itself against the effects of EMP by simply not being on in the calculated moment of the explosion. And the armor's last act before shutting down was to opaque the mirrored visors to full midnight darkness, preventing the Eternal operators within from being visually disoriented. A ghostly sensor-generated image of the battlefield appeared during the brief downtime allowing the Uplifted to continue to engage last known and projected positions of the enemy. It involved a slight delay, but it was good enough. The helmet's external auditory sensors were shut down as well, and so there was no compromise on that level either.

So it was that Zur and Smaug were not only protected but free to engage, employing fairly accurate guesses about where the enemy was, even as the flashbangs went off. Both Eternals immediately switched over to over-cycle auto-fire and let loose—for two reasons. Defensive measures was reason one. Effected in order to put as many rounds between the Eternals and their oncoming foes as possible. Reason two, accuracy through overwhelming firepower.

There were some survivors from the initial Spilursan assault team on that stairwell, but in no way, shape, or form did they manage to gain a foothold on eight. Wounded and pinned, the surviving Animals had advanced mere meters from the stairwell when the armor rebooted and allowed both Eternals full access to their enhanced targeting and acquisition systems. Seconds later those few survivors of the lead Animal squad died mid-sentence in their frantic sitreps back to command.

But these Animals were only the first. Within two minutes of first contact, heavy assault teams pressed down and forward, pushing through without remorse or thought of the dead dying all around them in the blur of incoming gunfire. Both wings of the Eternals' Chaos team were engaged in relentless combat.

However, both assaults, as hacked comm traffic would later reveal, were in the end merely probes from the Spilursan commander. The main assault was coming directly at the two Eternals who guarded the central lift hub. Crometheus and Marz.

The main lift was an open well in which a massive hexagonal-shaped freight platform descended. Standard in much of that era's utilitarian architecture, Ice Station Hades's central core revolved around the transport system. Surrounding the hexagonal shaft, large enough to accommodate a small sports field, was a recessed walkway.

The smaller personnel lifts opened up from the wall onto this walkway.

Once the Spilursan commander determined that he would meet Savage resistance on eight, he ordered the lift dropped to that level. At its center he'd parked the fortress's only tank. A Spilursan Type-Seven Tiger, anti-air variant. Not known for its superior firepower, because that wasn't what was needed on an island fortress in the middle of a frozen lake at the top of the world, but commended for its heavy armor shielding and quad anti-aircraft heavy pulse weapon systems. Which had also proven to be effective as anti-personnel weapons.

Surrounding the tank was an improvised fort. The Spilursan operators had erected portable blast field barriers, a recently developed defensive system that deployed charged shields that would stand up to both energy weapons and slug throwers in much the same way a starship's defensive shielding did. Huddled Spilursan soldiers, each platoon augmented by a special forces operator, waited to engage the enemy under the protection of the Tiger's quad pulse system. The level would be taken from within, starting at the lift.

Crometheus and Marz waited in the shadows, behind duracrete support pillars under the recessed walkway.

"Here they come," noted Marz. In the background of their comm Alantra was screaming something about Immaculus being down. Things were going sideways over at the southern stairwell. But that was their problem, thought Crometheus.

The Animals were coming now.

Gods:
Chapter Thirty-One

The Spilursan Tiger tank opened fire the instant the lift was down and locked into place on level eight. Four brilliant streams of high-speed pulse fire spat forth and undulating rays of what looked like searing lightning raked the industrial-gray concrete walls not far from the alcoves Crometheus and Marz were covering in.

At the same moment all of the lift doors began to open on empty shafts along the recessed walkways.

"They'll drop in on static lines in the smaller lift shafts," murmured Marz, cool as a cucumber despite the hectic scream of immense pulse fire flooding over ambient sound. "Stay ready, Crometheus."

The fire from the tank was prepping an area on the opposite side of the hexagon for the huddling Spilursan soldiers to move into. It was clear their on-site commander had no idea how many Uplifted they were facing, or where exactly their enemies were, so they were relying on overwhelming firepower to establish position until they could ascertain the disposition of the forces arrayed against them.

As if on cue a detachment of Spilursan Animals, their sergeants shouting at them, hustled forward in wedge formation, heading directly away from Crometheus and Marz. Red targeting lasers danced across the smoke-filled darkness as the quad guns on the Type-Seven Tiger fell silent for a moment.

"They're shifting fire," murmured Marz. "Hold position."

An expectant hydraulic hum could be heard as the tank's turret rotated to a new firing arc. And at the same time rope lines fell into the empty shafts along the walls of the main lift. The Animals would be coming down those rappel lines soon. Arriving at the backs of the two Uplifted Eternals tasked with defending this point.

Crometheus shouldered his primary and pulled both hand cannons off their carries. The work would be tight and close here under the recessed walkway. Better with sidearms.

"Good move," whispered Marz, noting Crometheus's switch to CQB weapons. "If we lose here… fall back to the flow control station. A highlighted route appeared in Crometheus's HUD.

Over ambient they could hear the thumps of the boots of the rappelers coming down the shafts. Then the quad pulse turret on the tank opened up again, blistering another section of the hexagonal main lift with overwhelming firepower. More troops rushed into the newly blasted area a second later. Troops were shouting, but it was clear they had comm going on and there would be a lot of intel for the taking if the Chaos team could hack in.

"Alantra," said Marz.

Nothing but silence came back over the comm for a long moment. Then... her voice was breathy and rushed. But not frightened. Crometheus had heard the exact same tone and rush from various junkies he'd once known. Possibly even himself, a time or two long ago.

"Die! Die! And you!" A series of loud bangs as the 1000 she was carrying unloaded on full auto in some tight space. The smash of gunfire echoed and repeated. "You're next, vermin!" she screamed. And then fired again. Whatever was going on at her loc was unclear, but it sounded like she was on the distributing end of an epic slaughter.

"Alantra..." Marz tried again over the cacophony. His voice firmer this time. Trying to get her attention despite the adrenaline rush of her kill streak.

"What? What?" she shrieked emphatically. "Busy as a bee here, Marz."

More automatic gunfire. Return pulse fire coming from close by.

"Need a hack on the Animal comm system. They're coming down the lifts in force. The fight will be on our loc. Intel would be useful."

"Immaculus is dead!" she shouted back as though she hadn't heard the request from Marz. "Game-overed by the animals when we got overrun. I'm falling back to reactor three." Then: "See what I can do!"

Two separate teams of Animal soldiers in the main lift were now working their way toward Crometheus and Marz from opposite directions along the recessed walkway, and the tank's massive quad turret was now swiveling on a hydraulic tone, coming close to bearing down on them.

"Now! Engage! Engage!" shouted Marz over the comm. They would try to take the momentum before the tank started firing.

Their plan had been to fight from beneath the recessed walkway, using the solid support columns as cover. The duracrete pillars, blocky and angular with small status displays for various station functions glowing in the drifting smoke and darkness, would stand up to pulse fire. Crometheus and Marz could cover and fire in succession as they moved from pillar to pillar. It was a good plan.

But they hadn't counted on that tank. That had been pretty brilliant on the part of the Animal commander, dropping armor right into the middle of a base.

Crometheus moved first and quickly, targeting the dark shadows coming down his side under the curving walkway that encircled the massive shaft. Enemy targeting lasers danced neurotically across every surface as rounds from both hand cannons, fired in succession, smashed into that advancing group of Animals. A second later, a hail of pulse fire, bright blue and almost like lightning moving in a thundering plain's herd, erupted out across the darkness in response.

Crometheus had multiple tangos down, according to the HUD. But the Animals had reinforcements and they weren't busy with the casualties he'd caused them.

Crometheus covered behind a pillar, poked one hand cannon around the corner, and fired without aiming. A blur of heavy caliber on full auto. Thirty rounds exploded down the walkway and it was anyone's guess how many found a target. That wasn't the point. The point was keeping their heads down while Marz shifted positions.

The other Eternal raced like a shadowy blur past him, firing and sprinting for the next pillar forward of his position.

Men... *Bad Thought*... just Animals really... were screaming in the darkness ahead as Marz shot them down.

An Animal came rappelling down the shaft nearest Crometheus, holding a subcompact pulse rifle in one hand. Crometheus hit him with five shots from his off-hand sidearm. Excessive, but why not make a point? Maybe someone coming down the lift shaft above the dead Animal would think twice about being tricky.

The operator died, dangling and bleeding in the well of the shaft, and more Animals dropped down beside him and fired through the lift's exit onto that level. But Crometheus was already gone, shifting for the next firing position as Marz covered.

They were in it now. Mixed in and among the Spilursan troops swarming the walkway. Within seconds, and faster than he'd expected, Crometheus was firing point-blank into the startled faces of the Animals as both sides unexpectedly met. One tried to deploy a grenade, and Crometheus batted at him with a powerful strike from the augmented cybernetic arm of his armor. The Animal soldier went stumbling back toward the tank, and the explosive device he was carrying went off against a defensive barrier.

Someone attacked Crometheus with a knife in the dark.

Pulse fire streaked past his helmet from close at hand.

He felt someone use their rifle to butt-stroke his armored midsection. The Animal's rifle shattered.

He fired back, riddling that one with wild fire that tore holes in his chest.

A dark shadow grabbed one of his hand cannons. Suddenly. Desperately. Crometheus tried to shake the man off, while firing with that same weapon into the face of another Spilursan soldier who'd pushed forward and tried to bring his pulse rifle to bear. The round from Crometheus's sidearm took that man's head off.

The dangler on his arm continued to try to drag the weapon down and out of the firing arc to no avail. His twisted rictus of a face was snarling, fear-struck, and angry all at once that he was helpless against the incredible strength the Eternal armor provided. The Animal knew that he was in the worst of all possible positions as Crometheus rammed his plated knee forward and broke the man's ribs. Gasping for air, the Animal collapsed into the other bodies along the floor.

Crometheus took a step back, steadying one hand cannon forward to engage any targets ahead and dropping the other to fire off finishing shots into the man on the ground.

That was when the tank opened up, filling the battle space surrounding Crometheus and Marz with an intense and overwhelming amount of fire.

Gods:
Chapter Thirty-Two

There are things that happen in battles. Amateurs get lucky. Grenades explode directly underneath something and fail to kill or even maim anyone. Artillery falls indiscriminately, mindlessly killing one while leaving another nearby standing. The trained and the untrained can both become corpses in a battle, and though reason at times has something to do with it... at other times, it matters not at all. Who can say what will happen when the shots start flying?

Such are the vagaries of war.

As the darkness of the recessed corridor that ringed the heavy-duty lift platform filled with the intensity of pulse fire from the Tiger's quad-linked turrets, Crometheus turned to see Marz literally disintegrate, the bright blue pulses tearing him to shreds in half a second.

Game-overed. No doubt about that.

In the sudden ghostly blue starlight created by the tank's fire, Crometheus saw all the Animals that had surrounded him in shadow... now revealed. Their twisted and leering and, yes, even haunted features made clear in that terrible moment. Determined to kill. This was a snapshot of a kind of the last seconds of the battle there at the main lift. A memory he would carry away—of them, the Animals, the worst of humanity, surrounding Marz, the best of what humanity was capable of becoming. *Homo deus.*

And everyone was torn to shreds.

All of them.

Save Crometheus.

The tank's turret operator cut a wide swath of searing bright destruction across that entire section of the corridor.

The pulse fire missed him for no discernible reason.

Such are the vagaries of war.

He hadn't ducked. Hadn't dodged. Just some fault in the timing of lethality meets target that caused the four bright streams of destruction to miss him entirely when everyone else was ruined in the same moment.

A moment that may have lasted, at best, seven seconds. A moment of apocalyptic blue hell.

And then the quad turret ceased and everything it had touched had turned to melting ceramic, smoking plastic, burnt flesh, and charred bone. Armor and weapons. Cooked flesh. Original and synthetic. A damaged power conduit flashed and erupted in a sudden shower of sparks. Damage control lights went off around it signaling a fatal rupture in the system it fed, or operated, or diagnosed.

Crometheus ran.

Dashing for the exit that led to flow control, their established fallback point.

The quad turret was not silent for long. The gunner allowed the guns to cool down and the barrels to finishing their firing spool, then spun it all up again to engage Crometheus as he sprinted for the exit.

Crometheus used both hand cannons to pull for all he was worth, arms and weapons dragging him forward and away from the arc of the four barrels of the quad turret and their hot fire that sprang at him once more. Legs pumping and heavy armored combat boots thumping, running from the battle that had just been lost, he made the opening and slammed the panel to shut the emergency blast door behind him. It knifed into place, sealing him off from incoming fire.

Moving forward through the infinity of cross-shaped sections that was the master flow control for reactor three, Crometheus opened the comm to find out who was still operational in the Chaos team. His HUD was getting signal interference and failed to provide squad bio readouts.

"Status report," he demanded over the ether.

After a pause, Zur came in.

"Low on ammo, Cro. We've ceded the access well and are dropping back to reactor three external venting. Going to set up a kill zone there. Smaug is hit bad but says he can hold."

"Copy," replied Crometheus, falling back into their pseudo-military gamer chat that had long ago evolved into the lingua franca of the Uplifted marines. "I'm in flow control but it's a bad loc to hold. May have to fight from reactor control. Alantra, what's your ten?"

Her voice was low and whispery. Breathy almost.

"Completing hack on their comm. My area is overrun. I've crawled into the outer hull of the station with one of their dead. Dissecting comm and should have an analysis of their traffic shortly. Stand by."

Crometheus heard plate cutters going to work on the blast door behind him. It wouldn't take the Animals long to get through. Then they'd breach in force. But the one thing he had going for him was that they couldn't get the tank in here. The tank would protect their access point in the lift well, but that was all it could do. The quarters were too tight for it to move deeper into the station. If he could fall back and link up with Commander Zero, he might be able to acquire an anti-armor one-shot. They'd brought a few with them in the long trek across the ocean bottom, but many had been used up to knock out hardened points of Animal resistance on the lower levels.

"Crometheus to Commander Zero."

He waited. The station's electromagnetic shielding to protect the cloud had made comm traffic between the levels spotty at best. But a moment later she came through, her voice tinny and far away.

"Zero here. What's your status, Crometheus?"

"We've disrupted their main assault. Marz and Immaculus game-overed. Hacking enemy comm at the moment… For now, we're holding at reactor three."

It was quiet as he ran along the cliffs of flow control. Four massive blocks that linked up to the reactor jutted out into a central well. The power that pulsed through them was ominous. And not for the first time did Crometheus wonder if the shielding was enough to deflect the high-explosive ammunition they were getting down to. He'd need to use that soon just to stay in the fight.

He checked his HUD. He was still on six point five. And down to half on the fifty cal for the Automags.

"Acknowledged, Crometheus," replied Commander Zero. "We're receiving satellite uplink traffic from the sensor grid we installed out on the lakebed. Our ships are in-system and commencing the assault. We don't have to hold much longer. But we do have to prevent the Animals from tracking down Maestro if they decide to go looking for what we did to their cloud while we had access. Which they will. Also… their special operations teams have just dropped submersibles via airborne assault group. They'll try to take us from below. I can't spare anyone to relieve you at this time. We have to hold the core. Hold in place until our allies breach the station from the surface. I need you to hold your position and keep them out of the main core."

In other words… they were surrounded on all sides without much room to maneuver. If they failed, the Animals were familiar enough with their own cloud core system to run a sweep and find Maestro. Then everything they'd attempted would have been for nothing.

"We'll hold," he said over the comm.

There was a pause.

Then, "For honor and glory, Cro," she said, as if it were she who had found the right answer. Fake it until you make it.

"For honor… and glory," he replied. Telling her she'd found it. The next step along the Path. Maybe the last. Maybe this was his last message to his tribe.

Then the comm went dead.

Gods:
Chapter Thirty-Three

Within minutes Alantra had created a live feed from the incoming enemy comm traffic. It was clear the Animals were sensing their moment of victory in retaking the station. That resistance on level eight had been less than expected was considered a sign that their enemy was reeling. And though there had been casualties, there weren't as many as expected. They were going to push hard now.

"What next, Cro?" asked Alantra as they both listened to the hacked feed. Crometheus said nothing as he swapped out new mags. She was working her way through an internal duct system to reactor three. Zur was pinned down in a vent under a furious crossfire from two Animal elements. There was no way to relieve or rescue him without leaving reactor three undefended.

Reactor three was the failsafe in the Animal plan, according to the hacked traffic. If they couldn't crack level nine where the cloud was being held by the rest of the force, then they'd det the reactor higher up in the station and solve the whole problem in one epic nuclear fireball. So holding reactor three until Uplifted reinforcements arrived was essential.

"The way I see it," began Alantra in the absence of an answer, "they'll be coming at you from sub-maintenance, main supply, and the dock on the starboard side. All three lead straight into the reactor. If they override the blast doors, or even just cut through them, they can come straight at you."

Again, Crometheus could think of nothing to say. Everything she was saying added up. There were no easy answers or tricky plans. Options were nil to non-existent. It's one thing to talk about death… it's another thing to actually face it.

What did that feel like?

It felt like you were speechless and strangling on words that wouldn't come. It was like having nothing to say and instead resigning yourself to the fate you'd so glibly chosen when the moment hadn't been as real as the one you found yourself in.

Crometheus looked around at the space he found himself in. The reactor was state-of-the-art. Housed within a massive cavern, the central bulb of the nano-reactor hung four stories above his head. On the floor of reactor control everything was dark save the flickering lights and glowing panels of the control systems. Massive superconductor coils arced away from the reactor, transferring energy to the rest of the fortress.

At that moment the station was rocked by some explosion in the levels far below. No doubt the Animals were attacking with their submersibles. A mere split second later, anti-personnel explosions erupted in the corridors elsewhere on Crometheus's level. Zur's biometric feed, recently reacquired, flickered out. Signal was still good. Indicating... the Animals were coordinating their attacks. They had a pretty good idea of what they were facing and they were working together.

"He's gone..." Alantra said forlornly over comm.

"I know," Crometheus replied.

"So... again... what's our plan now, Crometheus?" she asked after a long minute of silence. He could hear the fear trying to creep into her voice. He could also hear her fighting it back, not allowing it to get a claw hold inside her mind.

Crometheus couldn't chance damage to the reactor. Which meant the HE ammo was out. Everything would be for nothing at that point, never mind that they'd all get cooked. Honor and glory tasted like dry things in his new mouth at that moment and he wondered why he'd ever volunteered for this. He licked his lips and thought about the sensation. It was real. Just as it had been long ago.

That was... good. Something good from a good time long ago. As simple as licking your lips. Imagine that.

He remembered candy and snacks you could buy at Little League games. Powder that you dipped a candy stick in and licked.

Life... life was good.

"I'm going to attack the main body," he said. "I'll try and do enough damage to convince them to pull back before assaulting the reactor. That's the best I can do now. Give them something to think about and force them to reassess. Maybe that buys us a few more minutes for the main body to hit the station. Maybe. I don't know."

"Okay… I'm in. We can link up at—"

"Negative. Get to the reactor and disable all the control systems. It won't prevent them from destroying it, but it'll slow them down when they do take it. Either way it gives us a little more room for reinforcements to arrive."

"Cro… that's over a thousand coming straight at you. It's suicide."

His last words to her were, "It… always was." And then just before he cut the comm, "Do whatever it takes to stop them. If there's a way disable their ability to melt it down… I'll buy you as much time as I can."

And then he was gone.

Gods:
Chapter Thirty-Four

There was some song playing in his head. He couldn't remember it completely. Only just barely. Some song from when he was a kid. Before he'd left the place he'd called home. When it had been a real place and not just a digital reimagining inside a massive MMO playground they'd decided was more real than that same reality itself was. From when he'd been real too.

Real.

The song was some determined march, or dirge, or ballad maybe by a synth-pop band. Something that had always made him think thoughts of gravitas... duty... and fate. Even when he was a kid.

Soldier thoughts, he'd always thought of them as.

Things he thought were important when he was a child. *When I was a child I spake as a child* he remembered a preacher preaching. Once and long ago.

Funny, he thought. Funny how at the end... old things keep coming back no matter how hard you try to forget them. Or keep them alive.

And...

Would Holly Wood be there at the end? He'd always had that fantasy. That there would be some kind of final reckoning between the two of them other than the one where he'd...

Edit.

... where she'd left. Some apology from him. Some final absolution from her. That she would show one last time at the end of everything.

But was that impossible.

That had been the script as it was written in his head.

But he was trillions of miles and centuries up time's stream. And she'd stayed on lost Earth. Long ago.

No, he told himself, when you're storming an ice station on an alien world trillions of miles from home, chance meetings of a serendipitous nature with long-lost loves aren't very likely.

That should be a law right up there with gravity, he thought to himself.

So then, maybe a miracle—though he'd never believed in them. Some wise woman had once written something in a book he'd read between concerts. Halfway between Reno and Rome. Lying in a musty old hotel room waiting to come on stage. Waiting to come to life. She'd written... *Sometimes you pray, even when you don't believe.*

He was marching straight into the teeth of the oncoming enemy element determined to take back the station with everything they had. It would take a miracle to come out the other side. That was for sure. This was not a fight... it was that other thing. That thing he'd been contemplating before the weekend seminar at the airport Marriott.

Funny how all the old things come back around. No matter how hard you try to avoid them.

The Animals were moving in wedges, supported by marksmen fire. Coming straight at him according to the tac map overlay in his HUD. All of it glowing a ghostly white, reminding him of old first-gen computer games. Text adventures. That blocky white overlay where you were supposed to imagine the living breathing world of the game. Except that too was an illusion.

Over four hundred of them, heavily armed Animals, clogging main access to get at him. He was holding the 1000 rifle down and ready to engage. Loaded now with the high-explosive five-shot, as were all the ready mags in his carrying system.

He could damage the station. Not enough to blow the thing. Just enough for the reactor to protect itself via emergency blast doors and bulkheads. He could damage it and hoped they pulled back to avoid being sealed within.

Like he would be.

That was the only chance he had.

For honor and glory, right?

But he was banking on something different. On a hope. A hope that the Animals were confident enough in their numbers not to expect a frontal assault from a lone Savage marine. He'd done it to them once… he could do it again.

Not Uplifted. Not anymore. He'd become what they were afraid of now. He'd accept, and embody, their darkest nightmare.

The Savage.

A thing from the outer dark. The stellar boogeyman. He would be that to them now. He would embrace who he really was. The Savage. That's what he would become in this last attack. He'd shed the polite term of Uplifted. He'd become their nightmare. The Savage that carried away their women and ate their children. He'd embrace that now, here at the last. If just to save himself a few seconds longer and kill just a few more.

They'd be thinking they'd have to dig out defenders all the way to their objective. The last thing they'd expect was a single boogeyman straight from the Nether. Coming right for them.

He sighted the lead element of the Animal's main assault down the narrow central corridor. Targeting and data feed came in from the 1000, and he steadied himself, then pulled the trigger and fired. Full auto. Releasing an eighty-round mag in seconds. Caseless six-point-fives shot through the air between Savage and Animals, five-round groups flying almost as one, and smashed into the lead element. The explosive inside each round fired and another dumb slug launched itself forward at two thousand five hundred meters per second. It was like shooting a hurricane of nails.

The armor recorded multiple secondary and tertiary hits. No station damage yet.

Crometheus flung himself against one of the angular walls, covering behind a bulkhead, and reached for a new mag. His fingers doing the work of automatically releasing the dead mag. His muscles trained perfectly in sim for this unthinking task. His mind busy plotting his next killing move. He would go forward and drive on them. He would push them and push them again until they had to fall back.

That was what he'd do now.

The unexpected. Here at the last.

Within the HUD he watched the whole sensor layout of the advancing force come to a sudden halt. Someone opened up with heavy automatic pulse fire, and the corridor turned into a world filled by a thousand angry flaming hornets.

The moment there was a pause in the fusillade, Crometheus dove forward out into the corridor, not bothering to aim, and let the weapon fire with one hand as he scrambled for another bulkhead ten meters ahead. Closer to the enemy. Push them, he thought.

He landed against the wall on the opposite side of the access tunnel. He'd used up half a mag of HE for his own covering fire. Stopping them now was more important than worrying about collateral damage to the reactor. It could be repaired, but it couldn't be retaken. There just weren't enough of their force left. So he'd switched to high-explosive munitions.

Over the comm he could hear their ponderously slow NCOs freaking out that he was advancing on them. Which was perfect. They swore in disbelief that he was actually attacking.

He shucked the bando of frags from around his neck, pulling it over his helmet, and activated its daisy-chain mode. A long depress of the last grenade in the string gave him three flashing green lights indicating the mode was operative. He lobbed the bando down the corridor at the attacking force. Halfway between him as his targets.

Useless if it exploded just now.

Deadly if proximity mode was activated and someone came at him.

Which it was.

Which they did.

Already the element commander was ordering a charge forward to overrun. Covering fire turned up in volume and Crometheus hugged wall, feeling his chest within his armor heave like a desperate bellows, hearing their boots thumping-thundering to close with him. They were pressing forward and only the *crack*s of designated marksmen fire, farther down-tunnel and far too careful, announced their impending meeting with Death.

I am Death.

Because that's what a Savage is. Death personified.

He needed to give them something to be distracted by so they'd didn't see the bando. He stepped out into the corridor and cut loose with the 1000 again, firing from the hip, letting the HUD show him where his impacts would land.

Rounds slipped through men and smashed into a second line coming behind. But there were a lot of them. Some threw themselves to the deck or hugged wall and targeted him with return fire. Incoming pulse fire was inaccurate at first as both sides collided with each other. On the one side, four hundred in a narrow cone, funneling straight at him with high-grade military weapons throwing everything they had at him. And on the other, a lone Savage marine, working the 1000 dry and ejecting the mag. By the time the latest magazine clattered to the deck, empty, his perfectly trained body's muscle memory had a new one in. The weapon auto-racked the first round and began to spit forth relativistic death into the faces of the oncoming Animal horde.

There were advantages. The fact that he was facing vastly superior numbers in such a narrow space meant only so many could get an engagement window on him at a time. Lots of friendly fire. And the HE ammo was a game-changer. It tore through anything and everything.

But those advantages… weren't enough.

Crometheus took a pulse fire blast in the gut, and it burned like hot fire. The next one, or maybe the first one, they hit so close together it was hard to tell, smashed into his armored leg. It deflected, but the leg was surely broken. He knew that for sure even as he collapsed onto one knee, his mind roaring red murder.

The third round smashed into his helmet. The HUD cracked and sounded like an old-school television set hitting a parking lot after being thrown from a seventh-floor balcony.

He knew that sound.

From his rock and roll days.

He remembered the hotel entertainment system's arc and long fall off the presidential suite's balcony. And some perpetually unhappy bandmate, the bassist maybe, finding some small joy in that momentary destruction they'd shared together.

He stopped firing and pulled his fractured helmet off, wondering how badly he was hit in the head. Hearing nothing but a dull ringing in his ears and wondering if half his skull was blown off.

What did you think would happen? he asked himself in some subroutine of his mind. *That you'd actually beat four hundred to one odds?*

Rounds streaked past him, but it was clear the enemy was having a problem figuring out what the hell was going on. The front rank of dead were torn to pieces, the wounded were struggling away from the onslaught, and for a moment the troops at the rear weren't sure who was friend and who was foe.

And then the first Animal soldier reached the bando's sphere of detection.

He tripped all thirteen grenades at once.

Streaking hot needles exploded in every direction within the passage. But the attacking element bore the brunt. Micro-packed needles, over six hundred in each explosive device, thirteen devices in all... *walnut shell and temple bells worn around the neck*... streaked away from the device at incredible speeds, shredding flesh and tearing out eyes and ripping arteries and organs to pieces. Literally turning the closest bodies into nothing but raw hamburger while ranks of Animal soldiers as far back as sixty meters suddenly found white-hot shards of metal sticking out of their skin or armor or going straight through a helmet and destroying the fragile brain matter beneath. And the mind within.

It sounded like someone had dropped a thousand ornate crystal chandeliers all at once while setting off some serious high-grade fireworks. And the carnage wrought was incredible. Over a quarter of the attacking force was torn to shreds.

When he opened his eyes he could only see out of one. The other had been destroyed by a fragment. Some linked system within his mind, still talking to the armor's AI, told him he'd been hit by three other shards across his body.

The armor was busy pumping him full of painkillers and compressing wound punctures to stop the bleeding in the most heavily damaged areas.

He got to his feet, barely, one leg ruined forever. But the armor had doped that appendage to full and tightened it to allow some restricted movement.

He pulled the trigger on the 1000 at a distant Animal soldier staggering, armless, down-corridor away from him in the aftermath of the tremendous explosion.

He got a dry click from the 1000's receiver indicating the rifle's mag was empty. His fingers, not working too well as his mind tried to stabilize and find balance, found a new mag and slipped it in, covering it in his new blood. Then he set off, stumbling and limping through the field of ruined bodies and bloody pulp that had become this section of the corridor. Firing at distant targets running away from him.

The enemy force was reacting slowly. Not sure what had happened or why over a quarter of the force had suddenly gone off comm. Clearly something had gone horribly wrong as far as those in command were concerned. The lead element had just suddenly... disappeared.

Vaporized.

Poof.

A team of enemy soldiers, Animals, was coming forward cautiously, targeting lasers searching through the smoke and ruin. Maybe they thought he was one of theirs... one of them without the helmet. The profile of his image messing with their targeting acquisition. He didn't wait to find out and instead hit the heavy gunner at the tip of their spear with a burst from the 1000. He worked the weapon over this new threat as they scrambled for cover and when it ran dry of rounds he dropped to the deck and crawled behind a mass of ruined bodies, many of them still smoking from high-velocity needle-sharp wounds of the daisy-chain explosion.

To his right was a narrow intersecting maintenance shaft. He crawled into it, dragging his useless leg behind him, dropping the empty 1000 as a fusillade of pulse fire shot down the corridor he'd just left. Through his ruined armor's comm system, coming over a secondary speaker not connected to the helmet, a backup feature, he could hear Commander Zero, broken and distorted, telling him something. Something important.

But his ears were still ringing.

On his gauntlet a small panel lit up. The armor was trying to help him. Its secondary comm panel and downloaded training surfaced through his blasted mind and senses, reminding him he could use this to connect with his... tribe.

Uplifted? No.

Eternals... yes.

He raised the opposite gauntlet, saw one of the frag needles sticking out of his wrist, through his wrist really, and touched the comm contact. Then he pulled out the needle. There was no pain, but his muscles were shaking.

Again the armor was probably doing its job. But it was clear this body was ruined.

As long as my mind isn't, he thought distantly, as Commander Zero came through. He could hear weapons fire close and personal. Things weren't going too good down there either, or so it seemed.

"Cro ... Uplift ... allies here. Hold ... at all costs!"

He nodded. Tried to say something. Nothing came out. His voice didn't want to work. He tapped the confirm icon and slumped against the side of the tunnel in the dark. He could hear more of them, the Animal warriors, coming now, stepping over the dead. Wondering if they'd killed him. Hoping they had.

His old selves.

The Animals.

What they all once were. Had been. Once and long ago.

"Bad Thought," he rasped, and laughed raggedly. Then pulled the Automags from off his thighs.

"Honor..." he croaked to no one. And... "Glory."

He waded out into his last gunfight at almost point-blank range. Surprising them. Firing from just meters away. Knowing that even stopping them now, just for a moment, would slow their advance on the reactor, buy a little more time to protect the cloud. And if they could save the cloud... then when the rest of the Uplifted arrived...

Well then... That would... be... something.

He fired at the first soldier. A sweating black man carrying a pulse rifle. Three rounds smashed into the guy's guts and Crometheus flung him aside.

... That would be something. Infecting all the Uplifted with the Path. If they held the cloud they could win. Would win. Everything.

The flung Animal hit another soldier and Crometheus swept the men close at hand with fire from both weapons, the hand cannons booming out quickly in successive concussions. Massive rounds smashing into flesh and bone. Puncturing armor. Dispensing death in violent impacts.

The Unity Virus was the win.

Animals NCOs were trying to organize for this new fight that had broken out in all the carnage of the blown-to-pieces lead element.

Someone behind this first bunch freaked out—wisely, thought some distant part of Crometheus's tactical mind—and cut loose with a long burst of heavy pulse fire. Men were torn to shreds regardless of what side they served on. Crometheus crouched, fired back with his off hand and no targeting, and did a decent job of blowing off the heavy gunner's head.

Now they were all freaking out.

Like the dumb slow Animals they were, and always would be, they panicked as a herd because he was willing to stand up to them with everything he had. Within the space of ten seconds they were being told to "Fall back!" again. Someone had falsely estimated they'd run into a main body of Savages. Unexpected. An ambush. Too many to deal with. Regroup and assess. Whatever.

Crometheus stumbled after them, firing into their backs and knocking them down onto their ripped chests and bellies. Crushing their skulls as he stepped over them.

Dragging his leg, firing first one hand cannon and then the other. Dealing out death on this last battlefield.

"You're facing a god!" he screamed at them. But all that came out was a ragged gasping croak. All he could see was seen out of one eye. The other ruined. And he was probably dying.

But he had really lived. He had become a god in the end. At the end.

And that was life. A real life.

Wasn't it?

Could they, these fear-driven herd Animals, say as much? he thought as he advanced on them down-tunnel. Engaging as he went. They tried to set up a defense, but they were so panicked they lobbed a grenade first. He kicked it right back at them and it exploded within the perimeter of the control area they'd planned to defend. It went off and ruined them long enough for him to suddenly be in and among them, shooting them down at point-blank once more like some ruined savage horror from the nether where nightmares are real.

Both hand cannons were smoking when he exited the control station, hearing their boots thunder off down other corridors just to get away from him.

He heard distant firing. The telltale rattle and cackle of automatic gunfire. Old-school. The Uplifted.

Savages.

His mind was fading, and he knew if they came back for him now all he could do was maybe fire a few shots before he was empty. Whatever adrenaline the new body had been able to manufacture was gone now. Fading. And with it... him.

He leaned against a wall along a processor-filled corridor. Standing over the dead he'd shot down just seconds earlier. He looked back down the tunnel the way he'd come. Not that long ago. Just a few minutes.

"Time's a funny... thing..." he muttered. But really he just gasped a series of croaks no one would have understood.

Like the journey to the stars, from the Earth of long ago... that corridor was littered with the dead he'd left behind in all the long crossings from Reno to Rome.

And he didn't feel too bad about it. Not at all.

That was life.

Kill your way forward to the next level. You only get one quarter. So make it count.

He'd done that.

When he had that last thought, he could hear the gunfire getting closer. Coming for him.

Or coming to help?

Hard to say now. And it didn't really matter. He was done. That much was...

He slid down the wall, surely leaving his own blood, and lay with only his shoulders resting against it. Both massive sidearms resting on his legs.

... true. He could still kill a few more if they chose to come this way. But they'd need to come soon... because there wasn't much time left.

His eye, the last one this body had, closed.

"Master Crometheus..."

It was Maestro.

"Mission accomplished, Master Cro. The base is now under Uplifted control. Our forces are advancing on the core to secure the data they've come for. It's where I'm waiting to infect them with the Unity Virus that will show them the way to become what we all must be. Gods. Every one of us gods, Master Crometheus."

The dying Savage marine mumbled something.

Maybe "Holly Wood." Expecting as he always had that there would be some final moment between the two of them.

"I'm turning you off," said Maestro gently.

"Game... overed?" he croaked. Thinking of the arcade. Of all the tokens he'd ever dropped. Of the feel of them, each and every one and every time he'd slipped one into the slot and pressed play. A new chance to get it all right. Again. "Something... 'bout that," he managed. "Feeling."

Was the best feeling in the whole world. Was what he thought the shape of life would be when he was young and wanted to do it all.

The station shook. Nearby was another burst of automatic gunfire. Then a fusillade that seemed to cook the whole world. Alarms were going off.

"They're taking this level. Your brothers and sisters, Master Crometheus. Our fellow Uplifted. And no... not game over. But for now, the other Uplifted will need to think that you and the rest of the Eternals died in a pre-emptive strike against the station. They'll be less wary of accessing the core that way. So now you're going to sleep. And then...

we'll start over, young master. I'm accessing that trick I showed you. Message from Lusypher to follow..."

Menus began to flash across Crometheus's mind at lightning speed. Whether he liked it or not. And then... the voice of Lusypher. His message was simple. To the point.

"Well done, son. This is just the beginning."

Crometheus closed his eyes... and he was gone.

Gone from the battle.

Gone.

* * *

He was back home. Back in the world he'd burnt down.

It was late morning on a spring day. The sky was a chromatic blue and the quality of light was brilliant. There wasn't a sound. Just ruin. Charred ruin for miles around. The gas station that had exploded and burnt to the ground. The streets that had melted in the fire. The strip mall burnt to nothing but charred beams lying in piles of neat destruction.

The neighborhoods and schools of his youth, for as far as the eye could see... were nothing but drifting piles of ash.

And...

... it was beautiful... to him.

It was like... like that token-into-the-slot moment each time he played again and anew. A second chance. A second chance to get it all right again. A chance to rebuild the narrative and frame it right this time.

One more time. One more chance.

Regardless of the truth.

Regardless of what had gone before.

Regardless of what had really happened and who he'd really been. Those things could be edited.

I can be anything I want to be this time, he'd always thought. Standing there amid the ruin and destruction that was like a fading dream he only half-remembered… He did remember the last time… he'd been a twenty-first-century rock star that time. He'd created a whole life of albums and excess. Triumphs and tragedies. Some details were like what really happened. Some not at all. Some borrowed and riffed on like… what had they called it back on Earth… jazz. Like jazz.

What is truth? someone had once asked a condemned man.

It's what you decide it is, answered the Devil.

That had ever been the motto of the Pantheon. The motto that had lifted him up out of a life he'd found disgusting. Prisoner. Politician. Guru insider long ago. He'd started over so many times he couldn't remember what the actual truth had ever really been. Who he really was. Sometimes he got glimpses. Fragments. But they always made him uncomfortable. Best to edit those when you found them. Like Jim Stepp. The marine who died in a foreign war. The toughest kid in school. Who killed a kid in a fight one afternoon.

Or about her. Leaving him.

Hadn't gone that way exactly.

Or the glimpses of the execution chamber especially. The trials. The long imprisonment back on Earth. The chance he'd been given if they could just experiment on him a little. The promise to make all the horrors go away.

And in time, he would decide what was truth. What had really happened, and what hadn't.

He would decide what to call good and evil.

A god's prerogative. Of course.

He closed his eyes and smelled the burnt char and listened to the lonely wind caressing the ruins of a place he'd burned down a thousand times before. And always kept coming back to.

He could make it new this time.

Something to reflect his new status as an Eternal. What his new story would be this next time round. Not rock star. He'd done that one. He'd have to think up something else. Something fun.

He opened his eyes and she was there. Across the ruin and rubble. Just standing there.

She was wearing that white silk dress that made her tanned skin and blond hair look so vibrant.

She was smiling at him like she never had. Or had she?

Like he'd always wanted her to.

The girl he'd murdered.

And loved.

Holly Wood.

He always started with her. Every time he rebuilt. Every time he started over. Here, in the secret place even Maestro couldn't find…

… or had he the last time?

Hard to say what was known. Hard to say what was true.

But he always started over with her.

PART II:
LEGIONNAIRES

"That's what makes Tyrus Rechs dangerous. Nothing... nothing ever makes sense to him except his own iron will. Because there's ever only one way. His way."

—Casper Sulla

Legionnaires: Chapter One

It occurred to me that there are now only ten people in the history of the world who have lived longer than us. Shem, I think, is next on the list. Waiting to be overtaken.

Not many people talk about those stories any longer. I used to think they were just myths. And while I'm not saying I *believe* any of them, living the life we've lived does make me wonder. Is what happened to us all on the *Moirai*... was that the Savages unlocking something ancient that mankind lost? And how much more remains unknown? Waiting for us?

I know those questions have been trapped in your head like earworms. And don't worry, I haven't told him. Though he would disagree with me, I don't see harm in thinking about the possibilities. I'm eager, Reina, to know where your mind is in all of this.

The three of us knew better than anyone else in the galaxy the true threat of the Savages. What was really lurking within those lighthuggers. And now, what everyone thought wasn't possible, has happened. Diverse Savages are working in tandem. They've taken New Vega, and as best I've gathered, they're staying.

So how to stop it?

You know where I stand. And we both knew where Tyrus stood. It still seems to me a miracle that he went along and decided to *really* try things my way.

I think—suspect—that I know your mind on how to stop it. But, please, don't. And if you never intended, then forgive me for my faithlessness.

Methuselah lived to be nine hundred and sixty-nine years old. And when he died, judgment came. I wonder, if we pass him, the man who lived longer than all others… what does that mean for the galaxy? Does the judgment of God come with our deaths?

The galaxy certainly can't profess its innocence.

I know. I'm talking like a madman. But life and death, and especially you, Reina, have been on my mind much as of late.

You know about what happened on New Vega. The reports from the survivors have no doubt reached you, wherever you are in the galaxy. News travels fast from one freighter crew to another. I can tell you that all of it is true. Worse than you heard, I'm sure, but not as bad as you might imagine. The Savages on New Vega… they were still clinging to some semblance of their humanity.

They weren't the truly bad ones. The ones *we* knew.

Tyrus and I think we can take New Vega back. Give the galaxy something inspirational. But that means crafting soldiers capable of fighting what will prove to be the most violent conflict the galaxy has ever seen.

The blood of world wars, the Mongol Conquest, all the rebellions of China and all the civil wars of Earth will hardly reach the ankles of the Savage giant that has now swept into the galaxy.

But we can win.

Hard men will always be victorious. The Savages are brutal. Depraved. Ghastly. But they are not hard men. Not like those Tyrus and I have forged in the Legion.

I suppose, if I'm honest with myself, that's the larger reason for my writing you. That a Legion will rise and emerge victorious over the Savages, I have no doubt. That I will live to see it, that anyone will know the sacrifices undertaken to get where we are now... of that I'm unsure.

But I wanted someone to know. Someone who would care. And someone I still, deeply care about. And so I'm telling it to you, Reina.

Legionnaires: Chapter Two

The obstacle course was similar to the hundreds Casper had seen before. Sand pits—wet and dry. Razor wire. Oil-slicked walls. Ropes. Towers. Turrets sending electro-shock pulse fire for any would-be graduate unable to keep their head low enough. Simulated artillery fire controlled by bots, all designed to make it feel close enough that you think, *I might actually die doing this.*

Casper himself had thought that very thing. Just last night, he believed the rounds were too close and the bots were programmed improperly and that he was—finally—going to die. When he and the rest of what would become the officer corps for Tyrus Rechs's new Legion went through the course themselves—to prove they could conquer it before judging the others who would attempt the same in the daylight—he thought his time had come to an end. There in the darkness, on this forested planet Rechs had selected, Casper believed the course would kill him.

But of course he didn't die. He made it through, even scoring a respectable time when put up against the bell curve. Rechs was the course leader, of course. A few officers washed out. And there were too few to begin with.

There had been a lot of failure already. Rechs had dismissed Legion candidates with extreme prejudice. And Casper wasn't sure he agreed with that. This war with the Savages—which was exactly what it was, even if the galactic governments didn't want to admit it—would require blood and steel. Bodies. And Tyrus Rechs seemed to be shipping more bodies out of training than he was pushing them through.

The general stood at Casper's side, along with a small cadre of officers who had kept up with Rechs's exacting standards.

"You wanna be a legionnaire," Rechs bellowed at a group of men struggling through wet sand that Casper had never felt the bottom of when he'd gone through, "first you gotta make Ranger!"

The veins in Rechs's neck bulged. His face was hot and carried a permanent scowl of hate. Casper knew this face. Had seen it before. It was his warfighter face. The one he put on whenever he let the galaxy fade away. When he surrendered himself to the blackness of his inner being that made him the most efficient and ruthless soldier Casper had ever known.

"General, we *made* Ranger, sir!"

The man speaking those words was named Greenhill. He had been part of the detachment of Spilursan Rangers that "Colonel Marks" had commanded on New Vega. And he was right. Greenhill and many of the other men accompanying Rechs on the journey from Savage-controlled New Vega *were* Rangers. And in one of those cosmic ironies unbeknownst to them, the Spilursan Ranger School had been created by Tyrus Rechs hundreds of years prior.

Yet, to Tyrus Rechs, none of that mattered.

"You were a *Spilursan* Ranger," Rechs bellowed, such ferocity in his voice that Casper wondered if his old friend was about to dive into the quicksand and make some point of violence. "Now you'll become one of *Rechs's* Rangers. And God help you if try to shirk duty in my presence again!"

Greenhill bit his lip and went back to the task of pulling himself through the muck, his uniform sloppy and caked with wet sand. It had taken Casper a half hour to wash it all away in the moments afforded him before wake-up. Greenhill would have no such opportunity. He would live with the gritty, irritating crust. Eat chow in the crust. Run in the crust. And finally find some reprieve when he swam across a stagnant pond.

What Rechs was putting these men through was brutal. Even by his standards. And it was clear that Casper's fellow officers thought the same. He could feel them looking at him. Watching him to see if he would challenge the general.

That Casper and Rechs were old friends was now well-known. Tales of their heated exchanges on New Vega had reached the rank and file of those who had joined them on this journey to become something capable of standing up to the Savages.

And now those officers were wondering if Casper was capable of standing up to Rechs.

But Casper said nothing. He noted the interaction on his battle board and watched Rechs stalking the sidelines of the course, screaming his displeasure at everything. Breaking the men down. Bringing them to a place where he could build upon their training and make them into something more than soldiers. To make them into clones of himself.

Because that's what would be needed to win against the Savages.

Rechs pulled back from his raving and looked at Casper. "Completions?"

"One in ten are dropping out," Casper replied. "Better retention than I would have guessed."

"They're good men," Rechs growled, low enough that only Casper could hear.

"About half the class has completed the course and is staged for trail run."

Rechs nodded. "Captain Milker!"

The officer ran from the huddled group of would-be Legion leaders and snapped to attention at Rechs's side. "Yes, sir!"

"Head to the finish line and get the men up and running. Twelve miles, Captain. Punish them."

Captain Milker nodded and, somewhat less excitedly this time, said, "Yes, sir."

"General," Casper said, examining his clipboard as though he had found an anomaly. In truth, he felt the time had come to check his friend. Things were getting too… draconian. "A moment?"

"Stand by," Rechs growled. He looked at the gathering of officers, trying to spot the one enlisted man he kept in that company. "CSM Andres?"

"Here, Colonel," said Command Sergeant Major Andres, emerging from behind a black-haired lieutenant whose face seemed to have more scars than whole flesh. Andres had not shaken the habit of calling Rechs "Colonel." A holdover from his first introduction to what was then an alias: Colonel Marks.

Andres was what Rechs referred to as his *backbone*. The burgeoning Legion structure was limited, given their insufficient numbers. Rechs had named himself general and no one argued. Milker had served as a lieutenant under Rechs on New Vega and was now the only captain on staff. The rest of the men were a collection of first and second lieutenants.

Casper had not yet been told his rank. He found himself filling the position of major, colonel, and, in cases of strategy, a brigadier general. But ranks and honorifics were of no concern to the man who had served as, and still was, an admiral for the United Worlds.

This was about making sure there was a galaxy left alive now that the Savages had come together.

"CSM," Rechs said, using the abbreviation that the entire command staff had adopted for Andres. "Motivate these men. Anyone who doesn't finish is out."

"Yes, Colonel." Andres moved to the obstacle course, walking up and down and picking up the intensive motivation where Rechs had left off. His hand continually went to his stomach, a subconscious tic, reaching toward the near-fatal wound he'd suffered at the hands of Savages on New Vega.

Rechs addressed his remaining lieutenants. "I want you to put together a list of potential NCOs. Base your assessment on what you've observed from point of landing to now. Whatever came before is *not* a factor. Understood?"

"Yes, sir," came the replies.

"Good. Dismissed."

The lieutenants ran back to the United Worlds capital ships that had cleared the training zone and now served as barracks and command centers. There were a lot of crew on those vessels—navy spacers and marines—who had opted not to try for Rechs's Legion. But they had seen New Vega. They knew something had to be done. They would support the efforts here the best they could.

Casper and Rechs now had their privacy. But Rechs did not switch off.

"Sulla," he growled.

Casper didn't have a problem being subordinate to his friend. "Yes, General."

"More men are washing out." Rechs nodded at a group of candidates pulling themselves out of the pit of wet sand. "Process them. Place them somewhere useful."

Casper nodded. "Yes, sir. And, Tyrus, about what I wanted to speak with you…"

"Dismissed, Sulla."

Legionnaires:
Chapter Three

"Admiral Sulla!"

The marines guarding access to Sulla's flagship, the assault frigate *Chang*, barked the words in acknowledgment of the important man returning to his command.

Casper saluted and stepped aboard. It was an odd feeling. On board the ship, he was the highest-ranking man on this uncharted forest world. So remote that whoever had first discovered it hadn't even bothered to give it a name. But once off, once a prospective member of the Legion, what was he?

Rechs had treated him almost... disdainfully. And though Sulla knew it was a quirk of Tyrus's personality, the unfamiliar dismissal left him feeling vexed. Hadn't the formation of a Legion been *his* idea? And though Rechs was beyond a doubt the right man to galvanize and forge such a fighting force, shouldn't Casper be given some acknowledgment, some appreciation, for finally bringing about this momentous force that would bring the galaxy together?

Finally together.

Casper had dreamed of what was happening now. Had talked endlessly about how to *make* it happen. But there had never been a way that didn't involve conquering. A bloody, modern-day Alexander capturing planet after planet, Hellenizing the galactic culture until humanity—at last—was unified. Except that unlike Alexander, Casper would keep on living.

But Rechs had no stomach for conquerors. He saw them as tyrants, necessarily. And there was no doubt in Casper's mind that if he attempted to become a Caesar, Rechs would be the man to stop him.

The thought of fighting his oldest friend was painful. Why gain the galaxy if it would cost you your soul? And what destroys a soul faster than the loss of a true friendship?

The Savages changed all that. Not the random, nomadic hulks that appeared to spread terror and were destroyed by a coalition of superior naval firepower. But this new threat. A coalition to counter the human coalition. The Savages who would stay.

The *conquering* Savage.

And that... that at last was something the galaxy could join together over. A common enemy. From Hitler to the die-back, history had shown Casper what was possible when humanity found a common enemy.

Casper moved through the corridors of the *Chang*, nodding and saluting at those who jumped out of his way. The ship had been modified to serve as a central command vessel for the nascent Legion. The most notable change had been the general staff room, which had been converted into a processing center where candidates who quit or were cut from Legion training gathered to find out what came next. The large holotable had been removed, replaced with a multitude of chairs and a few ominous medical supply benches.

Training had not been without its injuries. Some so severe that the men would never fully recover. Another thing Casper wanted to talk to Rechs about.

The admiral entered the room and found approximately twenty glum men sitting in chairs, the dirt, sand, mud, and blood from the day's training scuffed into the carpet and plastered to the chair legs. The ship's rudimentary cleaning bots had to work the room multiple times a day.

"I'll be with you shortly," Casper said, cutting off any attempts the washouts might have hoped to make at conversation.

He strode directly to a door at the opposite end of the conference room, then through a security door that led to his staff officer's office. Beyond that was his own.

Immediately Casper knew something was wrong. His staff officer, a lieutenant named Cami Dutton, was pacing the room in a clearly agitated state.

"Admiral," Dutton said, gesturing to the door leading to Sulla's office. "I tried to stop him, but he barged right in."

"Who?"

"And I tried to call for a security team to haul him out of here, but he… he did something with the comms." Dutton glanced behind herself. "I didn't want to leave him unsupervised."

"Who?"

"He… uh, locked me out, sir."

"Lieutenant Dutton... who are we talking about?" Casper asked, thinking that this sounded like something Rechs would do.

But the description the lieutenant gave sounded nothing like the burly soldier.

"I... don't know his name, Admiral. He wouldn't say anything except 'Relax.' He was skinny and... I think part of the Spilursan Ranger element. One of the washouts perhaps?"

Sulla approached the door to his office. "You say he locked you out?"

"Yes, sir."

The door chimed, and the light above it switched from red to green. "That seems to have been remedied, Lieutenant."

"Admiral, I'm sorry. I should have—"

But Casper had an idea as to who was on the other side. And if it was who he thought, there was little Lieutenant Dutton could have done beyond tackling the wiry little man before he had a chance to slip past.

"It's fine, Lieutenant." The door swished open, revealing a slight and far-eyed man Casper knew as Makaffie. "I appreciate the action you took. Some candidates in need of out-processing have built up in the conference room. Would you make sure their files are loaded up for me? I'll need to reassign them once I finish chatting with my... *friend* here."

Makaffie looked up from Sulla's personal computer and gave a sly grin at the word "friend."

"Of course, Admiral," Dutton said. She frowned at the skinny man, his shirt unbuttoned to reveal a scrawny, hairless chest, then turned to her next task.

Sulla waited for her to depart and for the door to close behind her.

"What are you doing in my office, Private Makaffie?"

The skinny, hollow-eyed man held out his hands, fingers splayed and dancing as though he were feeling the colors and textures of some cosmic acid trip. "That's *Mister* Makaffie now, man. Private Makaffie died on New Vega. Part of the deal Rechs made with me. I'm a free man now... man."

"That in no way explains what you're doing in my office."

"Well, technically it's also big bad Tyrus Rechs's office. And he said to do what I needed, and I needed a look at these data files you got." Makaffie looked up and pantomimed an explosion about his head. "Which are like... *ker-powboom-chigga*, you know?"

Casper sighed. Technically, what the man said was true. He was sharing his office with Rechs—not that the general ever used it. He wasn't exactly the paperwork type.

"Oh and hey," Makaffie mumbled, his gaze fixed again on the screen before him. "Tell your secretary or whatever that I didn't wash out from Legion training. It's insulting."

"I'm sure Lieutenant Dutton didn't—"

"Because, like, I wouldn't be caught dead doing that gung-ho rah-rah stuff, man. The universe is karmic. There's like some serious payback for specializing in killing, man."

"Didn't I read in your file that you created some kind of super-narcotic? H8?"

"That's different. Death is like, a side effect. Not the main feature. I can hook you up with some, though."

Casper set his jaw. "That won't be necessary. What is it you need?"

He knew that the man before him was some kind of technical savant. Rechs had told him as much. And he knew the Legion would need some serious R&D to be able to stand toe-to-toe with the Savages. The armor Rechs had procured from the Savage hulk *Moirai* was proof of the advanced level of tech those zealots had created out there in the dark. He and Rechs had been cataloguing whatever technological schematics they could from their encounters with the Savages. Other planetary governments and coalitions had done the same, but Casper's database was—whether through espionage, firsthand encounters, or political bribery—the most complete in the galaxy.

"Just grabbin' some stuff. Don't know what I need 'til I see it. But these Savages. Man… them working together ought to have all of us pissing our pants because just a basic look tells me that marrying some of the separate tech will result in quantum-level advancements."

"That's what we need to beat them."

"Yeah, well, you're gonna get it. I mean, probably gonna get it. How long until weapons training?"

"Next week."

"Okay. Cool. Can it be in two weeks?"

"Why?"

"Because I have some prototypes. Real revolutionary stuff, man. Incredibly efficient. Lethal as hell. Gonna punch through Savage armor like it's weaved out of clouds." Makaffie tittered at his own joke, sniffed, and wiped his nose with the back of his hand. "So like, this stuff takes off, and pulse rifles are yesterday's news."

Casper nodded. "Spare me the technical details, but tell me about it... *Mister* Makaffie."

Makaffie's face lit up. "It uses a charge pack, and it's energy-based but not like a pulse rifle. It shoots legit projectiles I call bolts, only you don't have to load 'em like the old gas-fired slug throwers. It draws the bolts from basic matter through a specialized intake."

"Like... sucks the dust out of the air?"

"Right," Makaffie said, nodding with a trance-like enthusiasm. "Sucks in all the particulate matter that's constantly floating in the air and strains it out, same way your nose hairs do. Then the charge pack energizes the bolt and hurls it at insane speeds. Killer stuff, man."

Casper smiled. "What was it you were saying about galactic karma?"

"Huh? Oh, that doesn't count either, man. Not like I'm the one pulling the trigger, you know?" Makaffie curled his index finger back and forth, simulating a trigger pull. "So anyway, I got about four tested models in my lab. But they're bulky as hell. But then I was talking to Tyrus and he said something about a nanitic battery that some Savages was using to keep the lights on or some such. And I think I can use *that* to make the weapon easier for one of you legionnaires to carry."

Any sense of frustration Casper might have had over this intruder's presence in his office had blown away like an empty cloud passing above a parched desert. The Legion would be equipped in the same armor as the Spilursan Rangers—Rechs's armor was too advanced and cryptic to duplicate, at least for now—but with this new tech, the legionnaires would be packing considerably better firepower than their Spilursan or Savage counterparts.

"I'll see if I can delay weapons training," Casper said at last, suddenly mindful of the failed candidates still waiting processing and reassignment.

"Cool strings, man."

Casper nodded. *Cool strings.* "What's this weapon called? I want to tell the command staff about it."

"Oh. Well, like, Tyrus already knows, you know. But he's the only guy besides me. We're calling it the N-1."

Legionnaires: Chapter Four

This is a waste of time, babe.

The broad-shouldered sniper who had long ago lost his wife, family, and name grunted in reply, sending a white, bubbly glob of spit from his increasingly dry mouth to the ground as he added mile upon mile to his knees. Running was hard for him. Always had been. Not from any defect, just what came with being taller, broader, and heavier than most.

A lion could run with a herd of gazelles. For a little while at least. But not for long. And this pack of Legion candidates—the gazelles among them—had been running for so long now that the Wild Man could identify them only by the trail of dust they kicked up.

Still, the sniper carried on. Knowing that he would not find his way to the front of the pack with the lithe long-distance runners, but determined not to fall out of formation altogether. Because that was when the general or one of his officers ran up beside you and without fanfare or mercy would say, "You're out."

And then that was it. And then… well, then she'd be right.

But the Wild Man didn't think she was quite right about it. She, for some reason, couldn't see this training for what it was. She didn't have the proper sight picture.

You need to do another one, babe.

Wild Man grunted.

Too long, babe.

Wild Man huffed and rasped, sounding like something untamed. A reflection of the name he'd taken because it fit and because his true name was forgotten. Wiped away from the galaxy the way the Savages had wiped away everything he had known or loved from his home world.

They gave him a new name when they arrived on this forest planet, just after the orbital bombardment turned a great, fifty-mile swath of it into a wasteland.

Legion Candidate 0008.

LC-08.

That's how the general and the officers referred to him now. He didn't mind it. Though he preferred when the other candidates called him Wild Man. The officers never called him that. And neither did Tyrus Rechs. That bothered him a little bit, because he had gone to war with that man. And now the general acted like he didn't know anyone but the admiral and the command sergeant major.

But that was just how the army was, he supposed. Whether or not you call it a Legion.

A wrinkle of pain showed up in his ankle. Spiking every time he took a stride and landed on the foot. He hoped it would go away after another mile or so, but knew he wouldn't stop even if it remained.

Don't you love me, babe?

"L-love… you," rasped the Wild Man. He felt sweat fling from his nose and jaw for the effort.

Then go find a Savage… Go do another one, babe. I need it. We both do.

He knew she wasn't talking about him. Could see her standing there, little child hoisted up on her hip. Both of them asking for a vengeance that could only ever result in the death of every Savage in the galaxy… or the death of the Wild Man. There could be no compromise.

But compromise was what she saw this training furlough. Precious time withering away when New Vega was thick with Savages. Three hulks full.

The Wild Man saw how Tyrus Rechs fought. Saw the kind of damage the man had done with his volunteers, deep behind enemy lines. If killing Savages was his life's quest, the Legion would provide its fulfillment. With the Legion, he would kill more Savages than he could ever hope to by himself. He just needed to make it through the sadistic selection process.

"C-can't," he muttered, the same answer to the same request. The one that had started even before they landed to train. The one issued by his darling while he was still recovering on the ship. Still trying to shake off the nightmares those Savages plied him with in those terrible stasis baths.

"Yes, you can," panted another voice. Feminine, almost like his darling. But different. Not his wife. She wasn't demanding… she was encouraging.

The Wild Man looked over and saw Captain Davis. Only now she was LC-25. Legion Candidate twenty-five.

She'd helped everyone get down beneath the great hill on New Vega, then helped them get back to the surface. But Rechs acted like he didn't remember that anymore, either.

"We can do this together, Wild Man," Davis said. "I'm with you stride for stride. We don't let the leaders get out of our sight."

Only, she wasn't matching his strides. For each lumbering scissor of his own legs, Davis took at least two of her own. She was faster than him, but her legs shorter. Her endurance seemed on equal footing. And both of them were behind the elite runners that attempted to keep pace with the relatively fresh-legged Captain Milker.

They had begun with six miles along uneven terrain. Up and down hills. Constantly looking out for the exposed roots, craters, and other obstacles that littered the course following the ad hoc fleet's "clearing" of the fifty-mile crucible meant to turn professional soldiers into something new. Something better.

They ran those half-dozen miles still wet and covered with the sands of the obstacle course. Wherever a drenched United Worlds gray T-shirt touched flesh, the skin was raw and aggravated. Thighs chafed. Nipples bled. Feet blistered. That was the ugly truth of it. There were no stylish, high-end running outfits. No hydro-units, heart-rate chips, or other gadgets. No hot showers waiting for them at the end of those first six miles.

Captain Milker had led them to a lake fed by melting snow runoffs pouring down an imposing mountain all the candidates hoped they'd never have to visit. The lake was a mile across. Milker told them to swim to the other side.

It felt good to dive in the water. To feel some of the sand finally wash away. But then the chill of the water, born of the snow, began to bite into their bones. It took rapid, tiring strokes just to keep warm.

Those who arrived at the far bank sat and waited for the rest of the candidates to join them. Not wanting any to fail, but hoping they would take a long while yet. Some of the men exchanged quick vows that they wouldn't be left behind, and then fell to sleep as if dead.

Captain Milker himself looked tired. Whatever reserves of strength he had banked by not taking the obstacle course that day were seemingly depleted. He panted as hard as any man.

The Wild Man was far from the first across, but he was not the last. Which meant he got a moment's rest. But only a moment. He lay across a large stone slab, stealing the warmth it had drawn for the sun and noticing the pain on his skin and in his limbs. Feeling the heaviness of his socks and boots. He was not a good swimmer. Hadn't even known *if* he could swim until he went into the water. He'd floundered until he managed to watch a few of the faster swimmers move and figured out how his body ought to behave. Still, it was a hard go, much more work than it should have been. He'd swallowed enough lake water to make his stomach feel bloated and sick.

A few of the other candidates stood. Not yet broken or bowed. Ready, if not eager, for more.

And then more came.

Captain Milker straightened himself and shouted, "Swim back. Run for chow!"

The captain watched as the candidates picked themselves up from the rocky shore and trudged back into the rippling lake like ghosts of the sea returning to their watery grave. He watched and waited, resting as long as he could before going in after them.

And the Wild Man had tossed himself into the wetness. Whatever gains he had from resting under the sun were quickly taken away in the sobering sensation of ice-cold water immersing the flesh.

Kick and crawl to stay warm. And then run. Run to leave the water behind you. Replace its cold with the warm saline flow of sweat shaking off his brow with each thunderous step.

It was during the run back that he first saw the general. The old man glided by—a lion that ran like an antelope. He was moving against the stream, heading for the lake, far behind the school of candidates that had left long before him.

Four miles of the return run had gone by, Wild Man figured, when Captain Davis put a stop to the conversation he'd been having with his wife.

"Just a couple more miles," Davis panted. "No sense quitting after you've already killed yourself."

No. There wasn't any sense in that. If you killed yourself, you may as well keep on being dead.

They ran in silence after that, but Wild Man felt refreshed. He felt that Davis had led him to a new reserve of strength. Together, the pair of runners kept pace. The antelopes up front moved gracefully, but they didn't disappear.

Perhaps there were other candidates running nearby, but Wild Man didn't notice them. Didn't hear the thud of their feet planting and pushing. Not until a steady, easy gait—almost a jog—filled his senses.

Wild Man looked to his left and saw the general, soaking wet with sweat and from the swim, jogging past him. He wasn't running hard, though he must have, to have caught up already.

Rechs settled into an empty space about twenty meters in front of them and then just coasted, maintaining a steady speed.

"He's pacing," panted Davis. "We… gotta… get ahead."

She kicked her legs and lurched out in front of Wild Man. He dug down and found whatever it was that he had in his guts that let him catch up to her, feeling as though he was taking exaggerated strides in an attempt to close the distance. They reached the general, and he gave them no acknowledgment. Nor did he attempt to pass them again once they passed.

But now the pace was higher and harder, and Wild Man could taste blood coming up from his lungs. He wanted to breathe through his nose but found he could only suck in great raspy gulps of air that never seemed enough.

He didn't know why he turned around, but he did. And he saw Rechs facing the opposite direction—looking at where they'd just come from, his arms held out wide to slow those runners who trailed behind Davis, Wild Man, and the other pack leaders.

Those trailing runners, now separated from the rest by a notorious war criminal, slowed and halted. They grabbed their knees and doubled over. A few rested their arms atop their heads and attempted to walk out side stitches.

"You're out!" Rechs barked.

Then he turned and continued on after those who had made the cut. Those who were still Legion candidates.

There were no trucks waiting by the side of the road. Those deemed unfit for the Legion by Tyrus Rechs would walk back to the ships.

Legionnaires: Chapter Five

It was dark by the time Casper finished out-processing the washed-out Legion candidates. Most of them would stay on and provide shipboard support, serving as marines in the event of a Savage boarding party. Some showed aptitude in other areas—one of them had so much flight experience that Casper didn't know why he wasn't a pilot in the first place—so he set them up for additional training that could maximize their potential.

That was perhaps the starkest different between Tyrus and himself, Casper had decided. His old friend was so focused on creating a fighting force capable of backing down the Savages that he was losing sight of the fact that it took more than front-line shock troopers to win a war.

Casper would make sure that when the fighting began, Rechs's Legion would not be without the necessary support.

Rubbing his eyes from too much time behind a battle board or other screen, Casper made his way to the *Chang*'s galley, knowing that it would be full of candidates cramming themselves full of the calories necessary to even *try* to cope with the brutal training regimen they had found themselves swept up in.

But the ship was quiet and subdued, and for a moment Casper thought the candidates might not have returned yet from their training. As he walked through the ship's corridors and reached the main passageway that branched to the galley, he saw the telltale muddy prints, dirt, and sand. With custodial bots working tirelessly to clean it up.

Particulates like those were a liability on board a ship. Yes, artificial gravity kept them in place well enough, but find yourself in a slug-fest with a Savage hulk and gravity could wind up being one of many systems to fail. And all that sand and dust floating its way into some of the most sophisticated space-faring technology the galaxy has seen to date wouldn't exactly help in such a fight. Ships needed to be squared away for a number of reasons, and Casper had to suppress an urge as strong as instinct to get the corridors cleaned up posthaste.

But he had to be pragmatic. For now, the *Chang* was a training vessel meant to quarter Legion candidates—not a ship ready to respond to a threat at a moment's notice. There was a give-and-take with what was happening outside of the ship.

He followed the dirt trail to the galley, each crunch of sand beneath his boots an affront he was forced to let slide.

The galley doors hissed open, and to his surprise, Casper saw the candidates eating hurriedly but quietly. Many of them had intravenous drips in their arms, attended to by *Chang*'s limited medical staff. But that was to be expected after the grueling obstacle course, runs, and swim. Something else was the matter.

Casper saw Captain Milker picking over a side dish of gelatinous proteins, halfheartedly spreading it over calorie-packed slices of dense, nine-grain bread. The captain looked exhausted. He, too, was hooked to an IV, but no nurse was actively attending him.

"Rough outing?" Casper asked, keeping his voice low. It seemed not the place to do anything but speak softly.

Milker let out a sigh. "As much as you'd expect, and then a little worse. One of the candidates drowned in the quicksand."

Casper craned his head back as though trying to get away from the news. "I'm surprised none of the washouts mentioned it. This was a straggler before your run?"

"No. It was *after* the run. The general felt he'd been able to catch up to the element too quickly, so he ordered everyone to take the course one more time in reverse before falling in for chow."

Casper clenched his jaw. That was excessive. Even for Tyrus. These men weren't Savage-born like them. They hadn't spent all that time on the *Moirai*. They were just men. And what they'd accomplished already was remarkable. This was a flagrant disregard for safety. Tyrus was pushing things too far, as only he could.

The admiral wanted to tell his friend this, but he could see that Captain Milker was struggling to comprehend what had just taken place.

"I know you did your best, Captain."

Milker shook his head. "I didn't have to do the course again. I was watching from the side. Tried to jump in and help get him out. A lot of us did. But... by the time we found him..."

Casper nodded and gripped the man's shoulder. "You did your best and your men saw it." He looked around the galley. "Be there for them as they need it. They have their own affinities, but no NCOs to lean on yet."

Milker nodded.

"Who was it?" Casper asked.

"Cond—I mean, LC-196."

"I'm not the general. You can use the man's real name around me."

"Steve Condrey. One of the Britannian commandos. Saw the guy kill at least five Savages single-handed. Drowns in a stinking mudhole."

Casper's jaw clenched again. "Where's the general?"

"Outside, I guess. He told me to make sure everyone who finished got on board the *Chang* for chow."

* * *

Command Sergeant Major Andres considered two things to be his proudest achievements. One was recent: being promoted, by the colonel, to the pinnacle of non-commissioned officers in the fledgling Legion. The other had been with him for decades: completing the training as a boot back on Spilursa. Throughout his time in the Spilursan army as a Ranger, he never forgot those basic training lessons. Because in his considerable experience—he was an old man in the eyes of most of the kids he watched out for—those basics were what kept you alive.

So when the colonel handed him a shovel and said, "Help me dig," Andres did just that. He was good at digging. His back might complain for being bent from the labor, but Andres could dig a hole well. Which was no small thing, because Andres had seen the consequences of doing it poorly. He'd seen men peppered with shrapnel because they couldn't be bothered to burrow down in a foxhole deep enough when orders came to dig in.

You had to get it done deep enough so that when you ducked down during the shelling, no part of you remained exposed. Make whoever's on the other side of them guns work for it. Drop it right in the hole—gimme that direct hit if you want me dead. But it can't just be a place to curl into the fetal position. Because sometimes the shelling doesn't stop. Being bombarded—whether artillery or from an orbital gunship—is a miserable experience. And it's the little things like realizing you can't climb out of your hole when the need arises that make it more so.

Bowels and bladders don't much care that you're being rocked. In fact, the very act of it, the noise, overpressure, and rumbling of the ground all seem to conspire to evacuate your insides sooner rather than later. And as bad as digging in and hunkering down through a blitz is, doing it while lying in your own filth is that much worse.

So you gotta dig deep and you gotta figure out where you and your buddy are gonna answer nature's call. And you gotta do it fast.

Andres worked fast. As fast as he could whenever the situation called for it.

He knew exactly why he was digging. Earlier, when he came to stand next to the body of the candidate who drowned on the course—Condrey—he couldn't help but look down. The dead man's face looked swollen, like he'd tried to drink in all that mud and sand and when he finally filled up his stomach and every waterlogged pore in his body, there was no place left but the lungs. And the nose and mouth that seemed to ooze sand-encrusted trails down his face to gather behind his ears.

Andres didn't like it. The kid had been a fighter. Did damage against them Savages. One of them Britannian commandos who got out on the *Chang* but knew he had to come back.

But he ain't comin' back now.

His eyes were still open, so Andres knelt down and closed them. It wasn't as easy as in the entertainments. Them eyelids seemed like they wanted to stay open. Like the kid wasn't ready to go to sleep yet.

He probably wasn't.

But they closed enough. Made the kid look like he was winking up at Andres. Like he knew something the command sergeant major didn't.

Andres didn't like that either.

Then the colonel came, carrying two shovels.

"Help me dig," he said, and right away Andres knew he meant a grave.

He looked around. It seemed too close to the obstacle course. But the colonel was already at it, turning over fresh piles of patchy sod that filled the air with a musty, earthy aroma. Like a tilled garden. It covered a hanging scent of sweat and explosives that Andres hadn't realized was there until a competing smell visited.

Andres started digging the grave. And he dug fast because he was hungry and wanted to get inside the *Chang* for some chow and because it seemed like the kind of job you didn't dawdle on. The pile of dirt was over his head and Andres was standing waist-deep in the hole when the admiral came by.

The admiral called for a break, though he didn't say it in so many words. "Tyrus, what is this?"

Andres let his shovel bite into the loosened dirt he'd been working on. There weren't many rocks, which was good. The sergeant looked at the two square corners he'd dug out, then rested an arm atop the handle of the shovel.

The colonel kept digging.

"Diggin' this boy a grave, Admiral," Andres said before returning to work. Because if the colonel wasn't quittin', he wasn't neither.

"I can see that, Sergeant," Sulla said, looking at the body. "The *Chang* has the necessary incinerators to perform a proper disposal."

Rechs thrust his shovel into the ground and said to Andres, "This is deep enough. Go get some chow."

"Yes, sir."

Andres hopped out of the grave and strode toward the *Chang*, determined not to let his protesting back keep him from walking tall.

"Tyrus…" Casper began.

"Buryin' him right here," Rechs said, climbing out of the grave and then pulling the lifeless body to its edge.

"Some of Specialist Condrey's friends—"

"His name is LC-196." Rechs was cold and standoffish. Deadly serious. "Use it."

"Tyrus, his name is—"

"I know enough dead people, Casper. We both do. Not gonna add any names to that list until I'm confident they have what it takes to survive."

Casper sighed. "Well, the candidates have noticed. It's not doing you any favors. Do you want them to hate you, Tyrus? Because that's where this is headed."

Rechs pushed the body of LC-196 into the grave. And then proceeded to begin refilling it. "You gonna help?"

"No. I'm not going to take part in this. You're doing it again, Tyrus. You're going at this like you go at everything: full speed with no thoughts as to the consequences."

Rechs only grunted as he shoveled a spadeful of dirt over the kid's winking eyes.

"These candidates, they think of Tyrus Rechs as someone larger than life. Something out of myth that's spent a good portion of their young lives singlehandedly hunting Savages and destroying entire planets to earn a victory over them. Don't turn yourself into a monster before their eyes, Tyrus. Just… just think about what you hope to achieve with all of this."

Rechs kept shoveling.

Casper walked away.

* * *

Command Sergeant Major Andres had taken a sip of his coffee—that's what the United Worlds crew called kaff—and was about to bite into a Frankenstein sandwich with protein jellies and some kind of fried egg when the colonel strode into the mess hall.

"Legion candidates, listen up!" shouted Rechs.

The room fell silent.

"Outside is the grave of LC-196. He's buried next to the pit he drowned in. When you swim that pit, you will look at his grave and you will be reminded that you are physically unable to breathe water and live. This will keep you alive. Is that clear?"

"Yes, General!" came the shouted replies of the candidates.

They weren't dejected. Or at least they weren't letting their feelings be known. They sounded committed to becoming legionnaires. But Andres knew that some of them, mentally, would call this the last straw. They would quit.

The CSM took another sip, wondering how many the colonel was willing to lose to ensure that all who remained were as hard and as mean as him. How many legionnaires did he need to win this war? As it stood, they were barely a company, and only if they graduated all the candidates right now.

And then Andres caught a glimpse of Rechs's eyes and discovered the answer to his question. *However many can do it. And only them.*

"Legion candidates!" bellowed Rechs. "On your feet! You will run this course again and continue running it until those of you left alive learn not to drown!"

Legionnaires: Chapter Six

Casper walked with his hands clasped behind his back, addressing the small group of Legion officers. When the training had first begun, he thought they would be desperately short of officers. Now, as grueling Legion selection wore on, he began to think they would have too many.

"Most of you have seen the stark improvements in the candidates' conditioning," he said.

A chorus of heads moved up and down in agreement.

Rechs had made the grueling obstacle course a twice-daily ritual—at a minimum. Runs stretched for miles, weaving in and out of the forested paths so that it wasn't just running, it was jumping, lateral movements, crawling over and under fallen logs... exhaustive, dirty toil. The men were never without abrasions and blisters. Flat, nail-sized bugs would get inside the candidates' shirts on virtually every exercise that put them in contact with brush or the forest floor, and these bugs would dig themselves in beneath the skin, growing fat on blood until burned off or pulled out with tweezers.

The candidates were miserable. But they were also in the best shape of their entire lives. Men who had been standouts in their units—whether Spilursan, United

Worlds, or any of the other colonies and planets that had formed the Coalition that fought on New Vega—were now transcending all of that. Becoming something more. And though they loathed the taskmaster who forced that transformation upon them, deep down they saw the effect on their bodies.

The officers saw it as well. And, Casper hoped, so did the newly selected NCOs. Today was the first time they were being included in the start-of-week briefing. It was the dawn of a new day in the Legion training program that Rechs was constructing.

Casper checked the clock in the meeting room they used for briefing aboard the *Chang*. It was always hit or miss as to whether Rechs would be present. That CSM Andres was absent as well told Casper that he himself would be running the entire show, doing his best with what limited information Tyrus had given him the night before over dinner in private quarters.

"And now for some more good news," Casper continued. "We are officially done with the current training routine and will be introducing weapons qualification with the new N-1 model developed from Savage tech."

The officers and NCOs clapped, smiles on their faces. The relentless conditioning had been not only physically brutal, but also mentally draining. Every day was the same slog, with little variation. They had become stronger and faster, but the mental fatigue of unvarying routine seemed to be turning some of the candidates into zombies.

"In addition, I've reorganized the candidates into squad-sized teams. Each squad will have an NCO assigned to it, with a lieutenant overseeing things at the platoon level. As it stands, we have the men for seven platoons, which will form this Legion. We hope to expand that number as possible."

Captain Milker raised a hand. "I take it this is the First Legion, sir?"

Casper shook his head. "Negative. This is the Seventy-Fifth Legion. General Rechs's preference. A bit of personal history."

He handed each NCO a tablet containing their assigned squad and the officer they would report to. And though the rosters contained names, Casper stressed the point that Rechs's wishes were for Legion Candidate—LC—numbers to be used. There were no questions about that. The candidates themselves had grown used to it.

"I know most of you. And you know one another well. But General Rechs is completely serious about this. Call it another personal preference, but in writing up reports, giving orders, or any other time you find yourself around the general, it's LC-123. Roger that?"

"Roger that," answered the men.

"Good. It's an hour to sunup. Let's go introduce the candidates to their new squads."

* * *

Wild Man was having good dreams. Which was to say he was having *no* dreams. Just the deep, black REM sleep that came with utterly exhausting yourself. The crash and recovery that never seemed quite long enough.

But the lack of dreams... that was all right. Because usually those dreams were nightmares. Reliving the grisly, all-too-short defense as the Savage wave burned away his former life. He'd sort of gotten used to those nightmares. Didn't even mind them all that much. His wife would be there with the baby in those dreams. It would always be the moment he left them, when there was still hope. The worry and anxiety always made him feel a little sick if he woke up during that part of the dream. But in a way that wasn't so bad. Because the pressure hadn't come yet.

Wake up, babe.

The pressure of finding the Savages. Killing them. Staying alive to kill more. It didn't seem as hard to keep his wife happy before the Savages invaded Stendahl's Bet. They had their fights. But they were happy. He remembered them being happy. But now that happiness only came when...

Wake up and do one for me, babe.

He needed his finger on a trigger again. Needed to squeeze with a Savage marine in his sights. Needed to see the spray of blood, hydraulics, ichor, or whatever else was running through their debased and abhorrent veins.

Wake up...

Wake up...

"Wake up, candidates!"

Wild Man's eyes flashed open and his ears became aware of a cacophony of noise so loud that it seemed impossible that his mind was lost, drifting in the silence of a black, thoughtless sleep.

Legion candidates were scrambling to get dressed. Rushing to make beds. Screaming back answers to the red-faced instructors—the officers and Command Sergeant Major Andres. Someone was banging on something hollow and metal, a drum without its skin... just making noise. Like a baby set down next to the pots and pans, making a racket just because there was one to be made.

There was so much shouting. But Wild Man got the message immediately, even if his groggy mind didn't yet have the speed to hear the individual words. He had to get up and out of bed.

He swung his feet over the side of his bunk, careful not to disrupt the sheets and blanket too much. Wild Man had learned how to make a bed, something his wife had done the last time he regularly slept in one. Sometimes, on the nights when the dreams were incessant, he would sleep on the floor. Just to be ready. Just to stay hard.

Just to do another one. Babe.

Now he was wishing he'd chosen to do that last night. Because everything was chaos and noise and shouting and he wanted desperately to be out of the barracks, out of the *Chang*, and on to whatever was in store for the candidates.

"Get up, twinkle toes!" yelled CSM Andres.

Wild Man remembered when the sergeant had been gut-shot. Knew the wound still bothered him. Figured he used that pain in his stomach as a motivator, because he was as mean and direct a drill instructor as any of the other candidates had ever seen. That's what they told Wild Man at least. Or, that is, what they said while he was in earshot, cleaning his weapon. Usually the only people who bothered trying to actually converse with him were Davis and the others he'd fought with on New Vega. Except not so much Andres.

And never Tyrus Rechs.

"Get up!" Andres repeated. "I want every candidate in formation outside *Chang* in five. And I'm only gonna say this once: there's a color card on your footlocker. Memorize that color and fall into your new squad with the same outside. If you're color-blind, best ask someone! Don't nobody make the general wait!"

Wild Man quickly made his bed, then pulled on his pants, tucking in his T-shirt. He sat down on his footlocker to put on his boots, mirror-shined the night before. Then he glanced over at his card. It was kind of red. Maybe a little orange, he wasn't sure. It wasn't a primary color, and his stomach fell at the thought that this was all some trick and the candidates were on the verge of being chewed out for failing to get their shades lined up right. Any excuse to punish them.

Looking around, Wild Man checked to see if he saw any other candidates with the same color card as himself. There were blues, pinks, whites, shades of purple and green, but he didn't spy an exact match. Some of the candidates were stuffing the cards in their pockets, likely thinking the same thing as Wild Man—that this was a trick and so they took the extra precaution of taking their color along with them.

"Move your asses!" screamed one of the lieutenants. "Move your asses!"

It was odd to have the officers serve as drill instructors. But that's how it was working. Rechs did things his own way. Wild Man had overhead the other candidates saying that, too.

Wild Man picked up his card and held it in front of his face, studying it. He moved to stuff it in his pocket and then stopped. Placed it back on top of his footlocker and stood, inspecting his bed, his clothing, and the barracks.

Some of the beds were made. Had been made by the time Wild Man opened his eyes from sleep. These belonged to the men who had been selected to serve as the Legion's first NCOs. Wild Man knew he wouldn't be selected for such a task. Candidates didn't look to him for leadership, and he hadn't excelled at much of anything. Some of the choices surprised him, and some were obvious. Some of the men chosen he liked. Others he didn't.

He hoped his squad leader would be one of the good ones.

Legionnaires: Chapter Seven

"Holy hell, Sergeant. Why are these things so heavy?"

LC-330 had never served in the military. And now he found himself a newly minted sergeant, expected to answer the question put to him by the Legion candidate holding the new battle rifle assigned to his squad.

"The N-1 will punch a hole clean through a Savage marine," the sergeant answered. "That was a distinct problem on New Vega—having to go through copious amounts of ammunition and energy just to put 'em down. These rifles will make a difference."

One of his men, LC-08, called Wild Man by his peers, raised his hand. There was an anxious, almost eager look in his eyes. "Are we shooting them today, Sergeant?"

LC-330 shook his head and then looked down for a moment. "No. Not today."

His squad, called Echo, part of Second Platoon, was gathered at the edge of the obstacle course. They sat together in a small circle, their sergeant standing tall. The other squads from Second Platoon doing the same. First Platoon, along with Captain Milker, had moved out ninety minutes ago. Everyone had thought that today would be a change of pace. A chance to do something other than run.

"We'll be running the gauntlet," the sergeant said. "Only now your rifle, body armor, and kit are coming along."

There was a groan from Echo Squad.

"Hey. Legion won't send us to fight Savages wearing PT shorts… and we wouldn't like it if they did."

"Easy for you to say, Sarn't." It was LC-116. A PFC from one of the United Worlds planets by the name of Daniel Kimm. The candidates called him Danny. Then Danny Boy. Then Dan-Bo. They someone threw in Kim and that stuck, and now he was Kimbo.

Unless the general was around.

"Easy? How's that, Kimbo?"

"You was always at the front of the pack."

LC-330 shrugged. "Gotta hump it either way, candidate."

"You figure that's why they made you sergeant?" asked LC-25. Davis. She had been an officer prior to all of this. Pilot. Fought alongside the general and a few others on New Vega. But the way she was asking wasn't challenging, like she thought *she* ought to have been selected. Just curious.

"Might be," LC-330 answered. "And I'm no stranger to giving orders."

Before the Savages showed upon New Vega, LC-330 was on-planet to deliver a cargo hold full of archeological specimens taken from one of the pre-inhabited worlds. The galaxy was full of them. Temples and civilizations that seemed to have been long abandoned by the time FTL travel was discovered and mankind started to explore the stars with reckless abandon. Various professors and scientists jockeyed to label the lost and forgotten builders of these abandoned ruins, but the term that stuck was… the Ancients.

And LC-330 had done everything short of getting inside the impenetrable Ancient temple on a little multi-biome moon called Gable's Purchase. Mostly that meant supervising a dig and taking anything out of the ground that might be of interest. Bones would be examined for signs of sacrifice or consumption—burn marks or knife scars, respectively. And there were a few pieces that seemed obvious enough. Things like utensils, vessels, and bits of fused and clumped machinery. A few items were a mystery—things with no analogous modern counterpart and seemingly no purpose. Those were the kinds of things the buyers, be they museums, universities, or private collectors, got the most excited about.

And paid best for.

The buyer on New Vega was the head of a university anthropology department that had just received a generous grant—a product of the boom happening on-planet. LC-330 and his first mate, Zeb, had just delivered the load, and the payout for the crew was enough to keep them all in their cups or in the arms of some lover for hire until their captain found another job and gave them the usual ultimatum: stay until your money runs dry or leave the revelry for another months-long trip in the bush digging bones and fighting the elements.

Only, the Savages showed up and erased everyone's plans and hopes and dreams in an instant. A few ships—the lucky ones—got off-planet in those first moments. Those were the ones with enough of a crew on board that they were able to take off, departure protocols be damned, and make a mad run to the far side of the planet, looking to escape the looming Savage hulk.

No one minded that. Most would have done the same thing if they could have. And those escaping ships would be the only hope the rest of the populace would have of surviving what came next. Those first escaping ships would spread the news: Savages on New Vega. Send help.

The captain and Zeb were running for the docking berths when the bombers launched from the lighthugger sowed bombs like farmers' seeds over the area. The two adventurers watched as everything they'd worked for—and their only avenue of escape—went up in a spectacular ball of flames.

Savage marines dropped into the New Vega streets from orbital assault pods. It was instant pandemonium. Citizens gunned down in the streets. But not dead. Not unless they were the local first responders. Those were engaged and overpowered by marines using lethal arms. Gas-fired projectiles. Slug throwers. Same as the pistol the captain carried on his hip.

Everybody else fell as if dead. But teams of special Savages began gathering them up even as the marines advanced further into the city.

"Harvesting," Zeb observed. "With ill intent, I'd reckon."

"Never any other way with Savages," the captain answered.

He pulled his pistol. Zeb did the same.

The crew was somewhere in the already flaming city. Likely holed up in a whorehouse or saloon, trading gunfire with any Savage marines attempting to take the building as patrons screamed with fright and clung to anyone who looked willing to fight. That's what happens in those times of sudden violence. Those in need of protection flock to the protectors. Sheep to shepherds. Cubs to mama bear.

Zeb and the captain didn't venture into the city. Didn't make an attempt to link up with the crew to fight their way to freedom or start some underground resistance cell. Because that wasn't how you survived a Savage invasion.

Zeb and the captain had lived through two Savage invasions. Each time it required the same thing: reach the wilderness and live off of the land until help came to drive the Savages away or destroy their hulk… or until the Savages finished whatever they were doing and left on their own in an attempt to fade away before the United Worlds or whoever else could come and engage.

So the duo moved through the city, dropping Savage marines with their pistols and reloading as they went. It was chaos, but it was also clear that the Savages were herding the citizens of New Vega toward the Hilltop area where their hulk had landed. Easier harvest. And many of the locals seemed to be heading that way of their own volition. Heading for the underground bunker system New Vega had once employed to stave off pirate invasions as a fledgling colony.

Once the captain and Zeb slipped through the ring of Savage marines, it was a straight run into the wilds. The Savages aren't as different as you might think. They face the same limitations as any other finite force in the galaxy. Armies control cities, but the wilds... they're flyover territory.

Just don't get spotted by the drones. Stay away from the foot patrols that venture twenty kilometers or so from the city and then turn around and head back. And don't linger where you might be caught.

The two spacers, adventurers who'd chosen life on their own terms, didn't linger. And they didn't get caught. They moved so far out into the bush that the glow of New Vega—still powered by automatic generators long after its populace had been captured or gone to ground—had all but faded from the night skies. They stayed out there, fighting a savagery of deprivation. Cold. Wetness. Hunger.

Hair grew matted. Skin darkened as a layer of filth folded itself into every crease and pore. They lost weight.

Zeb's gums started to bleed because he wouldn't eat pine needles. He lost a tooth before relenting.

Then the Coalition came in all at once, setting down inside the city in numbers that were more than sufficient to finally drive the Savages from New Vega. Zeb and the captain marched through the night, the starlit sky flashing without end as Savage anti-aircraft guns attempted to slow or stop the inevitable.

Salvation had come.

Zeb turned his ankle somewhere along the way. Had to limp and hang on to the captain. It slowed them down, but they made it. Found themselves in the sights of two wary sentries armed with pulse rifles who worried incessantly about suicide bombers in their midst.

Zeb lifted up his shirt to show off a sunken chest, exposed ribs, and a belly swollen with hunger. And no weapons. "Only place left for the explosives is up my ass," he yelled at the sentries. "And you're welcome to check there so long as you let us through and get us the hell off this godforsaken rock."

They let the men through. Sent them to an aid station. Warm food. Kaff. Blankets.

Zeb was in a bad way. He almost died out there. But it turned out he died on a hospital frigate that was blown apart trying to escape New Vega after a bombing run gone terribly wrong.

LC-330 wasn't on that ship. He wanted to stay and fight the Savages. Felt strong enough to do it. Knew his help wouldn't be refused so long as he found a pragmatic officer. He was embedded as a scout with a platoon of soldiers from somewhere on Levenir—part of the United Worlds. They were seeking a route through the city that would take them around the Savage defenses.

The captain's helmet fit, but his United Worlds uniform was baggy, and those pants and shirt billowed as the bombs erupted well short of their target and the overpressure and dust storm enveloped him and his unit, hurling shattered pieces of buildings the size of cars, along with actual cars, in all directions.

He woke up a lone survivor. Covered in dust except for the whites of his eyes.

Everything everywhere seemed dead. But he made it back to the stadium. Found other survivors. Got out on the *Chang*. Volunteered for Legion training.

They looked at him a while. And he knew they were thinking he was too frail. Too skinny to make the cut. He had lost a lot of weight. And they didn't know his story. No one did.

Except Zeb.

And Zeb's dead.

It wouldn't be until he reached the Legion training planet called Hardrock that he started to put weight back on. Regain muscle. The general and the admiral, Rechs and Casper, they pushed you hard. But they didn't starve you. Not like the wilds did.

A man grew strong training for the Legion. LC-330, who had always been the strongest and fastest man he knew, grew stronger on his way to reaching the rank of sergeant. And now he had his own squad of Legion candidates who would rely on him to keep them squared away and get them through this nightmare that was Legion training.

"So," Davis said, bringing LC-330 back to now. Back to waiting, his squad assembled. "What are the orders, Sergeant? No way we aren't gonna be forced to run in all this."

"I wasn't kidding so stop asking," said LC-330. "We're running the gauntlet. Plus a little extra."

Someone groaned. The big man. The Wild Man. He wasn't a runner. It was a wonder he was still hanging around. Him and Davis both. But they had something. That extra checkbox in the makeup of a man that wouldn't quit.

LC-330 had that quit box unchecked, too. And it would be his job to make sure his squad kept going. Failure is a result. Quitting is a choice.

"Command Sergeant Major Andres will order us to fall into a timed run. We will make that time and from there will be instructed on proper handling and firing techniques for the N-1. And... Echo Squad: we finish this run together."

Legionnaires: Chapter Eight

It was agony. It was agony and the obstacle course was barely halfway finished. Wild Man grunted, crawling on his belly beneath razor wire, the cumbersome N-1 rifle cradled in his arms as he went headfirst down a gulch, sliding more than anything else. Feeling the sand build at his chest and roll back his shirt to deposit itself inside his clothing, where it would rub against his skin.

"Let's go, Echo! Let's go!"

The sergeant was yelling for them to keep up. He had to slow his pace several times. Force himself to stay back when he was used to flying through the course. Other squads were already through the course and on the run.

This is your fault, babe.

Wild Man climbed up the opposite side of the gulch and picked up speed, hurling himself at the ten-foot wall and just barely grabbing the sergeant's waiting hand, his rifle banging against his hip as he jostled up and over.

The landing was hard. Wild Man's knees could feel the shock. His ankle twisted, but not badly. Nothing he couldn't ignore. But that landing…

Wild Man looked around as he sprinted for the rope tower. The sands seemed to have been compacted since the last time he ran the course. Made harder. Probably by orders of that damn general, Tyrus Rechs.

That's how Wild Man thought of the man who'd saved his life on New Vega.

That damned general.

It was how all the candidates thought of Rechs. Who'd proven himself to be worthy of every hard word ever spoken against him. He was mean. He was vicious. And his way was pursued with the steadfastness of a zealous pilgrim following the direct revelation of God.

No wonder the man had personally destroyed thousands if not millions of lives by nuking Savage-infested planets. Who else but a sonofabitch could do something like that? Who else but a self-righteous egotist like Tyrus Rechs could declare himself justified in destroying entire populations of colonists and Savages alike, leaving them all to burn side by side in the post-apocalyptic fire?

Nobody liked him.

The officers pretended to.

The NCOs seethed with controlled rage, their tolerance necessary for keeping order.

The admiral was seen dining with the general, but rarely. Only CSM Andres seemed to genuinely enjoy the general's company. And Andres was almost as bad as Rechs himself.

"Hustle up, Echo!"

The sergeant had already caught up. Helped every member of the squad over the wall and sprinted back to the front, climbing up the rope net to the top of the tower structure as though he lived there. He turned at the structure's zenith and called for the squad to move it. But not in that damned general's way. In a different way.

The Wild Man huffed, feeling the net bend and sway in reaction to his weight. Having to pitch his neck and back so far out that if he craned to look straight above him, he would see the horizon.

Davis was struggling alongside him. He was glad she was in his squad. And he didn't mind the other three men either. Kimbo was friendly. And the Johnson brothers, James and Randolph, were fine, too. Most of the time they only talked to each other, and they let Wild Man be. Didn't get on him about the way he ran. His breathing heavy and his steps loud and clunking.

Wild Man turned to watch Davis climb past him as the sergeant hollered for them to "Keep going!"

He wanted to speak to her, but he knew his breath was coming in ragged pants that wouldn't do well for even a passing remark. But he wanted to tell her how it seemed like the sergeant was yelling not because he was angry, like Rechs, but because he actually *wanted* them all to finish.

Wild Man liked that about Sergeant.

Sergeant. The NCO ought to have a name other than just *Sergeant*. He was LC-330 whenever an officer or the CSM addressed him. And rumor was that the candidates called him "Fast."

Sergeant Fast. That would probably be okay so long as the sergeant didn't mind it.

Who cares what any of these people think?

"I... care..." rasped the Wild Man.

Then you're an idiot.

It was quiet for a long while after that. Wild Man kept climbing. Reached the top and went headfirst down the taut rope that led from the tower to a thick tree trunk in the ruined landscape along the obstacle course. Wild Man hated that part. Felt like the rope would break or bend and twirl and he'd fall into the sand pit below. A few days back a candidate broke a leg falling from the middle portion of the tightrope. Lost his grip while inching along and dropped like a ship without engines.

Wild Man didn't know what happened to the candidate after that.

Don't you love me, babe?

He nodded. Knowing that somehow, she would see it. Feeling that anticipation that came from her wanting his attention, his affection again. Just like the old times. The old fights. And the makeups that came with them. Sometimes those fights were worth it. Just for the way they made up.

Then do another one, babe. Leave and do another one. For me. If you love me, do it for me.

"Can't."

And then she stormed off for a long while.

The rest of the course wasn't any easier. Some dirt got into Davis's eye when a simulated mortar round sent some dirt into her face. She was squinting and crying. Rubbing and shaking her head. But it wouldn't come out.

Her eye was red as blood.

Wild Man took his canteen and pulled her to the side of the course the moment they finished it. Right when they were supposed to be starting the six-miler. He tipped her head back and flushed the irritant out.

"Better?" he asked.

"Thank you, yes."

And then Wild Man saw that Kimbo and the Johnson brothers had stopped and were watching them. Their heavy rucks heaved as the sweat poured down from beneath their helmets. Sergeant stood there, too.

"Sorry, Sergeant Fast," Wild Man said, stowing his canteen and fumbling to get it back on his kit.

The sergeant nodded, thereby accepting his namesake. "Hustle up, Echo. Long run."

A two-man all-terrain transport equipped with four omni-balls pulled beside the squad. Admiral Sulla was driving. And General Rechs was in the passenger seat, standing as the vehicle skidded to a halt, his face already red with anger.

"LC-330! What is the reason for your squad's delay?"

The sergeant stood at attention, eyes forward. "No excuse, sir!"

"Then get your squad moving, Sergeant! Set the pace!"

"Sir, yes, sir!"

Sergeant Fast began to run, the rest of Echo Squad falling into place behind him. But it seemed to Wild Man that the sergeant wasn't moving as fast he could. They were running hard, but this was not the speed the sergeant was known for.

Rechs had Casper drive the transport alongside the sergeant, who ran head up, looking straight ahead.

"Damn sorry turn of events, LC-330!" Rechs shouted at the sergeant's ear. "Went from front of the pack to way back here. Makes me sick! Does it make you sick, too?"

"Sir, yes, sir!"

But Sergeant Fast didn't increase his pace.

Whether the general noticed this was unknown. He arrived angry and he parted angry, warning Echo Squad that they were "expected at the range by oh-nine-hundred hours!"

Otherwise… don't bother showing up at all.

As the transport carrying what constituted the highest brass the young Legion had to offer sped forward in a cloud of dust, everyone looked to the sergeant. Wondering if he would kick it into that extra gear he seemed to possess. Force them to run beyond their potential. Or force them to fall behind, pushing themselves to catch up with their squad leader when they could.

If they could.

Wild Man looked at the huffing faces of his buddies. Davis. The Johnsons. Kimbo. They were all middle-of-the-pack. At least, they had been in the early days of Legion training. But washouts had made a new order. And Echo Squad was now the bottom of the pile. Slow through the course. Slow on the runs.

You're the screwups here, babe. And you're the biggest screwup of all. You ain't no Savage-killer. Not anymore. Not even for me. Ain't no man, either… babe.

"Shut up," Wild Man grunted.

Kimbo, who didn't understand, said, "Yeah, I hate the old man, too."

"We're… supposed to," huffed Davis. "That's… why… he drives… while… we run."

The Johnson twins hoarsely whispered between themselves. Wild Man couldn't make out what they were saying.

They were moving at a pace that, while slower than what Sergeant Fast was capable of, felt just as daunting. The weight of the gear and rifles made every step painful. Like they were sinking into the planet itself, driving themselves into its core with each stride like a hammer hitting a nail.

Kimbo shook his head. "Why... would he want us... to...?"

"Because he's... a bastard," Davis panted. "Isn't he... Sergeant Fast?"

Wild Man knew she was right. He remembered what Tyrus Rechs was willing to do to all those people on New Vega. Trigger-nuke. Burn up everything. No chance. No hope. No mercy.

But he wanted to hear the sergeant say it. Wanted at that moment the permission to stop running and walk away from a table where the game was so obviously rigged against them.

Sergeant Fast dropped back into the midst of the company. His breathing sounded light and easy. He was only now beginning to perspire; light beadings of sweat formed beneath his helmet.

"Only one thing you can do to get back at a man like the general," he said. "Prove him wrong."

He picked up the pace. Only a little bit. But faster than what Echo Squad had been accustomed to. And it felt much faster given the kit and the heavy N-1s slung over their shoulders.

They kept up. Blisters pushed against boots. Lungs burned. Backs ached.

But they kept up.

***

Echo Squad was the last to arrive at the shooting range. Sergeant Fast fell back behind his men as they jogged to take a place facing a long platform that seemed to have been built out rough-sawn boards. The range had been constructed from the abundant timbers on Hardrock, and the sergeant could see more than a few familiar faces working on constructing what had to be a kill house.

These men weren't Legion material. They were washouts. But the admiral kept them working toward the cause. Rumor was that they would form some sort of auxiliary force meant to support the Legion proper. If they chose to stick around.

None of the washouts would meet Sergeant Fast's gaze. Even the men he'd gotten to know. Especially them. It made the sergeant's stomach grow sick with pity, like he could feel the shame these men must now feel, seeing those who gutted it out ready to use their weapons. Ready to take on the next phase of Legion training.

Or maybe that was conjecture. Maybe they were secretly happy to not be running like slaves under the whip of a cruel master—the general—any longer. Maybe they felt the same pity for Sergeant Fast, too stupid to walk away from insanity.

"Here comes Echo Squad," one of the candidates called out, faceless among the throng.

The comment sparked a ripple of guffaws and pocketed conversation.

Oh well. That was to be expected. Echo would shrug it off. Do better next time.

"Fitting name," called out someone else—one of the other sergeants. LC-83. Charles Lower. Someone who knew better. "We all get here on time and then... the echo."

He said it loud enough for everyone to hear. And the laughs were that much louder.

Echo Squad set their jaws. Trying to act like they didn't notice. Or didn't care.

"Hey, knock it off, Lower," Sergeant Fast warned.

"Gotta be killing you, Fast," the other replied. "Used to beat every candidate in this outfit. Dead last today. Sucks, huh?"

Fast walked stridently to the man, shoulders back, head held high. He spoke loud enough for everyone to hear, addressing the candidates as much as Sergeant Lower. "Echo Squad arrived on time and together. You won't need just me to show up to save you from the Savages—you'll want the whole squad."

Lower shook with mock laughs, moving his shoulders up and down and looking for approval from the candidates he was expected to lead. Some of the men looked up, thrilled. Others looked away, aware that this... was not how it was supposed to be.

"Nah," Lower maintained. "You're the only one worth a damn, Fast. If First Platoon needs help, you have our permission to come solo."

"You're wrong," Sergeant Fast said, getting inside Lower's personal bubble of space. Standing a good six inches taller. Fast said those words loud enough for Echo Squad to hear. But what followed was just for his colleague. "And if you say another word about my team, I'll knock every kelhorned tooth you have down your throat."

There was an electric moment where it seemed a fight might break out, but that suspense was impaled by the bellowing voice of General Rechs.

"Captain Milker! What in the *hell* is happening between your platoons, Captain?"

"LC-330! LC-83! Is there a problem here?"

The two sergeants stepped apart.

"No, sir," said Lower.

"The hell there isn't," Rechs growled, pacing the raised platform that formed the range stations like a predatory cat stuck in a cage. "Everybody on your feet!"

The candidates obeyed, many of them still wet with perspiration, their uniforms soaked in sweat under their arms and against their necks.

"LC-04!" Rechs boomed.

"Yes, sir!" Sergeant Greenhill replied.

"Get *Chang* notified to start serving chow." Rechs put his hands on his hips. "*Chang* closes the galley in sixty minutes. What you make of the six miles back to the ship determines how much time you have left to cram grub down your necks. LC-83!"

"Yes, sir!" responded Sergeant Lower.

"Corporal. You are to lead both platoons back to *Chang* and have them ready to march back upon conclusion of the lunch hour. Is that clear, Corporal?"

Lower wavered a half-second, and then the realization of his demotion fell on him all at once.

"Yes, sir," he said, barely hiding the venom in his heart.

"Good. Captain Milker—you and the rest of your NCOs are to forgo lunch and remain here with me until both platoons return."

"Yes, sir!"

"CSM Andres, take the mule back to the *Chang* and make sure LC-83 doesn't get my platoons lost."

"Yes, sir!" Andres moved to the transport Rechs and Sulla arrived in and drove at breakneck speed past the column of waiting candidates.

"Corporal!" Rechs shouted, not hiding the annoyance in his voice. "You're wasting time and depriving your platoons of the opportunity to eat. Move out, now!"

Corporal Lower hurried to the front of an already-formed column of Legion candidates. "Ranger Company… fall out!"

Sergeant Fast watched them run and then looked back to Rechs, who held his fisted pose of rage until the column of Legion candidates was out of his sight.

"Fall in," called Admiral Sulla.

The remaining officers and NCOs did as they were told, standing below the raised platform that housed the shooting stations, each one numbered with ample room for the rangemaster to pace behind the shooters and observe their progress.

Sulla was standing next to a man so slim he seemed anorexic to Sergeant Fast. Makaffie. One of the soldiers from New Vega who'd decided the Legion wasn't for him. It was Makaffie who had designed the N-1. And made the thing too damn heavy. Fast was sure of that. He'd always preferred pistols in his former life. Quick and useful for trouble that was up close. Which was how things usually happened out there running crews on remote planets where a starship was worth killing for. Fast had made more than one opportunistic colonist die trying to "commandeer" his ship.

But a rifle had its purpose. Especially in war. Particularly against the Savages. You didn't want them too close. Fast had seen what they were capable of when it all boiled down to hands. The galaxy had discovered some powerful species since mankind started jumping through the stars, but Fast couldn't think of any who could hold their own against a Savage marine in a wrestling match.

"This is the N-1 rifle," Sulla began, showing them a weapon they'd been running with as though they'd never seen it before. "The forward and rear sights collapse in order..."

Fast saw out of the corner of his eye one of the men working on the kill house approaching General Rechs. A washout maybe, but Fast didn't recognize him. Maybe he dropped in those first couple of days. Before the faces had the chance to make an impression.

The two men, general and laborer, started to converse. Fast could hear them talking.

"I want in the Legion sir," said the laborer.

Not a washout, then.

Sulla continued talking. "The charge pack will provide eight shots before needing to be replaced. This is a semi-automatic weapon due to a tendency for a pack to disperse all its energy in a single blast in full-auto tests. R&D is working on a solution..."

Fast caught the tail end of Rechs's reply to the laborer. "...late in the game."

"I know sir, but..."

"In the event of an overload, you are to prime the..."

Fast saw the laborer nod, leave his tools and coworkers, and run off after the cloud of dust the candidates left on their run back to the *Chang*.

"Any questions?" Sulla concluded.

When no one provided them, the NCOs were invited to step up and demonstrate that they understood how to handle the weapon.

"Leave your issued N-1 below. You'll be firing the weapons at the firing stations."

Fast took a place at an empty station and stood, waiting for permission to take up the N-1 rifle waiting for him there. He was familiar enough with weapons to feel no apprehension. The N-1 weapon system seemed pretty much like a traditional gas-fired cartridge system. And while his didn't come issued with a charge pack, he'd studied the weapon enough to understand its function.

"Pick up your weapon," Sulla ordered.

The rifle was *much* lighter than what he'd been carrying through courses and runs. It felt like it was barely in his arms. Perhaps three pounds at most.

"Right now you're wondering why your N-1 is so light," Sulla observed. "The rifles you've been issued have been specially prepared and weighted at the general's orders. I'm guessing you like the feel of an *actual* N-1 more?"

Fast smiled and joined the other NCOs in answering, "Yes, sir."

"Good. This is an object lesson for you to teach your squads. When you're stretched to your thinnest, your N-1 will *feel* as heavy as what you've been marching with. As light as these are, they will feel akin to hoisting a Savage hulk to your shoulder when the fighting won't stop. You remind your candidates that they've carried worse."

The men nodded, the lesson not lost on any of them.

"Good," Sulla said. "Charge!"

Fast shoved a charge pack into the magazine well.

"Prime."

He pulled the priming handle and heard a high-pitched whine issue from the weapon.

"Eject."

The charge pack released from the weapon. Fast set the rifle and the charge pack down on the table in front of him, barrel facing the silhouette of a Savage marine a hundred yards downrange.

"Good. That's all you need with the N-1. It's streamlined, and as you'll see, it delivers quite the punch."

Legionnaires: Chapter Nine

The badge glinted in the moonlight as Wild Man held it in his hands, turning it over. N-1 marksman qualifications. Expert.

Only a handful of candidates achieved the expert qualification. Sergeant Fast had done it, and Wild Man wasn't surprised by that in the least. But only he, the Wild Man, had achieved a perfect score. Forty targets ranging from five to three hundred meters away. Iron sights. And god help him if he didn't drill each target right in the middle the moment it popped up.

He felt like he'd turned a corner. The other candidates would shake their heads at him. But not in the way they did before. Now it was with a smile as if to say, "I can hardly believe it."

Even the general seemed impressed that day on the range. He nodded at Wild Man. Said, "That'll do, LC-08."

Which still bothered the Wild Man, because he felt like he ought to be more than a number to Tyrus Rechs. But he wasn't. No one was.

And in a way that didn't matter. Because just getting a hint that the old man approved when every other thing in life seemed to make the general go apeshit… that gave

Wild Man a sense of pride. One he would never admit to feeling, though he expected that others who earned what passed as a compliment from the general felt it, too.

Echo Squad didn't hold back their congratulations. Even the brothers Johnson piped up.

"Nice shooting, Wild Man," James said.

"Yeah, nice shooting," echoed Randolph.

Davis told him repeatedly that he had done something special. That he belonged.

Kimbo wanted lessons. He had qualified as a marksman on the N-1, but was five points shy of reaching sharpshooter. Let alone expert. Wild Man could tell it ate at him.

And Sergeant Fast… he called it the finest shooting he'd ever seen in his life. And something about the man made Wild Man think that he'd seen a lot of shooting. Though he professed to have never joined a standing army until the Legion.

"I wanted to live free," Sergeant Fast had said. "And I did. Until it became clear that the galaxy was poised to take that option away from me. So… nothing left but to fight."

Wild Man figured he meant the Savages. And he understood that. He wanted to fight, too. But freedom never really came into the Wild Man's mind until Sergeant Fast mentioned it.

Revenge, yes.

And hate. Pure, unvarnished loathing.

There was a lot of that in his heart for the Savages. Figured it was there for everyone who ever really saw them. Except Sergeant Fast seemed too calm and cool to be hateful. Sometimes when they ran, and the time came to push themselves, Wild Man could see something like anger in Sergeant's face. But it disappeared as quickly as it arrived.

But everyone hated the Savages. After what they did. What they would do.

The hate felt distant tonight. Under the moon out in the woods. Part of a week-long march that was supposed to take them to the base of that mountain that they all hoped they'd never have to visit. Someone called it Mount Doom and the name stuck.

Mount Doom.

Wild Man couldn't see it through the darkness of the trees. But he could feel its cold blowing down, chilling the night air in a way that didn't seem natural given the summer weather they endured while running the gauntlet. Like ghosts were bringing their deadly cold down with them to haunt the living that lay in the forest beneath.

A campfire would be nice. The crackle of branches flowing sticky with tar and sap. Making you feel dry and warm. The smoke clinging to your hair and clothes.

But orders were lights out at all times. Pretend there are Savages. No light. No heat. No noise.

The moon didn't obey the orders of men. And Wild Man watched its light twinkle on the badge. It was something they had on the ships, he knew. Something for some U-Dub soldier that happened to be in supply on one of the ships that accompanied *Chang*. It was cheap, made with a material meant to look like silvene. He knew that, too.

But it was his. And it was beautiful for what it represented. Respect. Belonging. Purpose.

"Told you," he whispered to his wife, who sat somewhere behind him in the darkness. He could feel her there. She wouldn't come sit next to him. But she was there. "Told you this was important."

She wouldn't answer. She was mad at him.

He missed her.

"Who you talking to, Wild Man?"

Ivy Davis sat down to join him. He could hear her hips click and pop. The pain on her face didn't escape his notice, either. And while the general kept the candidates well-fed—they were all growing bigger and stronger—Davis seemed hollow and thin. Ever since they moved from PT gear to full kit. The toll it had taken on her body was evident.

Her spirit was still strong, though. And it shone through the night, making itself known through the question she asked. Davis didn't make small talk. If she asked a question it was because she wanted to know the answer. Because she cared to know.

"Uh," Wild Man said. Because he didn't know what else to say. He knew the answer and knew what people would think if he told them the truth.

That he was crazy.

But he wasn't crazy. She was here. She was real. Had been with him all the time as he waged a one-man war against the Savages. Came to Hardrock while he trained to be a legionnaire even though she didn't want to.

She was real.

"Myself, I guess."

And then she was gone. Wild Man could sense her getting up and walking away. Wounded by the slight. He turned to look over his shoulder at her, but she had disappeared into the darkness.

He ought to get up. Go after her.

But he stayed with Davis. His wife just needed some time to cool off. She never did like being wrong about things. And she *was* wrong. Even if she didn't want to admit it. The Legion… all this training… it was the right thing.

"Too much of that will make you crazy," Davis said, before letting loose an involuntary groan. "Oh, sket. I don't think there's a square inch of my body that isn't sore. How are you feeling?"

"Feelin' good," he said. And even though it was true, he wondered if maybe he shouldn't have been so up-front about it.

"I'm glad one of us does."

"Hang in there."

Davis leaned her head back on the tree she rested against. "Yep."

"No. Really. Made it this far."

Just then Kimbo arrived, collapsing into a heap and lying against the heavy ruck he'd been humping. Wild Man knew it was the marching with that pack that was causing the strain for Davis. But Kimbo didn't seem any more pleased with it.

"Why we gotta haul this crap around, Shooter?"

Wild Man shrugged because he didn't know. He did like being called Shooter, though. Even if Kimbo was the only one who called him that.

"Beats me," Davis said. Which was odd. She usually seemed to have answers. Like she had a window into the mind of General Rechs. "Most modern armies are able to haul everything they need in ten-kilo bundles. These are what, thirty? Plus the armor? I feel like I'm literally breaking apart."

"Hang in there," Kimbo said, and Wild Man could tell the fellow candidate meant it.

"Hang in where?" asked James as he joined the circle and sat down.

"Yeah, hang in where?" added his brother, Randolph.

"Davis is feelin' it, man," Kimbo said.

"Oh," said James. "Hang in there."

"Yeah. Hang in there."

Davis chuckled. An ironic, almost spiteful laugh. "Rechs won't break me. He's not gonna break any of Echo Squad."

"Damn right," said James, who Wild Man figured was the older brother.

"Damn right," repeated Randolph.

"I heard from Sergeant Greenhill," Kimbo said, leaning forward and keeping his voice low, "that we're coming close to the end of it all. A little more time on the range getting requalified on 'slug throwers' and some sweeps through the kill house. Then probably the last big march and we're in. It's all mental at this point."

"Speak for yourself," Davis shot back.

"Well, mental is what you can control, I mean."

Wild Man grunted. That was true. He'd come to realize it during all those pounding runs where his large, muscular frame screamed to his mind that it wasn't built to be used that way. But his mind never gave in, and wonder of wonders, his body didn't fail on him. No matter how often it swore it would.

He thought about adding to the conversation. Almost said, "That's true."

But then one of the brothers switched subjects and the moment was lost. That was all right, though. Just... just having his brain fire like it did, giving him something to say—that was nice. Things hadn't been that way for a long time. Wild Man hadn't felt this good in a long time.

He looked over his shoulder. Maybe because he thought he heard a rustle, but most likely because he wanted to see if she'd come back yet. She hadn't. He hoped she wouldn't get herself lost or into trouble. He gently bit his tongue.

How could she?

Still... he wanted her to be all right.

"Echo Squad."

The whisper came out of the darkness, and made all five of the candidates jump. Kimbo searched frantically for his N-1 while Davis held her hand against her chest.

"Holy hell, Sergeant Fast! I almost died."

"Sergeant Fast," said James. "Stop sneaking up on us like that."

"Yeah, stop sneaking up on us like that."

The sergeant moved right on without slowing to acknowledge anyone's fright or complaints. "Quiet. Something's up."

Everyone looked around, taking in the darkness. Wild Man focused on his sergeant's face, watching it under the moonlight. It was slightly damp with perspiration. And it was dirty.

"What is it, Sarge?" asked Kimbo.

"Every officer along with two squads from First Platoon are gone."

"Is that bad?" asked Davis.

"Maybe. Maybe not. CSM told us lights out and act like there are Savages nearby."

"We didn't start no fires, Sarge," James said. "Honest."

"Yeah, honest."

Sergeant Fast shook his head. "I know. But if Savages were here… this is a terrible defensive position."

Wild Man rocked back against his ruck, looking around. He could see the trees standing like moonlit sentinels all around him until their trunks disappeared behind leafy swaths of bramble and other ground cover. It gave off the impression that they were hidden, but that was all it did. Anyone with a mind to move through the forest would remain screened by those same bushes that gave this false sense of protection. And they would find Echo Squad and the rest of the platoon in the open with no defensive cover.

This time the big man, the man of sorrow who drifted from planet to planet, punishing Savages with his sniper rifle, found his way into the conversation. "You got a better place for us, Sergeant Fast?"

Fast nodded, his face expressionless. All business. "Just finished digging it."

"By yourself?" asked Kimbo. "Damn."

"These trees have been here dropping needles so long, you can dig down six feet before hitting rocks."

"So the platoon's moving into foxholes?"

Fast shook his head. "Echo Squad. Not the platoon. The other squads are as tired as we are and didn't want to get up."

Davis rested her head back against her tree. "I think they've got the right idea. I need a horizontal night of sleep right now. Not an evening on my feet."

"Well that's too bad," Fast said, standing before her and holding out his hand. "Because Echo Squad works as a team. On your feet, candidate."

Davis took the hand and Sergeant Fast hauled her up, causing more pops and snaps to issue from her hips and knees. "Let's move, Echo."

* * *

Casper moved through the still of the forest, feeling the invigoration that comes from a rush of endorphins following a march. Tyrus had led the officers of First and Second Platoons, along with CSM Andres and the best-performing squad from First Platoon—Sergeant Greenhill's Alpha Squad.

Greenhill was one of the men Rechs had fought with during the chaotic escape from New Vega. The same was true of the expedition's point man, Lucas Martin, who Rechs insisted on calling LC-05. In spite of knowing the man. In spite of having fought alongside him, having put his life in the man's hands during the fight with the Savages when he was Colonel Marks. Before Casper's hope for a galactic coalition fell apart in that doomed bombing run.

That might as well have been a lifetime ago from the way Rechs behaved. Might as well have never even happened.

But then, perhaps there was something Casper's old friend saw that transcended words. The general had specifically requested Greenhill's squad for this operation. Alpha Squad consistently outperformed the other squads in both platoons. Individual candidates might be better shooters, might achieve higher PT scorings, but as a whole... Alpha reflected its name.

The squad was quiet and professional. They hiked to the mountain with Rechs taking the lead, turning back only when Tyrus reached some unseen marker that told him they'd climbed enough. Then it was up to Martin to lead them back down.

But not before Rechs explained their objective on the windswept crags of what the candidates called Mount Doom.

"Tonight, we are the Savage marines. And there are two platoons probing the woods to our west. We will creep up on those legionnaires and we will murder them." Rechs paused a beat and then said, "Move."

Martin, used to following the orders of the man called Tyrus Rechs, began to descend the mountain. Rechs followed, as did the rest of the officers and Alpha Squad.

But Greenhill lingered, standing next to Casper. The admiral knew that the officer corps and the candidates themselves saw him as something of a lifeline, a voice of reason that could sometimes make sense of the enigma that was Tyrus Rechs. Someone who could even change the course Rechs set himself on, though Casper saw his ability to do that dwindle more and more.

"Admiral?" Greenhill said. The naval rank had stuck. Rechs still hadn't supplied him with a formal rank in the Legion.

"Go ahead, Sergeant Greenhill."

Greenhill, used to officers referring to him by his LC number, hesitated. "Ah… that's not the clearest of plans."

"You're thinking General Rechs should have asked if there were any questions?"

The pair moved together down the mountain, Greenhill's N-1 carried at the ready. Casper was armed only with his pistol, which he kept holstered.

"Suppose that's it, yes."

"The Savages don't ask questions, Sergeant. They do what they're told. The general wishes for you to attack like Savages. You'll find that, militarily, a Savage fighting force is often devoid of complex tactics. They are given a directive… and they execute."

Greenhill seemed to be thinking back to his time on New Vega. What the admiral said must have made sense because he nodded.

"Thanks, Admiral. Just… sometimes the general don't make sense to me no more is all."

And then the candidate picked up his pace, leaving Casper alone to bring up the rear. Perhaps aware that he had made what could be considered a colossal error in judgment in sharing his thoughts so freely.

And it *was* that. An error in judgment. Part of Casper felt that it required an immediate dressing-down. A reminder of the need for proper adherence to rank and its protocols.

Except the comment struck him because he had been thinking the same thing about his friend. It was Rechs's job to train this Legion. That there would be differences of approach was obvious, but Casper had moved into a realm of having to put blind faith in his friend's actions. Tyrus had moved far away from what Casper thought of as reasonable. And while Rechs may have been the finest soldier Casper ever knew, Casper was no neophyte. He was a better strategist than Rechs, had a better mind for organization and administration.

And this... this training. Casper had faith that it would produce a soldier of a higher standard and caliber. But there was a simple formula of diminishing returns. Rechs, in his opinion, was depriving his Legion of capable fighters. In his zealous purification rituals, his attempts to remove any and all dross, he was beginning to lose some of what was valuable in the process.

Casper thought of all that when Sergeant Greenhill voiced his reservations. Had thought it many times over. Even in giving his explanation of why Rechs was giving his orders the way he did, he was only employing guesswork. Tyrus hadn't shared his reasoning. And, like too many times in the past, Casper was left to clean up.

He was reminded of all the times he had forestalled or misled a strike cruiser of vengeful colony battleships, keeping them from hunting Rechs down after he'd heedlessly nuked a planet full of distant cousins and families. Giving his friend time to escape. And then tried to get him to see reason, to recognize the folly of destroying habitable planets in a galaxy that didn't have all that many to begin with. Especially those in easy jumping distance of others.

But Rechs was the sort of man who did what he wanted to do.

He'd never said thank-you for those rescues. For those times when Casper could have easily stepped aside and let any number of fighting forces show just how immortal they truly were—or weren't.

It's just how he is, Casper reminded himself. A man is no better than his nature. No better than the circumstances of how he came up in the world. Rechs is what he is. Excels where he excels and needs protecting where he is weak.

That's your job, Casper. As his friend, that's your job.

When they reached the candidates' camp hours later, it was evident that men who by all rights should be exhausted, weren't. At least not enough to sleep just yet. There was talking. Nothing loud and excessive. Quiet, easy conversation punctuated by laughs that, while held low, still escaped the thicket they bedded down in, betraying them.

No one in Casper's element had spoken. Not since ten kilometers back when Rechs had given his final instructions—and only then because Casper had pulled him aside to tell him that more was needed than the vagaries he had supplied in giving orders. They would move into the camp in a wedge formation, following Martin's lead. A head-on Savage attack designed to kill everything in first contact. There would be more to it if the intent was to kill. But the N-1s were the training models. They wouldn't fire. Only the officers carried live weapons, their pistols, and those remained holstered, their owners aware of the purpose of this exercise.

Martin dropped to a knee and looked over his shoulder, verifying that the rest of his "Savages" were in position. Casper nodded to him, and Martin rose and pushed through the obscuring underbrush, N-1 at his shoulder.

They moved forcefully through the camp, surprising the candidates in their repose. No one had even thought to set up sentries or pickets. They should have known better. They had been trained better.

Casper saw this as another consequence of Rechs's shortsightedness. So much of Rechs's focus had been on brutal physical training that basic military principles were being forgotten.

The wedge led by Alpha Squad hurried through camp unhindered, rifles aimed at the pockets of Legion candidates who lay dumbfounded on the ground. Martin reached the middle of the encampment and stopped, his N-1 pointed at the candidates before him, his squadmates' rifles covering those on either side.

Rechs nodded at Casper, who stepped forward.

"Ranger Company. You have been overrun by Savage marines and have suffered a one-hundred-percent casualty rate. You are all dead, the consequences of which are that you will now put your gear back on and prepare for a night march terminating at Mount Doom."

No one groaned or protested. The deep, sinking reality of what had happened, and what it would have meant had this all been real, had sunk in quickly.

And then there was a rustling coming from behind Alpha Squad and the officers. Casper turned and saw figures seemingly rise out of the ground behind them. The ghostly figures had their N-1s raised and pointed at Alpha Squad. The candidates had branches tied to their helmets and dirt smeared across their faces.

Slowly, Alpha Squad turned around and lowered their weapons.

Casper smiled inwardly. "Identify yourself."

"Echo Squad, sir."

"LC-330, is it, Sergeant?"

"Yes, sir."

"You have destroyed the Savage element, Echo Squad. Have your team rest here tonight. You will join us on the mountain at first light."

"Yes, sir. Thank you, sir."

LC-330 hustled his squad out of the foxholes, and Casper could see Rechs watching them as they moved, shadows in the night.

Sergeant Greenhill walked up to Rechs and Casper, rifle held at the low ready. "How 'bout Alpha Squad, sir?"

Rechs gave a look devoid of mirth. "You just got killed, didn't you? The dead march at night."

And then the general moved off back toward Mount Doom, leaving his officers to organize all those who died to march until they could catch what sleep they could among the freezing, craggy stones.

Legionnaires: Chapter Ten

The extra sleep Echo Squad was rewarded with seemed to be equal parts blessing and curse as the team struggled up the mountain to join the rest of the company of Legion candidates the next morning. When Sergeant Fast had woken them before dawn's light, Wild Man felt stiff and frozen. Like he was stuck back in that goop the Savages had baptized him in. He felt a sudden panic in the seconds before his body limbered itself up and began responding to Sergeant Fast's orders to get up and get moving.

But Davis was the one who really suffered. She marched with a pronounced limp—and not for sympathy. It was obvious she was trying to hide it. But every step seemed to be accompanied by an audible click of her bones.

Or maybe that was in his head. It seemed like he could hear things more clearly this morning. Like his ears had been waterlogged and had only now finally dried out. But he could make out the clatter of pebbles tinking their way down as Kimbo and Sergeant Fast led the way, the Johnson brothers staged behind them.

Wild Man paused and looked below. He puffed out exhausted breaths, the cold air making the vapor look like smoke escaping the mouth of a dragon. He was looking for his wife, but she hadn't come with them.

But he could see Davis, struggling to make her way up. Using her hands to pull her along where the others had only required their feet and a willingness to lean into gravity, those rucks weighing heavily on bent backs and tired shoulders. She slipped. Sliding down a few feet on her belly before pushing herself up and starting again. Rocks tumbled down below her.

Wild Man turned and yelled up the mountain. "Sergeant!"

And then he carefully climbed back down to reach Davis, holding out his hand. "Here."

Sergeant Fast scaled down the mountain in an instant. He grabbed the Wild Man's webbing to keep him steadied as Davis pulled herself up by her anchored squadmate.

"How we doing?" Fast asked.

"I got this, Sarge," Davis huffed, her voice raspy and dry. "I got this."

Fast's face was impassive, but Wild Man felt as though he saw the hints of concern in his eyes. Like his face was trying to make the expression, only the sergeant wouldn't let it.

"Echo Squad stays together," Fast said, positioning himself slightly above Wild Man, allowing Davis to pull herself up from the first man and then to the next.

The rest of the team fell in line, giving Davis the handholds and pulls she needed to make the climb.

They were a quarter of the way up when they reached the rest of Ranger Company. First light had spread its glow over the candidates long before, and every man was awake and spending his time either eating rations or simply watching Echo Squad slowly move up in their odd, chain-gang climb.

When Wild Man and the others rejoined the main unit, their uniforms were drenched with sweat. And while it felt good to finally stop moving, it gave way to a new discomfort as the mountain wind whipped into its newly stationary victims, making them feel as though their sweat would freeze to their skin.

Rechs was livid.

"LC-330! When were you ordered to rejoin the rest of your unit?"

"First light, sir!"

Rechs looked up into the sky. "It appears some time has passed since then, LC-330!"

"Yes, sir!"

"I'd ask if you slept in, but we could all see your squad poking up this mountain. So I'll ask something else: does Echo Squad wish to be in this Legion?"

"Yes, sir!"

"I don't believe you, LC-330! So far, all I've seen from your team has been a propensity to dig holes and set up ambushes. The moment I ask you to move your asses, it all falls apart, doesn't it, LC-330?"

"Yes, sir!"

"Well the Legion doesn't have a security guard division! I expect my legionnaires to excel at all fronts of warfighting. Is that clear?"

"Yes, sir!"

And then, to the rest of the candidates, Rechs shouted, "Is that clear?"

The mountain echoed with the reply: "Yes, sir!"

"Good! Then let me make another thing clear, you sons of bitches. This little vacation is drawing to a close and the Savages are still out there. Now I can count on two hands the number of you who have what I think it takes to be a legionnaire. But we aren't finished yet, and maybe some of you will surprise me."

Rechs turned his attention back to Sergeant Fast, who remained at attention, his squad scattered behind him.

"LC-330. You were a capable candidate before you got hitched to your squad, weren't you?"

"Sir?"

"Don't 'sir?' me. You damn well know how you went from the front of the pack to its ass. Why is that, LC-330?"

Fast repeated the mantra Rechs and his trainers had drilled into all the candidates' heads since dividing them up into squads. "Sir! A Legion squad fights as a unit, sir!"

"Except there ain't no fighting when you're late to the damn battle, is there?"

"No, sir!"

"You're a capable soldier, LC-330."

"Thank you, sir!"

"I wasn't finished!" growled Rechs. "Echo Squad has dragged you down to its level."

Wild Man swallowed at these words. Tried to catch Rechs's eyes. Wanted to see if he meant what he was saying. He was so different… so different from the man he had fought with on New Vega.

Which was the real version of the man?

Or was he both? Living in two worlds.

Just like you, huh, babe?

She was back. And she was enjoying the spectacle.

Wild Man wished she'd have just stayed down in the forest. Or waited for him back at the *Chang*. And then, for a moment, he wished she was more like…

You thinking thoughts of other women, babe?

Wild Man said nothing. Thought nothing.

That Davis girl got you all hot between your legs? Got you feelin' warm. Yeah. I see it. Me and our baby, doin' what we can. You playin' Romeo out here, chasin' skirts. Sure as hell ain't killin' Savages. I know that much.

"Not like that," Wild Man mumbled.

And then his heart sank.

"What?" shouted Rechs. "What the hell did you just say, LC-08?"

Wild Man, already at attention, stiffened. He didn't answer. Didn't know what to say. Wanted to be away. In that moment just wanted his rifle and a clear sight picture of a Savage marine.

I told you. You know I did.

"Well this just makes me sure of my mind." Rechs shook his head and returned to Sergeant Fast. "LC-330. You have your choice of reassignment. You want Alpha Squad, First Platoon—it's yours. Do you understand what I'm saying to you, LC-330?"

"Sir, yes, sir!"

"Good. What'll it be, Sergeant?"

Fast's posture softened ever so slightly. Like the general calling him "Sergeant" instead of his candidate number told him and everyone else just what the old man thought of him.

Here it comes.

Wild Man held his breath. Ready for the camaraderie and everything good to fall apart. And why shouldn't it? Sergeant Fast was a pro athlete playing with kids in the slums. Echo Squad was holding him back. They all knew it. Showed how much they were aware by the way they hung their heads.

"Sir!" Fast let the address hang in the air for a beat, then said, "I choose Echo Squad, sir!"

"Damned fool," Rechs growled, and then stalked past Casper and the rest of the company, CSM Andres falling in line. "Nothin' but a damned fool!"

And then the general stormed off, disappearing behind a bend. A moment later the whir of small craft engines sounded, and a light transport lifted off and banked down the mountain toward the *Chang*, far away.

Casper stood, hands clasped behind his back. He didn't speak until the sound of the ship's engines had faded away, leaving the deep quiet of the mountain to regain its hold on the minds of those present.

"Sergeant," he said to Fast, "have your squadron fall in."

"Yes, sir." Fast waved his candidates forward. "Echo Squad on me."

"The general mentioned that we are nearing the end," Casper said when they were assembled. "We are past the point where quitting should have any allure. You have all suffered too hard, marched too long, endured too much to toss it away for a moment's respite. Now is the final push. You will qualify on Legion-issued sidearms, will perfect the squad-based tactics you've trained on in the kill house, and will finish a final navigational course. And then you'll move from candidate to legionnaire."

The candidates cheered at the prospect.

"Today we made it a quarter of the way up Mount Doom. The next time we're here, you'll be expected to reach the summit. And for now… we march back down and to the *Chang*. Sergeants, give your men twenty minutes and then have them ready."

A lieutenant called for the men to rest, and almost immediately the candidates began to voice their opinions about what they'd just heard from the admiral.

Wild Man realized that his wife had left again. She was bitter that Sergeant Fast had stayed loyal to Echo Squad, when it would have been better for him to make another choice. But Wild Man was glad Fast had chosen the way he did. So was everyone else.

Everyone but her.

The Wild Man didn't dwell on that. Instead he dropped his ruck down where Davis and the Johnson brothers were resting and voiced the prevailing opinion of the candidates that morning. "Of course the old man would march us up here just to have us turn right around and march back."

* * *

Casper was tired and footsore when he reached the *Chang*. He and the candidates had marched all day and arrived as the sun began to set. There was a chair in his office that he desperately wanted to settle himself into with a glass of Espanian port.

But, as his aide told him upon his arrival, his office was "occupied by General Rechs and Mister Makaffie."

That didn't stop Casper, though. He entered his office, stepped inside, and was greeted by Tyrus's stern face. "Casper. Can we have a couple more minutes?"

"Sure. Of course."

That was fifteen minutes ago, and Casper was debating abandoning his daydreams of wine, perhaps a cigar, and some time in his chair in exchange for a shower and bed when the door to his office whooshed open and Makaffie stepped out.

"The whole world is unfolding before us, Admiral," the wiry, odd little man practically sang. "Big things are coming for the Legion. Big things!"

He repeated that phrase to himself as he left, presumably to return to his lab. "Big things... *big* things."

Tyrus was waiting for Casper inside the office, arms crossed.

"'Big things,' Tyrus?"

Rechs sniffed and gave a fractional nod. "Looks like it. Gonna take some work. Phase two of the Legion training."

This was the first Casper had heard of there being a whole other phase.

"Phase two? Holy hell, Tyrus. How much more do you intend to put these men through? They're supposed to fight Savages at some point. That is still the plan, isn't it?"

"It is."

"Well… good." Casper threw his arms out, exasperated. "Because lately, I'm not so sure. I find myself spending more time *outside* than in."

"We tied up your office for too long."

"Not just the office, Tyrus. *Everything*. I'm finding out what's planned next sometimes just minutes before the candidates. Same with the rest of your officers. And the morale… Tyrus, they're just as likely to shoot you in the back as they are one of the Savages at this point."

"They won't."

"They *despise* you. And you've earned it."

"That's their choice."

Casper opened the lid to his cigar box, then flipped it closed in disgust, not bothering to remove one. He sighed. "Help me see what it is you're attempting to do."

"Nothing's changed. I need men who can fight the Savages. We're getting there. And you need to keep doing your part."

Casper collapsed into his chair. It felt uncomfortable against his thighs and back. But his legs felt too tired to stand up again. "And what part is that?"

"Exactly what you have been doing. You and the rest of the officers and NCOs. That's part one."

"And are you going to fill me in on part two, or phase two, or whatever it is that's happening next?"

"In part."

"In part." Casper sighed and shook his head ruefully. "I know we've only known each other for centuries, but your confidence in me is truly overwhelming, Tyrus."

Rechs shrugged. And Casper recalled that his friend wasn't one for verbal sparring. He didn't get humor. Couldn't tell a joke properly. Missed most social cues. Had little empathy.

An argument would do little beyond cause frustration for Casper. Rechs probably wouldn't even know to be bothered. He would stolidly go on answering things literally, showing an endless patience until Casper relented and saw things the Tyrus Rechs way.

It was rather remarkable the emotion Rechs showed in chewing out the candidates. Casper wondered if that was a real expression of the man, or if it was for show. He'd known him for so long. It felt… odd to be so unsure. What else didn't he know about this man he thought to be so simple and straightforward?

"Tell me what you can tell me, Tyrus."

"Keep doing what you're doing now, and one other thing."

"Which is… ?"

"Get me a fleet and an army. Another coalition force."

Casper laughed. Low and involuntarily at first, and then a loud, deep laugh. He shook his head, unable to remove the smile. "And here I thought *we* were building an army."

"The Legion is a sword to pierce the heart of the Savages. I need you to get me the hammer to pound them to where we want them."

"Raise an army. Check."

"Assemble another coalition. Recall the one that broke and fled. They'll listen to you. You... can talk to people. Talk them into things."

"It'll be a short conversation once I mention who's leading this little Legion."

"Then tell them what they need to hear, Casper."

Casper formed a steeple with his fingertips. This step had always been a necessity, he knew. Part of his ultimate vision of uniting the galaxy against a common threat. But his assumption had been that this would happen *after* Rechs's Legion had won its first victory against the Savages. It was always easier to convince twitchy planetary governments or self-interested empires and alliances to join with a winner.

But that didn't mean it was beyond his abilities.

"I'll see what I can do."

Rechs nodded. "Two weeks."

"How's that?"

"They need to be ready in two weeks."

Casper shook his head in disbelief. "How—"

Rechs cut him off. "Have the *Chang* waiting at the top of the mountain in exactly a week. The rest of what came with us needs to be waiting in orbit. I marked some to stay behind and continue the training of new recruits and injuries cycling back in."

Rechs tossed a data tablet to his friend.

Casper powered it on and began to study the plans. He looked up to make a comment, but Tyrus Rechs had already left the room.

Legionnaires: Chapter Eleven

"Keep your weapon up here!"

Sergeant Fast adjusted the N-1 in Wild Man's arms. The big man was a shooter. The best he'd ever seen at range. The way he was able to consistently put shots on target was a thing of beauty, and it was obvious that he would be one of the platoon's snipers.

But today's work involved shooting at close quarters, and while Wild Man was hitting his shots, Sergeant Fast was growing concerned at the length of time it took the sniper to get his weapon into the action.

They'd run through the kill house twice now. The first time, nobody was armed. They held their arms out, mimicking an offensive assault and sweeping through the interior of the newly constructed training areas. And that construction had been something else.

While from the outside these looked like rough-sawn slat-board cabins, the interior was otherworldly. General Rechs and the scientist he employed—Makaffie—had taken spare parts from the *Chang* and other vessels and altered and installed them so the interior of the house had the looks of some bygone starship. That it was meant to look like the interior of a Savage lighthugger was lost on no one.

Even Sergeant Fast had to remind himself to focus on moving through the kill house according to the prescribed pattern, following the shouts of CSM Andres and General Rechs, who watched from catwalks above. No targets presented themselves during that run. As they moved from corridor to room, each member of the squad cleared their assigned corners as they moved as a unit.

The second time through they were given their N-1s. The light combat variant. Not the barbell they'd been humping to get Tyrus Rechs strong. The real thing.

Par for a complete and successful clearing of kill house one—made to look like a Savage docking bay that led through a transit corridor and then broke off into several rooms—was five minutes. Echo Squad took six.

Breaching was textbook. Likewise their entry into the docking bay, where Fast was in the lead, hitting targets with blaster bolts from his N-1 as the rest of his team poured in behind him. They moved smoothly from there, but slowed down with each new room. Each new encounter.

Fast found himself hitting the holographic targets at the far end of the room that should have been the responsibility of those on his wings. At first he thought it was a case of him simply moving too quickly for the rest of the team. So he dropped back and let Kimbo take lead. The results were the same.

After the second run, CSM Andres pulled Sergeant Fast aside.

"You're a good man, LC-330."

"Thank you, CSM."

"You know what's slowin' you down, don'tcha?"

"I have my suspicions, CSM."

"Maybe shoulda taken the colonel up on his offer?"

Fast gave a wry smile. More at the way CSM Andres insisted on calling General Rechs "Colonel" than anything else. "Seeing how that time has passed, what are you observing, CSM?"

"LC-08 is letting his weapon slip every time he moves. Has to bring it up into position with each engagement, and that's adding up. Not his fault. He wasn't military. Just a shooter. But it ain't how you clear a room."

Sergeant Fast nodded. He'd noticed the same from the back.

"And Davis—she's about spent, Sergeant." Andres frowned. Like he didn't like the words he was speaking. "She got heart. Helped save more than a few of my boys on New Vega. But this ain't it for her. Uh-uh. She's draggin' hard. Slowin' you all down. Your team is matching her pace. Like you don't even know it."

"Squad stays together," said Fast.

"Stay together, die together. Drift apart, die apart." CSM Andres dug in his pocket for a cigarette and lit it, pulling in the smoke through the side of his mouth and exhaling as he added, "But that's only if you make par."

Fast nodded again.

Andres rapped him on the chest with the back of his hand. "And, you didn't hear this from me… but last chance is your next go. Make par, or somethin' gon' happen what ain't good. Reassignment if you're lucky. Squad washout if you ain't. Colonel didn't tell me what."

"Thank you, CSM… Why are you telling me this?"

Andres blew out a cloud of blue smoke. "Colonel told me I ain't goin' with y'all. Says gettin' shot took away the last of the young man I used ta be. He ain't wrong. I'm slow, and that gut shot made me slower. So now it's my job to stay here and train your replacements."

"Replacements?"

"Word gets out. Plus we got some scrappers that want to take the chance. Some of them boys from the engineering corps."

"Like that Seaman kid?"

"Yeah. You know him?"

"Not really."

Sergeant Fast had run into the builder who had spoken to Rechs back before N-1 training. From day one, the kid was running the Legion training all by himself. Getting worked with no one to share in his misery. Lately a few more candidates had joined in with him. Soldiers who'd heard rumors and somehow worked their way to Hardrock.

"Well. I gotta train him and make him Legion. Gotta train the others too. That means I can't watch my boys. That's a sergeant's job, you know. Watch out for your boys."

Sergeant Fast nodded. He'd run into military types all throughout his career hunting for Ancient artifacts. Exploring temples. Uncovering what death and time had tried to keep hidden. A lot of times it was local systems or planets that wanted something checked out. Discovered. Explained. Found.

Fast had spent a lot of time as an interstellar guide in those days. Leading platoons of soldiers through hostile wilderness, looking for pirates who had pushed their governments too far. They relied on Fast because he was often the only other human who had set foot on those planets and moons.

Call it osmosis, but Fast was able to put together what made an officer or NCO effective and what didn't. He'd seen men with more valor than brains lead their troops to their deaths. And he'd seen the tears of men like Andres as they circled back around to recover the dead.

But CSM Andres wasn't far off, in Fast's opinion. The good leaders watched out for their boys. They made sure those under them were the best at what they did, to the best of their abilities, and made sure those people weren't wasted. Weren't used up in vain. They might die—that came with the job—but they should never be put to waste. Never sent to the slaughter because nobody could think of anything better to do.

Sergeant Fast hoped that Rechs wasn't the type to do that. But he didn't really know. Sometimes there was a glimmer of knowing in the old man's eyes. Sometimes he seemed like the type who would send a thousand men to die to gain a hill that command planned on abandoning the next morning. Sometimes.

But CSM Andres… he was being sincere. He was worried about the Spilursan Rangers who'd served with him. Worried about what would happen when he was no longer around to keep watch over them.

"They gotta have NCOs who can keep 'em from doin' somethin' stupid," Andres continued. "And that ain't gon' happen if men like you don't pass Legion selection. And the colonel won't hesitate to drop you if you can't get it done. No, sir."

"Roger that," Fast said, unsure of any other answer. His mind worked for ways to shave off time. He would go over what needed to be done, of course—talk to Wild Man and Davis about how they could optimize their assaulting. But if that wasn't enough…

What then?

"All right," Andres said, throwing his cigarette to the ground and stamping it out. "You got the rotation to come around. So fix what's broken, LC-330."

And that's what Sergeant Fast did. But still, as they stood outside the kill house, waiting for the signal to begin the breaching procedure, he found himself having to right the Wild Man's weapon. Davis looked dead on her feet, not recovering from the morning's push through the obstacle course and run. The rest between rotations may as well not have happened judging by the look on her face.

"Davis," Sergeant Fast said, snapping his fingers for her to pay attention to him. "You're in back with me. Big Brother, you breach. Kimbo first. Then Wild Man and Junior."

The candidates nodded and then activated the breaching charge. A blast that sent the door swinging open initiated the start of the exercise, and the team pushed in, clearing corners and dropping individual targets.

"Clear!" called out Kimbo.

"Keep moving," shouted Sergeant Fast. "Wild Man, keep your rifle up! Up!"

Wild Man grunted and followed the team out of the first room and into the long corridor. The walls were a sleek, shining robin's-egg blue—which seemed an odd choice to the sergeant. But he'd never been inside a Savage ship before. Maybe their aesthetics didn't match the whites, grays, and blacks that seemed to dominate space travel in his experience.

Down the hall, illuminated by harsh overhead lights, targets began to appear. Life-sized holographic projections of Savage marines that dropped dead when shot, lay on the floor for a few seconds, and then dematerialized as the projection system rendered new stationary threats. Wild Man and Kimbo moved forward and both took a knee, watching the corridor for additional targets.

There were three rooms on each side of the corridor. The squad was to clear each room as they moved down the hall.

"Clearing left!" called out James, whom the team had taken to calling Big Brother. Or Big Bro. Or simply Big. It depended on the mood.

The brothers disappeared inside the first room on their left, working together to clear it and return to the corridor and move up with Kimbo and Wild Man.

Sergeant Fast had to wait for Davis, who was limping to catch up, rifle lazily pressed against her shoulder. It was painful to watch.

"Davis, you good?" Fast said, knowing she was anything but.

"What's wrong, Sergeant?" Wild Man asked, peeking over his shoulder.

"Watch your lane!"

Wild Man refocused on what was ahead of him just as Davis reached the door. "I'm good," she panted, squinting in pain as she did so. "I'm good."

"Like hell. Kimbo, swap out with Davis."

"Up!" Kimbo called and hustled back. It was clear from the look on his face that he was concerned about Davis— and the seconds melting away from the mission counter.

Sergeant Fast wrapped an arm around Davis and helped her practically hop as she limped to replace Kimbo's position.

"Echo Squad," a voice boomed over the kill house PA system. "LC-116 has been killed by Savages and is to lie down. You have three minutes remaining to complete this training evolution or your squad *will* be cycled out of the selection program."

It was General Rechs.

"Sket," Sergeant Fast said, aware that Davis and Wild Man were watching him.

The brothers emerged from their room, announcing it cleared.

"Move up," Fast told his squad. "I'll clear this room and catch up."

"Not supposed to go alone, Sarge," protested Randolph, the younger brother they all called Junior.

"Sometimes we have to improvise." Fast slung his rifle over his shoulder and drew his pistol. He felt more comfortable with the weapon and had earned expert in its qualification. "Get going, Echo Squad."

They moved up with Wild Man in the lead and Davis limping to follow and then crashing onto her stomach and assuming a prone shooting position.

Kimbo lay on his back. "This sucks."

"Yeah. Sorry you died. Shoulda been me."

"No. Not you, Sarge."

Fast moved his way into the room, quickly clearing both corners, each of which was filled with the holographic projection of a Savage marine. A third popped up from behind a storage crate. The sergeant eliminated the threat with a double-tap, each round striking the marine in its dome-like reflective helmet.

The room clear, Fast moved back into the corridor and staged outside the next room. The brothers hadn't yet finished clearing their own room ahead and across the hall. Which meant Fast had gone through his own quickly, or that they were running into some trouble.

He didn't for sure know what he or the brothers might expect. The kill houses were modular and could be set up in a variety of configurations. Some of the other teams going through their final evolution had complained that it was like a whole new experience. Those teams had all passed, though. Something that Sergeant Fast was worried wouldn't be true of Echo Squad.

New targets were appearing at the far end of the hall that Wild Man covered with his N-1. They appeared to be moving to engage the boarders, pouring out from some holographic barracks. But Wild Man didn't miss at range, and he was able to knock the targets down as soon as they showed up.

Davis was clearly hurt, though from what, Fast couldn't tell. She was lying prone, putting shots downrange, but they were either missing or coming after Wild Man had already put the target away.

"LC-330!" Rechs shouted over the PA system.

Sergeant Fast knew at once that an already tough situation was about to ratchet up in difficulty. "Do *not* clear that room solo, candidate. You will breach with LC-25 or you will fail this training evolution."

Keeping low, Fast moved along the side of the corridor back to where Wild Man and Davis were covering. The brothers returned from clearing their room.

"Two down!" James called. "Moving up!"

"Move up with them," Fast called to Wild Man, and then covered the trio as they advanced.

Davis was struggling to her feet. Fast grabbed her by her webbing and pulled her up. "We gotta clear this room, Davis!"

She shook her head. "Something's wrong. Something's broken. My hip… I can barely move."

Fast could see tears of pain welling in her eyes. She was standing on one leg, leaning all her weight against him.

Rechs boomed a warning. "Time is short, LC-330. Move. Now!"

Sergeant Fast cursed under his breath.

"We can do this," Davis said, tightening her jaw against the pain. "I won't quit. We can do this."

Fast nodded, then slung one arm around Davis's waist, the other holding onto a pistol. "You clear left when we go inside."

"I'll try."

That would have to be good enough.

Practically carrying her, moving so fast that her good leg would sometimes drag as it tried to keep up, Sergeant Fast entered the room. He saw at least five targets and knew he had only seconds to clear them or be declared dead. He sent two shots into the predictably staged target in his blind spot on the right. Then he swept his sights inward and dropped a second target, the effect so rapid that it sounded like four shots being discharged at random. Like a drunk with a pistol shooting at the moon in the wee hours of the night.

Pop-pop-pop-pop.

The sound of Davis's N-1, wielded from the hip with one arm, added itself to the din. It fired again. And again. But Fast could tell that Davis's aim wasn't adjusting. She was trying to hit her first target.

Pivoting, Fast swung himself to face the left blind spot, dropping two more targets in his deadly arc. It felt like forever... like time had run out long ago and the only reason the general or CSM Andres hadn't declared him dead was because they wanted to add that little bit of suffering that came from *thinking* you'd done something only to find out that, no, you hadn't. He took the shot even as Davis did her best to make it her own.

The Savage went down. The room was clear. No violations. Fast had cleared a room of five targets with a pistol by himself, with an injured Legion candidate stuck to his side.

There was no time to dwell on the achievement. At least one more room needed clearing, and then they needed to exit the kill house by moving through the door at the end of the corridor.

Sergeant Fast left the room, not bothering to pretend Davis was helping. He simply lifted her up off the ground and fast-walked to reach Wild Man.

"Changing mags," Fast announced next to Wild Man's head. "Moving to final room."

"The brothers are already in!" Wild Man shouted.

That was good. They had managed to clear their final room and then move across to the other side to begin clearing it. Not as fast as a functioning team moving smoothly in unison, but it seemed to LC-330 that they had cleared rooms faster than ever before—once the shooting started. There was no telling exactly how long the delays had stacked up, but his internal clock told them time hadn't yet run out.

"I got this," Sergeant Fast called to the Wild Man. "Go back and grab Kimbo. We're finishing this together."

Wild Man smiled and ran back to Kimbo, picking the candidate up easily and placing him in a fireman's carry. The pair returned just as the brothers emerged from the last room, declaring it clear.

"Move up!" Sergeant Fast cried. "Move!"

Echo Squad formed a tactical wedge, the brothers taking the lead with those left standing former the rear. A few more holographic Savage targets popped, and were just as quickly put down.

"Keep pushing!" called out Big Bro.

Sergeant Fast felt as though his left leg was going to break from the added weight of carrying Davis, whose arm felt grating and irritating wrapped around his neck. He could feel pressure in his ankle, which constantly tried to roll out of his tight boots. But he kept running. The entire squad did. And when the doors on the far end of the corridor swooshed open, they exited as a unit.

"Time!" Command Sergeant Major Andres shouted. "Four minutes, fifty-four seconds!"

A cheer went up from Echo Squad. Wild Man set Kimbo down and the two were practically jumping up and down in elation as the brothers exchanged an embrace. Davis bowed her head, and Sergeant Fast breathed a sigh of relief.

They'd made it. Together, they'd achieved success. No stacking of the odds, no setbacks had been enough to keep Echo Squad from doing what it needed to do. Davis would need rest, to be sure. But Sergeant Fast felt confident that his team could achieve whatever was asked of it. They were one. As much a family as the Johnson brothers were.

Fast looked up to the rafters while his team celebrated. Searched out CSM Andres's eyes, because he'd done what the man had asked. But instead of seeing the fatherly, satisfied, maybe even proud look he expected, he saw concern. Then he looked from Andres to Rechs and saw that things were far from over.

Rechs nodded at the CSM.

"Echo Squad!" Andres yelled. "Atten-hut!"

The celebration stopped as each candidate snapped to rigid attention.

"About face!"

They turned, looking back down the corridor they'd just conquered. Still, there were smiles hidden in their eyes. Like this was some sort of formality attached to their triumph. The last step before the old man finally gave them some well-earned recognition and praise.

Only Sergeant Fast seemed to sense otherwise. His brow was furrowed, serious. Anticipating some new obstacle to be overcome.

"Echo Squad," General Rechs said, shouting down from the rafters at them. "You have cleared the Savage docking bay and planted explosive charges. You have thirty seconds to traverse from your current location and return to your point of origin. Each man will be expected to carry his own weight. Do *not* help the man next to you. CSM Andres?"

"Mark. Go!"

A second of confusion passed. And then Sergeant Fast ordered, "Move it!"

Wild Man, Kimbo, James, and Junior took off sprinting, reaching the opposite end of the hall with ample time to spare. The candidates turned and saw Sergeant Fast bouncing on his heels as Davis pulled herself forward, one leg dragging behind the other.

"C'mon, Davis!" Sergeant Fast called. "You gotta move now! Suck it up and finish!"

But Davis kept her pace where it was. A purposeful, pain-filled stride, like an ancient myth of mummies brought back to life, the degradation of the grave mocking each lame step.

"Davis, you can do this!"

Calls came from the opposite end of the kill house. From the candidates who had crossed the line. Met the standard. They were shouting, not for Davis, but for their sergeant.

"Sergeant Fast, you gotta move!"

"C'mon, Sergeant!"

Fast hesitated, still bouncing on his heels as if he were on an open court, ready to cut off a defender.

"Sergeant!"

"I'm sorry," Fast said, low and beneath his breath. And then he raced past Davis, sprinting down the hall and into the receiving hands of Echo Squadron.

Relieved, the men patted him on the back and shoulders, then stopped as Sergeant Fast turned and watched Davis.

Her head was held high, but no new gear was found. She slid her body along, using her one good leg to drag all else.

"Time!" CSM Andres shouted, giving voice to the sentencing everyone knew was coming.

"LC-25," General Rechs called, his voice loud but even and unyieldingly firm. "You're out. Report to Admiral Sulla for reassignment."

And with that pronouncement, Rechs and Andres left the catwalks. Left the kill house.

"Son of a bitch old man," mumbled the Wild Man. "Ungrateful son of a…"

He didn't finish the sentence.

Because Davis hadn't stopped. She kept pulling herself forward, the sweeping of her bad leg across the ground filling the rafters of the kill house like a knife pulled across a whetstone. It was a sound that cut into the hearts of those who'd formed a bond with her in Echo Squad.

Kimbo took a step out to help.

"No!" Davis shouted, struggling to breathe through the pain and exertion. "No. I'll finish… on my… own."

Sergeant Fast put out an arm and pushed Kimbo back behind the line. The remaining members of Echo Squad watched the slow scrapings of their friend as she shambled toward an achievement that held meaning only because she decided it did.

She had given everything she had.

It wasn't enough.

Legionnaires: Chapter Twelve

I confess that I hoped to have heard from you by now, Reina. Forgive me for that. It's an entirely one-sided imposition caused by me. I know this.

Still, it's in our nature to long for the unattainable. The old man who pines for youth. Who despises the young because he is no longer counted among them. And what can those younger men do in response?

And what can you be expected to do about my own hopes? For you. For me. For the galaxy.

I just hope—and I hesitate to mention this—that these missives are not beyond your reach. That your silence in responding is a choice. That you're not too far gone to be reached.

We are poised to strike back at the Savages. Tyrus concluded Legion selection training this morning. A final march that carried the candidates to the top of a mountain. Its peaks were modest, but the view of the forests and training grounds wasn't lost on those who made it through. I now have the entirety of the Legion aboard my command ship, *Chang*.

That these men didn't break under the withering demands Tyrus put on them, both physically and mentally...

it's beyond remarkable. I suppose many of them did break. But not all. And what's left… I marvel at them. These are all men who weren't exposed to what we once were. They've known terror, but they lack the benefits that came to us as a result of our terror.

They are mortal men capable of achieving immortality through their efforts. Timeless men who need only an Alexander or Leonidas to lead them. One capable of showing them what heights can be reached with vision, resolve, skill, and determination.

Ask me sometime if I still believe Tyrus is that man. I think now that he is. But… doubt has crept in. It gnaws at me, Reina. He's a man who will destroy lives—destroy worlds, even. Toss them into the air like sands to be carried off into the wind. But never to any purpose. Never for something greater than what is sitting directly before him. He remains a gladiator. Focused on surviving. On killing his opponent.

But after the Savages are dealt with… what then?

Who can lead the galaxy to a place where its potential can be finally reached?

The man with a hammer for his hand sees nothing but nails. The man with a gun… he sees only targets.

Legionnaires: Chapter Thirteen

Word had leaked that those Legion candidates who had left Hardrock aboard the *Chang* were not going to New Vega as they had imagined. But that they were staging for a fight was evident. Each man had been issued a new kit of body armor, worn piecemeal around their tactical blue battle dress uniforms—a color selected for maximum efficiency for wherever they were shipping off to.

Casper looked over the crowd of officers and NCOs that now waited to hear from him. Some of them held their helmets at their sides as they stood in the *Chang*'s main hangar. Others wore the open-faced helmets loosely on the back of their heads, the tactical information face shields covering their foreheads like visors. These were modifications of the United Worlds design. Each helmet had the LC number and squad identifier painted on the side in a muted gray paint that shone in radiance under infrared light.

"Gentlemen," Casper began, causing the group to hush. "I trust that you and your men have had sufficient time to recuperate during the jump. And though this may come as a surprise to you, New Vega will *not* be our first stop."

Casper paused and gave a fractional micro-smile. Just enough to let them know that he knew they knew, and that it wasn't going to be an issue.

"The time to put the rumor mill to bed is here. We are fighting the Savages, gentlemen, of that you can be sure. However, not the ones you might expect."

An image of a Savage lighthugger appeared on a mobile screen behind Casper, easily filling its twenty-by-twenty-foot area. Then the view panned out, shrinking the lighthugger until it was roughly the same size as the *Chang*, which was included on-screen for scale.

"This is what we call a Savage mini-hulk."

A full-sized lighthugger was superimposed behind the mini-hulk, dwarfing it in size.

"When the Savages initially took to spacefaring, not all of them had the massive hulks you are familiar with on New Vega. Ships cost money, and there were a lot of people who had enough resources to reach the stars before the hyperdrive was discovered but who couldn't scrape together what was needed for one of the big colony ships. People who didn't want to throw in with the corporations, for one reason or the next.

"Many of these were crewed by rudimentary flight programs. The passengers and crew kept themselves in stasis because generational reproductivity wasn't an option for a ship with such limited resources. There's no telling how many of those are out there.

"But our target… is different. The crews of this particular vessel didn't go to sleep, and they sure as hell went Savage in however long they've been out there. *Too* Savage."

Casper paused to scan the room. All eyes were on him. The men were at rapt attention. Like schoolchildren listening at story hour. And Casper didn't blame them. The Savages were fascinating. Or at least, they would be if they weren't so damn destructive and terrifying.

"The mini-hulk in question is named *Brentwood*. It was discovered by General Rechs some time ago. It is a derelict. Its initial vision was one of harmony, as best we are able to ascertain. This is important: Every Savage cruiser has an agenda. An ideology. A purpose. The key to defeating them is finding out what that ideology is and exploiting it to our advantage.

"*Brentwood* was seeking a way for animals and humans to live in complete harmony and community. The general's personal intelligence reports state that the hulk was working on a quantum communication device that would allow the crewmembers to communicate with any biological life at a conversational level. This led to experimentation, both on the animals aboard and the crewmembers."

Casper clasped his hands behind his back.

"What you will find on that ship are Savages who have made themselves into animal hybrids. They are no longer capable of higher brain functions or of controlling their cruiser. Highly cannibalistic, they simply survive.

"Your objective is to secure the *Brentwood* until it can be completely cleared of the Savage threat. Squad leaders are to report to your platoon commanders for further instructions. But before that, I have a letter from the general that you are to share with your squads upon completion of their briefings:

"'Legion candidates, today marks a turning point…'"

* * *

Kimbo held the letter in his hand, reading it aloud for the rest of Echo Squad to hear.

"'…a turning point. For today, those of you who survive this encounter with the Savages aboard the mini-hulk *Brentwood* will be counted as legionnaires.'"

The younger Johnson brother raised a hand. "I thought we already was legionnaires?"

"Nope," said his older sibling. "Gotta prove you're willing to die for the old man one last time before you're graced with his approval."

Kimbo held up the piece of paper the letter was printed on. "Can I finish this?"

"Do you have to?"

Kimbo looked up thoughtfully. "Good point." He crumpled the paper into a ball and tossed it over his shoulder.

"I don't know about you guys," said Big Bro, "but I have the distinct feeling that while we're tromping through some Savage ghost ship, the old man is gonna be hangin' in the back, yelling at us for not using our LC numbers over the comm."

Kimbo swelled himself up and impersonated the general. "You boys din't kill them Savages fast enough. Bring 'em back to life and kill 'em again in six seconds or less or you're out of my Legion!"

The whole of Echo Squad laughed. Except for the Wild Man, who was sitting on a supply crate, bent over and examining the expert marksman pin he kept in his pocket, turning it over again and again with his fingers.

"He's not a coward," Wild Man muttered.

"The old man?" asked Randolph.

Wild Man nodded. "Not a coward. I seen him fight on New Vega. He's mean in a fight. Good in a fight. Not like… not like how he is on Hardrock. I dunno. I want him to be there. Fighting."

"I wouldn't mind seeing him there, either," said Big Bro, acting like he was looking down his N-1 rifle. "Old man runs out in front of me and… whoops."

"Serve him right for how he treated Davis," chimed in the junior Johnson brother.

"And a lot of other candidates," added Kimbo. "But let's be honest, Big. You don't have the stones to take a shot at Tyrus Rechs."

The squad laughed again.

And then Sergeant Fast entered the room. "Savages should provide more than enough targets, SPC Johnson."

Big Brother stood up. "Sergeant… I was just jokin' around. I wouldn't—"

Fast cut him off. "As expected, Command doesn't have a replacement for us. So we're a five-man squad plus one. That means it's us along with a VIP we're to escort through the ship."

"Who?"

"Donal Makaffie. Scientist or something."

"I know him," Wild Man said. "He's… kinda funny. Not in the way that makes you laugh."

"Sounds great," said Kimbo.

"Does this mean Echo Squad is getting held back until the ship is secured, Sergeant?" asked Junior.

"You'd think so, but Command wants Makaffie in the thick of it. Apparently the mini-hulk may have some fail-safes and intruder protocols online. There's more to this mission than killing Savages. Probably some intel the old man wants prior to hitting New Vega."

Sergeant Fast looked at the crumpled letter on the floor. "Did you all read the general's note?"

Kimbo nodded. "Pretty much. What'd you think of it, Sarge?"

"Doesn't matter."

"When we rollin' out?"

"That's why I'm here. Grab your gear and follow me. It's time to stage at the ship-to-ship docking bay. We're being inserted first at the opposite end of the ship. Main force is going through the big bay doors while we get Makaffie to a place where he can assume control of the mini-hulk. You're about to kill a lot of Savages, Echo Squad."

The squadmates whooped at the thought.

Except for Wild Man. He merely let a wide, malevolent grin creep across his face and whispered, "I told you, darlin'. I told you."

Legionnaires: Chapter Fourteen

Echo Squad waited at the docking doors, alone even on their own ship as the rest of the Legion candidates massed for the main assault that would take place from the larger hangar bay of the *Chang*. Makaffie was supposed to have been waiting for them, but the scientist, who was supposedly in charge of Legion R&D and intelligence, was nowhere to be seen.

"We in the wrong place, Sarge?" asked Kimbo.

Fast shook his head. "No. This is it."

"Feels weird, doesn't it?" asked Big Brother. "Old man says we're candidates. Only this is the real deal. No one's watching over our shoulders. CSM Andres is back on Hardrock… feels like Mom and Dad left and put us in charge."

"That whole you're-still-a-candidate thing is the general's way of motivating everyone for this," Fast said, checking the charge pack on his N-1 a third time.

"Yeah, well someone should tell him he sucks as a motivator."

A new voice sounded from across the small, private bay. "Why don't you tell him?"

Echo Squad turned to see a slim man wearing the same kit as them, save for a mounted camera on his shoulder. Too large to be a standard cam. Sergeant Fast figured it must be capable of taking some kind of scientific readings in addition to recording and shrugged it off. Just as long as he didn't need to carry it.

"You're Makaffie?" asked Fast.

"I am. And *you* are Echo Squad. Ready to risk life and limb in pursuit of some great cosmic secrets… Echo Squad?"

Fast nodded. "Ready when you are."

"Why, is that…" Makaffie peered around Sergeant Fast at the big man standing with an N-1 in his arms and an imposing sniper rifle strapped to his back. "The Wild Man! It is!"

"Hey," mumbled Wild Man.

"Anyway," Makaffie said, turning his attention back to the rest of the squad. "You ought to just tell the general what you think."

Kimbo scoffed. "Yeah. Right."

Makaffie shrugged. "He's only an asshole if you let him be. He doesn't mind it when you push back. I say what's on my mind around ol' Tyrus Rechs."

"We'll take that under advisement," Fast said, eyeing the airlock door that would take them outside the ship and to the aft entryway of the mini-hulk *Brentwood*.

"You should indeed. Life's too short not to speak your mind. And between the general and the Savages, I'd rather risk being killed by the general. At least he'd make it quick."

"Funny guy," Kimbo said with a shake of his head. "You know how to use that kit you're wearing, or is the delay for you to get instructions from the sergeant?"

Makaffie smiled. "I happen to be a *veteran* of the *First* Battle for New Vega. Wild Man will vouch for me."

"Thank you for your service," Sergeant Fast deadpanned. "Is there a delay, though? We've been ramped up for action for thirty minutes. Time to go or stand down at this point."

"Oh, we can go. We can go. I just… wanted to get to know you all a little bit—other than Wild Man—before I activated the comm feed with the general."

"You mean we got the old man looking over our shoulder for this op?" Big Brother said.

Makaffie smiled. "This is the lynchpin of the operation, and Echo Squad are the ones tasked with making sure it happens. I thought that much was obvious—I'm here because I'm important to the Legion. And you're the ones Command thinks can keep me the safest."

Echo Squad looked at one another, their bewilderment evident. At no point had *anyone* in command given them the feeling that they were anything special. In fact most of them felt as though they'd just barely made it through the training on Hardrock. That they were reluctantly passed only because they eked out performances on tasks meant to send them packing.

But that was probably how everyone felt.

"Command, this is package, how copy?" said Makaffie into the comm.

"Copy, package." It was General Rechs. "Visuals confirmed. Proceed to breach point."

"Roger. Sergeant, let's go."

"Echo Squad," Sergeant Fast said, opening the airlock door, "we're up."

The team ushered itself into the airlock, which was magnetically sealed to the hull of the Savage mini-hulk.

Makaffie stepped up to the man-sized airlock door set into the hulk's hull. He produced a micro-tool and popped open a panel on the door, revealing a maze of wires. Makaffie attached several metal crimps onto terminals and then plugged them into a black box he magnetically attached to the hull.

"Such old tech," the slim science officer said. "It's quaint. How far we've come… how far can we go?"

Then, into the comm, he said, "Override secure."

"Proceed to entry," Rechs ordered.

Makaffie looked to Echo Squad, who stacked themselves on either side of the door. "Time to see what new terrors mankind has created out amongst the stars."

Kimbo and Junior exchanged a look before Sergeant Fast said, "Kimbo, you're on point."

A second later Sergeant Fast's comm chirped in his ear. It was the general. "Use your LC or squad identifiers, Sergeant."

"Yes, sir." He pointed at Kimbo. "Echo Two, move."

Kimbo nodded and pushed the door open. A light mounted to his helmet activated in the darkness beyond, shining a bright beam into an otherwise empty corridor.

Kimbo wrinkled his nose and stepped inside. The rest of the team quickly followed. The interior of the ship was dark and ominously quiet. Only the soft steps of their boots against the grating of the deck could be heard.

They were in a tubular corridor with dingy acrylic walls that were cloudy with age and condensation. On the other side of the clear acrylic, on both sides, looked to be an overgrown and wild terrarium filled with greenery. The leaves of the plants pressed up against the windows. Above was a metallic blue ceiling with hanging halogen lights hooded by long sheet-metal boxes. All the lights were dead.

"Hallway looks clear," whispered Kimbo.

"Move up," ordered Sergeant Fast. "Echo Five, seal the door."

"Roger, Sergeant," said Junior.

"Gods, what's that stench?" asked Big Brother. "My eyes are watering."

Makaffie sniffed and rubbed a hand beneath his nose. "Smells like these Savages ain't been using the bathrooms for a looong time."

"What're these?" Fast asked, nodding to the plants on the other side of the acrylic walls.

Makaffie shrugged. "Source of oxygen? Or maybe they just thought it was pretty when they set out."

There was a clanging from beyond the hull. A deep rumble that seemed to travel through the corridor behind and ahead of them all at once.

"*Chang* has disengaged," Rechs announced. "Proceed to secure aft bridge corridor and await further instructions."

"Copy, Command."

The team moved forward, creeping across the deck, lights revealing piles of dirt and filth in the curved spaces where the walls met the floor. Kimbo held up a hand and the squad killed their lights and took a knee.

Sergeant Fast switched on his IR overlay on the clear shield that extended down from his helmet. He could make out the faint glow of unit markings on the helmets as he hustled past his team and knelt beside Kimbo.

They spoke in whispers.

"What did you see?"

"Corridor has some doors on either side up ahead, Sergeant. Can't tell if they're open or not."

"No signs of life?"

"Negative."

Fast patted Kimbo on the shoulder. "Hold here."

He moved back to the end of the dispersed squad of Legion candidates, clapping each man on the shoulder as he squat-walked past them to reach Makaffie.

"Doors on either side ahead appear to be unlocked."

"Good," Makaffie said, his voice just a little louder than Fast would have wished for. "That means we guessed right."

"So you know where we are?"

"I do now."

"I have the feeling you know a lot more than you're saying."

"If I told you all what I knew... everyone would be too afraid to come." Makaffie sounded like he was smiling as he spoke. "Can't have a Legion with no legionnaires. And this is the final test, right?"

"Sure." Sergeant Fast stood. "Lights back on, Echo Squad. Let's clear these rooms and move up."

He turned to Makaffie. "Unless there's something else we gotta do."

"No. Clear the way. We can't make the next move until the general takes the rest of you fabled warriors into battle through the main hangar."

"Teams of two," Fast ordered, wondering if the old man was still listening in. "Echo Three, stick with Makaffie since you're old buddies. Echo Two, you're with me."

Wild Man jogged back to his new position by Makaffie. He gripped his N-1 tightly and Sergeant Fast could see beads of perspiration forming on his face.

"Here, Sarge," Makaffie said, unslinging the camera rig from his shoulder. "Put this on so I can see what you see in those rooms."

Sergeant Fast stifled a sigh and held still as the slim eccentric fastened the device to his shoulder, its lens positioned beside his head so the viewer could be afforded a first-person view. He could hear the sound of miniature gears and gyros working as the camera swiveled and stabilized itself. "We good?"

"Yes," Makaffie answered. "Visuals are being transmitted to my battle board. One more thing, though."

"Echo Squad, hold up," Fast said before the brothers could make their way to the first room. "Looks like we're prepping for this mission *after* it starts."

Makaffie laughed. "No one ever accused me of being a good soldier."

He activated a box-shaped device that hung from his belt. A black screen powered to life, showing two perpendicular lines extending out and reaching a curving wall showing max range—like the lines of a seamball field driving to the outfield wall—and the device began making a steady, rhythmic *oomp, oomp, oomp.*

"What's that?"

"Motion detector, see? Much better range than the usual battlefield HUD report."

Makaffie grabbed Fast by his shoulder pauldron and forced him to sidestep in front of the device. A blip appeared and then faded away when he went still again.

"Goes through walls, ceilings, and floors in a forty-meter radius. Three-dimensional. Anything moves inside that bubble, we should detect it."

Fast nodded. "Good. Kimbo, you ready?"

The sergeant winced inwardly at his forgetting to use the proper identifier. But the old man didn't say anything. Which meant he was probably busy with the next phase of the operation.

Or he was just holding back the butt-chewing until after the op. Maybe he would bring it up as an excuse to fail them. Who could say?

"Let's do it, Sarge," Kimbo replied.

The brothers nodded and slipped into the first doorway on the left. Fast and Kimbo did the same on the right, the sergeant moving in first so the camera on his shoulder would have an uninterrupted visual of what lay beyond the simple top-down pneumatic door. The door had been partially closed, and Kimbo had to physically push it up into its housing in order for both men to enter without ducking.

Sergeant Fast swept his light across the dark room, lighting up a desk and a pair of office chairs. After a quick visual he said, "Room looks clear."

"Burn a chem light," Makaffie instructed. "Need to see the room as a whole."

Fast nodded to Kimbo, who pulled a chemically charged diode stick from his hip pouch, ripped its top to activate, and held it up. The stick bathed the room in a soft light that seemed not quite yellow or green, but a blending of the two colors that somehow made the shadows appear dark blue.

"Like something out of a museum," mumbled Kimbo.

Fast nodded. "Echo Four, what's your status?"

"Room's clear, Sarge," responded Junior over the comm. "Just an empty office. Not a big one, either."

"Are there any nameplates in that office, Echo Four?" Makaffie asked. "Anything identifying whose it was."

"Stand by."

There was a tense silence as the Johnson brothers checked their room. The low clang of boots against metal decking was the only noise in the deep quiet as Fast looked over the office they'd entered. Kimbo had been right: the place did look like a museum piece. Like one of those carefully staged exhibits that showed life as it was believed to have been lived in the first years of a new colony. Or on the last years of Earth—though there was now some debate from the academic community as to whether that planet had ever truly existed. But most people took for granted that it was real.

The desk was a rectangular glass sheet with a clean, beveled edge. It was mounted on brushed chrome legs, with minimal storage, and its surface was sparse and untouched. Like it was waiting for whoever usually occupied it to return after a weekend away. A cord ran up through a hole in the desk's surface and plugged into one of the legs.

Fast picked up a wooden frame that had a still photo of a woman with auburn hair snuggling a toy-sized dog.

"You seein' this, Makaffie?"

"Nice dog."

Fast frowned. "Seems a little small. This mean anything to you?"

"No. Keep looking."

Fast obeyed, moving past concave disc-like chairs with white upholstery that, despite having what was likely a futuristic design, seemed hopelessly dated to the ancient past. "It would help if we knew what we were looking for."

"A name. The right office."

"What's the name?"

"Carlson, Humberto E."

Kimbo broke in. "This place looks like it belonged to a chick. Never heard of a girl named Humberto."

Fast approached the coat rack Kimbo stood next to, little more than a round, metallic rod with flattened hooks that bent upward. A women's cardigan hung on one of the hooks, its threads hanging loose and unraveled, holes bored throughout. It had been there a long time.

Big Brother reported in over the comm. "Found something in a closet. Looks like a... diploma. Name on it is Kyle McCarley."

"That's one of his assistants," Makaffie said. Clearly the man knew something of the history of this ship. "C'mon back out and regroup. One of the next two offices should be Humberto's."

"Copy."

As Fast and Kimbo moved back toward the corridor, Kimbo bent down and picked up a frame that had fallen from the wall at some point, shaking off the broken glass before reading it. "Ivellisse Mateo. PhD, Molecular Biology. University of California, San Francisco. Dude. This scrap of paper is gotta be worth a fortune. I'm takin' it."

The Legion candidate pulled it from its frame and folded into quarters before stuffing it into his pocket.

Fast gave a half smile. "You're not wrong about that." He turned and focused his camera on a pot that was knocked on its side. Barren, dry soil still lay spread out against the metal decking near the pot's broken rim. Next to it was an interior door, sleek and white—a pocket door that slid inside the wall itself. It was marred by long, ragged scratches, all the way from chest level down to the deck.

"You seein' this?"

Makaffie swallowed and said, "Oh, yes. Open the door."

Fast positioned himself in front of the door, N-1 up and aiming for whatever was on the other side as Kimbo stood to the side and dug his fingers into the manual open. Fast nodded and Kimbo pulled hard, forcing the door into its pocket inside the wall with a grunt that seemed to be absorbed by the room itself.

The sergeant sucked in a deep breath and then exhaled. A mummified body wearing a tattered white lab coat and shredded black trousers hung in the air, long black hair partially covering a skeletal face with taut patches of desiccated flesh stretched in a silent, open-mouthed scream.

"Think I found Ivellisse."

Kimbo peered around the open door and did a shake. "She hung herself?"

"Looks like it."

"And then somethin' sniffed her out and tried scratching the door open?"

Sergeant Fast frowned. That was the part that bothered him. "What now, Makaffie?"

"Inside the closet... do you see anything resembling an access or electrical panel?"

"Stand by." Fast took a step toward the darkened closet, shining his light in the corners and to the ceiling that the scientist had hanged herself from. His boot bumped into a footstool she'd been standing on during those last minutes of her life.

"Check behind her," offered Kimbo.

Fast pushed the swinging corpse to the side. It felt as though it weighed nothing at all. Like it was constructed of paper. A macabre piñata. The movement, after so many years of stationary existence, caused some long-decayed fiber in the belt or whatever she'd hanged herself from to snap, and the corpse tumbled to the floor. A cloud of dust billowed up into the faces of the two Legion candidates.

"Oh, sick," coughed Kimbo, fanning the cloud away.

Fast likewise coughed and blinked the dust from his eyes, looking through watery eyes at the panel. "Found it."

"Pop it open," Makaffie said, his voice revealing an edge of excitement. "But don't touch anything inside."

Fast pulled the panel open and stepped back, shining his light on two columns of round, glossy buttons. They were a variety of colors, and none of them were labeled.

"Now what?" he asked.

"Left side. Third button from the top. Should be yellow. Press it."

Fast stepped back up to the panel, looking down as he stepped over the corpse. He pushed the legs away to better be able to stand, mumbling his apologies to the body.

He found the yellow button where Makaffie said it ought to be, and pressed it. There was a series of clanks, then the room lit up with soft red emergency lighting.

"Okay, don't press anything else. Come on back out here."

"Copy." Fast nodded to Kimbo, who took point and led the way out of the office and back to the newly illuminated corridor.

The brothers were waiting with Wild Man and Makaffie.

"One more room up ahead and then the hall splits at a T-shaped intersection a ways further down," said Big.

"Tried the door before we came back," added Junior. "Locked."

"Electrical locks are tied into the emergency system," Makaffie said, watching his motion scanner as he got up from a knee. "Should be unlocked now. Can we move up, Sergeant?"

Fast nodded. "This'll be Humberto's office?"

Makaffie nodded. "Process of elimination says so. There were just the three scientists on this hulk. And their devotees."

Grumbling in the background, Wild Man mumbled something that sounded to Fast like, "I'll ask."

"Ask what?" Fast whispered as they moved toward the last office door in the corridor.

"Thought we were gonna kill Savages," the big man replied.

Makaffie gave a knowing smile. "Be glad you haven't had to yet. I hope it stays that way." He looked down at the motion screen. The only blips on the display belonged to Echo Squad. "So far… so good."

They moved in a tactical formation to the final office door. The only sounds to be heard were their rapid, purposeful steps against the metal decking and the *oomp, oomp, oomp* of the motion sensor.

Fast remained on point. As he approached the door—which was much larger and more durable-looking than the two previous—his eye caught a series of bullet holes on the wall opposite the door. The thick acrylic had spider-webbed where bullets had struck it, shattering in some places and spilling out soil and vegetation onto the deck. The effect was a barren dead spot in the otherwise lush tropical biome. Long, ivy-like vines had stretched across the decking, as if they had grown until turning brown and red from a lack of water—the ruptured section had probably lost its ability to retain moisture, and the plant's growth was stymied as it ventured onto the deck.

"Some fighting happened here," said James, stating the obvious.

His younger brother knelt and moved his hand over a stained section of decking. "Wasn't just against plants, either. Looks like old bloodstains. It goes on up the corridor, see?"

"Or you're imagining things," said Kimbo.

"Someone was shooting at something."

Fast shook his head. He looked to Makaffie, who was considering the blood, chewing on his lower lip. Lost in thought.

"All right, Echo Squad, we'll—"

A thud sounded somewhere far away in the ship. General Rechs came back on the comms. His voice sounded weak and distant. "We're about to begin the main assault, Makaffie. Are you in position?"

"Just about, Tyrus."

Echo Squad exchanged a can-you-believe-this-guy look. Who called the old man "Tyrus"? His own mother probably called him sir.

"Pick it up," Rechs growled. "We're about to breach. Command out."

"Well," Makaffie said, his eyes wide in mock surprise, "I guess that means it's time to see what's on the other side of this door."

Rather than waiting for the team to stack and breach, Makaffie simply pressed the switch and stood dead-center as the two heavy doors slid apart.

"Echo Squad," hissed a clearly annoyed Sergeant Fast. "Go!"

The team stormed the room, N-1 rifles dragging white beams of light through the red glow of the emergency diodes. There was a tinkling of spent brass cartridges as they pushed inside, but no signs of life.

Fast moved straight ahead to a desk that matched the one he'd found in the previous office. Glass top, futuristic in the old and corny style of those who'd first begun to jump across the galaxy. He found Humberto right away. The man had a revolver in his hand and a gaping hole in his head, which lay on the desk amid a grisly scene of suicidal carnage that had long since dried up and become a permanent fixture.

"Office is clear," Fast called.

"Hey, Sergeant." It was Kimbo. "Get a look at this."

Fast turned and saw a pair of mounted automated machine guns just inside the doorway, positioned to give converging fields of fire at whatever might come through. The spent brass they'd trudged through in storming the room clearly had been expelled by these stationary weapons.

"Explains those bullet holes outside," said James.

"Yeah, explains those bullet holes," confirmed his younger brother. "Glad these weren't still on."

"They're powered by a separate circuit," Makaffie said as he stepped across the threshold and into the office. "Part of a security package that—"

He was interrupted by the sound of his own motion device. Its *oomp, oomp, oomp* that had become part of the background noise was now a *ting, ting, ting*. And somewhere, deeper in the office, behind another set of doors, a new blip of motion had registered.

Legionnaires: Chapter Fifteen

Staged outside the door leading from Humberto's office, Sergeant Fast motioned for Kimbo to get into breaching position. He looked to Makaffie, who stood just outside the doorway, next to the sentry machine guns. "What are we dealing with?" asked the sergeant. "How many?"

Something was on the other side of the door, and other than what they could imagine based on the fact they were aboard a Savage mini-hulk, the Legion candidates didn't know exactly what.

"Just the one, still," Makaffie said as his motion sensor *ting*ed. He was beginning to sweat. Looking over his shoulder despite the lack of a sensor reading behind the group. Like he expected trouble to come from back there, even if his device said there was nothing to be found. "It's moving, but in one place. Like… I dunno, rocking back and forth."

"I take it that we need to get to the other side of this door whether you sense movement or not," said Sergeant Fast.

Makaffie nodded. "That's right. Humberto ran the brain of this ship. Handled the research lab and then later the… the experiments. His office leads to the control room, central computer, navigation, and piloting stations, plus the lab. Everything else is just living space for the people who paid to make it happen."

"None of this is making sense to me," James said, shaking his head.

"You hear that?" asked Randolph.

The team, having already been whispering, quieted down. The lab door was thick, dense enough that conversations should stay on the other side. But Sergeant Fast *did* hear something.

"It's like some kind of... clicking."

Wild Man looked up at the ceiling. There was a brushed-nickel air diffuser directly above them. "It's coming from the vents. Carryin' the sound."

Everyone looked up. The vent barked its clicks. Steady. Rhythmic.

"All right, let's see what we're dealing with," Sergeant Fast finally said. "You got a way to open this door, or do we need to blow it?"

"It'll open," Makaffie said. He stooped and picked up a lanyard with some kind of passkey card that looked to have fallen from the long-dead Humberto's hand. "Use this." He flung the card side-arm, its yellow string tail fluttering behind it.

Fast caught it out of the air and handed it to Kimbo. "Slide it into that slot."

Kimbo pushed the card in. Everyone tensed, ready for the door to open. It didn't.

Kimbo let out a sigh. "Doesn't work, man."

"Flip it over and try again," said Fast.

"For real?"

"I got a little familiar with old tech before I got caught up in playing soldier. It's... finicky."

Kimbo pulled the card out, flipped it over, and reinserted. A green light lit up and the door began to open, pulling apart with a protesting creak from being sealed for what may have been decades... centuries even.

From the other side, the clicking grew louder. More pronounced.

As soon as the doors pulled open wide enough, Fast ordered, "Go!"

Wild Man pushed himself through, then the brothers, then Kimbo, and lastly the sergeant. He entered the room and found all of his squad standing at ease, staring at an interior corner, their heads tilted up.

The clicking sound was coming from that direction. Fast quickly confirmed that the rest of the room was secure.

They had stepped into some sort of decontamination bay. Large glass walls and doors lay ahead, revealing a darkened room. Its only light came from hundreds of glowing buttons at workstations.

Satisfied of their safety, Fast inspected the source of the noise. It was a fifty-caliber machine gun suspended from the corner ceiling by a rod. Its barrel swept back and forth, covering the entirety of the room as its pin dry-fired repeatedly.

Click-click-click-click-click. A full-auto tool with no ammunition—thankfully. Fast could see a belt hanging limply from a cavity in the ceiling, drooping down like some constricting snake from a jungle treetop. It must've gotten loose over the years and fallen out of the feeder.

Fast turned and saw a matching defensive setup in the opposite corner. This one had its belt still fed into the weapon. But it wasn't moving.

"Must've been a bad wiring job," Makaffie said over comm, remaining outside in Humberto's office. "Probably came back online with the low-level emergency power I had you switch back on. That's a no-no."

"Echo Four, disable both of these," Fast said.

"On it, Sergeant."

The Legion candidate went to work bringing the weapons down, joined by his squadmates.

Tyrus Rechs's voice returned. "Beginning main assault. Over."

Sergeant Fast passed the info on to his squad, then motioned for Makaffie to join him. In the distance, a boom sounded. Fast's ears strained for sounds of battle, but evidently the main hangar where the assault was happening was too far away, even in the relatively modest-sized mini-hulk.

"Did you make contact?" Makaffie asked Rechs over the comm.

"Negative. Main hangar is empty. Pushing up. Have you got access to the system?"

"Working on that now, Tyrus. Five minutes."

Makaffie moved to the glass wall that looked out into the darkened lab and control room. The area beyond was swimming in shadow, its dimensions and architecture only faintly hinted at by the dim, pulsing flash of long-unused consoles that flickered in a coded language of their own.

The enigmatic soldier-turned-Legion-scientist leaned closer to the glass, squinting. "That's odd."

"What's odd?" Fast asked, trying to look past the glare of his flashlight as it shone against the glass and sent its shaft into blackness. His face was inches away from the partition.

"I thought I saw something. Way back." Makaffie inspected his motion sensor. It was giving off its *oomp*, but it identified nothing moving beyond the door.

"Out of the sensor's range?"

"Maybe. Tough to tell in the black. It looked like... well. Never mind."

Kimbo stepped forward. "Guns are disabled, Sergeant."

"Good," Fast said, eyeing Makaffie. He wanted the man to give them a heads-up about what he was expecting to see. His evasions were more worrying than him just coming out and telling them what they might be up against. "We're set to secure the next room."

Kimbo used the same key card that had opened the door from Humberto's office. The thick glass doors parted, letting in an electronic hum from the numerous essential devices still drawing power from the mini-hulk's core.

Computers and consoles were set up in rows, with swivel chairs bolted to the floor beside them. Echo Squad moved down the three steps that led into the sunken pit that was the control room and then split apart into two-man teams. Each team moved along one of the three walkways, moving parallel, separated by the rows of workstations between them.

Behind them, Makaffie moved slowly, his eyes fixed on the motion sensor screen which lit his face a ghostly white. He'd set it to ignore the motion of Echo Squad and was listening to the *oomp*, *oomp, oomp* of it searching out hostile elements. It was a sound of safety. A promise that they remained alone in the dark.

A rustling in front of Makaffie caused the man to look up. Sergeant Fast and the rest of the team had taken knees. Fast's fist was raised in the air. Their lights were sweeping the far end of the lab and control area, looking wide and weak because of the distance. Big, oblong shadows of the consoles in between them and their point of search stretched out along the walls.

"What?" Makaffie whispered into the comm.

Sergeant Fast's voice was utterly calm. "Saw something move behind those tower things ahead. Just got a glimpse."

"Those tower things," Makaffie said, "are meant for splicing genomes."

The comforting *oomp* emanating from Makaffie's hands gave a short-lived *ting* as a blip appeared on the edge of the screen. It faded almost as soon as it arrived.

Feeling a fear that seemed to deaden his legs, Makaffie edged forward. Another *ting*, and then nothing. Then two *ting*s.

"Somethin's in here with us, Sergeant," said James.

"Need to know what we're dealing with here, Makaffie," Fast said over his shoulder. "Other than Savage."

"I don't—we don't know. Not exactly. A hybrid. Human and animal. Savage records are hard to come by and even harder to understand in some cases. But... this group wanted to find the way to achieve harmony with animals. With their pets, specifically. Wanted to be able to communicate. Telepathically or whatever. That led to—I mean, I think it led to—some genetic experimentation which got out of hand and led to a loss of sentience. Whatever is still alive on this ship—it's not human. It used to be, but it's not. It'll be feral and wild. But an N-1 should put it down."

"So… monster hunting?" Kimbo said. "That sounds fun."

"Can you get the lights on in here?" Fast asked. "Maybe that'll scare 'em away."

"Hang on." Makaffie moved to a console and begin to type. "Come on…"

The screen flickered and pulsed, like it was having difficulty powering on. Finally, the words "Aja Enterprises" appeared on the screen, and Makaffie intuitively worked his way through the system from there.

"Okay. I'm taking this a little bit at a time. Just gonna try and bring on the lowest power suite beyond emergency lighting. Should just activate lights and a few essential systems."

Overhead fixtures began to hum, and soon the lab was bathed in a sterile, industrial white light.

"Going to try and bring on more systems. Get an idea of what's going on."

Fast nodded, blinking away the newfound brightness as his eyes adjusted. "Let's go see what's hiding back there, Echo Squad."

They fanned out so they were capable of sending fire at anything in front of them across the entirety of the elongated room. There was a scurrying sound ahead of them, just behind the large genome towers, which stretched from floor to ceiling and looked like columns dividing the control room from the more lab-like sections. Small, sealed modular rooms, mobile base cabinets, numerous high-capacity venting hoods... everything back there looked very scientific. And wrecked. Cabinets were overturned, with papers and shattered glass covering the floor.

A crash sounded from that area, and one of the overhead lights went out, its hood swinging as if something had battered it. That was followed by another crash, like a table falling over and spilling its contents to the floor.

Echo Squad paused at the genome towers. There was yet another crash, and more lights went off further ahead.

"It's trying to get back into the dark," Wild Man said.

Fast shook his head. This wasn't what he'd been mentally preparing himself for. He'd figured this would be a typical combat encounter—tactics, maneuvering, the exchange of weapons fire... but no. This was more like being stalked through some pristine jungle by a local apex predator. Trying to keep his crew alive long enough to finish the job and get paid.

Fast put his back against one of the genome towers and killed the light on the shoulder-mounted camera. He motioned for his squad to take firing positions behind the cover of some consoles. "I'm gonna take a look."

Echo Squad hustled into position, N-1s ready for anything that might try to flank around the towers and go after their sergeant from behind.

Sergeant Fast leaned around the corner, slowly exposing his head as the ruined lab came into view. That part of the room was darker, but still light enough to for him to see... *it*.

It had pale, wet-looking flesh. Naked except for a wild and matted mane that tufted from its head and carried down to the base of its neck. It stood on all fours. And it was big. As high as a man's chest when measured claw to shoulders. Its shriveled human-like breasts, one set on its chest and another lower, at the end of its ribs, marked it as female. A fleshy tail swept behind its hindquarters.

"What the hell..." Fast peered hard into the shadows.

The thing had its face turned away, but it froze as if sensing that Fast was watching, then turned toward him.

What the sergeant saw was an abomination. The face was shaped like a woman's, with large coal-black eyes and high cheekbones. But its nostrils were mere slits that puffed open and then sealed shut with every inhalation of air. And when the eyes locked on the sergeant, it opened its mouth—seemingly unhinging its jaw—to reveal a mouthful of crooked and decayed teeth. A combination of predatory canines that looked capable of tearing flesh and breaking bone, and twisted incisors that looked all too human.

The thing reoriented itself, squaring its shoulders so it faced the sergeant, making itself a smaller target, and backed away slowly on all fours, never removing its gaze from Fast.

Then it opened its mouth and screamed.

It wasn't a bestial scream like that of a lion or wolf. But the high, shrill, bloodcurdling cry of a human female. It echoed across the lab. Then sounded again.

Fast felt some primal fear tug at his insides. Part of him wanted to shoot the dreaded thing, but the scream made him feel as though he ought to… help it. Save it.

It screamed once more and then turned and loped out of sight.

"What the hell was that, Sergeant?" asked Kimbo, moving up and joining him. "Was that… was that a woman?"

"No. I don't know what it was. It wasn't human. But it made that scream and—"

Fast's words were cut short as more screams sounded from beyond. From around the darkened bend where the creature had retreated. The piercing cries of women and the agonized howls of men.

And they were all approaching together.

Legionnaires:
Chapter Sixteen

Tyrus Rechs stalked through the empty hangar of the Savage mini-hulk *Brentwood*. He stopped behind a pair of Legion candidates who were attempting to cut through a sealed blast door with torches. The task was taking entirely too long, which meant the doors had been reinforced beyond what this lighthugger should have been equipped with.

"Captain Milker," Rechs called into his comm.

"Yes, sir."

"We're at a standstill at bay door 03. What's your progress, over?"

"Sir, we're barely making a scratch. These doors must be ten meters thick the way they're resisting."

"Copy. Command out."

Rechs cursed under his breath. This was *not* how the mission planning was supposed to go. The intel he and Makaffie had analyzed from indexed Savage cores recovered from destroyed hulks and kept with Sulla showed that *Brentwood*, which Rechs had found by chance eighty years prior, was a Savage ship full of sentient but non-intelligent Savages. The result of experimentations gone awry. It needed to be cleared of its little beasties, something Rechs was confident his Legion candidates could easily accomplish, and then scoured for intel that could be used for the assault on New Vega.

The plan had been for Makaffie and Echo Squad to covertly gain access to the ship's systems and open the way for Rechs's main assault force to clear the ship. The thought occurred to Rechs that perhaps he should have given Makaffie and his team more time to take the controls, but he didn't like the idea of a team that small being solo on the ship for too long. The creatures might pose a significant threat if they banded into a pack.

Jogging to the farthest reach of the hangar—the only place he could get a comm connection with Makaffie—Rechs reviewed his options. Cutting his way into the main corridors of the mini-hulk was taking too long, and blowing a hole was too risky on a ship this old. It wasn't built to military standards. It was a civilian science vessel. That is was still intact after centuries of space travel was remarkable in itself. He could call back men, re-board the *Chang*, and then enter behind Echo Squad. But those were tight quarters for the force Rechs had brought with him. Still, sending in squads one at a time seemed like the best option, unless Makaffie had some good news for him.

But the moment the comm transmission went live, Rechs knew that no good news was forthcoming.

"Tyrus," shouted Makaffie over the sound of N-1 rifles firing without pause. "We could use some help here, man!"

"What's happening?"

"Those things are charging us non-stop. And no matter how many we put down, they're still coming."

"We're bottled up down here. Can you open the blast doors leading from the main hangar?"

"Negative. I'm fighting with some kind of program that was left behind. Just working to keep what I've got up from going back down. Mainly just lights. Oh—and fighting to keep the central core from wiping itself of all data."

Rechs shook his head and then motioned for a passing lieutenant to reach him. He muted his comm and told the lieutenant, "Tell Admiral Sulla that we need to re-board immediately."

"Yes, sir!"

The lieutenant activated his comm where he stood, and Rechs went back to Makaffie, the sound of blaster fire still ringing over the comm speaker in his ear.

"I'm working to get reinforcements to your position. What do you mean a program that was left behind? Someone was on this ship before us?"

"Looks like it, Tyrus. Don't know what they did or why, but I—" There was a boom followed by Makaffie letting loose a string of profanities. "Oh, man. They're using their grenades. That can't be good."

Rechs gritted his teeth. No. It couldn't.

"Do what you can, Makaffie. We're pulling out of the hangar as soon as *Chang* gets back into position."

* * *

The Wild Man's N-1 lay at his side, waiting and ready should he need it. But for now, his big-bore sniper rifle was all he could ever want. The things, the Savage… perversities, were swarming in a massive pack, all howling like the damned souls of the unrepentant. But Wild Man felt no pity for them.

They were Savage.

This was what they'd wanted. Maybe not what they'd foreseen, but nobody left on a Savage cruiser unless they thought they knew what was best for the world. That's what it boiled down to. They knew what was best and they'd force you to know the same.

Like they'd forced everyone he'd ever known on that small and unimportant planet that should have been of no consequence. Except the Savages always found consequence if it meant more killing.

Which was exactly what it meant on Stendahl's Bet.

They killed her. His darling. Killed his firstborn.

But they couldn't kill him. No matter how hard they tried. Whether with guns or teeth and claws… they couldn't kill the Wild Man.

The big man's sniper rifle belched out a flame as he squeezed a shot at one of the things running toward them. The bullet hit between the clavicles and tore a gory hole right through. The same round dropped at least two more of the things behind his target. They all went down as if a bolt of lightning from the Almighty had ripped through the charging mass. Immediate judgment.

The Wild Man liked that. He was a tool used in the hands of some cosmic craftsman. One that declared the Savages and their ilk to be a blight on the galaxy. He squeezed the trigger again and sent a tuft of mangy hair and bloody mist into the air, spraying red on the transparent lab walls. And more of the beasts dropped.

Do another one, babe.

She'd come back once the shooting started. He knew she would. Knew that, even though they hadn't been getting along very well lately, when it came right down to it she'd be back.

Because he loved her.

And she loved what he could do.

The rifle boomed, and she seemed to sigh in ecstasy.

Do another one, babe.

She didn't bring the little one this time. Wild Man felt a twinge of sorrow about that. Maybe this was too much for one so young to see. It would cause nightmares. Best to let him sleep in his crib.

That's best.

No need to hurry up and see all the horrors of life. All the wages of evil. Those would push their way to the front of your life long before they ought to on any account.

Hadn't the boy already lost his ma? Hadn't the little baby already been murdered once?

Why make him see more of life's cruelty?

Wild Man fired again. Yes. He was glad she didn't bring him this time. A child that young... he didn't need to see monsters. Didn't need to know that, when his blood was up, his pa was capable of becoming one.

Boom.

Do another one, babe.

* * *

Makaffie worked frantically over the command console that had once been used by Humberto Carlson, the genetic pioneer who'd had the vision to con a wealthy neighborhood into funding a miniature lighthugger to embark on a colonization voyage beyond the stars. Away from an Earth that was growing more volatile, dangerous, and unpredictable by the day.

The promise had been an easy one to make, one yearned for by those who were seeing a life of fantastic luxury begin to fade, whether through the threats of material loss that always seemed to accompany the politics of voting, or through the politics of armed gangs who took what they wanted.

And of course, there was always the more traditional foil of time robbing them of their youth. Forcing them to face down mortality.

Humberto had told them of a land free of ingrates. Free of those who would seek to ridicule and shame them for their mansions and luxury cars, their ornate lawns and pampered pets.

It turned out that the pets were the key to getting what he wanted.

All he'd needed to do was promise a breakthrough in his research allowing direct communication between animals and humans. That, plus the promised life of safety and luxury out among the stars, got the money rolling in.

But Humberto wasn't a simple con man. He *wanted* that breakthrough. That one, and many other darker, more nefarious ones that the passengers of the *Brentwood* wouldn't discover until it was too late. Until the medicines they'd consumed began changing them.

And by the time one of his two partners grew a conscience and tried to warn everyone, the colonists were all so confused, they didn't even realize that timid Mr. McCarley had gone missing.

Makaffie found a recording of his murder. Humberto did the deed himself. With the same handgun he ultimately committed suicide with. After the experiments had run their course. Once he and Ivellisse had come to grips with the reality that the colonists were something irreversibly terrible, and it was only a matter of time—

This was all interesting, but not life-altering information. Makaffie tagged it for backup and moved on, letting the files migrate to the data card he'd converted for use in this ancient computer system as he went searching for the really useful bits of information.

He found a partition that contained data on a new communications device. A project Humberto had worked on before growing so frustrated he scuttled it in favor of DNA manipulation. Immediately Makaffie saw the potential for an independent and self-reliant comm system in the Legion. He tagged it for backup. Priority: High.

Then he found unanswered comm logs from other Savage vessels. These too were tagged for backup, same priority.

And then a partially cleaned recording of what appeared to be Savage marines boarding the ship, rounding up a number of the creatures, reinforcing the doors, and leaving.

Tagged for backup. Priority: High.

"Tyrus," Makaffie said, ducking his head instinctively as the Wild Man's sniper rifle boomed. "I'm finding stuff that we need, man. But I'm worried we ain't gonna live long enough to get it all. Hurry up!"

"Copy," Rechs said.

Makaffie looked to where Echo Squad was making its stand. They had fallen back in tactical retreat, moving themselves much closer to where he worked than he would like. Sergeant Fast had been the last man at the team's old line, but now he was running back, just ahead of a snarly and snapping Savage beast, weaving slightly in an attempt to give him men a clear shot at the thing even as they cut down more of the creatures that lingered still farther behind. Finally the Wild Man dropped the thing with a headshot that left no head at all.

Sergeant Fast hopped behind cover and began firing again, looking completely unfazed by the ordeal.

Makaffie went back to his screens. A corner box beeped to tell him that his decryption program had finally granted him access to the ship's automated defenses. This would help.

He brought up the defensive schematics for the lab. There were the turrets that Echo had already disabled, and there were more of the same positioned throughout the lab. Capable of descending from the ceiling and opening fire in complete three-hundred-sixty-degree arcs.

All the guns had a red box superimposed over them on the screen. Indicating that they were offline. Makaffie pressed the guns that were set up away from Echo Squad, switching them from red to green in the hope they would start blasting at the rear of the pack and cause it to break, allowing Echo Squad to wipe out what remained up front.

He double-checked his work, ensuring nothing was green that could hit him or Echo Squad.

Then he pressed the activate button.

The distant guns lowered and came to life, barking heavy machine-gun fire into however many of those monsters were gathered. Makaffie visually checked the ceiling tiles inside his own area of operation, just to be sure they were offline. He saw no movement.

Good.

And then... not good. A ceiling tile slid aside and one of the defense guns came down. This one wasn't even in the program. Wasn't listed as an asset.

Makaffie swore and went back to his screen, frantically trying to shut the weapons system down before—

And then it happened. The machine gun barked its rapid claps and Makaffie watched in horror as it sent round after round into one of the Johnson brothers, stopped, and then receded back into the ceiling.

Legionnaires: Chapter Seventeen

"James is hit!"

Sergeant Fast turned his head at Kimbo's shouts and saw the Legion candidate lying face down, his N-1 dropped at his side and multiple bullet holes in his back. The blood was already soaking his uniform.

The sergeant turned his attention back to the nightmarish onslaught that raced toward him. The things weren't hard to kill—a well-aimed N-1 blast did the trick—but there seemed to be a lot of them, and they seemed unconcerned with the heavy casualties they were suffering; already the carcasses of the Savage monstrosities littered the lab. Fast looked for some kind of alpha—something he could kill to make the rest stop coming. But none of them stood out any more than any other. They weren't identical, but they were similar enough. Grotesque, humanoid bodies that moved on all fours, swollen pot-belly stomachs that hung down, flesh the gray of a man who'd spent his life in a cave.

And the screams...

Fast felt as though he was rapid-firing his N-1 just to drown out the murderous shrill cries of the females and the howls of the males. And the wounded were just as bad, moaning and crying like the wounded on any human battlefield. Only there were never any words. Never a sign of intelligence. Just a guttural, primal humanity.

So primal that it couldn't rightly be called human. But neither could it be called something else.

The field of fire was slackening. Echo Squad was concerned with James. Already his brother was rolling him onto his back. The moment he did so it was obvious that the older brother was dead. Blood poured from his mouth and down the side of his face. His eyes stared up, void of any twinkles of life.

Fast wouldn't yell for Randolph to get back into the fight. Didn't think it would do much good. But Kimbo…

"Kimbo! Get your ass back on the line and fire your weapon!"

The shouts rattled the Legion candidate. He popped up and started firing.

Wild Man was the only who seemed not to even notice what had happened. He was entirely fixated on killing more of the beasts that came in his direction.

"Changing packs!" Fast yelled, pulling his last charge pack from his pouch. This wasn't good. They hadn't gone in expecting to fend off a wave attack. He tried to get the younger Johnson brother's attention. "Randolph! Dolph! I need charge packs!"

Dazed, Randolph searched his kit and recovered a charge pack. He tossed it to his sergeant and then looked back at his brother. And then it seemed that something inside him snapped. He turned, standing straight and erect, and began to fire his N-1 as quickly as he could, yelling in rage as he did.

A brief burst of turret fire from elsewhere combined with this furious assault completely halted the charge of the Savage creatures. They began to scatter and turn, looking for routes of escape. But still more gunfire sounded from behind the creatures, and several of them fell.

"Is that us?" Kimbo asked, hoping it was the rest of the candidates arriving to help.

The bullets answered by snapping and whizzing past them with such ferocity that even Randolph was broken from the spell-like trance of his rage. He dropped to the deck as bullets chewed up the console stations they covered behind.

"What the hell is that?" Kimbo shouted.

They were all ducking for cover, even Wild Man. An unholy amount of fire was concentrated on them, like they were facing down an entire platoon of enemy soldiers armed with assault rifles and machine guns.

A stray round smashed into the console screen Makaffie was working at, causing the scientist to drop to the ground and crawl to reach Echo Squad.

"Hope that didn't ruin your reason for being here!" Fast yelled.

Makaffie shook his head. "Don't need a screen to be on to copy files. But we do need to live long enough to use them!"

Fast took a breath and popped up, firing his N-1 as he tried to see what was shooting at them. He fell back down. "Some kind of bot moving on treads."

Makaffie shook his head. "More security defenses."

"Can you turn it off?"

"I turned off everything I could."

Fast nodded. Not angry. Not despairing. Only a cold acceptance of the facts as he formulated what to do next.

"Okay, we're going to have to fall back."

"No, no," Makaffie said. "I haven't finished downloading the data I need. This Savage mainframe is ooooooollld, man."

"Tough," the sergeant replied. "That thing's gonna destroy us if we don't move it."

"Negative, LC-330." It was Rechs. "You are to hold your position. The *Chang* is moving to dock at your location and send in relief."

"Sir, we're almost black on ammunition, James Johnson is KIA, and I—"

"I don't need to know his damned name, LC-330! I need that line held and I don't give a rat's ass if costs *all* your lives to get it done. Hold the damn line until you're relieved or ordered to fall back!"

"Yes, sir," Fast said. Again, not angry. Cool and in control. As though he'd been facing down death—doing this—all his life.

"Echo Squad!" he shouted to be heard above the heavy fire that continued to slam into the thick consoles they covered behind. "We hold that thing here!"

"How?" shouted Kimbo. "I got like four shots left in my N-1."

Wild Man rose and sent a blast with his rifle into the chassis of the armored bot. The blast caused it to rock to one side, but then it turned, apparently unharmed, and unleashed a new volley of fire that sent the big man ducking for his life.

"Here," Fast said, pulling out his last charge pack and tossing it to Kimbo. He drew his pistol and peeked out, looking for a way to get behind the rolling killer, but machine-gun fire skipping across the deck forced him to pull back.

"That bastard," Randolph shouted. "Damn that old man!"

"We hold the line," Fast said, moving a pistol magazine from his waist pouch to a bandolier around his arm. "It's what we do."

"Not that. I heard what he said. About my brother. Like he didn't even matter. Like he wasn't even a person!"

Everyone looked down. Except Fast. The sergeant locked eyes with the grieving soldier. "So screw him. Screw the old man. This isn't his Legion. It's ours. We're fighting for each other now. Don't let him get to you, because what he thinks doesn't matter. What matters is that we make sure James didn't die for nothing."

Echo Squad was looking at their sergeant now. "Okay," Fast said. "Not gonna stop this thing at range, so one of us is gonna have to get up close and shut it down. Or at least try to. That's on me. Wild Man, Kimbo, Randolph—move right and draw fire. I'll flank the thing before it can bear down on me."

"You hope," clarified Makaffie.

Fast nodded. "That's the plan. Go!"

Wild Man ran to the opposite end of the room, drawing fire. Kimbo and Randolph did the same, drawing still more fire. Once in place, they put their weapons up over their consoles and sent blind fire at the armored tread-bot's plating, just to keep it occupied.

"Go!" Fast yelled, so his team would know to stop shooting long enough that he didn't become an object lesson in the dangers of friendly fire.

He moved along the wall, running with pistol in hand for all he was worth. He could see the machine identify the new threat and begin to swivel its chassis to put rounds on target. Banking hard and cutting inside, Fast saw the fixed heavy MG barrel on the robot spewing tracer rounds that zipped out and sparked along the deck plate as it adjusted its fire to catch up with the sergeant.

Hearing the snap of the bullets at his feet, Fast spun and found himself behind the machine. It was stocky, a little shorter than a man, but easily seven hundred pounds. The sergeant grabbed a welded handle on the back of its armored plate and pulled himself toward it. As it attempted to bring more of its powerful weapons around on the intruder, he shoved his pistol down into the inner reaches of the machine, and fired.

He didn't stop until the weapon's magazine was spent and the weapon dry-fired.

Fluid leaked, followed by a gout of smoke and flame—likely a battery being exposed to oxygen. The flames burned Fast's hand. He pulled it away and tumbled from the machine, which seemed to be suffering seizures, jerkily attempting to move its mounted machine gun but no longer firing. The fire consumed it from the inside out, cooking circuitry and sending up smoke that activated alarms inside the lab. A spray of white foam jetted from above, covering the robot in a pillowy cloud of white.

For a moment the sergeant feared that the fire had been extinguished too quickly and the machine would be able to come back online. But it didn't. It just sat there, the foam vaporizing from the heat of the fire and smelling like cherries in the air.

Fast let out a sigh of relief.

Then he heard Wild Man's gun boom.

"'Nother one!" the sniper shouted.

Fast turned his head and swapped out pistol mags, expecting to be perforated at any second. He was out in the open. Without cover.

But the machine Wild Man had shot at wasn't moving toward him. It was moving in the opposite direction. And fast. It had tucked itself into a compact square and was rolling on treads at high speed.

The Wild Man's rifle barked again.

No. Not the rifle. Something else.

"*Chang*'s docking to join us," Makaffie said. He sounded happy at the news.

Fast's heart sank. All he could think was that the machine somehow knew that too, and was moving to repel boarders. And given how tight that entry corridor was, if the candidates were bunched up it could be disastrous.

The sergeant jumped to his feet. "Rifle!"

Wild Man understood at once and tossed Fast his big sniper rifle. The sergeant staggered from the weight of the big thing slamming into him. He ejected the round and made sure it was loaded and then took off after the rolling death machine.

Fast shouted final instructions. Not wanting to alert the machine that it was being pursued, if that was possible. "Tell them not to board!"

Makaffie activated his comm. "Tyrus, you need to delay boarding. Repeat or, uh, I say again… do not board!"

Legionnaires: Chapter Eighteen

Tyrus Rechs put a hand to his ear. He was lined up with several squads of Legion candidates waiting for the doors to the mini-hulk to open so they could storm the lighthugger and secure the data Makaffie had found with Echo Squad.

And now Makaffie was yelling, frantically telling him to delay boarding. But Rechs couldn't understand exactly what or why.

"Say again?"

Makaffie repeated the message just as Sergeant Greenhill shouted from the front with Alpha Squad, "Doors opening!"

No sooner had the doors spread apart than a sudden and violent fusillade of machine-gun fire ripped into the opening. The bullets cut through the air with zips and zooms, slamming into columns of hapless Legion candidates, blowing holes in their helmets and ripping through hearts and lungs. Those in the front line dropped where they stood.

Rechs grabbed the man next to him and pulled them both against the wall, hugging it tightly as the bullets snapped down the corridor. Candidates dropped to the deck, some dead and others alive and trying to get below the line of fire. Still others dove to the sides of the airlock and corridor, pressing against the wall and pulling themselves tightly inward, hoping nothing was left exposed to be shot off.

"Lieutenant!" Rechs shouted to one of his officers, just a few feet behind him, hugging the wall.

The lieutenant leaned forward to reply. "Yes, si—"

A bullet slapped into his helmet and the man collapsed limply into death, his blood spraying the legionnaires nearby.

"Someone shut the doors!" screamed a panicking candidate, but the unyielding fire prevented anyone from reaching out.

"Dammit," Rechs growled. He activated his comm. "Casper!"

There was alarm in the admiral's voice. "What's going on, Tyrus?"

"I need a crew-served weapon down here. A rocket launcher. Something heavy-duty."

The general wished for his armor. Wondered at whether outfitting himself the same as his candidates was as wise as it had seemed when the bullets weren't flying. With the protection and weapons suite at his disposal, he was sure he'd have had no trouble destroying whatever was shooting at them. It had all happened so fast that Rechs didn't even know what he was facing beyond that it was shooting big, fifty-cal bullets at his men.

"Mobilizing," Casper said at last. "I'm heading there personally."

More bullets snapped down the corridor. They were completely trapped.

"Just make it fast!"

***

Sergeant Fast ran with the big sniper rifle carried at the ready. It felt every bit as heavy to him as the mockup N-1s they'd been forced to train with while on Hardrock. Whether that was because he was tired, or because Wild Man's gun was actually that heavy, he didn't know.

The bot had been slowed somewhat by the dead and dying Savage animals that lay strewn across the lab floor. Fast was moved into a part of the ship that was still under the red glow of emergency lighting. There were fewer of the dead beasts here—just the ones that had been wounded in the onslaught and had managed to slink away this far before finally succumbing to their wounds.

And then Fast heard the rapid discharge of the robot's machine guns. It was echoing from around a corner—it must have looped back to the airlock and was shooting at his fellow legionnaires.

Fast picked up his pace accordingly. The longer that thing operated, the worse it would be for the unlucky bastards on the other side of it.

He ran, jumping over a fallen creature, only to feel himself hurled sideways by a blindsiding impact from his right. He landed hard on the deck, and the rifle clattered out of reach.

The sergeant knew right away what had knocked him over. Could tell before the beast opened its maw to reveal that slimy mix of human and animal teeth. Before it let out its horror movie scream of a woman about to die. Only this time the scream belonged to the killer.

The thing's claw-like hand—it felt more like a hand than a paw against Fast's forearm—pinned him to the ground. But his right hand was free, and that was all that mattered. He reached down, unholstered his pistol, and fired several shots into the Savage's head, involuntary squeezing his eyes shut with each trigger pull.

The thing stopped screaming and fell to the side.

Without a word Fast pushed it off, recovered the rifle, and resumed his run. He kept the pistol out, holding it ready in his right hand while the rifle barrel was gripped in his left. It wasn't exactly an easy carry, but Fast couldn't afford another delay.

He saw the next Savage beast before it could pounce. Watched it leap as he approached. Trained his pistol on the thing and shot it out of the air. He left it dead or dying behind him. He kept running.

The machine-gun fire was louder now. Fast was right on the tread-bot. And the time of everything was upon him. Men had surely died. Were certainly dying with each passing second. Maybe newly hit, maybe bleeding out because medics couldn't reach them under the withering rain of destruction.

He turned a corner and saw the thing, a backlit shadow as it blazed tracers down the corridor, into the airlock, and deep into *Chang*'s hangar. Dead Legion candidates were stacked in the open, and Fast could see the living huddling against the sides of the airlock, peeking and then ducking back to avoid the stream of firepower. Waiting for death or for the machine to run out of ammunition. And who could say which would happen first.

Maybe the thing had rear defensive capabilities. Maybe Fast slowing and dropping to a knee was a mistake that would get him killed. But he was breathing heavy and needed a stable shooting platform. He lifted the weapon. It felt unbelievably heavy, as though hewn from rock. Through the scope, he found an actuator that he thought connected the machine's "head"—its optics and camera—to its body.

He held his breath even though his body only wanted him to suck in more air. He buried the part of his psyche that was screaming at him that maybe another of those creatures was behind him.

And he pulled the trigger.

The boom resonated loudly. The overpressure cleared his sinuses. His ears rang despite the comm-capable plugs shoved into them.

But the robot fell silent. The guns stopped. And, slowly, the Legion candidates emerged from their cover.

Cries for medics filled the air.

Sergeant Fast checked behind himself for more Savages.

He was alone.

Legionnaires: Chapter Nineteen

The old man was the first to pop from cover. He had an ancient-looking pistol in his hand. Sergeant Fast had seen them before on digs, from wrecked colony ships or lost scout explorers. A 1911, it was called. A fine gun.

"Captain Milker," Rechs shouted. "Clear this ship."

"Yes, sir! First Platoon, Second Platoon, on me!"

The surviving Legion candidates pushed out of the airlock and began to move through the ship. Clearing rooms that Echo Squad had already cleared and then moving further in. Occasionally the scream of a Savage could be heard along with the blast of N-1s.

Fast felt spent. But he saw Echo Squad emerge from Humberto's office, carrying the body of James. They set it down when they ran into the general. Rechs gave them a quick salute just as the sergeant rejoined his team.

Makaffie's eyes were bright. He was elated. "Tyrus! You need to come with me. Everything we hoped for... we got it."

Rechs nodded and then looked down at the body of the oldest Johnson boy. The scientist retreated for the lab, safely following two squads of Legion candidates who'd moved in that direction. Rechs motioned at the dead man with his 1911. "What was his name?"

Randolph answered before anyone else could. "LC-125, sir. He was my brother."

The grieving candidate gave a look to the rest of Echo Squad as if to say, let it be. Don't anyone call him James. Because the old man don't deserve to know his real name. They all understood.

Rechs worked over his jaw like he was chewing, but there wasn't anything in his mouth. He grunted out a "Hm," and then looked to Sergeant Fast.

"You did a hell of a job, Sergeant."

Fast unslung the Wild Man's rifle and handed it back to his friend. The sergeant's face was wet with the sweat of combat. His chin straps were loose and his helmet hung askew, its battle visor pulled up. "Thank you, sir."

"Gonna need men like you to fill in the officer corps, LC-330. What's your name?"

Fast looked at his squad, who all looked back patiently. Expectantly.

"LC-330." He paused a moment before adding, "Sir."

Rechs clenched his jaw and followed Makaffie to the control room. A moment later Casper arrived, leading medics and an unneeded heavy-weapons crew inside the ship.

"The general?" he asked Sergeant Fast.

Fast pointed. "Control room."

Casper nodded and, apparently sensing Echo Squad's wear and fatigue, took the time to clap each man on the shoulder. "You boys head back to the *Chang*. Get some rest.

You're legionnaires now. I want you to know that. You've done everything asked of you and then some. None of that is lost on any of us."

Randolph nodded to the body of James. "How 'bout him? He a legionnaire, too?"

Casper looked down at the corpse. "You're damn right he is."

And then he left after Rechs.

Medics came in and tried to pick up James. To carry him off the *Brentwood* and back onto the *Chang*. But Randolph wouldn't hear of it.

"He's my brother. I'll carry him."

But he wouldn't carry him alone. First Fast, then Wild Man and Kimbo, took hold of their fallen comrade. Together they gently lifted him. Fast had an arm wrapped under James's shoulder and kept his head from dropping down by cradling it in his palm. In unison, Echo Squad moved toward the *Chang*.

Randolph stroked the face of his older brother. "I know it's funny, but I don't... I don't feel so bad. For me, I mean. It's... it's how Mom will feel that makes me upset."

Fast nodded. "Yeah."

They carried the body of James to a hastily built aid station set up in the hangar, where medics and shipboard nursing staff were loading the dead into body bags. Kimbo, Wild Man, and Sergeant Fast left Randolph to be alone with his brother. To see him off for the inevitable.

After a few moments of silence, Kimbo spoke. "I thought the old man was gonna cut off your balls when you answered him with your LC number back there, Sergeant.

Then again, standin' up to the old man like that... he probably knew you had too much balls to cut off."

This made the Wild Man chuckle. And then he grew serious. "How come... how come you didn't tell him?"

Wild Man was thinking about himself. About how he couldn't remember his real name anymore. Maybe the sergeant was the same way.

Fast shrugged. "I dunno. Just seemed like, after all that, the old man didn't have the right to ask that question. We earned being legionnaires, but that don't mean he earned the right to suddenly act like he knows us."

Kimbo nodded. "Yeah. All of a sudden he wants to act like we're more than numbers? Forget about it. Still the same guy that made everyone run when Condrey drowned, remember?"

Wild Man nodded. "Davis and I... we fought right next to the old man on New Vega. I didn't... I never liked how, how he pretended not to know us. Didn't seem right."

Sergeant Fast raised his eyebrows. He understood all that. But more importantly, he understood why his men needed someone who would fight for them. Because fighting would soon be all any of them had. And he knew that was how things would be until they all drew their last breath.

"So, Sergeant Fast," said Kimbo. "That ain't your real name. Wild Man didn't just get a lucky guess the first time."

Fast smiled. "No. That's not my real name."

"So... what is it? Sergeant."

Fast looked at both men and smiled as much as he could. "Aeson Ford."

GALAXY'S EDGE
SAVAGE WARS
THE HUNDRED

ANSPACH & **COLE**

the SAVAGE WARS Trilogy will conclude with book 3: **THE HUNDRED**

https://galaxysedge.us/product/savage-wars-3

JOIN THE LEGION

You can find art, t-shirts, signed books and other merchandise on our website.

We also have a fantastic Facebook group called the Galaxy's Edge Fan Club that was created for readers and listeners of *Galaxy's Edge* to get together and share their lives, discuss the series, and have an avenue to talk directly with Jason Anspach and Nick Cole. Please check it out and say hello once you get there!

For updates about new releases, exclusive promotions, and sales, visit inthelegion.com and sign up for our VIP mailing list. Grab a spot in the nearest combat sled and get over there to receive your free copy of "Tin Man," a Galaxy's Edge short story available only to mailing list subscribers.

INTHELEGION.COM

GET A FREE, EXCLUSIVE SHORT STORY

About the Authors

Jason Anspach and Nick Cole are a pair of west coast authors teaming up to write their science fiction dream series, Galaxy's Edge.

Jason Anspach is a best-selling author living in Puyallup, Washington with his wife and their own legionnaire squad of seven (not a typo) children. Raised in a military family (Go Army!), he spent his formative years around Joint Base Lewis-McChord and is active in several pro-veteran charities. Jason enjoys hiking and camping throughout the beautiful Pacific Northwest. He remains undefeated at arm wrestling against his entire family.

Nick Cole is a Dragon Award winning author best known for *The Old Man and the Wasteland, CTRL ALT Revolt!,* and the Wyrd Saga. After serving in the United States Army, Nick moved to Hollywood to pursue a career in acting and writing. He resides with his wife, a professional opera singer, south of Los Angeles, California.

Honor Roll

We would like to give our most sincere thanks and recognition to those who helped make *Galaxy's Edge: Savage Wars - Gods & Legionnaires* possible by subscribing to GalacticOutlaws.com

Artis Aboltins	Antonio Becerra
Guido Abreu	Mike Beeker
Garion Adkins	Randall Beem
Elias Aguilar	Matt Beers
Bill Allen	John Bell
Tony Alvarez	Daniel Bendele
Galen Anderson	David Bernatski
Robert Anspach	Trevor Blasius
Jonathan Auerbach	WJ Blood
Fritz Ausman	Rodney Bonner
Sean Averill	Thomas Seth Bouchard
Matthew Bagwell	Alex Bowling
Marvin Bailey	Ernest Brant
Kevin Bangert	Geoff Brisco
John Barber	Raymond Brooks
Logan Barker	Marion Buehring
Eric Batzdorfer	Matthew Buzek
John Baudoin	Daniel Cadwell
Steven Beaulieu	Van Cammack

Chris Campbell	Ellis Dobbins
Zachary Cantwell	Ray Duck
Brian Cave	Cami Dutton
Shawn Cavitt	Virgil Dwyer
David Chor	William Ely
Tyrone Chow	Stephane Escrig
Jonathan Clews	Adolfo Fernandez
Beau Clifton	Ashley Finnigan
Alex Collins-Gauweiler	Jeremiah Flores
Jerry Conard	Steve Forrester
James Connolly	Skyla Forster
James Conyers	Timothy Foster
Jonathan Copley	Bryant Fox
Robert Cosler	Mark Franceschini
Ryan Coulston	David Gaither
Andrew Craig	Christopher Gallo
Adam Craig	Richard Gallo
Phil Culpepper	Kyle Gannon
Ben Curcio	Michael Gardner
Thomas Cutler	Nick Gerlach
Alister Davidson	John Giorgis
Peter Davies	Justin Godfrey
Ivy Davis	Luis Gomez
Nathan Davis	Brian Graham
Ron Deage	Gordon Green
Tod Delaricheliere	Shawn Greene
Ryan Denniston	Erica Grenada
Douglas Deuel	Preston Groogan
Christopher DiNote	Erik Hansen
Matthew Dippel	Greg Hanson

Jason Harris	James Johnson
Jordan Harris	Randolph Johnson
Revan Harris	Scott Johnson
Matthew Hartmann	Tyler Jones
Adam Hartswick	John Josendale
Ronald Haulman	Wyatt Justice
Joshua Hayes	Ron Karroll
Adam Hazen	Cody Keaton
Colin Heavens	Noah Kelly
Jason Henderson	Caleb Kenner
Jason Henderson	Daniel Kimm
Kyle Hetzer	Zachary Kinsman
Aaron Holden	Rhet Klaahsen
Clint Holmes	Jesse Klein
Joshua Hopkins	William Knapp
Tyson Hopkins	Marc Knapp
Christopher Hopper	Travis Knight
Ian House	Ethan Koska
Ken Houseal	Evan Kowalski
Nathan Housley	Byl Kravetz
Jeff Howard	Brian Lambert
Nicholas Howser	Clay Lambert
Mike Hull	Jeremy Lambert
Donald Humpal	Andrew Langler
Bradley Huntoon	Dave Lawrence
Wendy Jacobson	Alexander Le
Paul Jarman	Paul Lizer
James Jeffers	Richard Long
Tedman Jess	Oliver Longchamps
Eric Jett	Charles Lower

Brooke Lyons	Mitchell Moore
John M	William Morris
Richard Maier	Alex Morstadt
Ryan Mallet	Nicholas Mukanos
Brian Mansur	Vinesh Narayan
Robert Marchi	Bennett Nickels
Deven Marincovich	Trevor Nielsen
Cory Marko	Andrew Niesent
Lucas Martin	Greg Nugent
Pawel Martin	Christina Nymeyer
Trevor Martin	Grant Odom
Phillip Martinez	Colin O'neill
Joshua Martinez	Ryan O'neill
Tao Mason	Tyler Ornelas
Mark Maurice	James Owens
Simon Mayeski	David Parker
Kyle McCarley	Eric Pastorek
Quinn McCusker	Dupres Pina
Alan McDonald	Pete Plum
Caleb McDonald	Paul Polanski
Hans McIlveen	Matthew Pommerening
Rachel McIntosh	Nathan Poplawski
Joshua McMaster	Jeremiah Popp
Colin McPherson	Chancey Porter
Christopher Menkhaus	Brian Potts
Jim Mern	Chris Pourteau
Robert Mertz	Chris Prats
Pete Micale	Joshua Purvis
Mike Mieszcak	Max Quezada
Ted Milker	T.J. Recio

Jacob Reynolds	Sharroll Smith
Eric Ritenour	Michael Smith
Walt Robillard	John Spears
Joshua Robinson	Thomas Spencer
Daniel Robitaille	Peter Spitzer
Chris Rollini	Dustin Sprick
Thomas Roman	Graham Stanton
Joyce Roth	Paul Starck
David Sanford	Seaver Sterling
Chris Sapero	Maggie Stewart-Grant
Jaysn Schaener	John Stockley
Landon Schaule	Rob Strachan
Shayne Schettler	William Strickler
Andrew Schmidt	Shayla Striffler
Brian Schmidt	Kevin Summers
William Schweisthal	Ernest Sumner
Anthony Scimeca	Carol Szpara
Aaron Seaman	Travis TadeWaldt
Phillip Seek	Daniel Tanner
Christopher Shaw	Lawrence Tate
Charles Sheehan	Tim Taylor
Wendell Shelton	Steven Thompson
Brett Shilton	Chris Thompson
Vernetta Shipley	William Joseph Thorpe
Glenn Shotton	Beverly Tierney
Joshua Sipin	Kayla Todd
Christopher Slater	Matthew Townsend
Scott Sloan	Jameson Trauger
Daniel Smith	Cole Trueblood
Michael Smith	Scott Tucker

Eric Turnbull
Brandon Turton
Dylan Tuxhorn
Jalen Underwood
Paul Van Dop
Paden VanBuskirk
Daniel Vatamaniuck
Jose Vazquez
Anthony Wagnon
Humberto Waldheim
Christopher Walker
David Wall
Justin Wang
Andrew Ward
Scot Washam
John Watson
Ben Wheeler
Jack Williams
Scott Winters
Jason Wright
Ethan Yerigan
Phillip Zaragoza
Brandt Zeeh
Nathan Zoss

Lightning Source UK Ltd.
Milton Keynes UK
UKHW021517040321
379781UK00010B/2337